D0200426

Booty Nomad

SCOTT MEBUS

Booty Nomad

MIRAMAX BOOKS

FOR INFORMATION ADDRESS:
Hyperion, 77 West 66th Street
New York, New York 10023-6298

ISBN 1-4013-5204-9

10 9 8 7 6 5 4 3 2 1

Contents

to my parents

(in no particular order,
since they argued over who'd be listed first)

CHAPTER ONE

The Mannequins

I hate walking by the new Victoria's Secret on Eighty-sixth Street. It used to be safe to walk to the subway. There was the small clothing store with the little lingerie display in the corner, but if I walked quickly I was by that in a sec. This Victoria's Secret, on the other hand, is fucking huge. There's enough underwear in that store to clothe all of Massachusetts and have some left over for Christopher Street. And it taunts you. For the length of three normal storefronts, it taunts you. It doesn't matter how fast you walk, or how low you bow your head; you can't keep yourself from swiveling to the side and sneaking a peek at all those frilly underthings. I'm not a transvestite. I want to make that clear. I am also not a pervert, at least not in the parlance of the relaxed moral times we live in today. I just don't like being mocked by all that red and pinkness. The mannequins all lean in invitingly, thrusting their armless torsos out in jaunty, arousing poses. They shout at me, "Look what everyone else is going home to! Hot sex with sexy women wearing me! And you know what? The women love to wear me! They dance around in me for their lucky guys! Then they have more of the sex! And then they fall asleep together and wake up and drink orange juice and eat waffles and feed each other apple slices. And then they go out on the veranda and look at the ocean and the beautiful women still wearing me rest their heads on their guys' shoulders and he smiles. And then they have sex again." I hate it. Every morning on the way to work. Every night on my way back home. This store is the size of a warehouse and it's all window out front! You can't escape it. I can't escape it.

I used to buy lingerie for the one woman I ever loved, who will hereafter be called the Eater of Souls. She never liked to wear it. Once or twice she would, but it was obvious she was doing it for me. Which would have been sweet, if she hadn't spent the entire time telling me she was doing it for me (which is what made it obvious). How could I have loved the Eater of Souls, you might ask? She played games with my head, she mocked my insecurities, she spent my money, she refused to have sex with me because she said she felt like her dog was watching. Her dog was in New Jersey. She just felt like he was watching. You know, across space and time. He was that kind of dog. She loved her fucking dog. In all fairness, the dog was cute. He would jump up on my lap and lick my face. He never barked. He was nice to me. If he really was watching, it didn't bug me all that much. Let the poor ball-less boy get a thrill or two. I'm not unkind. But the Eater of Souls felt the need to protect her supernatural dog from the distant sight of our lovemaking. So no booty for me. And needless to say, no lingerie.

But back to the question: Why did I love her? Who knows? She was everything I wasn't. Outgoing, but shy, whereas I am shy, but outgoing. Popular but forgettable, whereas I am tolerated but remembered. Authoritative but easily satisfied, whereas I am easygoing but power-hungry. She laughed at my jokes. Or at least, at me. What else could I ask for? She was perfect for me.

So what happened, you ask? Why are Little Miss Perfect and I not together now, forever not getting it on in deference to the X-ray vision of Supershitzu? Well, one day I woke up and looked over at her sleeping face and noticed something. I was unhappy. I loved her, I ache for her to this day, but I wasn't happy. So I did the hardest and most courageous thing I have ever done. I broke up with her a month later by e-mail. Okay, in many ways, I'm small. But I'm trying to get bigger.

Four months later I was fine. I barely thought about her. She'd been sent away to stand in the Ex-Girlfriend section of my brain, which I only visited when drunk. Sure, she kept calling me, but hey, that's an ego boost, right? Sounds cool at the bar. Who's that lighting up your cell? Just a psycho ex-girlfriend. You know how it is. They just won't leave you alone. And all the guys will be impressed with how manly I am. And that's the point, isn't it?

I'm surprised my lips are moving I am so talking out of my ass. I was a wreck. What did I expect? A clean, painless break? That just wasn't an option. I had performed an amputation and I could still feel her like a phantom limb. You put a lot of yourself into your first real love. Years and years of daydreams and plans get jammed into her like all your old furniture into your new house. The longer you go without a first love, the more crap accumulates.

I was twenty-six when I met her. That's a long time to gather romantic antiques. A lot of the stuff didn't even fit her. She couldn't paint like Georgia O'Keefe or write like Virginia Woolf. She couldn't sing or do karate. She didn't read eight books a day or know every Woody Allen film by heart. She couldn't bend in unusual ways or whisper like a phone sex operator. Long walks through the woods gave her cramps and moonlit swims freaked her out. She didn't even like chocolate. But a late, soft morning lying in bed together passed effortless. So I adapted. Because something was there. Something different. Some kind of foreign language I found myself understanding without ever taking a class. I didn't pretend to know the reasons. I just responded. And each day that slipped by bound us tighter. I made promises. I planned wide, sweeping futures. I lowered my guard and let her move some of herself into this new place we were building, into me. So by the time I discovered that I wasn't happy, we were intertwined. And when it had to end, when I ripped us apart, I bled like crazy. I flailed around for bandages. I slept with someone a week later. That was like poking the fresh wound with a saltshaker. I talked to friends and family. Behind their sympathetic language I could hear them whisper, *Just get over it already and be fun again.* I let time pass. All the experts agree that time heals all wounds. It's a very famous saying. People at a loss have been spouting it for years. It's bullshit, of course. The pain is still there. I'm used to it now. I can function in spite of it. But when I stab at it like an unthinking, masochistic child, it still shocks me. And the ache can still keep me awake at night.

So what can I do? How do I get better? I needed to get over her as quickly as possible, I reasoned. But how? How did people move on? I did a poll of my friends, but didn't get anything helpful. They threw out useless words like "closure." That sounded like a lot of pain to me. I was trying to get over this girl, for Christ's sake, not let her kick me in the balls. When you escape the tiger you don't hang around to give him a long last look goodbye. That's when he'll eat you alive. You need to keep running until someone takes you down with a tranquilizer dart. That's how the survivors do it. And I was determined to survive.

So my friends proved useless. I turned to my own common sense. This had never helped me in the past, but I was desperate. Maybe the six hundred and forty-eighth time was the charm. What to do, what to do...Of course! It's so simple. You know what you need? You need a new woman to obsess about. You need to find another love of your life to eventually screw over. She had to be out there. It couldn't just be the Eater of Souls and then loneliness and death. That would be too cruel. So the best way to move on would be to find that girl and ride off into the sunset.

It was settled. I was on the prowl. Hell, just the search itself would distract me. It's not really running away when you're headed towards something, right? Then it's called trying to catch up. And the rest of my life was almost within reach.

I sat up in my bed in my minuscule apartment. My clock read 2 A.M. Work waited for me at ten. I couldn't sleep. I had to do something. I picked up my cell phone and scrolled through the names. Maybe one of them would pop out as the one. It would make it so much easier if I already knew the next girl of my dreams. Looking could tire you out. I've seen those movies. You meet once, by chance, and you spend the whole night just missing her at a thousand parties, restaurants and gas stations while being chased by Hells Angels and ninjas. Finally, you give up after watching the plane she's supposed to be on fly off. Of course, you turn around and there she is, smiling, and you say something witty like "There you are" and you kiss. Still, by that point a million humorous adventures have left you penniless, wearing someone's pink bathrobe and stinking from the smoke of your demolished Volkswagen. It's enough to give you a heart attack. I'd rather just look at an old friend a new way. It's a much less exhausting film.

A few names popped out at me as I skimmed through my cell's phone book. Moose Girl, The Screamer, Kareem Abdul Jabbar. I'm not good with girls' real names. I always nickname them in my head and I stick these monikers in my phone so I can have a mental picture of who I'm talking to. Of course, if somebody else answers, I'm screwed. I have no idea who to ask for. More than a few startled roommates have picked up the phone to a girlish scream and a dial tone. I continued scanning. Gumby, Ru Paul (she only looks like a drag queen), Diseased Girl. Okay, maybe not that last one. I had a few more numbers jotted down on various pieces of paper shoved into my back pants pocket. I keep a travelling wad of paper that I carefully transfer from back pocket to back pocket, without ever really checking the contents. Consequently, my back pocket now contained such vital personal effects as an empty stamp book, a perforated strip torn off a paycheck long since deposited, and the key to my high school gym locker. I just never got around to cleaning house.

But what did I plan to do? Call one right now? I pictured the conversation in my head. I'd wake her up in the middle of the night to tell her I needed help getting over my ex-girlfriend.

Could she meet me for a drink so we could talk, fall in love and make me forget the Eater of Souls ever existed? Of course, five minutes into the conversation, I'd be going over in detail the Eater's habit of petting her dog while flossing and presto!, dial tone. Now was probably not the right time to start in on my plan. I had the whole week to be desperate. But I felt so bone-achingly lonely. And to be honest, a little horny. I couldn't think about the Eater for ten minutes before I started to get a little randy. I really needed to talk to somebody. I needed to hear a female voice which would comfort me and make me feel important. A sexy voice, if possible, to make me feel desirable. Where oh where could I find such a voice?

I lay in bed for a while considering. An obvious solution presented itself. I'd never done anything even remotely like that before. Of course, I'd never gone through any of this before, so all bets were off. The Eater and I had tried it once. Or should I say, she let me get started. She lives in New Jersey, so we spent a lot of time on the phone. Naturally, after a few weeks of late-night calling, I began to steer the conversation into racier waters. But it never went the way I wanted it to. I'd ask her what she was wearing. She'd tell me a T-shirt and shorts. I'd ask her if it was a tight T-shirt. She'd say no, it was an extra large. I'd ask if it was soft, thin cotton. She'd say no. It was fifty-percent polyester. I'd ask her to name her favorite part of my body. She'd say my forearms. I'd ask her what she would do if I were there with her. She'd say give me my U2 CD back because she burned it and she keeps forgetting to bring it into the city. I don't know if she was doing this on purpose or if she was just phone sex retarded. Eventually, I'd end up way down the wrong conversational road discussing her shoe collection. Only once did I ever manage to approach the audio thrill. She had come back from some party drunk. I didn't play any games and just told her what to do. Even this didn't go down without a hitch. I asked her to say a dirty word. She whispered *shit*. I sighed. I asked for a real bad one. She hesitantly came back with *kike*. I gave up. We ended up discussing the Supershitzu's tooth decay. Sucks to be me.

I stared at the phone. This would be a professional. She'd know what to do. She'd know plenty of naughty words. And what order to put them in. This would be something I could never have done with the Eater. A first step towards freedom. And some dirty talk would be a nice bonus. Let's do this thing.

I didn't know any phone sex numbers offhand, so I turned on the TV. In New York, there's a special public access station that, after midnight, turns into a porn extravaganza. You'd think this would be a young man's dream, but unfortunately, this porn is nondiscriminatory. Thus, many a horny young lad has flipped to this particular channel late at night in the hope of some sweet release only to be confronted by a horrific close-up of a huge dick. That is the last thing any sexually aroused straight man wants to see. The dick does not stay long. It is usually followed by a vagina of some kind. But waiting out the dick often raises some uncomfortable questions, so sometimes the best policy is to leave the station alone. I rolled the dice, however, and punched the numbers into my remote. To my everlasting sexual relief, the screen filled with giant titties. The number of a phone sex line scrolled underneath. I was in business.

I wrote down the number and quickly turned off the television before my luck could turn sour. So I had gathered my ammo. Time to fire. I picked up my cordless phone and dialed. My stomach reenacted the USA Gymnastic Team's Gold Medal–winning routine at Seoul. Somewhere out there in Dirty Talk Land a phone rang. My heart beat audibly. One ring. Two rings. Three rings.

"Hello?"

I hung up. It wasn't panic. I just didn't like the sound of her voice. She sounded too tall for me. I'd look silly next to her. Like some kind of Oompah-Loompah. I sat there staring at the phone. Was I a man or not? I hit redial. One ring. Two rings. Three rings.

"Hey, sugar."

Click. Too Southern. What do I know about cotton? I sighed. My testicles were shrinking as I wavered. I stabbed redial. One ring. Two rings.

"Hey, baby, and who is this?"

Another hang up. Too insincere. I'd spend the entire time picturing her burping a baby. I needed a voice I could believe in. Plus, she sounded bossy. And who needs that? It could be that none of these women were good enough for me. One more try. Since I've probably already spent fifty bucks on around ten words, I should get something for my money. Redial again. One ring.

"Hey, could you hold on a sec? Thanks."

She took me by surprise. I waited, taking the moment of silence to steady myself.

"Sorry about that. My cat was falling off the counter. What's your name?"

"Bill."

The fake name popped out before I could help myself. I hoped I could remember it later on, when I was ordering her to scream it like a banshee.

"Hey there, Bill. My name is Autumn. And yeah, I'm a redhead."

All right. I love redheads. And her voice seemed nice. Just enough grate to get my attention. More importantly, she didn't sound fake. She was just talking.

"Well, hi, Autumn."

"Hi."

I didn't know what to say. How did one do this sort of thing? Should I do some kind of verbal foreplay? Or should I stampede towards the clitoris? I was lost.

"My damn cat just won't stay off the counter. Hold on. Get down! I think he has a death wish."

This was safer ground. I knew all about discussing pets.

"Cats like to climb. I used to have a cat. He peed on my jacket."

"Cats like to pee. If I leave Junior alone for too long he goes all over my hamper, just to show me. Don't you, little cutie! It's because you love me, don't you?"

Baby talk to the animal while on the phone. Déjà vu city.

"Do you leave him alone a lot?"

"More than I'd like. I'm at school all day, and then I'm out with friends. Thank God this job keeps me home at night."

"School? Where do you go?"

"University of Las Vegas. I'm studying business."

"Good for you. Sounds like you've got a plan."

"Yep. Make a whole lot of money and then travel until I die. It's not a big plan, but it works for me."

This was easy. Just talking away like old friends.

"I love Europe. You ever been?"

"Nope. But I have a map on my wall with pins in all the cities I want to see."

"Which ones?"

"Let me see. . . Paris of course. And Rome, London, Madrid, Venice. . ."

She began to list her dream vacation spots. There were a lot of them. She really had quite the travel plan.

Hold on, this wasn't right. Somewhere in the conversation we'd gone astray. We'd made a wrong turn and in my rearview mirror I could see dirty talk receding rapidly. I needed to make a U-turn. But how? I didn't want to seem crass or impolite. I couldn't just flat out ask her to rub Vaseline all over her naked body and call me Papa Smurf. (Not that I would. It's just an example. A wildly inaccurate example.) But on the other hand, I didn't want to pay five bucks a minute to hear her list all her favorite cities in Europe. I could get that from the bum on the corner for a nickel. And he'd throw in Asia and Africa. I decided to play it cool. I cut her off before she could get to the Balkans.

"That sounds great. Man, it's cold here tonight. I've got my blankets up to my chin. What about you? Is it cool there?"

"Actually, it's a little warmer than usual."

"How do you dress for that kind of weather, anyway?"

"Are you trying to ask me what I'm wearing?"

Busted.

"Yeah, I guess so."

"That's so cute. I'm wearing a tight white halter-top and short black shorts. My heater's cutting on even though I don't need it or want it to, so I'm sweating all over the place. My clothes keep sticking to my skin."

Now we're getting someplace. We just needed to do a little getting to know you talk before moving on to the big show. Now I was back on track. My way was clear. Which made what I said next even more frustrating and stupid.

"Is it central heat or do you have your own radiator?"

"You know, it's central and I can't even adjust it from my apartment! I'm a slave to whatever my landlady decides the temperature should be. Does that seem fair to you?"

"No."

"Do you live in an apartment?"

"I live in New York. That's all we have here."

"Can you control your heat?"

"No."

"So what do you do when it gets too hot?"

"I open a window."

"That just doesn't seem fair to me. It gets me so mad. It's like I live in the Gobi desert or something."

"Why that one in particular?"

"Cause I'm looking at it on my map. Now that's one place I don't want to go. Though India would be cool."

And we were off again. I had no one to blame but myself, really. She'd lobbed me the ball and I'd swung right through it. Like some bullied kid who comes up with the perfect comeback days later, hundreds of responses to her sweaty description popped into my head. They were all sexual and very dirty. But when it mattered, I choked. So instead of a moaning succubus in my ear, I got a travel agent. I had one more chance. I decided to be bold.

"Can I ask you a question?"

She halted somewhere in Australia.

"Sure. What's up?"

"What's your favorite body part?"

She laughed.

"Okay. On a guy or myself?"

"Your own body."

"You'll laugh."

"I doubt it."

"I love my nipples."

And I'm back!

"Why would I laugh?"

"It's a strange thing for a girl to like about herself."

Not on a phone sex line it isn't.

"Why do you like them so much?"

"They're just really round and sensitive and perfectly centered. I just love looking at them."

It was now or never. Time to be dangerous.

"Are you looking at them now?"

And here we go. Her voice got all playful.

"Yes, I am, and they're starting to get hard."

"Really? What are you doing now?"

"I'm slowly moving my finger down to my..."

Click.

"Thank you for calling Intimate Whispers. Please call back again sometime."

And silence.

What the fuck?

Did she hang up on me? But it was mid-sentence. I didn't think so. I looked up at the clock. I had been on the phone for a half an hour. The service must have some kind of cutoff after thirty minutes. They probably figured that was enough for any red-blooded male to get his freak on. They didn't take wussy gabbers like myself into consideration. This wasn't fair! It took me a half an hour just to work myself up to the dirty talk and now nothing? That was like hiring a hooker and spending the hour playing Scrabble. If I wanted a one-sided conversation about pets and heating systems I could have called the Eater! Hell, I was reliving the same feelings: frustrated and broke. I did the math in my head. Five bucks a minute plus a two-dollar connection fee. My little half hour of small talk cost me a hundred and fifty-two dollars. And that's without the countless extra bucks spent hanging up on those other aborted good times. I had spent too much to stop now! I needed to hear a little nasty in my ear, Goddamn it!

Of course, only Autumn would do. I had already invested too much time and mental energy to start over. Proceeding with a new voice would probably only lead me back down the same half hour of circling overhead that screwed me up the first time. So I hit redial, hoping to hear her voice.

"Hello?"

Not her. Hung up. Called again.

"Hey, sugar!"

The Southern girl again. Hung up. Redialed.

"Hola."

Nope. Again.

"Who is this?"

Not her. Damn it! Again.

"Hey, sugar."

The Southern girl yet again. I guess nobody liked her. Redial.

"Hi, big boy."

Where is she? Where is my Autumn?

"Hey, sugar."

What was with this Southern girl? Couldn't she take a hint? Again.

"Hello, good looking."

This was a cruel joke. The bucks were piling up as I called and called and called. But no redheaded, unaffected voice was to be heard. I must have called thirty times. That pathetic Southern belle answered at least eight of the calls. I found myself hating her. Why was she hiding Autumn from me? She probably despised me for something the Union Army did to her great-grandpappy. Let it go sister. Let it go. I wasn't excited anymore. This had ceased being about sex after the second callback. I just refused to let the phone sex company have my money without giving me any satisfaction. But it wasn't up to me. Finally, I put down the phone and fell back in bed. I'd probably have to sell something to pay my phone bill. How did perverts do it? You needed to have some serious cash to be a deviant. I flicked off my light and called it a night. The new me would have to wait until tomorrow to start walking the walk. For all my efforts, the Eater still floated around me like some clingy, obsolete guardian angel refusing to take a hint. As I fell asleep, I could feel myself bleeding. I wished I could make it stop.

CHAPTER TWO

Jim

I woke up the next morning feeling heavy. I was already five minutes late for work when I finally stopped hitting snooze and got out of bed. I don't mean late the way suburban commuters mean it. I wasn't five minutes off my schedule. I mean work starts at ten o'clock and it was now five after ten.

I'm the king of snooze. I love it. I set my alarm a half an hour early, just so I can hit snooze and still get up on time. I end up running at least twenty minutes late anyway. I've tried everything to combat this. I put the clock clear across the room. Of course I live in a studio in Manhattan, so I could still reach the alarm from my bed. I set a second alarm. I proved just as skilled at hitting snooze on that one. And on top of that, I would often forget I had the second alarm set, resulting in an annoying beeping sound that started right when I got in the shower. I'd have to take my entire shower listening to it drone on and on. My neighbors would bang on my wall. But I wasn't running out dripping wet to turn off my clock. I could get electrocuted and die. It's happened before, you know. I'd wait until I'd gotten out of the shower and toweled off. And by that point I'd be used to it, so I'd brush my teeth and, if it was a Wednesday, shave. (I have a shaving system. I think I look best with a slight amount of stubble. Ergo, shaving on Wednesday means I would have the right amount of stubble in time for Friday and Saturday night. By Tuesday, I start looking like I belonged in ZZ Top and it's time to shave all over again. Okay, I'm lazy. Is that what you want to hear?) By this point, my neighbors are shouting and throwing things at the wall. I mosey in, put on my clothes, and then, right before I leave, I'd turn off the alarm. A few times, I've left completely forgetting to turn the alarm off. Once, I came home to a three-inch-deep dent in my apartment door. By the way, if you're wondering, half the people in my building are musicians or actors of some kind or another, so nine-thirty is a little early for them. My landlady actually wants artists in her apartments. It makes her feel Bohemian. Of course, she doesn't live here. She lives in Queens. She can go to bed at nine at night without the fear of being woken up at two-thirty by a ten-piece Klezmer band playing down the hall. Bohemian, my ass.

I got to work forty-five minutes late. It was so cold out, my hair had frozen in the bizarre pattern my quick handful of gel had forced it into on the way out. By the time it thawed out, my hair had set. I spent the day looking like Yahoo Serious.

I sat at my desk and checked my fantasy baseball scores. I didn't really want to think about women and my ineptitude with even their voices. So instead, I focused on something more important: baseball. I'm obsessed with my fantasy baseball team. There are twelve teams in my league. I'm in last place. I suck at it. My buddy Jim talked me into it. The league is called "Ride the Snake." My team is Monstrous Pillow. I really want to win and knock Jim off of his make-believe baseball throne. I call him every day to tell him about some move I'm going to make that will completely change my team's outlook. As it happens, today I've figured out the player who will make my team great.

"Hey, monkey."

"Hey, Gonzo. Enjoying the basement?"

My job entails working with puppets (more on that later). Jim equated puppets with Muppets and me with Gonzo. I just like calling him a monkey.

"I've got the perfect plan."

"Not as long as Randy Johnson waits, kicking and snorting in my formidable stable. He is the Big Unit, you know. He is my first, my last, my everything. I have tilled the ground and now I reap the bounteous harvest."

"I'm picking up Kevin Millar."

"He's a broken-down, little man!"

"He plays right and left. He's versatile."

"He's a sad, frightened, little man."

"He's hitting .300."

"Because he's afraid Daddy will beat him if he fails. Anyway, it's only been one week of the season. My Nana could hit .300 for five games."

"Your Nana could bench 250."

"My Nana is a great woman. She hits for average and power."

"So you don't think it's a good idea?"

"It's up to you. It's your team. You follow the scores every day. You know as much as I do."

It was clear from his tone that no one knows as much as he does. I held my ground.

"I think he'll turn my team around."

"Then pick him up."

"I will."

"Good."

"You don't sound busy."

"I worked all weekend watching tapes. So now I'm resting."

Jim works as a production assistant for a documentary filmmaker. He's the only employee of a control freak. He does all the support work and in return is given little to no real responsibility. He has recently begun spending his weekdays talking to Goth women on the web. And his weekends. He says he likes them for their skewed outlook on life. I suspect he likes them because their low self-esteem makes them pliable. But I'd never say anything.

"So how's the job? Fired yet?"

"Not yet. I'm working on it. Hopefully by the end of the month."

This was not a joke. Jim has a plan. He works especially long weeks, which artificially inflate his paycheck to double its normal size. Simultaneously, he tries to get himself fired. His subsequent unemployment will then equal his original paycheck, since the government gives you half your last week of pay, or something like that. At least that's how Jim explained it to me. Of course, unemployment runs out after six months or so, but Jim isn't looking that far ahead. He just wants his dole check so he can move out of the city and up to Providence, Rhode Island, where all the Goth chicks live, apparently. They have a harem or a coven or a gaggle or whatever you call it. Providence is crawling with them. And Jim can't wait to be the mayor of Freakytown.

"How're you gonna try it this time?"

"Well the insolent attitude didn't work. The accidental trip and covering him in scalding-hot coffee didn't work. The whole badmouthing his wife thing didn't work since she ended up really having an affair."

"You didn't tell me that part."

"I just found out today. I was hoping to get the axe this morning. I worked all weekend and I did late nights all last week."

"I think I found the flaw in your plan. You keep working so much and he'll forgive anything to keep you around. But you need to keep working to bring up the paystub. Do you see the paradox?"

"I just need to find his button. Everyone has a button. Maybe I'll sleep with his mother."

"Just be inept. Dude, that's all you need to do. Trust me."

"Hey, I don't see you getting laid off. So leave the planning to the experts."

I laughed. If I thought there was an actual chance he'd be let go, I'd be worried for him. He didn't seem to take into account what losing your job really meant. But his job was no less secure now than it had been for the last few years, no matter what he said. So I played along.

"Okay by me. You gonna be around tomorrow night?"

"Can't do it. I'm going to immerse myself on-line in introverts wearing too much eye makeup."

"If they ever figured out how to plug the modem directly into your neck, I'd never see you again. Come on, man, you can do that anytime."

"Janine invited me up to Providence this weekend and I need to lay some groundwork."

"Has she met you yet? In person, I mean?"

"Once."

"And she's still talking to you?"

"I can be smooth."

"You gonna get some?"

"As long as I don't admit anything about us to any of her friends, I may get to dive into her wide Sargasso Sea."

"That's pretty smooth, all right. She doesn't even want her friends to know she's into you."

"I'm having fun."

"I need someone to take to a party at this girl's apartment."

"Which girl?"

"Opera Girl."

Opera Girl wouldn't hear a word you said if she couldn't ascertain how it fit into a conversation about her. It was a little ridiculous. I mean she was attractive, but not that attractive. She wouldn't ask a question about your life if you came into the room and coughed up blood on her carpet. She would just start talking about the time she accidentally swallowed her gum. I had no interest in Opera Girl at all. I found her barely tolerable to be around. Of course, she was the girl I had slept with a week after the Eater breakup. Now I was obligated to go to her party, and I needed to take someone with me.

"You were my last resort."

"Ask some girl."

"Just come for an hour. She may have pale friends. Maybe even anemic, if you're lucky."

"What about Bendy Girl?"

Bendy Girl taught yoga. She was too nice. But very attractive.

"I don't really know her that well. Her extreme flexibility scares me."

"Wussy. What about that other girl, the one with the rich parents?"

Totem Pole. An obvious suggestion. Totem Pole's parents were so rich they had authentic Native American totem poles arranged throughout their living room, tastefully set off by track lighting. Just like the shamans intended. They live on Nantucket. My dad loves Nantucket. My dad really likes girls whose parents live on Nantucket. He wants me to marry them. It bodes well for his retirement. She was a little too sunny. Like nothing bad had ever happened to her. It bugged me a little. Sometimes I wanted to pop her balloon, purely out of spite. But she was cute.

"Can't. She's decided to wait until she's married."

"I thought she was a slut."

"So did I. Apparently she just had a good press agent. I grabbed dinner with her a few weeks ago and she dropped the bomb on me. She's converted to Latvian Christianity."

"What the hell is that?"

"From what I gathered it involves a lot of praying, big black hats and chastity."

"Sounds like a party to me."

"She's all guilty about her money and she's working with the poor and sharing her cash. Why can't she feel guilty about her body and share that?"

"It's a loss to hard-up men everywhere."

"Amen. So obviously I can't ask her. I couldn't stand the frustration. So you have to come."

"I can't. I've got things."

"It'll only be for an hour or so. I'll buy you dinner. Come on, help me out."

Silence as he pondered.

"Fine. But it has to be a nice dinner. No Popeye's this time."

"Popeye's is good shit, my friend. It's the Nobu of cheap chicken joints."

"If you want me to put out, you're going to have to pay up."

"Okay. Just don't flake on me."

"Fine."

"Later."

Actually I could have called a few women, but I hadn't figured out which old female friend I was going to try to fall in love with and I didn't want to confuse some poor girl with my misplaced affection. I needed to keep things clean. The healing process demanded speed and precision.

I want to clarify something here. It may sound like I have thousands of women waiting with baited breath by the phone, wailing to the sky and mother earth while beating themselves with bamboo when I don't call. But I don't sleep with too many women. And when I do, too often I end up with the Opera Girls of the world. And that was such a mistake. The next morning she tried to hold my hand. I had to tell her I still wasn't over the Eater of Souls, which was true. Sex with someone else was weird after two years of non-sex with the Eater of Souls. She launched into what had happened when her last boyfriend broke up with her. We should have music implants in our ears so we can switch on some Talking Heads whenever we need it without tipping off the assailant. As she blathered on, I thought to myself how I wished I was one of those well-adjusted people who break up and remain friends, dealing with their anger and pain thoughtfully and maturely. I just can't do it. I'm sure there's a happy medium between regrettable sex and unending love, but I'm not good with happy mediums. Extremes make more sense to me. You see results quicker.

CHAPTER THREE

The Goddess

Opera Girl lived in a fairly large one-bedroom in Brooklyn. It was packed with upwards of fifty twenty-to-thirtysomethings, none of whom I knew. Beer, hard alcohol, chips, eighties music; the party was in full swing.

In his huge black overcoat, Jim looked like Darth Vader. A ring of space surrounded him, completely free of people, impressive for such a small place. I guess they thought he looked imposing. I thought he looked uncomfortable.

"You should take off your coat, man. It must be eighty degrees in here."

"Can't do it. I've got an image. Besides, I'm enjoying my Corona."

Darth Vader with a Corona and lime. Kind of like Arnold Schwarzenegger nursing a virgin strawberry daiquiri. Of course, when I ordered a whiskey sour, Jim acted like I was letting down red-blooded men everywhere. He wouldn't listen to me when I tried to point out the double standard, his bald-faced hypocrisy. Shaking my head at his refusal to see how sad he really was, I changed my order to a gin and tonic. And a shot of JD, for the masculine hell of it.

So many unfamiliar faces. I hadn't spoken to Opera Girl yet and without her introductions I felt a little adrift. I'm not good at meeting strangers at parties. I need an in first. Normally, I tried to show up at these affairs with a strong wingman who could help me get past my innate shyness. Tonight, however, I brought Jim.

"You know why this coat is so effective? No one bothers me. It's great. I can drink in peace."

"How do you plan to meet any women?"

"I've met plenty of women. My kind of women. The web is my cocktail party. Don't giggle. I hate this kind of thing. A room filled with people I don't know and would never like having inane conversations about Dave Matthews and places they've thrown up in."

I looked around.

"Okay, it's true, there are a large number of baseball hats in evidence. I see some serious Goldman-Sachs action going on. Maybe it's a little Upper East Side. But that doesn't mean they're bad people."

"Yes. Yes it does."

"That's kind of harsh. Maybe if you met some of these people, you'd start to have a good time."

"I'm sorry, you're wrong. I would not have a good time."

"You could mock them to their face. That could be fun."

"Cruelty to dumb animals is not nice, David."

"Man, I bought you a nice dinner. Doesn't that get me anything?"

"After a half hour standing here, it feels like I sold you my soul for some ribs and cornbread."

I couldn't tell you how much of this was Jim's natural elitism and how much was Jim's natural reticence. Jim's approach to party situations is very self-protective. I sometimes think he's so afraid to be hit by a pitch he stands two feet off the plate. And mocks the pitcher for having a mullet. Quietly, to the guy in the on-deck circle, of course.

Not that I was living it up at this little shindig. Besides Jim, I had only exchanged words with the bartender and some poor girl I pistol-whipped with my drink as I turned around. Not a great track record. I felt depressed. I could see the guys in hats Jim despised all over the place, and I looked down on them too, I'll admit it. But they chatted up the attractive ladies like it was as easy as breathing. They'd probably get some tonight. I comforted myself with the thought that they'd probably wake up tomorrow morning bathed in regret next to a horse-faced harpy. But that felt hollow. Who cares about tomorrow morning? I wanted the thrill of tonight. I was trapped in a windowless room with memories of the Eater hanging on the walls all around me. I kept trying the door, but it was locked. I needed someone to open it from the outside.

"Jim, what do you think about my female friends?"

Jim shrugged.

"Who do you mean? I don't know too many of them."

"Do you think any of them are attractive?"

"Annie's pretty."

"Besides Annie."

"I guess some of them are. What are you getting at?"

"I've been thinking about looking at a female friend in a new way."

"You've got the hots for one of your buds? Which girl?"

"That's the thing; I don't know yet."

"I'm lost. You don't know if you really like this girl or not? You're afraid you're going to screw up the friendship or something?"

"Not exactly."

Jim went back to his drink.

"I can't help you if you're going to be an idiot. Get back to me when you've figured out what the hell you're talking about."

"I haven't picked the girl yet."

"What does that mean?"

"I haven't picked which of my female friends I'm going to fall for yet. I'm just seeing if you think any of them are particularly attractive so I can narrow my choices down a bit."

"You're planning on falling for one of your friends?"

"Yeah. In a *Some Kind of Wonderful* sort of way."

"Have any of your female friends shown any interest in you?"

"Well, no."

"And you don't have any real preference?"

"Not right now. I'm still reviewing the choices."

"I know that girl fucked you up, but this is just stupid. Trust daddy, it just doesn't work that way."

"You pick which girls you want to go after from descriptions on the Internet."

"That has nothing to do with what you're talking about. I'm meeting new people and trying to have kinky sex. You're trying to manufacture romance."

"I'm not trying to manufacture anything. I just think I may have been too hasty with one of my female friends. Never took the time to look at them as a dating choice, you know? I slammed the booty door shut before I really thought about it."

"Is this a booty thing or a love thing?"

"I don't know."

"David, man, I know you're going through some serious shit. I hate to see it. But you can't arrange to fall in love. The only thing you can do is work on your swing and try not to fuck up when it's your turn to bat. David?"

I wasn't really paying attention to Jim because somewhere between "booty thing" and "serious shit" I became transfixed by a goddess. Brown hair, exotic cast to her features, small frame, sly smile, sharp eyes—she was fucking hot. I tried not to stare at her, so I kept my eyes on some big guy standing in her vicinity until he got weirded out and went to the bathroom to wash.

"She's a goddess."

He followed my gaze.

"She's all right. I don't know if psychotic staring is the best way to pick her up."

"She's fucking hot. And she looks pretty smart. Don't you think so? I bet I could have a good conversation with her."

"Let me take a moment to look into her soul. Come on, man. There's no way to find out without talking to her, David. Remember the Hawaiian Tropic Bikini Contest?"

Jim and I had judged a bikini contest at this beach bar up on Cape Cod a few years back. I voted for this dark-haired beauty because I thought she looked fairly intelligent. I pictured her paying her way through med school on her Hawaiian Tropic Bikini

Tropic winnings. After she won, I walked over to congratulate her. She was in the corner feeling this guy's biceps and telling him how this money was nothing compared to the cash she made stripping. She asked someone to buy her a Long Island Iced Tea because it made her "all silly." I went home a beaten man.

"I guess I should talk to her then."

"I'm gonna hit the bathroom. Let me know how it turns out."

He walked away, leaving me to stare helplessly at this vision.

Unfortunately, she wasn't talking with anyone I knew. And I am not the kind of guy who can just walk up to some goddess and start talking. What would I say? "Hey, I was just standing in the corner staring at you in a creepy way. Marry me, Goddess!" The word *goddess* tends to make women uncomfortable. It brings to mind the poor saps who think grand romantic gestures are the way to a woman's heart. I call it the Say Anything Syndrome. Meaning: The need to win a woman's affection by holding up a boom box playing "In Your Eyes" outside her house in the middle of the night. This works in the movies. In real life, it gets you prison time. A dozen roses from a complete stranger delivered to her at work is not romantic. This is not *Red Shoe Diaries*. She won't take them home and rub them all over her body wishing you would break in and ravish her. She's giving them to the girl at the reception desk and screening her calls. Strange suggestive notes that compare her body to Aphrodite aren't erotically poetic; they're grounds for a restraining order. I cannot emphasize this enough. An old buddy of mine suffered from this disease. He actually snuck over to some girl's apartment complex at two in the morning, stood on his car, and sang a song he had written about her called "Forbidden Love." She lobbed an old VCR out the window and gave him a concussion. He still lives with his mom.

So I couldn't just walk up to her. I needed someone to introduce me. And then it got worse. Opera Girl found me. I didn't want to talk to Opera Girl. I wanted to be seen by Opera Girl so she'd know I showed up. Then I wanted to be left alone by Opera Girl.

"How are you doing, David? I mean, really? I know I still think about Ray. It's been two years, and I still think about him. A part of me really loved him, you know. And even though he's gone, that part of him is still in here. I can remember the way he looked at me. It is hard, David. But it gets better. I just woke up one morning, and I felt better. Ray was still with me, but he wasn't all of me, if you get what I'm saying. I guess what I'm trying to say is. . ."

Blah blah blah. Across the room, the Goddess was talking to someone of the male persuasion. I felt a swift flash of jealousy. At least he wasn't wearing a baseball cap. Opera Girl droned on and on about this Ray guy living in her or something. I glanced around. Where the hell was Jim? He was probably watching from the corner, smirking. Blah blah blah. I started to play the song "Everybody Wants to Rule the World" by Tears for Fears in my head. I always liked that song. Nice solid eighties tune with a wistful edge. I started sinking deeper into the song. I had just gotten to the guitar solo when I noticed Opera Girl was introducing someone to me.

". . . David. David, this is my old friend from college . . ."

I didn't hear anything further. My mind stopped. My eyes had refocused on Opera Girl standing there with one hand on the shoulder of the Goddess. I was being introduced to the woman of my dreams by the last girl I'd slept with. It was the Circle of Life.

"Shit, I have to go check on the beer. I'll be around again."

Opera Girl scurried off, leaving me alone with the Goddess.

Panic. Must resist my Say Anything tendencies. I went for something innocuous.

"College, huh?"

"Yeah. I used to hold her hair back when she threw up."

I had no reply to that.

"Are you the David who broke up with some evil bitch and then slept with Maggie and then told her you weren't over the evil bitch and didn't call her again? Just wondering. It's a very male story."

Maggie? Who's Maggie? Opera Girl. Maggie is Opera Girl's real name. I'm just not good with names. Oh my God! I had no idea what the Goddess' name was! I had been so busy trying not to sing "Seeds of Love" out loud that I didn't catch it. Don't obsess! I'll skillfully get it out of her without sounding any idiot alarms. But first I must mock her feminist leanings.

"So you hate the men, do you? You're not going to throw paint on me, are you?"

"That's PETA."

"You're not going to throw anything else on me, are you?"

"I just have one question. Why did you sleep with Maggie if you weren't over this other girl? Didn't you feel weird?"

It had felt weird. I'd felt awful. I'd made a mistake. Don't goddesses make mistakes? I laughed it off.

"You don't know until you try."

That will work.

"You are such a guy."

"I guess I am."

Silence. I was not on the road that leads to booty. I needed to try something different.

"What do you do?"

"I work in publishing. *Now* Magazine."

"That sounds pretty cool. You must know all the models."

And that won't make me sound sex-crazed.

"Not really. They don't come to the office much."

"Is that what you want to do?"

"Actually I want to go to law school."

"You want to save the world?"

"What?"

"Most of my lawyer friends, they wanted to save the world, but then they ended up in, like, tax law."

"So what are you saying?"

I'm insulting her life's ambition and her integrity. I should win some kind of award for this kind of all-encompassing fucking up.

"I'm just saying stay away from tax law. What kind of law are you interested in?"

She looked at me a little funny.

"Tax law."

I laughed.

"You got me. No, really."

"Tax law."

Hah hah.

"Are you kidding?"

"I wish for your sake I was."

"I'm embarrassed."

"I'm embarrassed for you. What do you have against tax law?"

"Nothing, I guess. It just doesn't seem too exciting."

"Well, that's what I want to do."

"Are you sure you're not kidding?"

"Are you on some kind of mission to completely bury yourself?"

This was a new experience for me. Usually when I inadvertently insult a girl, she gets all huffy and storms off. She doesn't hang around and watch me drown. But this girl...hell, she was pushing my head underwater with a stick.

"I'm sorry. I don't know anything about law, tax or otherwise. I've known people who wanted to save the world and they gave up on it to do the opposite of what they wanted, which in my mind is tax law. But since you want to do tax law, you're not giving up on your dreams or anything. You're doing what you want to do. So you have my respect."

"So the opposite of saving the world is tax law? It's the refuge of hypocrites?"

"You are *so* fucking with me, right?"

She gave away nothing. I continued.

"I know nothing about law of any kind. Please don't eat any more of my entrails."

She smiled wryly and opened her mouth, probably to deliver the final push to my floundering, sinking body, but I was saved. Jim returned.

"Man, that bathroom line was longer than the one to see the Sistine Chapel. I was a little disappointed by the payoff, though this ceiling did have nice tile."

"I'm sorry you got taken in by the hype."

"I'm just a whore to the latest thing. Aren't you going to introduce me?"

The Goddess stood patiently, waiting to be introduced.

"Sorry. This is Jim. Coincidentally, I've known him since college. And this is..."

Sweet mother of Christ! I still didn't know her name! What on God's green goodness do I do now? Thank God I have such a long history with forgetting people's names. My body took over for me out of instinct and I started to cough.

"David, you okay?"

"Sorry, I just need a drink of water."

"Jim, grab that glass over there."

Jim handed the glass to me and I drank. I lifted the glass slowly and took a big swallow. While I'm steadying myself, she'll take the opportunity to introduce herself to Jim, and indirectly, to me. I'm so sly. I put down the glass and took a few cleansing breaths. Silence. I looked up. They both stared at me. The Goddess looked concerned.

"David, are you okay now?"

Jim patted my back.

"Yeah, that looked painful."

I wiped my mouth.

"I think I'm okay now."

I waited a second. Nothing. They were still just looking at me. Doesn't she know the rules of etiquette? How can she be so rude? They both looked at me expectantly, waiting for me to finish the introductions. I panicked.

"Actually, I feel a little light-headed. I'm gonna just hit the bathroom quick. Excuse me."

And I ran off like a frightened little bunny.

After a good twenty minutes, I came back out. The Goddess had moved on. I looked around, but I didn't see her. Fucking idiot! Jim stood where I'd left him, alone.

"You sure you're okay?"

"I'm fine. I didn't know her name. I was too busy staring at her to pick it up when Opera Girl introduced us. That's why I had to cover up. You know, create a diversion."

Jim snorted.

"Quick thinking. Nothing like an attack of tuberculosis to get you out of an awkward situation, huh?"

"Just tell me her name."

"I don't know it! You didn't fucking introduce me! After you left, Opera Girl showed up and dragged her off. We're both in the dark."

Perfect. I looked around the room, but she was nowhere to be found. I had fucked it up again. Jim patted my shoulder.

"Hey, I thought your plan was to look at a close female friend in a new way."

"You're right. Yeah, that's right."

"She would've just screwed that up. Stick to the original plan, which is a beaut, by the way."

"Yeah. It's a good plan."

We fell into silence. I was furious with myself. How could I ever expect to move on if this was how I acted around women? I scanned the room again. Jim put down his drink.

"I'm going to head home. You okay?"

"Yeah. I'm fine."

"You coming with me?"

"No, I'm going to finish my drink. I should at least get a hangover out of this evening."

"Whatever makes you smile."

⬡

An hour later, I was hammered and ready to go. Opera Girl had cornered me, drunk as all hell, and tried to explain to me that she was worthy of love. For forty-five minutes. This had to be one of the nine levels of Hell. Probably the fifth one, the one with the bad popes in it. I didn't see the Goddess anywhere. She must have gone home. I finally got away from Opera Girl by starting to talk about myself. After she staggered off, I grabbed my coat and slipped outside. And stopped up short. And thanked the deity of second chances.

There, trying to hail a cab, was the Goddess. One more chance. I probably should have just let her go. I had screwed things up enough already. Instead I took the fool's course, tapped her shoulder and opened my mouth.

"Hey, sorry about all that."

"Hey. Sorry for what? The choking? Yeah, that instinct for self-preservation, that was kind of rude. At least you didn't die. Ms. Manners would have had a fit. Well, nice to meet you. Goodnight."

"Wait. No, I'm sorry about the whole law thing. I had no right to mock what you want to do. I know nothing about it. I have a habit of thinking the best way to dig myself out of a hole is to make it deeper, hoping I fall out the other side somewhere in China. Anyway, I enjoyed meeting you, too."

"All right."

I took a deep breath and stepped off the cliff.

"Do you think I could grab your number?"

She looked at me funny again. Inside, my entire body was on full panic alert. Outwardly, I remained calm. Or so I told myself.

"Why don't you give me your number instead?"

"Okay. Sure."

A cab pulled up and the Goddess opened the door to climb in. I didn't have a pen, so I just grabbed a business card out of my back pocket and handed it over.

"That's my work number. I'm there all day, anyway. Give me a call. We can have lunch or something."

"Sounds nice."

She hesitated.

"By the way. I should apologize to you, too."

"Why, you didn't do anything wrong."

"Well, that depends. Environmental Litigation."

"Excuse me?"

"That's what I'm really interested in. The tax law thing was to see if I could make you cry. I hate it when people make assumptions. Sorry about that. Bye."

She closed the door and the cab screamed off like a wooden rollercoaster.

That little bitch. I was impressed. She got me. I wanted her to get me again. But I had no name, no number, and worst of all, the ball was completely in her court. I would be waiting by the phone for a call from some nameless girl I had barely even talked to. No! My drunken brain rebelled. This was too much. I would stick to the fall-in-love-with-a-friend plan. This girl had just spent an entire conversation fucking with me and never letting on. I didn't want to get into a relationship with someone like that. She'd eat me alive. No, my original plan was the best plan. I would stay on target.

◆

People from Manhattan often get confused when visiting the outer boroughs. We don't know them well; we avoid going to them at all if possible, so we don't really understand the spatial universe they reside in. Which is what led to my drunken decision to visit my friend, Annie, since I was "in the neighborhood." I felt depressed about my Goddess encounter and I needed a cookie. I couldn't just go home to my tiny apartment and pass out. That would be too dignified. I had been embarrassed by a girl and I needed to spread that around a bit before bed.

Seems simple enough, right? Brooklyn is right across a bridge and so is Queens, so it must be easy to get from one to the other, correct? Park Slope is practically *in* Astoria. Hell, I wouldn't even need a cab. I'd just take the subway. There'd probably be a subway stop in Annie's apartment, I wagered. Just a hop, skip and/or jump away. Piece of cake.

An hour and a half later I was running down the breakdown lane of the Brooklyn-Queens Expressway while hiding from the Korean mob. It's a long story. Let's just say it involved a wrong subway stop, a hibachi grill, an issue of Barely Legal and an ill-advised joke. Thank God for that insomniac Kenyan marathon runner or I would never have gotten away in one piece. I scared the hell out of some poor cab driver when I jumped in his cab while it was speeding down the expressway at fifty miles an hour. He dropped me off at Annie's building before rising up into the air and going back to the future. Okay, fine, I just got lost. I like my version better.

I rang the bell. And waited. Nothing. I rang again. Nothing. I rang a third time. An encyclopedia landed on my head. Felt like a volume from the front end of the alphabet. Something from the *C*'s maybe.

"What the hell are you doing?"

Annie was leaning out of her second-story window. I shrugged haphazardly.

"I'm saying hi!"

"It's four o'clock in the fucking morning, asshole!"

"I would have been here sooner but the Koreans got involved."

"Whatever. Come on up. And grab my encyclopedia."

I should have been sober by now, but I wasn't. I guess my body didn't really want to have to deal with reality quite yet. I stumbled through the buzzing door and made my way upstairs on all fours. Annie opened the door and shepherded me in.

"Be quiet, drunk boy. Jacob's asleep."

Jacob is Annie's not-boyfriend. They live together in the same apartment as "roommates." Oh, and they do it all the time. And neither of them makes any attempt to date other people. But it's a handshake deal. Annie's been very careful not to put anything in writing. I don't understand it myself. She keeps her distance in public. If anyone mentions that they look good together, she'll loudly deny everything. Jacob's told me that after one of these "girlfriend accusations" it can be weeks before she'll even sit next to him on a couch. Never mind that they both look happiest around each other. Because logic is obviously not wanted here in Queens. Annie says that she's just commitment shy. If so, she must have heard some awful things about commitment. Like that time in elementary school when Billy Jones told me that girls had a vacuum cleaner between their legs that sucked off your willy if you got too close. I knew he was lying, but I still removed my first girlfriend's panties with a stick. I was fifteen by that point. Sad.

"How is the not-boyfriend?"

"He's asleep. And don't call him that."

"How about your 'special friend'?"

"Shut it. You make him sound like my period."

"Okay, then. Your green card?"

"We're both American."

"I'll call him Rosemary. And that's my final offer."

"Put this in your mouth."

She tossed me a cookie.

"Fantastic."

I chomped away happily. My evening's harrowing adventures now seemed worthwhile. Annie poured me some Coke.

"So what happened with your little party thingy?"

I filled her in on the Goddess situation, taking great care to make it sound even more embarrassing than it actually was. She handed me another cookie in sympathy. Score!

"So I came here, for some friendship and baked goods."

My phone rang. We both looked at it. Annie bit her lip.

"Is that who I think it is?"

"She won't stop calling me. It's driving me nuts. She is fucking nuts. Sorry."

"Hey, don't worry about what I think. Sometimes I agree with you."

Oh yeah, the Eater of Souls is Annie's first cousin. Forgot to mention that.

"I wish she'd let up."

"I don't think that's likely. She sure as hell won't let up on me. I hadn't talked to her in years before I introduced her to you. Now she won't leave me alone. She pretends to be interested in me, I mean she asks maybe one question, and then she's off talking for hours about you. You don't want to know what she's saying."

"And yet I can't turn away."

"She talks for hours about how you never did this for her, and how you never did that for her. And the whole sex thing. I really don't want to hear about it at all, but she doesn't even bother to ask. She just launches into this diatribe about how she made herself have sex even when she didn't want to. And get this, apparently she's convinced herself that you abused her."

"What? How did I abuse her? I never even raised my voice around her. I didn't even mention the word 'sex' for the last four months."

"Well, she's decided you abused her."

I grimaced. This was lovely.

"You know, sometimes I really miss her. I get to thinking about when we went skiing together, and the weekend in Montauk. Great times, right? And then she goes and ruins it! She is so small that she can't even let me have my happy memories. I've only been in love once. I'd like to think there was a reason for it. But now all I can think about is how she's selfish and psycho and small-minded. When I close my eyes and think of her that's what I see. Every time I try to save one memory of the woman I loved, she has to gnaw it apart. Now I think I was delusional the whole time."

"I'm sure you weren't."

"Why can't she move on?"

"It's easy for you. You can ignore the phone when she calls. I have to answer and listen to her bitch for four hours."

"Why don't you hang up?"

"Then my aunt would call my mom and it would become a big family incident."

Annie would do anything to avoid a family incident. She has three aunts, each of whom is crazier than the last, and between them they don't have enough skin to cover a thumb. They get insulted by every other word they hear. They're constantly feeling slighted by each other. Auntie One wouldn't talk to Auntie Two because Auntie Two didn't notice that Auntie One had lost five pounds. Auntie Three made the sign of the evil eye whenever Auntie One walked in because Auntie One didn't finish her piece of the apple pie Auntie Three had made special for Thanksgiving. Can you even imagine Thanksgiving? It must be like trying to make peace in the Middle East. You don't know when someone will take something the wrong way, flip out, and invade the Gaza Strip.

Coming from a very small family I can't understand this, so I always recommend that Annie just tell them all to shove dildos up their asses. But Annie can't do it. She'd rather be stuck on the phone for hours with my ex-girlfriend who she doesn't even like rather than make trouble in the family. I think it has something to do with the name. When you're called Annie, and life is looking down, you're almost genetically required to burst into a cheery song about tomorrows and sunshine and sunshiny tomorrows. Even when what you really want to do is smack the headmistress with a shovel. So Annie makes peace, and doesn't rock the boat, and has a spastic colon.

"I'm sorry you have to deal with her."

"Me too. It's like she forgets that you're my friend."

"I think she knows. That's why she wants you on her side."

"I hate being in the middle. I'm always in the middle."

"Annie!"

The cry came floating in from the next room.

"Shit, we woke him up. I'll be right back."

Annie slipped out of the kitchen. I stared at my phone. Before I even realized it, Annie had a hand on my shoulder.

"Okay?"

"Sure. Fine. Just drunk as a skunk. Who's been drinking a lot. Stupid alcoholic skunk."

"Do you want to sleep here?"

"Sure. Thanks. What did not-boyfriend want?"

"He's just bitchy because we woke him up."

"If I didn't know any better, I'd think you guys were married or something."

Annie sat down. She stared at her hands on the table.

"He almost told me he loved me tonight."

"Wow."

"Don't get too excited. He almost tells me that every night. I'm grateful he never actually says it."

"What would you do?"

"I don't know. Just because two people live together and sleep together, that's no reason to start dating. There's no rule, right?"

"It's more of an unwritten code, really."

"I look at you and my cousin. I remember how happy you guys were. Always holding hands. Always calling each other. Every five minutes, it seemed like. We all made bets on when you would get married. The same way we'd make bets on how long until a guy in a speed-eating contest would vomit, true, but still. It seemed certain. I may not have liked it much,—I never liked her for you though I wouldn't say it at the time—but you guys were in love.

Hell, I don't have now what you had then. Jacob and I are so...pragmatic. If passion is a burning building, then we're fire-proofed. You know? There has to be more. You had more. Oh Jesus, I'm sorry, David."

Tears fell down my face like deserters, betraying me. It was true. I *had* had more. It's so easy to be cavalier when she's on the other line, pathetic, calling over and over again. She's not even real. She's some crazy woman I can't even picture in my head anymore. But she was real. I was too drunk to deny it. My voice came out cracked and childish.

"I'm sorry. We were talking about you."

"Don't worry about it. Are you okay?"

My crying scared me, coming in uncontrollable bursts. These weren't movie tears, streaming gracefully down my cheeks. I cried like a scared, frightened child.

"It's okay. Do you want another cookie?"

"You're going to have fat children."

"True."

We sat there in silence for a moment.

"I remember when she told me she loved me. It wasn't in some special place or after some big event or anything. We weren't in bed or sitting on a beach at sunset or lying on the hood of my car staring at the moon. It was so ordinary. We had gone out line danc-ing, if you can believe it. Country line dancing. She made me do it. There's a roadhouse type place in Jersey City that has a live band every Thursday night. When we got there, I sat us in the corner and watched for a while. Her feet were tapping and she faced the dance floor with this cute little eager face. I didn't want to dance because I didn't want her to move. She was so beautiful, so alive.

She turned to me and begged me to dance. I left my pride with my jacket and hit the floor. She stood on my right and some weird old guy stood on my left. He had on this huge hat that was three times bigger than he was. He looked like the mascot for Arby's or something. I watched his feet and I watched her feet and gradually I picked up a few moves. By the third song, I had gone crazy. Throwing my hips into it, which you don't do in country dancing, that is a no-no, and shouting like a movie cowboy. It was fun. Eventually, I noticed that she wasn't next to me anymore. I looked over at our table and there she was, watching me with this little smile. I bet you that same smile flashed across my face when I'd watched her wanting to dance. And it struck me how amazing it was that two people could feel exactly the same way about each other. How odd is that? How unlikely. But it had happened to me. On the car ride home, she leaned up against her door. Tired, I guess. I asked her if she'd had a good time. She said she loved me. She didn't even look at me when she said it. I'm glad she didn't. It felt like more of a gift that way, you know? Does that make sense?"

Annie's voice came out like cotton.

"Sure."

"So ordinary and so perfect. And now look at me. She still feels like that and I don't. I call her crazy, but who's more unfair? I'm the one that changed. How can I call her crazy?"

Annie wiped her eyes.

"I wish I could feel that."

"Give yourself a chance."

"Don't beat yourself up about changing. There's a reason you guys broke up."

"I know."

"Good. Just try to remember it. Let me grab you some sheets. You can sleep on the couch."

"Thanks, Annie."

After she had gone to bed, my phone rang. I let it ring. I vacillated, then decided to check the message. The Eater alternated between tears and anger.

"There are a few things I never got to say. I think I need to say them to feel better. I told my friends what happened and they all agree you were a bad boyfriend. You must never have loved me to do this to me. This is not my fault. You are such an asshole! I hope you get hit by a car! Call me back."

I've gotten a few messages like this. My cell has caller ID, so I don't answer when she calls. Sometimes I have to shove my hand under something heavy, just to make sure. I'm not calling her back.

CHAPTER FOUR

The Joys of Children's Television

So what do I do? For a living, I mean? I work in television. I produce a children's show called *The Puppeteers.* They're a band of
pirate puppets that sail around teaching children how to read and
not bite each other. "Books are your friends, me mateys!" Captain
Blueboots loves to tell the boys and girls, his felt head nodding
wisely. "Don't bite. Aargh, it hurts!" The truth is I never burned
to do it. I had no desire to work on a TV show, let alone produce
one, and especially not some kids' show starring buccaneers with
hands up their asses. I wanted to write a screenplay. I'd win an
Oscar and thank my mom and give the Eater of Souls the finger
on national television. Maybe I'd win an Oscar for best song too,
for composing the title tune to my own blockbuster movie. Of
course, I'd have to learn how to play my guitar first, but I'm getting there. I can do "Twinkle Twinkle, Little Star" and you can
almost guess it. And the only thing I've written so far is a one-act
play I put on with my own money shortly after college, which I

will never see again, ever (the money, the play and, thank God, college). It was so soul-suckingly bad that the one poor bastard who had to review it simply wrote, "Further proof that there is no God" and left it at that.

So I'm producing a kids' show for public television. Never wanted to do it, had no interest in it at all, but here I am. I keep getting raises without asking. I've become the top guy in production after starting there three years ago as a lowly production assistant. It's like dating, I've decided. If you want it, you become desperate and it shows. People are never attracted to desperation (except for a certain breed of sad little men). If you don't give a rat's ass one way or the other, then you exude confidence. So I'm the top guy. And I couldn't care less.

Let me explain how our show works. It's not very complicated. I've worked on fifty-eight episodes of *The Puppeteers* during my time here, and it hasn't ever really gotten any easier. Or harder. It doesn't change much one way or the other. Can't you tell how much I love my job?

An episode of *The Puppeteers* begins with a story meeting. The writers and producers, including moi, sit around a big oval table and eat bagels. Occasionally someone has fruit. We talk about which associate producer is sleeping with which intern. We make fun of the executive producer's awful car. Harold Pruitt, our executive producer and creator of *The Puppeteers*, is color-blind. Even that fact doesn't excuse the hot pink and neon blue colors that pervade our puppet ranks. Sometimes I think the only thing our show prepares children for is a career in designing clothes for aging drag queens. What does that have to do with his car? He loves status symbols. He has his Rolex and his minuscule cell phone that he has to hold up to his ear with tweezers and his six-hundred-dollar haircut, which still looks like his drunk aunt attacked him with shears. And he has his Rolls Royce. He had to have a Rolls Royce. Nice car, you might say. Of course, he didn't realize he got it in shit brown. The car salesman didn't tell him. God knows we would never say anything. His hundred-thousand-dollar luxury vehicle looks like a chrome-lined turd.

For an hour, we gossip like gay entertainment reporters. Then, five minutes before we have to break, someone will remind us we need a plot. So we turn on PBS and catch the end of *Sesame Street*. Whatever the lesson was that day becomes the lesson for our new episode. It sounds underhanded and dirty, but it actually makes a lot of sense. There are only so many things that kids need to know. Don't talk to strangers. Not all Asians are good at math. Don't staple your dog to a bus. There's nothing on *The Puppeteers* that hasn't been on *Sesame Street* or *Reading Rainbow*, or *Blues Clues*, or *Wild on E!* or vice versa. So this just saves us an hour of thinking, which is always a good thing.

Now that we have our lesson, we need an actual storyline for the episode. For that, I go out and hire a writer. He or she writes the episode and gives it back to me. I read it. I make lots of notes, whether I need to or not, just to show I'm paying attention. They revise it. I then hand the script to Harold. He always assumes it's the final draft, so he never makes any changes. I don't think he even reads it. He barely shows up on set anymore, unless we're shooting one of his pet project episodes. Once he okays the unread script, the crew assumes it's good to go. This can backfire. One week when I had the flu, we shot an entire episode set at Negro Falls. I didn't notice it until my ears cleared up. By that time we were in the edit room. I was wondering why everyone had been shooting me those looks. And why Tyrone the sound guy kept giving me the finger. I had to bring in the actors to dub over their lines. This was fine for the puppets, but the real kids looked like actors in a bad kung fu movie. And we found out later, hundreds of angry calls and letters later, that lip reading is not the lost art that we told ourselves it was. Tell you one thing. To this day I can't think about Niagara Falls without feeling awash in deep racial guilt.

So now the show is written. Jake, our music guy, writes some cheesy "learning" songs to go with that episode's theme that I'll be unable to keep out of my head for the next eight months. Then we rehearse it with the actors, build the cheap sets, and shoot it. We usually shoot six to eight episodes over one week to save money on the actors. Finally we edit it. This means I hire an editor and watch him work for two weeks. After that we send it to the network, they approve it without really watching it since it is a kids' show and we've been doing it a while now. I know that because as a joke we once gave God a producer's credit and no one said anything. You might figure the credits are hard to read, maybe they just missed it. It was bright yellow. And flashing.

There is a theme here, and you've probably caught it. Not a lot of quality control goes into our little program. We've won three Emmys, by the way. I think, after the first season, people just kept voting for us out of habit. Who watches kids' shows anyway? There's another theme here, if you look close. I don't seem to do much. I don't write. I don't direct. I don't act. I don't edit. What do I do? How did I ever get hired to do this job? Why doesn't anyone notice I am completely useless, the appendix of the television world? It's simple, actually. I make decisions. Of course, if I kept making the wrong decisions I'd get the axe. This is a business of scapegoats. But I work on a show aimed at four-year-olds and I have the mind of a four-year-old. I think poo is a damn funny concept. I can stare at my hands for hours. I believe water balloons are the only way to tell someone you love them. So I do okay. Go figure.

That's my work life. Not very glamorous, but not bad either. There's worse, believe me. I get my own office. I get three weeks paid vacation. I have a really nice laptop that has a lot of games on it. Do I love my job? No. Is this my life's passion? No. Would it break my heart if I were fired? No. Is it a cool and easy way to make eighty grand a year? That would be a yes.

It was Friday. The Goddess still hadn't called. I was in an edit session supervising the cutting of our latest episode, so I was forwarding my calls just in case. This was a mistake, since I usually never answer my phone at all. I found myself speaking with people I never had to talk to before, like vendors, writers, actors, my Aunt Kathy. But I couldn't let voicemail get it. So instead of playing a game of Tetris or figuring out how to give someone the finger with my toes, ways I usually spent my edit sessions, I was actually doing more work than I had done in a year.

I took a break and called the parents.

"Hello?"

"Hey, Mom."

"Hey, David. How's my boy?"

"Hey, son."

"Hey, Dad."

You can't call just one of my parents. You're stuck with both. Ever since my brother left for college, my parents have started competing over us. Whenever I call, they both answer within seconds of each other. They must walk around all day, phone in hand, trying to catch the one time the other misses a call. Then they put a big mark down on the chalkboard they have up in their bedroom and, apparently, I love the loser a little less. So I always end up talking to both of them on the phone at once. Have you ever tried talking to both your parents at the same time? Especially in competition? They're so busy trying to one-up each other in the categories of insightful questions and sage advice that they spend most of the conversation yelling at each other. I'm on the line merely as the moderator.

"How's work, David?"

"Yes, son, how are things at the office?"

"Did you decide to talk to your boss about that raise like I mentioned?"

"Elaine, if he talks to his boss right now, so close to that whole Negro thing, he could get fired. David, wait a little."

"I don't appreciate you putting down my ideas."

"I'm not putting you down. Your mother is so oversensitive."

"You're always putting down my ideas!"

"Elaine, calm down. You'll throw out your back again. Though I don't know how you threw it out in the first place. The hardest thing you do all day is order in dinner."

"Why should I cook when you make enough money to order good food?"

This is a good point. My mom is many fantastic, wonderful,

life-affirming things, but she is no cook. What my mom does to food actually tops ethnic cleansing on the UN's list of crimes against humanity. I still wake up in a cold sweat after one of my "filet of sole" nightmares.

"Your mother is such a JAP."

My mom's Presbyterian.

"I have a high level of stress. My back problems all come from stress. I've been saying it for years, but your father won't listen!"

"Your mother is a hypochondriac."

"I want to know how David is doing. Do you mind? Ed? He hung up. He is such a baby."

"I actually have to go, Mom. I have a meeting."

"And we didn't even get to talk. Call me soon. I need my David fix."

"Okay."

"Love you."

"Love you too. Bye."

I hung up. I just couldn't handle them sometimes. Don't let this conversation fool you. My parents are very happily married. I would bet you that right after my mom hung up, they probably had sex. How do I know this? They tell me. They won't shut the hell up about it. They say that communication is important. I yearn for the good old days of sexual repression. According to my parents, they've had sex almost continually since they got married. They love mentioning it and watching my and my brother Alex's faces turn green. It's the most awful image in the world and I hope your parents shield you from it. It may be a natural thing, but that don't mean it ain't nasty.

Actually, I'm glad they argue. It means they still have passion.

I'll call on Monday and they'll fight again and whoever doesn't hang up in disgust will get to hear about my day. Today, however, I didn't have the strength. I looked over my editor's shoulder to see how it was going.

An interesting tidbit about children's television: The people who work in it have some of the foulest mouths anywhere. They could make a construction worker turn red and try to change the subject. My editor, Chuck, is one of the worst. In the middle of cutting a scene where Captain Blueboots was telling little Jimmy it was all right to cry, Chuckie began to wax philosophical.

"I love the way cunts taste."

I hate that word. But I felt I had to say something. To be friendly and encouraging.

"They are tasty."

"I was going down on this chick last night, really lapping it up, right, and she just started coming all over my face. It tasted fantastic! You know what I mean?"

"Sure."

"They should make soup out of that."

I did not need that image. Thousands of women filling up soup cans, a smiling housewife rubbing her tummy on the label. Not pretty. To make matters worse, Tyrone the sound guy stopped by to check the levels.

"You telling him about the soup idea?"

This was an actual concept? This was a money-making scheme?

"Yeah, he doesn't look too thrilled, though."

"That's probably cause he's not getting any sweet pussy. He's too busy making his own chowder to buy our soup."

I felt the need to defend myself.

"I met a girl, actually."

"You hit it?"

Tyrone did a complex dance involving hip movement and slapping. Chuck started laughing. I had to put a stop to this.

"No, I'm a gentleman."

Tyrone kept a-shaking. Chuck brought himself under control and decided to dig deeper.

"You call her yet?"

"I don't have her number."

"So how are you supposed to go out again?"

"She's gonna call me."

Tyrone stopped dancing and shot me an incredulous look.

"Oh man. Why didn't you tell me? You've been here all week and the whole time your dick has been somewhere out in the world, stuck in this girl's pocketbook. It's a damn shame!"

"She's just waiting the requisite three days."

Tyrone scoffed.

"Only guys play that shit. If a girl likes you, she calls you up right away. This girl is never gonna call you, dog."

"She's gonna call."

"Okay. But you remember when she doesn't call that I told you she wasn't going to call. And then picture me doing this."

Tyrone started to do his patented happy white boy dance, which he stole from Carlton from *The Fresh Prince of Bel-Air*. Chuck couldn't breathe. Maureen, my coproducer, stuck her head in.

"You boys doing all right?"

Tyrone danced up to Maureen.

"Just talkin' about soup."

Maureen rolled her eyes.

"Please promise me you'll never tell me what you're talking about. I love not knowing."

Tyrone just smiled and danced. I had to put a stop to it.

"Get out of here, you're distracting my editor."

Tyrone boogied towards the door, waving.

"Good luck, Mary."

"Go away."

Tyrone danced out. Chuck wiped the tears from his eyes and looked me in the face.

"You look a little green. Want some soup?"

Maureen sat down next to me.

"David, has Harold said anything to you about me?"

"No, why?"

"I just have this funny feeling. That he's going to fire me."

Maureen had an alarmist streak as wide as the great Mississippi.

"He's not going to fire you. He'd fire me before he'd fire you."

"You're a guy."

"Exactly. And you're a girl."

"You wouldn't understand."

"What did you do?"

"You know how I was out sick yesterday?"

"You mean when you pretended to be sick so you could hit that sample sale?"

"Yeah. I left him a message saying I had food poisoning."

"I know. So?"

"So he called me later that morning to ask how I was! Who does that?"

"Good human beings."

"Not only that, he asked what I had eaten."

She looked at me triumphantly. She was in fine freak-out form.
"And?"

"And why would he do that unless he knew I was lying? He was
obviously trying to catch me in a fib."

"He was just seeing if you were okay. That's all."

"Then why..."

"That's all."

"But..."

"That's all, Maureen."

"But I could tell..."

"Calm down."

"I just know it meant that he..."

"It didn't, Maureen. Trust me."

She seemed almost disappointed.

"I guess so."

"Okay?"

"All right."

We lapsed into silence. Throwing water on Maureen's wig-out
fires had become part of my job description. I looked at the phone.
At least her attacks took my mind off the absence of ringing.

"Still hasn't called? You know, she may be married. Always a
possibility."

"Thanks. I'll try to keep that in mind."

"Just don't get obsessed over it. And don't forget our meeting
with Harold today. I'd hate for you to get fired, too."

Maureen patted my hand, got up and left.

The Goddess was going to call. But what if she didn't? I didn't even know her name. I guess I could call Opera Girl, if it gets to that point. But it won't.

The morning passed. No one called. Well, two editors, a kid from my college looking for a job, Sprint PCS, the head of Paramount Home Video, a suit from the network, and my landlady, but no one important. I gave Jim a ring.

"Hey, monkey."

"Hey, Gonzo. Daddy's this close to grabbing that half a point. My baby Mike Sweeney had a huge night last night. I think I'm gonna give him extra pudding tonight, just for being so good to me."

"The Goddess still hasn't called."

"I'm sorry. Ah, well..."

"What if she doesn't?"

"Then she doesn't. You'll live."

"I'm thinking of dropping Millar."

"I thought he was your new guy. Your family's provider. I thought he was putting food on the table."

"He hasn't hit anything out of the infield all week. He sucks. I'm dropping him."

"You are a moody little bitch, David."

"The Eater called last night."

"Does she obsess much?"

"She sounded all sad. Made me sad."

"Trust me, if I know her, that's all she's trying to do."

"So you're going up to Providence tonight."

"Yep."

"Do you need any practice denying involvement with that girl?"

"Throw me one."

"I'll be one of her light-fearing friends. 'Say, you and Janine look awful cozy. You guys doing it?' "

"Not at all. I sleep chained to her desk. She kicks me awake in the morning, feeds me from a dog bowl, and then lets me out the back to go wild on her crabapple tree."

"That sounds pretty sexy to me. You're supposed to be denying involvement, not describing it."

"Fine. Ask again."

" 'Big boy! Are you sticking it to that Janine chick, or what? She looks like she needs to be filled to the rim with Jim!' "

"I have no relations with the aforementioned."

"Better. Did you like the rim with Jim bit? I thought that flowed well."

"It was okay. You should have said it in the coffee guy's voice, though. That would have been funnier."

"You're probably right. I suck."

"True."

"I'm going. There's things."

"Bye."

By mid-afternoon, I'd decided I didn't care if she called, that she wasn't all that anyway, and that I was the biggest manbitch there ever was. So I gave in. I called Opera Girl. I got her machine.

"Hey, this is Maggie. I'm out of the country for the next two months backpacking through Europe so unless you are calling to tell me I inherited some serious cash, you'll just have to wait. Beep."

Hopeless.

❖

I pulled myself away from the phone and headed off to this stupid meeting. We were supposed to go over a new concept Harold was keen about. Apparently, he's gotten into yoga. (I shudder to think what color his sweats are.) He wants to incorporate his new obsession into the show. I didn't know how you get hand-operated puppets dressed like pirates to do yoga, but I guess that's why he pays us the big bucks. He was meeting with me, Maureen, and his yoga instructor. I couldn't wait.

I was the first to walk into the conference room. The walls of our conference room were a dark purple, like Barney had burst in as a suicide bomber and we just let him dry on the walls. The conference table was a monstrosity. It dominated the room with its sheer awfulness. You sat down in the matching purple chairs, whose backs always seemed to be broken so you had to fight to stay upright, and conducted your important meetings over a glass table that reminded me of a frozen lake in which thousands of dead toys were trapped for all time. You looked down at hundreds of action figures, stuffed animals, dolls and puppets, all arranged in hideous poses wrapped around each other. It looked like Dali's vision of childhood. It freaked me out. One Saturday I hung out in there with my PA, Don, and got very high. I won't tell you what we saw when we looked in the table, but ever since, I can't look at Ren and Stimpy without thinking bad, bad thoughts.

I sat down, and almost tumbled to the floor as the chair back proved just as defective as I'd feared. I pulled myself upright, and waited. Maureen slipped in five minutes later holding a coffee.

"They're still not here? Good. Do you think I have time for a smoke?"

Maureen took thirty-five smoke breaks a day. Each of them

lasted about ten minutes. Do the math. She still worked more than I did.

"I don't think so. They should be here any minute."

Maureen sat down, prompting another chair ballet.

"So, David, what do you think about this idea of his?"

"I'm lost. How are we going to make it work?"

"Don't look at me. A hand can only move in so many ways. How can you do lotus position with your index finger and your pinky?"

"Maybe they can just watch his pet yoga instructor doing the moves."

"Yeah, that won't be creepy. Great lesson for the kids. 'It's okay to stare at women while they bend.' I can't take many more of these ideas."

"Maybe the watching thing will work. We'd have to try it."

"David, just think of it. A woman lying on the floor bent over. Four puppets surrounding her silently staring. Those googley eyes could be looking anywhere. It would look like puppet porno."

"Well, he's going to want something."

Right then, Harold burst in followed by a familiar face. Bendy Girl! Who knew? I almost shouted out her name in surprise, before I remembered that I couldn't remember it.

"David, Maureen, this is Kelly Haverlock, the new yoga enthusiast for *The Puppeteers*."

"Actually, Harry, David and I have met before."

"Really? Fancy that. So you know how fantastic she is, right, Davey?"

I hate being called Davey. To me, it's the masculine form of "Toots."

"Sure do."

"So, how do you know my yogi?"

"Through a mutual friend."

"Great, right?"

"Definitely. She's very good."

Bendy Girl smiled.

"Thank you, David."

Maureen was smirking at me. But I hadn't slept with Bendy Girl. She was a friend of a friend of Annie's. We had met at a party at their apartment and hit it off. We had dinner once after that, but she had to get up at five A.M. so our date was over by nine. She was very cute, and I liked the yoga thing. It spoke of being in shape for years to come. I'm a far thinker. For some reason, though, I hadn't really thought about her all that much since. Home by nine can do that to you.

"So how can we get Kelly into our little program?"

Harry loved to call it a little program, especially in sight of the Emmys. Maureen took point.

"We've been talking about it, and I'm not sure how to incorporate it. Puppets are not very flexible."

"They don't have to do a full Warrior Three!"

He and Bendy Girl shared a yoga laugh. Maureen persevered.

"But we don't want it to look too fake, either. And we don't want them standing around watching like some kind of puppet perverts."

Harold cut her off.

"Davey, what do you think?"

"I don't know. I can't think of anything off the top of my head."

Harold sat back.

"Here's what we'll do. Maureen—work with Kelly here, run the rehearsals, and figure out a way to fit yoga in. We've done some research and yoga is the biggest fitness trend since Tae-bo!"

"For four-year-olds?"

"Don't be a smart-ass, Maureen. Davey, try to figure out how we'll shoot this. Make it beautiful! I know you can do it."

With that, he walked out. I did my own version of muttering.

"Fuck me."

Maureen was very sensitive.

"This is gonna be better than the Negro thing. I think you got the shit job, boyo. I just have to make sure everyone's bending correctly. Kelly, let me walk you out."

Bendy Girl put her hand on my arm.

"I'm sure you'll make it look wonderful. We should talk later and catch up."

Maureen rolled her eyes. She can be such a witch. They both walked out. Damn, I wasn't even going to get to work directly with the flexible hottie. Shit out of luck.

I made my way back to my office in despair. How do you make felt bending look interesting and believable? This was not part of my job description. This was way more than just another quick decision. This might involve creativity. I was fucked.

Maureen stopped by to gloat.

"Think of anything yet?"

"I'll think of something, don't you worry."

"So..."

"So what?"

"I sensed a certain...energy. Anything you want to tell me?"

"Not really."

"Fess up. You have so had sex with her."

"Actually, I haven't. Nor am I going to."

"She seemed pretty into you."

"I didn't notice."

"Didn't she touch you on the way out?"

"Yeah. So what?"

"She's into you."

"I'm a professional. I don't mix work and play. Anyway, she was just being friendly. She's a very crunchy person. They love everything. She would have acted the same way if I was a can opener."

Harold popped in.

"If the sexual tension in there had been any thicker, I would have fired you. Way to go, Davey!"

"See, even Harold saw the passion burning in your faces."

"Leave me alone, Maureen. Don't you have your influenza to attend to?"

"I'm just as addicted to your dramas, my friend."

"You guys are full of it."

Harold hit me on the back. It hurt.

"We'll see this weekend."

"What? What's this weekend?"

"We're going camping!"

What the hell?

"Tomorrow? We're going camping tomorrow? I'm sorry, I can't go. You didn't say anything about this before..."

Harold cut me off.

"I just thought of it. I think it'll be great for us to do a little team building and brainstorm this whole yoga thing out in the middle of nature. It's perfect. The three of us roughing it, communing with the natural world. You'll love it."

Maureen's face was pure terror.

"I'm sorry, Harold. I can't. I have plans."

"Cancel them. This is work."

"But I don't know how to camp..."

"It's easy. You walk for a while, then you put up a tent, and then you go to sleep. You don't need to be McGyver. It'll be great."

"But I..."

An idea popped up in my mind like the head of a prairie dog. Bendy Girl liked me. I thought she was cute. We were already friends, sort of. It was perfect! She could be the friend I look at in a new way! So what if she was too nice? Maybe once she'd been exposed to me long enough, I'd transform her into a puppy kicker. I didn't know. But this was the perfect way to find out. I piped up.

"Hey Harold, maybe we should invite Kelly. She'd probably have some good ideas."

Harold smacked my back so hard I involuntarily spit on my knee.

"You dirty bastard. I see right through you. But it's a good idea! I'll give her a call and invite her along."

Maureen was still sputtering.

"But..."

"I'll see you both tomorrow morning, then. Don't forget your backpacks! And bring lots of water. We're going to come back with some great ideas, I just know it!"

He left.

Maureen was not happy.

"This is your fault. Goddamn it! What the hell am I going to wear?"

She stormed out. I did not want to go camping with my boss. On the other hand, this would be a great chance to get to know Bendy Girl past her curfew. I just had to keep Harold away from her. He tends to get a little chummy with the ladies. Whether they invite it or not. He's particularly solicitous of breasts and legs. He's often spent entire conversations without taking his eyes off of one or the other. Low-cut blouses and skirts, long or short, have led to many a young girl's social discomfort. Hopefully, he goes to bed early. At the very least this outing will take my mind off of the Goddess not calling. Fuck. Now I was thinking about it. Ah well, at least thinking about the Goddess kept my brain free of the Eater of Souls. Fuck. Now I was now thinking about her. It never ends. I need a lobotomy. Everything would be easier. Spitting up peas would be the highlight of my day. The world would be perfect.

I decided to visit Annie to cleanse my pallet before the camping trip, like mango sorbet before the curry. When I got there, she was baking more of her wonderful cookies. Annie bakes some fucking awesome cookies. She puts marzipan in them. Most people I know don't like marzipan all that much, but they still love her cookies. That's because they're fucking awesome. I love those cookies. Annie, if you're reading this, never stop making cookies! If you do, I will stop caring about you! That's how much I love your cookies. Bake some right now, in fact. I'm coming over.

So you've gathered that I like the cookies. Annie's the kind of girl who bakes. Besides great cookies, she whips up fantastic banana bread, and cupcakes, and gingerbread houses, and popovers, oh those fucking awesome popovers! I've ruined pairs of pants just thinking about her popovers. I'm not friends with Annie just because she bakes. But it sure helps. Hell, I went all the way out to Queens. There is no stronger endorsement than that.

Annie encouraged me to taste the dough.

"How does Jacob not weigh four hundred pounds?"

"I don't know. Maybe he's bulimic."

Jacob the not-boyfriend was at work that night, so we were alone as we got sick on cookie dough. I sat at the kitchen table while Annie did something with eggs. I offered to help, but thankfully the mixer drowned out my whisper. I'm more of a moral support baker.

Annie picked up the bowl for a better mixing angle.

"This camping trip thing sucks. I was hoping you could hang out tomorrow."

"Why?"

"Jacob keeps hinting that he wants to say something or do something. Something I hope he doesn't say or do. So I wanted you there to help keep things under control."

"Would it be so bad?"

"I don't think I want to find out."

She seemed reluctant to say more, so I changed the subject.

"Do you remember Bendy Girl?"

"Sure, Vanessa's yoga friend. Why?"

Vanessa. That's the friend's name.

"It turns out my boss hired her to help us do a very special yoga *Puppeteers*."

"How are you going to pull that one off?"

"I don't know what I'm doing! Who hikes for four hours to brainstorm? I would think you'd be too exhausted to think about anything. And what happens afterwards, when I haven't thought of anything? That's when the shit will hit the big ol' fan."

"Don't start with that crap again."

"This time they'll realize I don't know what the fuck I'm doing."

"You'll think of something."

"The puppets will look like they're performing bizarre sex acts on themselves. I'll get fired!"

Okay. So, deep down inside, I was no more secure than Maureen.

"You'd better not. I only hang out with cool television people."

"This is what happens when you make decisions! You're lucky, Annie. You don't make any decisions, so you stay out of trouble."

"Thanks."

"Take my advice. If you're ever faced with an important decision, like if Jacob walked up to you right now and asked you to make your non-relationship a recorded fact, or even demanded to hold your hand in public, or else he's gone forever, you vacillate! You hem and haw and beg off! Because once you start making decisions, you can't stop. Next thing you know, you'll be picking which restaurant to go to before you leave the house, instead of playing it by ear and ending up at the same diner every time. You'll be wearing clothing that matches instead of standing in front of the mirror until you're forty-five minutes late for work and you have to throw something on at random. It will be the beginning of the end. The end being teaching yoga to felt."

"Are you done insulting me?"

"Sorry I...I was just kidding."

"I am a good dresser."

"It was a joke. I just got on a roll."

"You look like you got dressed by a malicious street performer."

"I'm sorry. I'm just venting. You know you're a fox."

"Sure."

Annie put the cookie dough in the oven and set the timer. She sat down and stuck a small wad of marzipan in her mouth.

"I like the diner."

"Obviously."

We sat in silence. Annie looked over at the oven.

"You have weird dreams, right?"

"Of course. I had a scorcher last night, actually. I was peeing outside, trying to write my name in the snow. But it wasn't my handwriting. It was all ornate, like calligraphy. And then I noticed that it wasn't even my name. It was someone called Arnold. I was about to check to see whether it was my penis when I woke up."

She didn't smile.

"I've been dreaming about flying again. Like back when my dad died."

This was not good. Annie's dad had been a pilot. He died when we were in high school. It wasn't even a plane crash. He had a heart attack while waiting on the runway. I remember how Annie just disintegrated. Totally fell apart. She was out of school for a month. She passed all her classes, though. I don't know how she did it, but she passed. She was always smarter than me. For a while, she had nightmares about flying. Normal, they reassured her. And eventually they went away. She went on living her life.

"What do you think that means?"

"I don't know. The dreams weren't scary in and of themselves. I'm just flying. Not like the old dreams at all. Last night, though, I noticed something. I looked around at the clouds. They weren't drifting by, like I thought. They were soaring upwards. I wasn't flying, I was falling. I looked down, but there was nothing there. I was falling forever. But it felt like flying. Then I woke up."

"That doesn't seem too weird."

"Everyone can't dream about severed heads trying to translate the Declaration of Independence into Braille."

Another of my winners.

"Do you think your dad has something to do with this whole fear of Jacob thing?"

"No. I hope not. Why does it all have to be my dad's fault? Everyone can't wait to pin it all on that one event. It's like a huge "get out of jail free" card. Every stupid decision I've made is because of that one thing. You knew me before and after. Did I change that much?"

Of course she had. Who wouldn't?

"I don't know. It was puberty. We all changed."

"I just don't buy it. I bet you it has nothing to do with him. I'm afraid I'll never be happy. Just like everyone else. That's all. I'm not some textbook case. I'm just screwed up like every other person in the world is."

This conversation was making me uncomfortable. Both my parents were very much alive. I had no frame of reference to work from. What did my opinion mean, anyway?

"I bet you're right."

"I just want to be happy."

"Me too."

"The question is, what's standing in our way? Is it really some outside influence, or are we doing it to ourselves?"

The oven timer went off. Annie got up to check on the cookies. I watched her, unable to answer.

I had almost fallen asleep when the phone rang. I let it go to voicemail and immediately checked the message.

"Hey, David. I don't think it's cool the way you're avoiding me. You're going to have to deal with me sometime. It's really hard, you know, going from talking to you every day to not talking to you at all. I miss you. I miss the way you made me feel. I miss the way you listened to me and made me feel like I wasn't crazy. I sent you a letter today. Please don't throw it out without reading it. I don't like the way you're ignoring me; it makes me feel like you think I'm crazy or something. Just read the letter. Bye."

I erased the message and curled up on my side. Just when I was getting to the point where I could really look down on her and put her away in my psycho folder, she did something like this and reminded me of things. I remembered holding her hand walking through Central Park. I couldn't just hold her hand. I had to play with her fingers, constantly touching her. I remembered lying underneath my parent's Christmas tree and talking about the future. I remembered the way she smelled (freesia) and the way she looked her best with her hair pulled back in a ponytail with one lock of hair hanging down free. I remembered her crying and me sitting there watching like an awkward boy afraid to break something. She didn't like being comforted when she cried. Since I couldn't hold her, I'd just watch her silently, trying to radiate good things. Clean, good things. Eventually she'd stop, and I could stroke her hair. We'd just lie there. This was why I loved her. Because I did.

I fell asleep trying not to cry. Who knows if I succeeded or not? I tell myself I didn't cry and that will have to be good enough.

CHAPTER FIVE

Fun With Mushrooms

Saturday morning found me in the car with Maureen. Don, one of our production assistants, lay across the backseat sleeping. Harold and Bendy Girl were in the car ahead of us. Poor Bendy Girl. Good thing she was wearing pants.

I just wasn't built to be awake at six in the morning. The plan was to drive up to the trail, get there by eleven, hike in and set up camp by nightfall. I wasn't sure what happened next. What is team building? I hoped it didn't involve falling and hoping to be caught. I didn't trust anyone I worked with.

I didn't know why Don was with us. He was only a PA. Even though he and Harold got along ridiculously well, he still shouldn't have been invited. I hoped I didn't pass out while hiking. My chances with Bendy Girl would probably lessen if I threw up on her shoes in a fit of dehydration.

Maureen was driving and looking as bad as I felt, if not worse.

She sucked on her fifth cigarette of the morning and her last cup of coffee was a distant memory.

"Why the hell am I here?"

"You shouldn't mutter while driving. You look crazy."

"This is the dumbest idea ever. This is worse than yoga puppets. There are so many things I could be doing with my Saturday. I could be sleeping."

Pause.

"And?"

"And what? I could be sleeping..."

I looked out the side window at the passing trees.

"I'm not too happy either. I'm barely awake."

"Good thing you're not driving, then."

"I agree."

"You will be driving. I am not driving the whole way. I will get out and ride with Harold before I let you ride shotgun all the way to the trail."

"It's nice to see you so passionate about justice."

I curled up against the hard door and tried to sleep. Maureen had other plans for me.

"So. How's the Stalker treating you?"

I didn't want to talk about this before my head had fully defogged.

"It's fine."

"Really? She's isn't calling you eight times a day anymore? That's too bad. Ladies are fickle."

"She's still calling. I just don't answer. Let me sleep."

"Yeah, I know all about psycho exes. Did I ever tell you about the Asshole?"

Jesus, just let me sleep!

"Yeah, yeah. You have."

"With my best friend!"

"A tale as old as time. It's practically a Bible story. Real tough luck."

I kept my eyes closed in a fierce hope that my exhaustion would win out over Maureen's incessant chatter.

"I ran into them a few weeks ago. At a party. I saw them first. When they noticed me, they got all sheepish looking. People are such bitches, you know?"

"Amen to that, sister."

I was almost there. Her voice was getting all fuzzy.

"Do you think I should have said something?"

Leave me be, harpy!

"No. It's all over. Just move on."

"Easy for you to say. Have you moved on?"

"I'm trying."

"Yeah, I've noticed that, Mr. Mopey."

A voice floated in from the back.

"You should just go out and bone some chicks, bro."

Fuck, Don was awake. This was a lost cause. I opened my eyes and straightened up in my seat.

"I don't want to just go out and have mindless sex."

"It's the best kind, bro. I had a sweet chick last night. Damn, she was so fucking hot."

Maureen looked disgusted.

"Don't you have a girlfriend?"

Don smiled.

"You bet your ass I do. When it comes to poontang, I am covered for every occasion."

"You're disgusting."

"I am laid. That's what bossman here needs. A little lamb on his shish kabob. That Kelly chick is pretty hot. Are you hitting that?"

"No, I am not hitting that."

"If you're not gonna, then I'm trying. We'll be all tired from the hike and she'll need a shoulder to rest her head on. Next thing you know, we go for a ride on my slip 'n slide!"

"Do not, and I repeat, do not try anything with Bend...with Kelly tonight. This is an office retreat. We need to behave."

"If you say so, dude. But I can't help it if she grabs it."

Don is not an attractive man. He's got a potbelly and his grin leaves something to be desired, namely intelligence. Still, he's not a bad guy to hang out with. Kind of like a trained seal, he's good for laughs. Except when he gets drunk and takes off his shirt. Nobody wants to see that. But he is a dog with the ladies. I don't know how he does it. I've seen him in action, and he ends up with some hot women. I mean model hot. He took home a Knicks dancer, I kid you not. And his girlfriend is very cute. It really makes no sense. I guess there's something to be said for being just smart enough. He's just smart enough to be smooth, but not smart enough to know he's out of his league. So he succeeds. Remember what I said about confidence. Don makes that work for him. Of course, he also asks literally every girl in the room. There's something to be said for taking the Uzi approach and spraying the area. You're bound to take down somebody. It just pisses me off that the somebodies he ends up with are so fucking hot. It isn't fair.

Maureen was offended.

"What would you do if your girl cheated on you?"

Don was taken aback.

"Why would she do that? I satisfy my woman."

"Really? It sounds like you're barely ever home. How do you know she doesn't get bored waiting for you? Maybe she's waking up in some strange guy's bed right now."

"That isn't funny. She would never cheat on me. She loves me."

"But it's okay for you to cheat on her?"

"I can't help it if I'm in demand."

I laughed. Don scowled.

"Screw you, man. And you too, Maureen. My girl is true. You're just jealous 'cause we're in love."

I shot Maureen a look.

"Yeah, Donnie. What you have with your girl and the greater New York metropolitan area is special. I wish I could taste the magic."

"I'm going back to sleep. Screw you both."

He closed his eyes defiantly. I smiled.

"I'm glad we brought him along. I needed to feel better about myself this weekend."

"He is good for that."

"You suck!"

We drove on into the brightening morning.

We got to the trailhead ahead of schedule. Harold was pleased.

"Let's get on those packs, people. If we push, we can get there by mid-afternoon. Then we'll have time to do some serious team building."

Maureen rolled her eyes. She struggled to don her backpack, eventually resorting to my assistance. It galled her, I could tell. Bendy Girl was in her element. She kept walking up and down the first twenty feet of the trail. She looked like a puppy who needed to be walked. Don had obviously camped before. He looked fairly comfortable. Harold, of course, was raring to go. He even wore a cap with "Born to Hike" written on it. Though the hat was bright pink, which made me feel better.

I staggered to my feet, pack on shoulders. I shouldn't have any problem finding some time to talk to Bendy Girl during the hike. She looked pretty fit, but I was sure she'd get tired sometime and I could hang back with her. No problem. Harold struck an adventurous pose with walking stick in hand.

"Are we ready to embark? Then let the hiking begin!"

And we were off.

An hour later, I wanted to kill everyone around me and then myself. I wasn't made for this hiking shit. Harold and Bendy Girl were way up ahead, talking brightly while skipping along. Don was close behind, walking briskly. I had been dragging Maureen for the last hundred yards.

"Shoot me right here, David. I don't want to live."

"Take a sip of water."

"I don't need water. I need vodka. I need something to take away the pain."

Harold shouted from up ahead.

"Hey, slowpokes! Don't be little sissies! We've got another four hours of hiking ahead of us. I'd hate to have to fire you for being so worthless and weak!"

Bendy Girl gave me a brilliant smile.

"Isn't this beautiful country? I love it up here!"

They turned and continued on. Don was talking to Bendy Girl, probably trying to get her to "grab it." I hoped that if she did, she'd throw it ahead like a stick for a dog. Maureen was attempting to light a cigarette. I held her steady until she succeeded. We pressed on.

The next four hours were a blur to me. I kept my eyes on my shoes trudging forward as I led Maureen along like she was blind. She ate both her powerbars and both of mine. At least she was too tired to bitch. I wanted to talk to Bendy Girl, but she was too far ahead. I couldn't keep pace. I'd almost reach her and then I'd run out of gas and she'd motor ahead, oblivious. I half-expected her to do backflips down the trail, like a hiking Mary Lou Retton. Harold yelled back what he thought were witty encouragements.

"Just put one boot in front of the other boot. That's about it."

"I thought you guys were team players. Come on, step on it."

"If we don't make it by mid-afternoon, you're both fired."

By that point, I would have sacrificed my job in a second for some sweet relief. Maureen was delirious. She kept asking her mother to stop poking her. I would have been more worried if I hadn't been dancing with Dame Judi Dench.

At one point, Maureen and I were so far behind we could barely hear the others ahead of us. Maureen looked at me imploringly.

"Just one second. Please. They'll never have to know."

"Okay. But we have to be quick."

We both leaned against trees. I wiped my forehead.

"A powerbar would really hit the spot right about now."

"I hope you saved yours, then."

I gave her a dirty look. She drank her water, oblivious. She blotted her mouth with her sleeve. I pulled out my cell and dialed.

"Who are you calling?"

"I'm just checking my messages at work."

My mailbox was as empty as it had been late last night and early this morning.

"That girl still hasn't called, huh?"

"Nope."

"What do you care? I thought you were going to hit on Kelly."

"I will. Give me time."

"If you wait any longer, Don will have already dumped her for a younger woman."

"She's a tiny bit more…energetic than I am."

"She's a machine. And I'm a fat pig."

I glanced over at Maureen. She looked like she hadn't had a snack in five years.

"I don't think you have to worry."

"She's so fit. It sickens me."

"Drink some more water. You'll be fine."

She took my advice.

"You'd better make your play soon."

"Don't worry. I'll make my move at camp."

"It'd be a shame to lose her to Harold."

"Harold, too?"

"He's been macking her like crazy. Of course, he probably wouldn't recognize her headshot. He'd need a little more of her below the neck in the picture to make a positive ID."

"He does that with everyone."

"I know, I know. There are shirts I can never wear to the office again, and it kills me. But he's liking her stuff in particular."

I didn't want to talk about this.

"Let's get going."

"Fine."

She smiled to herself as we peeled ourselves off of the tree trunks and headed off into the wilderness. I looked around at the trees surrounding us.

"Do you see the trail?"

"I see dirt."

"Fantastic."

Finally, an eternity later, we got to camp. The other three had already put up their tents. Harold was arranging a firepit out of loose stones while Bendy Girl and Don gathered sticks. Maureen lit a cigarette, leaned back on her pack and passed out. I didn't like playing for this team. Harold clapped his hands.

"Hurry up and pitch your tents."

My weak voice floated up from the ground.

"What are we going to be doing?"

"You'll see."

"Does it involve consciousness? If so, I don't think I can play."

"Stop fooling around and get to work."

It took me an hour to get my tent upright. I had borrowed it on the way home the night before from my buddy Cameron, who went camping all the time with his family. It had sounded easy enough when he explained it. But now, here in the wild, the tent was a sadistic Rubik's cube I could not solve. Finally, with unwanted help from Harold, I got it up. That last sentence is pretty damn scary when taken out of context. Maureen lay passed out in the center of a tangled pile of canvas and poles, cigarette jutting upwards like a smoldering white flag. Harold looked around in disgust.

"You know what? Never mind about that team-building crap. Screw it! Let's get naked and go swimming!"

Harold ran off towards the river. No one followed him. Presently, he came back, dripping wet in his shorts and a towel.

"You guys are all pansies. Well, I enjoyed my swim. Now who's cooking supper?"

Throughout all of this, I hadn't gotten much of a chance to talk with Bendy Girl. Harold and Don had been monopolizing her all day. I needed to make my own opportunities, I told myself, so when she volunteered to cook, I offered to help. Harold had other ideas.

"Nah, I don't think so. David, why don't you go out and grab some more wood. I'll help Kelly here. If I can do a Chatarunga, I can cook some beans."

They laughed. I walked off to grab wood, muttering some creative uses for said wood under my breath.

People say that the food on camping trips always tastes fantastic. Something about everything being tastier in the great outdoors. Those people are dirty, dirty liars. The food was awful. Beans and soup and shit like that. If it wasn't for the whiskey Maureen had brought, I wouldn't have been able to down any of it. Thankfully, the Wild Turkey numbed my throat and knocked out my taste buds for a few blessed minutes. Otherwise, we would have been catching repeats of my meal soon after the main broadcast. Harold ate with gusto, of course. Bendy Girl didn't complain, though I could tell her eyes were getting teary from all the beans. Maureen didn't touch her food. She just drank and drank until she felt no pain.

Once dinner was over and the plates cleaned, we gathered around the fire. Harold poked at it with a stick before speaking.

"This is the time for the real team building. I need you all to think outside of the box with this yoga thing. Donnie, did you bring the box openers?"

"Sure did, boss."

Don pulled out a baggie filled with fungus. Ah, drugs. That explained why Don got an invite. I can't say that I was surprised. We had all speculated that Harold was a fun boy. He was famous for his mood swings and no sane, uninfluenced man could ever eat that many chips. It also explained the time he'd conducted an entire meeting massaging the production accountant's head. Nor was I surprised that he would be so unprofessional as to bring them out at a company function. He knew we wouldn't say anything. Our jobs were much too cushy to rock the boat.

"Mushroom time, people! Down the hatch! This will help clear your mind and give you some new insight into yoga and the *Puppeteers* and maybe even into some stuff you weren't expecting! You can thank me tomorrow. Don't worry, they're supposed to taste like shit."

With that, Harold grabbed some mushrooms and gobbled them up. Don downed a few, as well. Maureen stared at the shrooms in her hand. Harold gave her an encouraging nod. She brought her hand up to her mouth and threw her head back with a forced gulp. Bendy Girl looked frightened, but she took a small one and swallowed it gamely. She must really need this job. When it came time for me to partake, though, I must admit I cheated.

There was no way in hell I was going to go tribal with my boss. So I palmed the mushrooms and took a big, fake swallow. I sat back and waited for the fun to begin.

A half an hour later, Harold was massaging my head.

"Do you know what a didgeridoo is, David?"

"No, Harold."

Harold reached into his pack and brought out a long hollow stick, about eight inches in circumference. It was decorated with bright symbols.

"It's an Australian musical instrument. The Aborigines would blow into it for hours. They'd never have to take a breath because of something called circular breathing. Kenny G can do it too. He once held a saxophone note for forty-five minutes."

I didn't know if I wanted to live in a world where Kenny G had that power. The spaces in between his notes are the best part of his playing. Harold continued.

"This didgeridoo is half-sized to fit in my bag, but it's still blessed by a real shaman. Touch it. David, touch it!"

I touched it. I wasn't proud of myself.

"Tonight I'm going to achieve circular breath. I can feel it. What are you going to achieve?"

"I don't know. Stuff."

"Focus, David! And then one day you'll be in charge and you can do whatever the hell you want!"

He danced away clutching his long, hollow instrument tight to his chest.

An hour passed. The shit was really kicking in, I could tell. Harold had disappeared. Don had his shirt open, revealing his impressive beer gut. On his head he wore his dinner bowl like some kind of army helmet. He carried a stick in his hand that he waved around while making machine-gun noises. All the while he danced like he was in a seventies disco movie. He kept pointing his stick at Maureen and riddling her with imaginary bullets seductively. I could see why he did so well with the ladies. Bendy Girl sat in a lotus position staring off into space. I sat down next to her.

"How are you doing over here?"

She smiled at me.

"Have you ever noticed how wonderful joy is?"

"Why yes, I have."

"It's fantastic. Joy is so wonderful. I want to take a long luxurious soak in joy."

"I'd settle for a quick sponge bath."

This was very good. She was talking about water. Bendy Girl was nice, but wet Bendy Girl was the grand prize. Wet, naked Bendy Girl was the grand prize plus whatever's behind curtain number three.

"Have you ever noticed how alive dirt is? Look at it! I wonder if it would make me more alive?"

She started smearing dirt on her face.

"Hey, calm down there. You're starting to look like Martin Sheen in *Apocalypse Now*."

I was going to stop her, but my mind jumped ahead to step two, namely the rubbing of the dirt over the rest of the body. Unfortunately, Bendy Girl's mind wasn't playing the same game of hopscotch as mine.

"Have you ever noticed how silly knuckles are? They make me laugh! So...much."

She proved it with a huge laugh. Not even a mind as nimble

and one-track as mine could figure out how to turn this into nudity. She took care of it for me.

"Have you ever noticed how needy nipples are? They just... look! A camel!"

She pointed at her big toe. Damn! So close.

"Have you ever noticed..."

It wasn't fair.

Another hour passed. Bendy Girl turned me on to everything from the night sky to the Dewey decimal system. Harold was still missing, though I kept hearing what sounded like Louis Armstrong being violated by a confused buffalo off in the distance. If that's the didgeridoo, then I wasn't sure what the Aborigines were trying to prove. Maybe they were just angry. Maureen and Don were arguing about whether one particular stick looked like a penis. Bendy Girl tapped my shoulder.

"I want to see more!"

She held out the bag of mushrooms. I held up my hand.

"No thanks! I've had enough already."

She continued to smile at me. She grabbed a handful of mushrooms and placed them in my mouth, tracing my lips with her finger. I was helpless. Before I could spit them out into my hand, she grabbed the back of my head, and kissed me full on. I couldn't help it. I swallowed. I didn't want to, but sometimes common sense comes a distant second to impressing a girl. She let me go and looked around in wonder.

"Have you ever noticed how flirty air is? Look at this leaf! Have you got a quarter? I want to hear it sing!"

She chattered on. She seemed to have forgotten about the kiss. I wanted more. I leaned in and kissed her again. Time slipped away as we made out, sitting in the dirt. Eventually, I noticed that she was still talking as we kissed. Then I noticed that her feet were behind her head. Finally I noticed that her head had been replaced by a watermelon. I stood up sharply and spun around in confusion. Oh shit, I was on drugs!

Oh well. At least I was getting some. I dropped to my knees and crawled back to the watermelon, begging forgiveness. She seemed to welcome me in. I leaned in and lost myself in her lips.

Time danced by. Eventually, I opened my eyes and looked to the side. Don was teaching someone how to make a bong out of his belly button. That must be Maureen, I figured. Must be. The girl leaned back after taking a hit of Don's stomach. Wait a sec. I know that smooth, flexible body. Don was smoking up with Bendy Girl. Than who was I . . . ?

I pulled back. Maureen looked back at me, lips shimmering in the faint moonlight.

"Oh, shit."

I scrambled to my feet and staggered over to Don.

"How long have I been over there with Maureen?"

"Dude, time has no meaning. But you've been sucking face forever!"

Maureen stared at me. When I stared back, she quickly dropped her eyes toward the ground. I turned around, dodged the bodies of Don and Bendy Girl going at it by the fire and ran out of there.

As I made my way through the trees, the air got heavier. I could feel it pushing down on my shoulders. Eventually, it forced me onto a small boulder. Women's faces hung in front of me. Bendy Girl, Maureen, Opera Girl, The Eater. My phone rang. Even out in the middle of the fucking wilderness, she could still reach me. I screamed into the night.

"That bitch better stop calling me!"

That felt pretty good.

"I never want to see her again!"

Maybe this whole circular-breathing lesson was a good idea after all.

"She looked so nice in a bikini!"

Whose voice was that? That wasn't my voice.

"She kissed like her lips and yours were jigsaw pieces that fit perfectly."

Who the fuck was talking!? I was starting to freak out.

"When you made love, she fit you perfectly. It was like you were slipping it back into the box it came from."

I scrambled to my feet and turned around, back away. There, reclining on my rock like it was an easy chair, sat a Victoria's Secret mannequin in a see-through bra and a thong. Her mouthless head stared at me with world-weary condescension.

"That is not the point! She never understood me."

The mannequin didn't care about my protestations. Her rigid nipples pointed at me accusingly.

"All you wanted was sex sex sex sex sex! Maybe she wanted someone to stroke her hair and make her orange juice."

"I did those things! I did everything I could. So I wanted sex! What's so wrong about that? I don't want to be with someone who doesn't want to sleep with me. Does that make me Mussolini?"

Her featureless face wasn't having it.

"Second chances, David. You can't escape her. Why do you want to?"

"It was all wrong! Love isn't like that! That was too hard!"

The mannequin shook her plastic head sadly.

"It's never easy, David. You know that. You've seen Oprah. *You gave up before you gave it a real chance. She is unfinished business. You can't run away from that. It doesn't matter how many women you put between you and her, it will never be enough."*

"What do you know? Why won't you leave me alone? Stupid Victoria's Secret mannequin trying to tell me what to do."

"She's the love of your life."

"She's a confused, self-centered girl who never took the time to even get to know me. She's frantic now because someone took her toy away."

"So she could change. It wouldn't be that hard."

I stumbled around angrily.

"You're twisting things. That's the point. She won't change. And even if she did, it wouldn't be enough. It was just wrong."

"Of course she could change. Look at me. I can change in an instant. Put a long flowing silk nightgown on me, I'm an elegant princess. Dress me up in flannel pajamas, I'm the smiling coed you wake up to on a Sunday morning. And in a hot red corset and garters I'm your most depraved daydreams come true. I can become any of those women, I just need the right clothes. She just needs to know what to change into. That's your job. You need to give her the chance to be what you want her to be. You need to show her the right clothes."

I could see the mannequin's face changing, becoming familiar. I turned away in self-defense.

"That's not right. That's not how it's done."

"That's exactly how it's done."

"Leave me alone!"

I whirled around and ran, heading straight for camp. Frantic thoughts shot through my head like bottlerockets. I didn't need to throw up a thousand women between me and the Eater. I only needed one. Maureen had kissed me once, she'd do it again. That'll show her. I burst into a clearing, ready to take Maureen like a wild animal. I stopped up short. Shit. Wrong clearing.

Harold sat alone, playing the didgeridoo. Circular breathing must have continued to elude him since he sounded like he was getting the Heimlich while he was puffing. But there had been one development. Harold was now buck naked. He saw me and waved.

"Come sit down! Take off your pants! I'll let you have a blow!"

I got out of there. By the time I made it back to camp, the early morning light had melted all shadows and I couldn't remember what I was running towards.

The next morning, no one said much. We all avoided each other's eyes. I couldn't even look in Maureen's direction. I kept picturing her face as I pulled away from her. Harold seemed unaffected by his night of nudity.

"Get your gear together! We hit the trail in ten minutes, people!"

I looked over the ground to make sure I hadn't left anything behind. I found my metrocard over by the fire. It must have fallen out while Maureen and I were being tricked by the evil narcotics. As I picked it up, I noticed a little pile of fungus on the ground. Right where Maureen had been sitting. A handful of mushrooms, surprisingly undigested. I drank in the implications.

"Let's get a move on! Time's a wasting!"

We made it back down the trail in record time. Not even Maureen dawdled. Before we knew it, we were back at the cars. Harold gave us some final words of wisdom.

"I hope last night helped you guys as much as it helped me. I feel pretty great this morning. I worked on my circular breathing. I hope you all worked on something too. I can't wait to hear your ideas on yoga; I'm sure they'll be off-the-wall fantastic. See you in the office!"

He hopped in his car with Bendy Girl and Don (who had decided not to ride back with us, surprise surprise) and they sped off. I looked at Maureen. She looked a little to the right of me and spoke.

"I'll drive."

As we approached the city, she finally broke the silence.

"Drugs can make you do strange things."

I waited for her to continue.

"And last night...I guess the shrooms took us both for a ride."

"I guess so."

"But it doesn't mean anything, right?"

She glanced at me. I didn't know what to believe. But I knew what to say.

"Of course not. It stays in the wild."

"Good."

I took a good look at her while she drove. She was pretty. I'd noticed that when we'd first started working together, but I had filed it away under "Don't Go There." We got along fairly well, mostly relying on the teasing banter that coworkers of the opposite sex often adopt. And we'd been working together for a while now. She was an old friend. And I was looking at her in a new way. Those pieces did fit. But if I felt worn out by her wig-out sessions from the sidelines, how would I handle the full brunt? She'd eat me alive. Plus, nothing had changed. We still worked together. As the great Plato once wrote, you don't shit where you eat. I returned my eyes forward resolutely. But my gaze kept darting sideways as we flew back towards the city.

I made it back to my apartment by mid-afternoon. As for all of those uncomfortable thoughts, I did the healthiest thing I could think of: I repressed them. Burying uncomfortable thoughts always makes me feel creative, so I sat down at my computer to work on my screenplay.

I think I would be a fantastic screenwriter. For one thing, I love movies. I love words. I love the words in movies. And that is, for all intents and purposes, the essence of screenwriting. I had endless stories and characters floating around in my head, and when I told these tales to myself, I was delighted and amazed. But looking at what I'd actually managed to put down on paper, I had to admit something was being lost in the translation. What sounded in my head like an impassioned speech about heartache turned into a whiney rant against meter maids. I couldn't translate the passion. I'd work myself up, constructing these intricate plots in my mind involving Mafia chiefs and supermarkets and Cadbury Easter eggs that would be both funny and moving, with killer special effects. Tears would be in my eyes thinking these Oscar-worthy thoughts. But what ended up on paper seemed more like the product of a woefully deficient public school system. But every once in a while, I'd write something memorable. A funny line that really flowed. A short speech that captured the moment perfectly.

And that encouraged me. I know I can do it because I've done it. The next step towards fulfilling my genius and grabbing my Academy Award is to somehow string these isolated sentences together into an entire script. In an effort to be bold, I'd even thrown out my plot. Whatever I write is what I write. This was supposed to let my mind soar free like the eagle so it can come back bearing profound insights into the human condition. More often than not, what I got back was a dead mouse.

My writing was going nowhere, so I turned off my computer. I reached out and banged on the wall. Then I spun around in my chair and grabbed my guitar and flipped on my amp. I heard the buzz from Rory's amp next door. Rory is a locksmith-slash-filmmaker only two years removed from Pakistan. And his name really is Rory. He won't explain it. That's cool. We've been jamming through the wall for a month and a half. We're both beginners. Try not to imagine it. You'll only hurt yourself.

I set my amp to play a heavily distorted, almost heavy-metal sound. Rory went for more of the traditional fuzzy blues. We tuned to each other without really knowing what we were doing. We just turned knobs until we felt like we'd accomplished something. Then we started in on one of the greatest rock songs ever. The kind of masterpiece that has such a memorable guitar riff you almost cry when you hear it. At least my brother cries when I play it. It's the kind of riff that you pray you never hear from the twelve-year-old next door whose mom just bought him an amp and a mini-Fender, took a Valium, and passed out. That's right. We played "Wish You Were Here."

I don't know why our neighbors never complain. Maybe they think it's construction. Surely it isn't music, they probably say. It must be some kind of new car alarm. One time I taped it and when I went to play it back I couldn't tell if the tape was playing or if the recorder was stuck on scrub rewind. It's kind of like what I think mentally unbalanced mass murderers hear right before they kill again. Good times.

I finished jamming with Rory, screamed "Rock on!" through the wall, and climbed back into bed. The Eater hadn't called tonight. She must be redirecting her energies towards poor Annie. I felt bad for Annie. Though deep inside, the little bastard survivalist in me danced the stepdance of joy. As I got ready to fall asleep, I purposely banished all thoughts of women from my head. It was too much and I needed to stop thinking about it.

It's all the same to me. I was Zen and that was my new mantra. It is all the same to me.

I fell asleep around four in the morning. I had gotten into bed at ten-thirty. But it's all the same to me.

CHAPTER SIX

To Shit or Not to Shit

Monday morning. I hate it so. I had fun with the snooze and didn't get out the door until a quarter to ten. So I was more or less on schedule. I averted my eyes as I passed the Victoria's Secret, but I couldn't help but notice the mannequins were decked out in black thongs and translucent white nighties this week. I walked faster and tried not to think about all the sex being had. Fucking lingerie. You don't know what you're talking about.

I got to work twenty minutes late and checked my scores. Still in last place. Why can't fucking Aurilia hit a fucking baseball?! That's what they pay him for. That's why he gets to take the winter off! Fucking slacker! I dropped Aurilia from my roster and picked up Orlando Cabrera. He was my savior, I knew it. I'd ride his superior defense all the way to first! I called Jim to gloat. An unfamiliar voice answered. It must be the control-freak boss.

"Hello?"

"Hi, is Jim there?"

"He took today off. And tomorrow."

"I guess I'll try back later in the week."

"Sure thing."

He hung up. Jim took days off? Right in the middle of the firing campaign? This sounded serious. I hoped he wasn't getting played by that Goth chick. A small voice inside of me hoped he wasn't getting laid either, for obvious reasons (to wit, I wasn't) but I ignored that voice. I focused on my concern for my friend. Maybe he really was chained to the kitchen table! Maybe he went to some strange Goth club and got involved in some kinky, "Eyes Wide Shut" shit. Led down some stone steps into a deep, dank cellar where his Goth guides gave him black eye makeup and pierced his tongue. Then the wall slid away and he could see all the creatures of the night, writhing in ancient, malevolent ecstasy and playing D&D. They dealt him in as a wandering bard. When he accidentally rolled a seven on the twenty-sided die and got the entire expedition killed, they turned on him, chained him to a giant wheel, and then left him for dead. Two days later, Janine finally crept back in and thanked him quietly for not telling anyone that he was with her. He told her it was nothing and could she please get him down, but she had already left. And there Jim remains to this day, chained to a huge wheel in the basement of a Goth club (which was probably a Gap during the day), punished for all time for his ineptitude with a twenty-sided die.

Or he got laid. I preferred to think it was the former. It was more cinematic that way.

Maureen walked past my door, conspicuously not looking in. Fuck. I had successfully avoided thinking about the women in my life for the whole morning. Bendy Girl was no longer an option.

Flexible or not, I refused go where Don had gone before. It had to be unhygienic. But Maureen...I looked at the message light on my work phone. If the Goddess would only call, my decision would be simple. But that was feeling more and more like a pipe dream. There would be no easy ways out for me. I could feel the Eater breathing on my neck.

Could I fall in love with Maureen? A montage of Maureen moments flashed by me.

She gets hired as an associate producer. She spends the first six months convinced that Harold hates her. She only calms down when I explain that she had been wearing turtlenecks, which limited Harold's interest in talking to her.

She makes her first major mistake, like all of us do. Hers involves forgetting to book a car for a special guest. The guest, an affable children's author, is fine with taking a taxi. Maureen is less forgiving. We find her a day later buried under eighty-four empty pints of Cherry Garcia. The amazing thing is that she actually weighs ten pounds less than the day before.

Maureen gets promoted to producer. Her first day, a PA loses a guest release and it takes a Sounds of the Forest album and Don furiously puffing cannabis into the vents in her office to calm her down. The PA quits in shame and later resurfaces as a television psychic.

Maureen gets dumped by her boyfriend. She goes insane, caught between so many different ways to wig out that she faints at the sheer number of choices. When she comes to, she goes out and buys the entire M.A.C. makeup display at Macy's. It will be two years before she can go shopping there again.

Maureen has dinner with me to discuss new show ideas. She

goes through napkins like she's Nixon's document shredder. She doesn't even think about it. That's just what she does. When we leave, she takes one for the road, leaving a napkin trail down Forty-fifth Street.

I couldn't date Maureen. That would be suicide. Maureen passed by my door again. I jumped guiltily. She didn't look at me. She stopped to talk to a coordinator. I found myself noticing her smooth skin and long, pretty legs. Maybe because she was so neurotic, she was in great shape. Not fit, really. More fragile than that. But attractive. Her back was to me. Slowly, unconsciously, my eyes slipped down past her waist. I had to admit it. Nice ass. Like she could feel me, she turned. My eyes darted up like lightning, but I wasn't fast enough. She blushed and rushed out of my sight. It felt weird being caught checking her out. Almost unholy. But not quite.

We got along well. We'd known each other a while. She definitely fit into the old-friend-in-a-new-way mold. We made each other laugh. We were very comfortable around each other, or at least we had been before the mushroom incident. I enjoyed hanging out with her. Maybe...

Don't shit where you eat! Don't shit where you eat!

But wasn't this how some of the greatest love affairs started? With two good friends finally seeing what had been in front of them the whole time?

You'll regret it! Find someone else! Totem Pole! Even Diseased Girl is better than the woman you will see every day long after it blows up in your face.

But who am I kidding? I'll never find love with those women. Maureen, on the other hand...there was a chance there. A slim chance, but a chance. Those other doors kept getting slammed in my face. What should I do?

I stared at that darkened message light. Damn phones. At least in the old days, you could blame the mailman, or the stagecoach, or Indians. Now, it's either she's lost my number, which doesn't speak very highly of her regard for me, or she's been mauled by tigers and doesn't really want to go out until the scars fade, or she just plain doesn't want to date me. I don't like any of these scenarios, though number two would be a pretty fucking good excuse, actually. Nothing I could say to that, really, without looking like a total bastard.

Maybe I could be gay. That would solve everything. And I think I could be gay. Except for all the sex. The gay sex would definitely be a problem. But I could be a nonpracticing homosexual. I'd hang out with the girlfriends, go clubbing and eat salad. So it was decided. From that moment forth, I was a nonpracticing homosexual. But I wasn't going to tell anyone. No need to start rumors.

This wasn't helping. I called the parents.

"Hey, Mom!"

"Hey, honey!"

"Hello, son."

"Hi, Dad."

"How's the muppet yoga going?"

"They're not muppets, Dad. They're puppeteers. Muppets are the enemy."

"Did you figure out how to shoot it yet?"

"I'm working on it."

"I know you'll make it work, honey."

"Thanks, Mom."

"So, your father's been smoking his cigars in the bedroom. I think I'm allergic."

"You are not allergic, you are a hypochondriac."

"My eyes swell up, and I can't sleep. Now that's an allergy."

"I've been smoking cigars for fifteen years and now your mother suddenly gets an allergy."

"The body starts to break down as you get older."

"Yours sure does. You're falling apart like an East German car."

"See what your father does?"

"Don't get so worked up. It's like last night in bed. You started to complain about your back during your favorite position. We do that all the time. Why does it hurt now?"

I started to sing the La La song in my head.

"I didn't stretch properly. I need to stretch beforehand, you know that."

"Nothing kills the mood like the sight of you stretching. What's that sound? David, are you singing the La La song?"

"David, honey, there is nothing more natural than two people in love having sex. How do you think you came about?"

"I had always hoped for Immaculate Conception, actually."

"Honey, do we embarrass you?"

I was painting my parent's bedroom when I was sixteen. It was a big job and I had to move all of their furniture. That's when I saw it. Tied to each bedpost was a necktie. I almost threw up. Most people have to deal with the thought of their parents having had sex at one time, long ago. I had to deal with the thought of my parents having weird sex right now. What's weird about it, you may ask? It's just a little innocent bondage, right? This was a king-size bed. The neckties were maybe a foot long. In order for my mom to reach both of them, she would need the wingspan of a pterodactyl. I'm grossing myself out just talking about this. Other people don't have to deal with this. Their parents stopped having sex after they had kids, like normal people. My parents put up a sign on the kitchen door that says "Give us ten minutes...Make that twenty." And they loved to torture us with it. They made out at dinner. They gave each other backrubs. They sang porno themes and giggled as they ran up the stairs to their bedroom. It was so healthy it made me sick.

"Son, you don't have to worry. With your mother's back, we'll need a chiropractor on call for the next time we get busy. Hello? I think she hung up. So, what's up?"

"I have female problems."

"Is she still calling you?"

"Yeah."

"Are you okay? We worry about you."

"I'm fine. I'm actually thinking about dating somebody else."

"Okay."

He sounded hesitant.

"It's been a weird weekend. There's this one girl who's nice and pretty and flexible. But she kinda bent herself around someone else. And there's this other girl that I work with, well, I think she likes me. I know, I know. Work people are bad. But I don't know. There may be something there."

"David. Calm down and listen to yourself."

"I am listening to myself."

"Maybe this isn't the right time to go dating all these women.

Maybe you should take some time to get your life in order. To get back on track."

What the hell was he talking about? What would he know? He'd gotten it right the first time. He didn't understand about the struggle.

"Maybe. I don't know. Anyway, I'm sure I'll figure it out."

"What are you looking for with these women? True love? Quick screw?"

"I'll figure it out."

"I don't want you to go rushing out there and get hurt, David. Be smart about it. That's all I'm asking. There's a reason your mom and I are still together."

Pause.

"Yeah? Which is?"

"Once I figure it out, I'll let you know."

We had reached the time limit for how long my dad could go without making a joke. It wasn't long.

"You'd better not let Mom hear that."

Once, when I was a cynical fifteen-year-old world-weary sage, my mom was driving me home from chorus practice. We were talking about my dating life. I was feeling particularly morose, so I declared to my mom and any women in earshot that I did not believe in love. My mom slapped me right across my face. I was stunned. She pulled the car over to the side of the road and faced me.

"No son of mine would ever say that. Don't you ever say that again!"

"Mom, you clocked me! What the hell…"

"How can you look at your father and me and say that you

don't believe in love? It stares you in the face every night at dinner. Are you saying that I'm just delusional? I don't ever want to hear you talk like that again. What do you know about love? If I've raised you for anything, I raised you to believe in love."

"Okay. I'm sorry. You didn't have to hit me."

"Yes, I did."

She pulled out onto the road again and drove home. That was the only time she ever hit me. I've crashed her car. I've burnt down her garden shed. I've kicked her dog. I've screamed at her that I hated her. But the only time she ever raised her hand to me was when I denounced love. Whenever I felt like I had no chance of ever finding anything real to love or to make me happy, I would remember that ringing slap and the world reasserted itself. It was the birth of my optimism.

"Dad, I gotta go."

"Okay. I'll talk to you later."

"Bye."

Maureen passed by again. Apparently there was some important shit going on over by the supply closet. There she was again, heading back. That was quick. I heard her enter her office and close the door. Should I go over there? What should I do? I stayed chained to my chair, imprisoned by indecision.

An hour or so later I remained stuck in the same position when someone knocked. I looked up hopefully. What the hell?

"Hey. How you doing, man?"

Jacob stood in my doorway.

"Hi. Um. Hey. Come in. Hi. What are you doing in this part of town?"

Jacob walked in. The not-boyfriend himself! His hair stood straight up in punk blond spikes. His pants had more holes than threads. His shirt, at least, was a respectable ripped flannel, though his leather jacket could hold up a convenience store by itself. He looked like he bit the heads off of puppies, just to teach them about the cruelty of life. His big metal-tipped boots seemed destined for some poor uptight yuppie's ass. A cigarette sat behind his ear, waiting to give the finger to our no-smoking policy. He was a scary motherfucker.

"I need some advice about romance."

Poppa didn't see that coming.

"Okay…do you want to sit down or would you prefer to loom in a threatening manner?"

"I'd loom, but these boots are killing me."

He sat down. I've hung out with him a few times, so I knew he was really a sweet guy. Who has happened to, on occasion, rip the spines out of fake bad boys when they tried to fuck with him. He's a true punk. He has an ideology. He really believes in things. And he hates poseurs. Thank God I've always been what I appear to be: an idiot.

"Why me? My track record sucks."

He propped his death boots up on my desk. I refrained from comment.

"Better than mine. My last girlfriend left me for a fucking banker. Said I was too intense for her. But then I met Annie…"

"She's great."

"Yeah, she is."

"You guys are great friends."

He snorted.

"Friends. That's the magic word, isn't it. You know Annie really well, right?"

"Sure. We've been friends forever."

"She keeps talking about passion. How she really needs it and wants it and on and on. Has she always been like that?"

I thought about it and picked my words carefully.

"I remember when she was thirteen. She decided she wanted to date me. She didn't even know me, she just decided. So she went down every romantic gesture like it was a list of require- ments. She left roses on my locker. She wrote me a poem. She found out where I lived and serenaded me under my window. But I never got the sense she really felt comfortable with it. She read the kinds of books that told her that things were done a certain way. So she did it that way. If a book told her to hit me on the head with a club, she'd have done that too."

"Did you guys date? I didn't know that."

"I refused. I just didn't feel it. It took half the school year before she finally gave up and we could be friends. And now we laugh about it."

Jacob's boots tapped against my desk, making the whole thing move.

"So what are you saying? She's not really romantic?"

"No. She's very romantic. That's very important to her. I just wonder sometimes whether it's what she really wants."

To the relief of my elderly desk, Jacob returned his boots to the floor and sat forward.

"That's my question. What do you think she wants me to do? I can't keep going on like this. I've put up with it so far because, well, for a lot of reasons. But I can't anymore. I want more."

"I don't know what to tell you."

"What would you do to win her over?"

"I wouldn't even know where to begin."

"Please. I need help, here."

The sight of the man with black fingernails looking so despondant broke me down. I couldn't help him, really. It had nothing to do with him at all. It was all in Annie's court. And I knew that Annie was dreading this very thing. But I also knew how it felt to sit powerless and wait upon someone else's whim, so I decided to give him a little hope, unfounded though it might be. Anyway, I couldn't help but think that Annie just needed a push towards what would make her happy, even though it scared the shit out of her.

"We both agree Annie's got this high romantic bar she wants to live up to. Maybe she needs to see you that way. Maybe you need to do something so crazy romantic that she has to admit to herself that there's passion there."

"What, like give her a card?"

"I think you need to kick it up a notch."

"Okay."

I looked at the man wearing spiked bracelets sitting before me.

"But don't try to be something you're not. You shouldn't have to change yourself. Just do what feels natural."

"That's good advice, man. I appreciate that. Please don't say anything to Annie, okay?"

"No prob."

"I just want to be with her, man."

"I had no idea you were such a romantic pussy."

"The baddest punks usually are."

With that, the chain- and leather-clad shit-kicker with the heart of a soft teenage girl clutching her pink teddy bear stood up and stomped out. I hoped for Annie's sake he pulled it off.

He had balls. I had to give him that. Risk. It was all about risk. Did I not have a big pair of stones as well? Hell yeah, I did! Big as mountains! Big ball-shaped mountains! Emboldened, I stood up and strode tentatively out of my office. It took me a while to make my way to Maureen's closed, forbidding door. I paused. What would I say?

I fought down a feeling of desperation. I had to look at this logically. What I had to get around was my natural inclination to fuck things up. Sure she likes me now. But I had never looked at her this way before. I never cared. When I care, I fuck up. The only reason I didn't drive the Eater off right away is that she talked so much, I didn't have a chance to verbally fuck up until we'd already been dating two months, and by then she kind of expected it. I was a disgrace to virile men everywhere. I had all the moves of an epileptic at a fashion show. This was why I needed not to care. Because when I care, I say stupid things. I fill silences. It doesn't matter if I really want the girl. Hell, I'm usually on the third date before I notice her hair color. It's about making her want me. I'm so busy trying to win her over, I don't bother with my own thoughts on the matter. There's always some little David inside of me, jumping up and down and screaming, "She's got the intellect of a lima bean. She thinks boy bands are catchy. Her favorite sitcom was *Full House*. She's a kind, generous, hopeful person. She's all wrong for you! You need cynicism. You need biting sarcasm. You need a *Freaks and Geeks* fan. Don't you see!" But I ignore it. I'm too busy trying to get her to ignore her little shouting person to listen to my own.

So I needed to go back to being the David who looked at Maureen as the kooky coworker. Back to the guy who just liked to hang out. Back to the David who didn't think about Maureen's lips. No pressure. Piece of cake. I knocked and opened the door.

Maureen sat behind her desk, talking on the phone with her head in her hands. She was speaking in a low tone, as if she didn't even trust her own office. A pizza box lay at her feet with one slice left, the last survivor of a horrible natural disaster. The TV was tuned to *General Hospital*, the comfort food of women everywhere. When she saw me, she quickly straightened up.

"Bye, Mom. No, I'll talk to you later. I've gotta go. Mom, I swear, I'll call back. I gotta go. Bye."

She hung up and smiled weakly. I gestured to the other chair.

"May I?"

"Sure."

I sat down. She stared at me. I stared at her. The last piece of pizza got uncomfortable and flipped over so it didn't have to watch. She broke the silence.

"So, the rehearsals are going well."

"That's good."

"We don't get the puppets 'til next week, but that should be plenty of time to figure stuff out."

"Sounds good."

"Still gonna look stupid, but that's more your department."

"Yeah."

I couldn't say anything. She was really cute. The pretty eyes and the full mouth coupled with her wry, uncertain smile and nervously shaking leg somehow formed a sexy whole. I had never really looked at her like this before. I almost wanted to kiss her. Her smile grew more and more uncertain under my stare until it fled completely. She began to chatter.

"Look, I'm sorry about the camping thing. I don't know what happened. I must have thought you were someone else or something. I would never do something like that under normal circumstances. Really. Are you weirded out? I wasn't the only one. You were kissing back, don't forget that. We both crossed the line. Look, let's just forget about it. We're professionals, right? We made a simple mistake. It's not like we slept together. Let's just move on. Please stop staring at me like that."

Attach a pump and her leg could have powered Con Ed. With every word she fired out, I grew calmer.

"Don't worry. I'm a little weirded out, true. I'm sorry about freaking you out."

She relaxed a little, meaning her hand stopped twitching. She really did have beautiful eyes. Frightened, but beautiful.

"No worries, right? As long as we're okay. I know neither of us meant anything by it."

She sounded almost pleading. She was embarrassed. She had been found out. She had a crush on me! It was written all over her. My stomach jumped. Her lips were slightly wet. She licked them nervously. I couldn't help it. I stood up, leaned over the table and kissed her.

She didn't really kiss me back. Maybe she was too busy trying to keep her leg from kicking a hole in her desk. When I pulled back, she gripped the sides of her chair. This was just what I needed. No rejection, no games. I knew she wanted me, so I had no fear. She pulled herself together, kind of.

"What the fuck was that?"

"I kissed you."

"No fucking shit! What the fuck was that?"

"I wanted to kiss you. So I did."

"Do you want me to have a heart attack!"

"I'd rather you avoided it. CPR could be construed as sexual harassment."

"Why did you do that?"

"I told you. I wanted to."

"You can't do this to me."

"I'm sorry."

"This can't happen. We work together."

"I guess we do."

I leaned in to kiss her again. To my everlasting surprise, she stopped me.

"I mean it. We work together. We can't do this."

"But we've already done it."

"That was out in the wilderness. This is right here in the office. Can you imagine what the minds of people like Tyrone would do with this? The soup products they'd come up with?"

"But sometimes you have to take a chance, right?"

"Not with my job. I can't."

I couldn't believe it. She still wanted me. I could practically feel it in the air. She wanted to reach out across her desk and stick her tongue through my head. But she didn't. The queen of wigging out kept her cool. What could I say to that? I stood up.

"I'm sorry for making you uncomfortable."

"No, we're fine."

"Of course we are."

I walked to her door. I looked back. Her eyes shot up from staring at my ass. She looked like she wanted to say something. But she didn't. I opened the door.

"Keep me posted on the rehearsals."

"I will. You betcha."

As I closed the door, she was already on the phone, ready to let it all out.

When I got back to my office, I sat staring at the wall for a while. I needed to stop it with all these risks. The minute I took one, I got kicked in the crotch. My life seemed to consist of a thousand kicks to the crotch. There was no relief in sight. And my message light remained dark, mocking me.

CHAPTER SEVEN

The Letter

I left work ten minutes early for no good reason and headed homewards. Before I trudged up the stairs I opened my mailbox. Sigh. The Eater of Soul's letter had finally appeared. Was she watching me? Or was fate telling me something about who I really belonged with? Everything she had never gotten to say in her twenty previous phone messages was laid out in ink. It made me nervous. I didn't want to hear all the things she never got to say. When she thought of something, she tended to blurt it out, so this letter had to be filled with the things she didn't mention in one of her messages. Meaning she had thought long and hard before sitting down to write. I could handle the Eater of Souls off the cuff, but I didn't know if I was ready for the reflective, reasoning version. She'd spent almost two years playing me like a banjo. She knew which strings to pluck.

I made my way up the stairs to my apartment, opened the door, and threw the envelope on the kitchen counter. Then I ordered Chinese. This was an emergency and I needed Beef with Broccoli to deal with it. Twenty minutes later the food arrived and I sat eating it, all the while staring at the unopened letter. I started to feel a little dirty. I turned my back on the envelope and switched on the TV. I changed channels until I found a Yankee game. Nothing could distract me from my life like a good Yankee game. The Yanks were up 5–0 on the Devil Rays. Fuck. Not the Devil Rays. That was like watching the Lakers play the Girl Scouts. I mean, sure you get to see some physical play, but at the end of the game you were left with a forty-point differential and an urge to eat Thin Mints. It was 5–0 in the first inning, by the way. Nope, wait a sec, 7–0. Giambi just hit a homer. Mussina was pitching for the Yanks. The Devil Rays threw out some fifty-year-old ex-science teacher who topped out at sixty-four on the radar gun. I couldn't concentrate. I'd rather watch hunters club baby seals; it's more humane. Why couldn't it be the Red Sox? I wouldn't give that letter a second thought if it had been the Red Sox with Pedro pitching. Okay, not Pedro, that would make the Yankees the Girls Scouts. But still, the Red Sox would be a distraction. The Devil Rays gave me the same kind of vague guilt that I'm sure Germany felt when they invaded France. It was just too easy.

So I was back to looking at the letter. I reached over to open it. I called Annie instead.

"Hey, help me out."

"Why, what's up?"

"I don't want to read this letter."

"So you finally got it, huh? She's been calling me all weekend.

'Did he get it? Did he get it?' I've started hearing her in my sleep. Well, maybe now she'll stop."

"She won't."

"Yeah, I know. If I were you I wouldn't want to open it either. She seems very proud. She told me it encapsulated everything she felt."

"Great, just what I need. An encapsulation. Should I tell her I'm a nonpracticing homosexual? Do you think that would help?"

"She'd probably say if you were nonpracticing, why not date her, too, since the sexual dynamics wouldn't be changing."

"Jesus, why won't she leave me alone?"

"Read the letter, send her a note telling her you're sorry and move on. Rip it off like a Band-Aid."

"I know, I know. I'm just building up my strength. You're an emotional pushup."

"I'm everyone's emotional pushup. Between the two of you I feel like I've been used for ten sets of fifteen."

"I'm sorry. Do you want me to tell her to leave you alone?"

"God, no. I promised her I wouldn't tell you I was talking to her."

"Do you break the promises you made me so easy?"

"No, no, you're my friend. She's just my cousin. But if she found out she'd tell her mom, who'd tell my mom, and then boom! Passive-aggressive city."

"One of these days you're going to have to say something. You keep getting stuck in the middle like this and you're never going to want children, just to stop the succession of guilt."

"I'll do that the same day you date a girl for her personality."

"Hey, I only date women I like as people."

"Name one."

"I liked Sandy."

"Oral sex and the subsequent outrage don't count as a relationship."

I went down on Sandy on Long Beach the summer before I started dating the Eater. She was a beautiful girl with perfect breasts and brilliant green eyes. She wanted to be a singer. I told her I played guitar. We shared a lot of long silences that I chose not to think about. After I went down on her, we laid back in the sand and scrupulously avoided touching each other. I wanted to hold her, but I could tell she was somewhere else. I wanted her to want me. So as we were walking back to the car, I tried to dazzle her with my beautiful words. I ended up showing off my scorching case of verbal hemophilia. I wanted to dream up some sexy, romantic thing to say that would show what a suave, sexually experienced man about town I was. Something D. H. Lawrence or Henry Miller. So this is what I said.

"You know, I've got this taste in my mouth. I don't know how to describe it. It's part sand... and part you. Hmm."

I'd never seen that expression on a woman's face before and I hope I never see it again. If I had dropped my pants to reveal a live hedgehog jutting out of my crotch she could not have looked more horrified. She dropped her jaw like she was an anaconda about to swallow a large rat. The sad thing is, I meant it to be a compliment. I like the way a woman tastes. But as usual, what sounded like Anais Nin in my head came out all Howard Stern. And my subsequent assurances of "It's a good thing!" didn't help matters. I never saw her or her beach-filled vagina again.

"Annie, I'm offended."

"Don't blame me. I'm not the one picking sand out of my teeth."

"If you're not going to be constructive, I'll just go."

"I'm sorry. Read the letter. If you want to talk later, I'll be up."

"Thanks."

"Good luck."

"Bye."

The letter still sat there, despite all my positive thinking. Time to face the music. I tore it open.

As I scanned the tightly packed handwritten pages, I felt a wave of unreality wash over me. This couldn't be her. Not the self-absorbed Eater of Souls. Not the girl who once talked for twenty minutes before she realized her cell had lost the signal. Not the girl who told me that two friends of hers were coming into town and that they were going to stay with me, and when I told her that might be inconvenient, she replied that she had told them how small the place was and they were okay with it. Not the girl who once put down the cordless during a long-distance phone call with me so that she could play with her dog because he looked "a little droopy." When she called me back a half an hour later after a game of fetch the ball, she was actually pissed that I had hung up. That couldn't be the same girl who'd written this letter.

The letter was an apology. It didn't actually specify what it was apologizing for, but you can't expect miracles. She promised to try harder, to listen to me, to be a better girlfriend. I couldn't believe what I was reading. She was willing to change any way she could in order to make this work. Our love was stronger than mountains, apparently. She didn't know what she had done to drive me away, but she would try to fix it. It was the most nonspecific apology letter I'd ever read, but it sounded sincere.

This was exactly what I had been afraid of. This letter was graffiti on my inner wall. It marred the picture I had painted of my ex. I started to wonder if maybe she really was the one. My eternal soulmate. And I was ruining it for myself. All this time I'd thought I'd fooled myself by creating this perfect girl I was lucky to be dating, when maybe, after the breakup, I had gone in the other direction by fabricating this horrible witch that I had no choice but to break up with. I was doing so well! I had gotten all Zen about women. I was feeling good! Why did she have to wreck it? I kept reading.

Don't you remember? You're so busy thinking about why we don't work. Don't you remember the hot tub behind the swimming pool in Montauk? Don't you remember lying under your parents' Christmas tree and talking about winter weddings? Don't you remember the game you made up for me on Valentine's Day? The quiz on how much I remembered about our relationship? I got almost all of them. I just couldn't remember the name of the Italian restaurant. Don't you remember swing dancing when everyone else was doing the two-step? Don't you remember that see-through bra I wore for you that night we went to . . .

She wrote on, relentless. I skipped ahead.

How can you remember how happy we were and still push me away? But I won't wait forever. I'm still at the point where I can forgive you, but wait too long and it'll be too late.

She'd forgive me? I knew she'd eventually do herself in if she wrote long enough. We both had a form of verbal hemophilia. Any offspring would have it for sure. I'd rather find a nice stoic and try to breed this out of my gene pool. But then she got me again.

No matter what you did or what you said, I still loved you. I still

love you. I don't know what I said or what I did. But I think some-
where deep down you still love me, too. I look forward to the day we
can tell each other that.

I stashed the letter away with the photos I still kept of the two of us. One day I'll throw them out. Maybe this weekend. I picked up one of the pictures and stared at it. We looked so happy. We were on the boardwalk by Coney Island and I was making a face. She was laughing and mock-punching me. Later, I remembered, we went back to my apartment, played Scattergories, made love perfectly and fell asleep. It was the beginning. I had no idea things would turn out like this. Would I still have fallen if I'd known? Do those walks on the boardwalk and late-night Scattergories sessions justify the incessant phone calls and schizophrenic letters? Was it better to have loved and been harassed than to never have loved at all?

I wanted to forget our entire history. It made it harder to think straight. I have moved on. And part of moving on is burying the good times until it's safe to dig them back up. It wasn't safe yet. It's easier when she blames me. Angry and upset I could handle. But the past... the past was dangerous. The past made me forget why we broke up. It just reminded me how good it was to be together. This was what I wanted to avoid. Of course there had been good times. We were together for almost two years. I'm not a masochist. I was happy for some of it. Very happy, at times. But it went wrong. And I needed to concentrate on the part that went wrong or I'd go crazy missing the parts that went right. That's where doubt lived. And where there's doubt, there's always the possibility for repentance. If I started thinking about Italian restaurants (named La Mela, by the way) or see-through bras, I'd start thinking about my loneliness and her comfort. So I don't look at the mannequins. I look down. I stay strong. I'll have all the time in the world to remember about how nice my first love was when I'm married with two kids. But for now, I was still susceptible to relapses. So I couldn't think about Christmas trees or boardwalks. I couldn't think about how nice her head had felt on my chest, or how beautiful she looked all bundled up against the cold with her hat and scarf on. I couldn't think about how easy it was to lie back and talk nonsense with her on Sunday morning, without feeling stupid for not saying anything worthwhile. I had to remember her angry and spiteful. I wished I could remember exactly how that looked, because I was losing it. I was softening, and that was the path back to the wrong future.

I picked up my cell. The Eater's number seemed to pop up like magic. My fingers seemed to move of their own accord. I was so tired of fighting. So tired of reminding myself. I just wanted to give up. It would be so easy. So easy. Like slipping back into the box I came in. I lifted the cell up to my ear. Somewhere out in the world a phone rang.

"Hi, I'm not in right now. Leave a message."

Maureen's voice. Bubbling up to save me.

"Hey, it's David. I'm sorry about today. I swear, I'll act like a gentleman from now on. I'll have to read up on it, but I'm sure I'll get the hang of it once I practice. Anyway, I just wanted to say sorry I embarrassed you like that and I hope you're not mad at me. But I'm not sorry I did it. Just so you know. I'll see you tomorrow."

Keep running until they take you down with the tranquilizer dart. Looking back just slows you down.

I never dream about sex. It's kinda weird, actually, because I dream about women all the time. Women I've known, women I've slept with, women I can only imagine I passed on the street that day. But I never sleep with them in my dreams. I dance with them sometimes. Swing dancing or slow dancing or once a tango during halftime at a Knicks game. We talk a lot in my dreams, usually about useless things like ranch dressing or the Belgian Congo. These dreams are extremely vivid. I can remember every pore on the woman's face after I wake up. I remember the cockeyed smile she threw me after the monkey ate my guitar, or her bright eyes shining as we got off the car at Space Mountain. The surroundings are always fluid, ranging from the Sahara to an eighteenth-century pirate ship to Circuit City. We can be trapped in pudding or freeing the slaves. But I'm always me. And she's always her. Whoever she is. And I never sleep with her. Maybe, once in a while, I'll kiss her chastely. Then I throw her out of the plane and jump after her, right before it explodes. I don't pretend to understand why I dream this way. I hope it's healthy. I'd hate to dream in an unhealthy manner.

That night I had a vivid dream about the Eater of Souls. We were food shopping at the A&P. I wasn't wearing any shoes since I had just donated them to charity. She was dribbling a melon like a basketball. We knew the race would start at any moment. I stretched. She shot some hoops. We were both getting limber. A kid I went to elementary school with handed me a water bottle. The Eater was toweled off by my great-aunt Peggy. We turned and took our positions at the starting line. At the other end of the track waited a telephone. I knew that whoever got to that telephone first would be believed. I glanced at the Eater. She looked terrified, but she was still going to race. Nothing would get in the way of that. We waited at the line for the starter's gun. It went off and I began to run.

I felt like all my muscles were being flexed simultaneously. I couldn't get them to work together. In my bare feet, I staggered down aisle six. I looked to my left and she was neck and neck with me. I couldn't pass her. She couldn't pass me. And then she started to throw words at me. They were made out of papier mache and they broke when they hit me. Her face would change with each one. First she'd be crying. Then she'd be angry. Then she'd be pleading. Then she'd be happy. Then her eyes would shine the way that I remembered. And with each word, I'd stumble. But I kept running. And though I couldn't pass her, she couldn't pass me. The telephone inched nearer and nearer. Finally, in a move of desperation, I made a huge leap and landed on the phone. I could feel her right behind me as I lifted the receiver to my ear and heard my own voice say, "I believe you."

It would be more poetic if I had woken up then. But instead I went on a rollercoaster with my brother and some girl I had a crush on in college. After that I went swimming, learned how a baseball was made from John Lithgow, and jumped off a cliff. Then I woke up, wrapped so tightly in my sheets I couldn't move.

CHAPTER EIGHT

The Belly of the Beast

As the rest of the week zoomed by, my relationship with Maureen took an unexpected turn. She never mentioned our little incident, which I expected. But instead of avoiding me like I thought she would, she kept stopping by to go over work details. She started flirting with me. It was an odd sensation. I guess she felt emboldened by my frank admission of interest. And our little games drew me in. If I said this would she say that? If I accidentally touched her like this, would she brush up against me as she walked by? I began to really enjoy myself. I still checked my message light, which would light up for a thousand vendors and crew but never the Goddess. Yet it didn't bug me quite so much. I was caught up in the Tango Maureen.

I still hadn't heard from Jim. He'd apparently taken the rest of the week off and turned off his cell. I hoped he wasn't on a boat bound for India, about to be sold into white slavery. I pictured Jim. Well, maybe someone would buy him in one of those two-for-one deals. He could be a gift with purchase. I'm sure those white slavers would come up with some clever marketing plan in order to move him quickly. I'd have to call on Monday to see how it all came out.

Annie called me at work on Thursday. Maureen had just laughed too loudly at a stupid joke I'd made, so I was feeling pretty powerful. She smiled as she left me to my call. Annie didn't sound quite so merry.

"Hey, have you let her know you got that letter?"

"No, not yet."

. "The sooner the better, my friend. For both of you. Send her an e-mail or something. Oh man, I am in pain. My back is killing me and my wrist feels like I've been opening up beer bottles with it."

"What happened?"

"You remember Tommy? I think I've told you about him."

"Which one was he?"

"He's the booby grabber."

"Oh, that's right. My hero."

"We were running late with snack, so he tried to take a cupcake from the counter where Denise had stupidly left them out. I saw him, grabbed the cupcake first, and put it up high out of his reach. He bit my wrist so hard I had to pop his jaw to get him off me. Thank God he didn't hit anything vital. I turned to pick up a napkin to wrap my wrist in and then, out of nowhere, he smacks me across the back with a folding chair."

"Like in the WWF? Or is it the WWE? I can never remember."

"It hurt like a motherfucker! And I couldn't do anything. All I wanted to do was whack that boy so hard, but I let Denise deal with him while I grabbed a Band-Aid."

Annie works with children with autism. Not autistic kids, by the way. If Annie hears you talking like that, she won't feel any remorse about whacking you. She runs a playgroup every Monday, Wednesday and Friday. The other days she works with kids privately. She's very good with the children. She slowly draws them out of their little worlds by painstakingly crawling into their closed minds and leaving trails of Oreo cookies for them to follow. For every word they say, they get a piece of cookie. For every toy they ask for, they get a piece of cookie. The hope is that their love of cookies will entice them out of their shells. It's a ridiculously long, repetitive process with uncertain rewards. Annie's been doing this for eight years and she's "cured" one child. Most of the kids she works with will never be normal, but they'll be a lot better off for having known her. When you think smaller, the rewards are huge. She makes a child notice the world around him. And she's the one who points it out. She's the track lighting in his dark little room. I can only imagine how that feels.

There are downsides. Like chairs across the back. The bitch of it is that she can't do anything about it. She can't react. If she gets mad or yells at the kid, it only reinforces the bad behavior. He knows that doing this thing will get a response. So he'll do it again and again. This would be bad. Therefore, if he pees on her leg, if he picks her nose, if he grabs her boob, if he bites her hand, if he licks her eye, if he pulls her hair, Annie can't do a damn thing to retaliate. To put this in terms that I understand, these kids can feel up as many boobies as they want and no one will do a thing about it. They are my gods.

So Annie is always limping, or bleeding, or buying new bras.

But, as I remind her, there's job satisfaction, and you can't put a price on that, now can you?

"That sounds awful, Annie."

"And I had been so happy with him. Earlier he had asked for his truck without any prompting."

"Did he ask you for the World Wrestling championship belt after he laid you out flat?"

"That's not funny."

"I couldn't do your job. I would be drop-kicking children left and right, and that is just not humane."

"You get used to it."

"How do you get used to constant beatings by five-year-olds? It must wear on your soul. A three-year-old could kick me in the nuts and I'd just have to pat him on the head and say good boy."

"No. You just couldn't react."

"What about tears? Is that reacting? Can I at least cry, like a man?"

"You can if you're smiling."

"So that's what they mean by the 'tears of the clown.' It's being kneed in the berries by an autistic kid."

"A kid with autism. It's not his religion. If you had syphilis I wouldn't call you the syphilis guy."

"Why would I have syphilis? What are you implying?"

"You'd be that asshole with syphilis."

"I am very clean, thank you."

"Don't make fun of my kids."

"I'm not making fun. Even though I'm too self-involved to ever do something like that, that doesn't mean I don't respect what you do."

"It's not about me. Don't make fun of my kids."

"Of course not."

"And call her! Tell her you got that fucking letter."

"You know, you hold in all that anger with your job, you hold in all that anger with your family, do you see a pattern?"

"Don't talk about my family. I'm in hell. I'm supposed to be heading over there tonight for my grandma's birthday and Jacob just pulled out."

"What? That's not cool."

"No, it's okay. He has to work. He felt terrible, I could tell. Plus, now I feel a little less like I'm taking advantage of him. It is a lot to ask when both my grandma's birthday and Easter come so close together. If he were to disappear on Easter, then I'd have problems."

"So what are you going to do?"

"I've been calling people, but no one's around. I may have to go by myself."

"You're not going to ask me?"

"Of course not. Let's just say you're not exactly the pope in the eyes of my family right now."

"I thought they liked me."

"They did. But your ex-girlfriend is the golden child. And you've defiled the idol."

"Is she going to be there tonight?"

"Eventually. She's working. I'm actually hoping I can sneak out of there before she shows up. I don't think I'll have the strength to field David questions on top of the inevitable Jacob queries."

I really owed Annie a lot. She dealt with my mess every day.

"Look, I'll come with you."

"Dude, that's suicide. I'll go alone."

"Maybe my presence will take some of the heat off you."

"You could murder her right in front of everyone and they'd just ask me why I never got killed by an ex-lover in a fit of passionate rage. That's just my life."

"I'm coming. As long as I'm out by the time she gets there, I'll be fine. Besides, I like your grandma. I want to wish her a happy birthday."

"She is the greatest grandma alive."

"No argument here. Come on. Let me do this for you."

"Okay. I'm not going to lie and say I couldn't use the support. Just be warned."

"Duly noted."

"All right, then. Be at my place at seven. We'll drive up. And thanks."

"My pleasure."

"This doesn't let you off the hook, you know. You still need to call her."

"Okay, I'll call her. But she's not going to like it. And neither am I."

I hung up.

"Busy?"

Maureen stood in the doorway. She was wearing a tight skirt and what must have been twenty-inch heels. I forced myself to focus on her face. By her smirk it was obvious that she could tell the effect she was having on me. She sauntered over.

"Here's the rehearsal schedule for next week. I wanted you to have it, just in case."

Her hand brushed up against mine as she handed the paper over to me. The electricity almost made the schedule burst into flames.

"Thanks. If I need anything, I'll know where you are."

"Good."

She smiled at me. I smiled at her. Breaking eye contact, she turned smoothly and walked out. She gave me one flirtatious glance before she left my doorway. I heard her reach her office.

"Motherfucking shoes. Where's my fucking chair?"

I heard her door close. I had to smile.

I picked up the phone and called the Eater. I knew she was at work. I left a message.

"Hey, it's me. I got your letter. I know what you were trying to say, but I still don't think we should get back together. Anyway, I gotta go. Bye."

Something tells me that wasn't what she wanted. But it was all I was willing to give.

On the way to Annie's, I farted on the subway. It really is an awful thing to do to your fellow passengers. And it was right after the doors closed during the rush hour crunch, so no one could run. I felt horrible about it. It was a bad one, too. I could see the realization dawn over the other people in the car. First their noses twitched. What is that? Then they pulled their heads back, instinctually running from the bad air. But there was nowhere to go. They looked around, as if knowing who had done it would make it all better. Did I mention that I was standing? So some poor sap sitting behind me had his nose at ground zero. It's a wonder he didn't pass out. No one said anything. But I could tell they were suffering.

They began to breathe through their mouths. But even that didn't protect them. The infected atmosphere simply crept into the mouth and then up into the nose from behind. There was no escape. This was a subway ride to hell. I wrinkled my nose too, just to fit in. Truth to tell, though, I didn't mind it at all. It didn't smell so bad to me. It didn't smell good, but I still enjoyed it a little. I guess you could say it smelled decadent. Something all the better for being wrong. I felt invincible. We were on a subway car filled with tear gas and I was the only one wearing a gas mask. We were at the bottom of the ocean and I was the only one who could breathe underwater. I was still moral enough to feel guilty. Especially for that sad bastard behind me going into cardiac arrest. But for all my empathy, there was still a small part of me breathing deep and smiling. On the outside, I breathed shallow out of sympathy. And a fear of getting caught and having the passengers force me to the floor while they each let one go in my face, one after the other, until I cried out for someone to kill me.

When we hit the next stop, my car emptied like a sinking ship shedding rats. I could see the remaining passengers doing the Clue thing in their heads, trying to figure out which of the remaining subway riders was the murderer. They never pegged me. I was too shrewd for them. Plus some poor badly dressed teenager drew most of the suspicion. I rode to the next stop and I stepped off. I was Jack the Ripper, and they'd never catch me.

I met up with Annie at her apartment. Her car was in the shop again, so she borrowed Jacob's while he was at work. I searched the glove compartment frantically for the emergency joint I had been told about, but no luck. Annie gave me a sympathetic pat on the knee.

"I was looking earlier. He must have smoked it before the New Year's party."

Jacob needed something to get through the horrific ordeal of the Annie family gathering. I wouldn't have been surprised to find everything from a flask of JD to crack cocaine. Anything to take the edge off.

"I'm not sure I can make it through this without chemical assistance of some kind, Annie."

"I anticipated that. Open my purse."

There, nestled between a Neil Gaiman novel and a Tampax lay my messiah.

"Sorry about the white trash-ness of the narcotic, but it was the best I could do on short notice."

"Hey, it's like I'm fourteen again."

I grabbed the bottle of Robitussin and downed half the container in a single gulp.

"Quit bogarting the sweet stuff! Hand it over."

I passed the bottle over and Annie finished it off. It was feeble protection against the harpies, but every little bit helped.

Annie hated to face her family alone. They had a way of making her physically ill. Consequently, her aunts were convinced she was sickly and went to great lengths to comment on it frequently during family get-togethers. And contrary to popular medical belief, repeated questions of "How about a carrot, will that hurt your tummy?" and "If you don't like my veal, just say so! Don't just go running off to the bathroom!" are as dangerous as exposure to nuclear waste. Annie's aunts were the equivalent of the Chernobyl meltdown. And Annie said nothing. Kept the peace. Kept her mouth shut. Gritted her teeth during the muscle spasms that followed each passive-aggressive needle her family poked her with. It took a lot out of a body to keep all of that inside. And her body was wearing down because of it. She was getting old before her time. Her back hurt, her immune system worked on the "Hide under the table so they won't get me!" method of protection and, of course, there was the colon thing. Spastic colons are an evil affliction, because it's so hard to prove you've got one. Annie's unsympathetic loved ones dismissed her condition as everything from food poisoning to menstrual cramps. It took a short hospital stay to persuade them that maybe she wasn't faking. And they still weren't completely buying it. Somewhere inside lived the certainty that it was all a big hoax. A bid for attention. Why would they think that? Because it's something they would do.

For the past few years, Annie had finally gotten some small protection from these vultures. Jacob the not-boyfriend to be precise. He left his leather and chains at home, threw on a hat and tried to be one of the squares for an evening. He deflected their ire through his very presence. They couldn't taunt her about her unlovability, since here stood somebody who could raise his hand as a card-carrying member of the Annie fan club. For these events, Jacob was very firmly Annie's boyfriend. Any ambiguity would be leaped upon and gnawed apart. This didn't completely derail the machine. Annie's aunts would still try to undermine the situation in what they thought of as subtle ways.

"So Jacob, where did you meet Annie? Were you one of her kids?"

"You're so strong, Jacob. I bet you don't take any of Annie's lip!"

"She sure does enjoy her cake. I hope she doesn't go throw it up again. Because of her colon, of course."

Jacob just smiled and stayed silent. Annie depended on him to be the dam in the river of familial bile. She could hunker down behind him and stay dry for a little while. Since he couldn't make this merry occasion, I'd have to show off some of my all-weather protective qualities. It was enough to give me a spastic colon.

It took us an hour to reach the house way up in Rockland. Annie thanked me for coming at least forty some odd times during the ride. It would be cute, if it wasn't so ominous. I had met her family before, and each time I came away a good five pounds lighter. I just sweated it out under their constant barrage. I think they operated under the "There must be something wrong with him if he's friends with our Annie" supposition. I operated under "Annie must be adopted."

We pulled up the driveway slower than I thought a car with a standard shift could go without stalling. Annie grabbed the Robitussin, upended it above her mouth while smacking the bottom to encourage any stubborn drops of cough syrup to give up the ghost for a good cause, and violently threw open the car door. I knew better than to say anything. You don't poke the scared cat, not if you wanted to keep all your skin. Annie muttered under her breath.

"Murder is a sin. Murder is a sin. I'd never get away with it. Just say hi to grandma, drink some punch, and leave. Oh God I wish I was...Hi! How are you?"

Aunt Rosa stood in the doorway, a huge fake smile painted on her face.

"Hello, Annie! How's my little ray of sunshine! Have you been eating? You're a little pale. But what am I saying? Of course you've been eating. I mean, look at you! Hi, David! Don't worry, Annie made us promise not to say anything about the horrible mistake you've made. So mum's the word! Though I wouldn't be caught alone with Aunt Tina, if I were you. Just a bit of advice."

Aunt Tina is the Eater's mom. I regretted not bringing a switchblade for my own protection.

Aunt Rosa disappeared back inside and we followed her into the lion's den. It was packed with the entire clan. Annie's family just loved to reproduce. They weren't happy unless they were popping another poor bastard out into the world, ripe for the psychological damaging.

The clan celebrated a bunch of holidays. These included Christmas, Easter, New Years, Fourth of July, Cinco de Mayo (don't ask) and Grandma's birthday. The aunts circulated the holidays between them, much like the National League and the American League trade off the World Series. Everyone gets a shot at home field advantage. Annie's mom lived in California, so she only came out for Christmas. I was the only cavalry Annie was going to get tonight. I looked around nervously, but thankfully, no Eater. I whispered in Annie's ear.

"Remember, two hours at most. I don't want to be here when she shows up."

"Don't worry. She doesn't know you're coming, so you'll be fine. She doesn't get out of work until eight-thirty."

Aunt Rosa's voice flew across the room like a javelin and skewered us.

"Come into the kitchen, Annie, and say hello!"

All three aunts were in the kitchen arguing over whose fault it was. Annie and I couldn't figure out what the problem was, and they probably couldn't have told us. But it had to be somebody's fault.

"If you had waited a minute…"

"This is so like you."

"Don't look at me. I'm not the one with the fancy education."

Their arguments made very little sense. They spent most of their time offended. Aunt Tina hated fancy educations. She got very defensive when people acted all smart around her. And I wonder where the Eater had learned it… Aunt Rosa was the youngest and she was always on the lookout for anyone getting something more than she got. Aunt Antonia (sounds like a mountain range in Texas) lost her husband to sanity. He'd woken up one morning ten years ago and realized that even though he was a devout Catholic, when faced with a choice between hell in the next life and hell in this one, he'd rather take his chances with Satan. So he divorced her and became a Buddhist out in Arizona someplace. He was Annie's hero. Aunt Antonia couldn't stand the idea of happy relationships. With the Eater being broken up with and Annie showing up without Jacob, she was going to think it was Christmas.

Aunts Rosa and Tina both had husbands who didn't say anything at all. Aunt Rosa's boy Eddie sat quietly in the corner. He was a quiet, sensitive lad who twitched a lot. Every year he seemed to get a little closer to autism. It wasn't supposed to be possible to gradually become autistic, but if anybody could drive a boy to mental illness, it would be these three. Annie told me she wouldn't be surprised if Eddie showed up at her playgroup one of these days. She didn't know if she'd be helping him or hurting him by drawing him out. It might be safer inside.

Aunt Tina gave me the kind of look usually reserved for child pornographers and dentists.

"David. What a surprise. How did you get invited? From what I hear, you don't have a phone."

"Aunt Tina, you promised."

"Your grandfather took me hunting once when I was a girl and I shot a deer in the stomach from clear across a field. Nasty wound. It would have taken him days to die, so I came up to him and popped him in the head to put him out of his misery. Do you like deer, David?"

"Aunt Tina!"

Aunt Rosa stepped in.

"Why didn't you bring that nice Jacob boy? We like him."

Considering she usually referred to him as "That weirdo Jew," I knew I was now officially at the top of the shit list.

"Jacob had to work, so I brought David."

Aunt Rosa gave a loud theatrical sigh.

"Why do you always bring these boys around? Can't you just come up and visit on your own?"

"I like company for the drive."

Aunt Antonia snorted.

"Company, huh? Is that what you call it?"

"David and I are just friends!"

Aunt Rosa clucked sympathetically.

"Of course you are. I'm sure David has his pick of the ladies."

I thought that was nice.

"Thank you, Aunt Rosa."

"He sure goes through them like Chiclets. I'm surprised he

hasn't chewed through you yet. But then again, I guess he is pretty successful..."

Annie took umbrage.

"Are you saying I can't get someone like David?"

"Of course not."

"I could, you know. Easily."

I did the supportive thing.

"She could, if she wanted."

Aunt Antonia was skeptical.

"Is she too uptight, David? Annie, you need to loosen up. Separate those ankles every once in a while."

"Jesus, Aunt Antonia! Please. My sex life is not a conversational topic."

Aunt Rosa caught the pass.

"I'm sure Annie saves herself for the guys more her speed."

"Hey, I bet I could have gotten David if I had wanted to."

"I'm sure you could, dear."

I didn't want to keep supporting this. It was getting uncomfortable.

"You have a lovely kitchen, Aunt Rosa..."

"I think I could even do better, if I wanted."

"Hey!"

Aunt Antonia smiled crookedly.

"Really? That's nice to hear such confidence in our young people."

"It's not like it's hard to do better. You could at least find someone who knows how to treat a lady."

Aunt Tina was still gunning for me, I see. I had to stop this before Annie blew that throbbing vein on her forehead.

"You know what would be hard? To find a better-smelling dish. What's for dinner? Smells yummy!"

Nothing derails an Italian mother quicker than a culinary compliment. Aunt Rosa immediately turned and smiled.

"We're having Caesar salad, rigatoni and broccoli, and my special lemon chicken."

"Sounds wonderful. Annie, we should go say happy birthday to your grandmother. Come on."

I led her out of the kitchen. Aunt Tina was fondling a huge kitchen knife, so I thought it would be a good idea for both of us to go for a walk. Annie shook under my hand.

"Annie, are you okay? Are you okay, Annie?"

"Sure. I mean, I haven't been hit by a smooth criminal, if that's what you're asking. I just get so frustrated."

"I can tell. Come on, let's say hi to Grandma."

Grandma sat on the couch in the living room watching the Mets game. Her sister, Aunt Clara, was smushed in next to her. Aunt Clara scared me. I sometimes got the impression she wanted to do awful, dirty things to me. I didn't want to think about it. We walked up to the couch. Annie plopped a huge wet smooch on her grandma's forehead.

"Happy eighty-seventh birthday, you crazy lady! How did you do it? What is the secret to this eternal youth?"

Grandma cracked a smile.

"I try not to pay attention. You'd be surprised how far that can get you, dear. Thank you for visiting me on my birthday, you're a good girl."

Aunt Clara smiled at me disconcertingly. Something about her leer said if not in this life, then the next. Well, if we both end up in heaven, I am avoiding her. Annie turned to me.

"You remember my friend David, right?"

"Of course, of course. Hello, David."

"Happy Birthday, Grandma."

We all called her Grandma. What other name made sense?

"Annie, dear, where's your man?"

"Jacob couldn't make it, but he wishes you a wonderful birthday."

"He's a good boy. You should hold onto that one."

"Whatever you say, Grandma, you're the expert."

Aunt Clara was still smiling at me. I think she kept checking out my ass. I shifted uncomfortably.

"Annie, your friend here looks antsy."

"No, no, Grandma. I'm just trying to see the score."

"Aren't you a Yankee fan?"

Not bad for eighty-seven. I can't even remember a girl's name.

"Yeah."

"Then what do you care what the hell happens to my poor Mets?"

"Just curious."

"Then why don't you sit down and watch an inning with a ridiculously old lady?"

"All right."

Aunt Clara made as if to shift over but I wasn't playing that. I sat my ass down on the other side of Grandma before it was too late. Aunt Rosa's voice sailed out in our direction and hooked Annie like a trout.

"Annie, come in and help with the salad, will you?"

She gave me a pleading look. I made as if to get up. Grandma put a hand on my arm.

"Let the boy watch an inning. It won't kill you to help out your aunts. Tina got fined at work last week for talking back to the customers if you need some ammo."

Annie let loose a resigned sigh.

"Okay. I'll be back in a bit then. I need to make...salad."

She slunk off towards the kitchen, fighting the line all the way. My eyes followed her until I accidentally made eye contact with Aunt Clara, who was still smiling at me. I turned to the TV so quick I got dizzy. Mike Piazza looked like he was batting with a rake.

We sat there for a bit, Aunt Clara, Grandma and me. Grandma was an enigma. A fun old lady, she didn't seem to let anything bother her. Her family raged around her as she floated in the center of the maelstrom, unharmed. I think she knew everything that went on. But I couldn't tell if she cared. How could such insane women have popped out of such a calm mother? But then again, it could always be a clever reinvention. She births the kids, messes them up, then realizes the error of her ways and tries to make it up to the grandkids. Her children go insane trying to explain to their children how their beloved grandma was once a psycho mother, just like their moms. But the grandkids never listen. They only know their sweet, beloved grandma. And Grandma gets away scot-free. The kids keep getting screwed up and never learn from their parents' mistakes. It's an unending cycle. The American way.

Floyd hit a double with two outs. Grandma didn't react. She just watched. Whatever her secret, both Annie and the Eater adored her. They talked to her more than they talked to their own mothers.

"So, Grandma. How's she doing?"

Grandma didn't look at me. She kept her eyes on the game.

"Her heart's broken and she doesn't know how it happened. She calls me and cries for hours."

"Do you think it's all my fault?"

"I'm no detective. I can't tell whose fingerprints are whose. I'm her grandma. I love her. And I can't help her. I tell her, like I would tell you, that this is nothing new. This happens to everyone. It's happened to me. But right now, her pain is the only pain in the world."

"Do you blame me?"

"Of course I blame you. We all blame you. If it had been some other boy, which it would have, we'd blame him too. Quite frankly, I'm surprised to see you here. This is enemy territory. You're lucky I'm too tired to hold a grudge. If you had pulled this with one of my daughters, thirty-five or forty years ago, it would have been a different story. I would have hunted you down and mounted you on the wall like a marlin. Tina is too lazy to hold the kind of grudges I held. Rosa, now she would have ripped you apart. But you lucked out. I'm too tired and I've seen it too many times to get all fired up about it."

"I'm sorry I hurt her."

"I know you are. You're decent enough. You're just clumsy. If you're going to go around telling women you love them, you need to have a surgeon's hands."

I said nothing. We both watched Jose Reyes throw out Tino Martinez.

"She's coming later, you know."

"I know."

"You should talk to her."

"I don't think that would be such a good idea."

"It's up to you. But I think it would do you both good. You both need to be clear. Isn't that why you're here?"

"No. I'm just keeping Annie company."

"That's noble of you."

I could feel Aunt Clara smiling at me. I didn't want to know what she thought about it. Grandma patted my hand absently.

"I am tired. I can't go holding grudges like I used to. But I have to tell you, sad as it is to say, you have to take sides in life. And as much as I like you, she's my granddaughter and I love her. So until something changes, and you both get a little older inside, you'll have to be on my shit list. Sorry to say it, you are a nice boy, but there it is."

"I understand."

We watched Leiter retire the last batter. I stood up, wished her a happy birthday one last time, and walked away. Aunt Clara's gaze followed my ass on its way out.

Annie tossed salad in the kitchen, eyes darting this way and that like a rat cornered by dogs. She wouldn't be able to eat a thing. No one noticed me. Maybe I was being a coward. I didn't need closure, but what if the Eater did? I didn't want to keep hurting her for no reason. I didn't want to be on Grandma's shit list too long, either. I had a mental picture of her rediscovering her inner angel of vengeance and bursting into my apartment like some crazed grandma ninja, beating me senseless with her nunchucks. So maybe the thing to do was to wait until the Eater got here and have it out with her once and for all. I had about an hour to prepare myself. You know what, it was time I ended it. This was the right thing to do, I could tell. I'd be fine. Hell, a girl liked me. I was doing fine. I didn't need her. I was going to be a man for once and just take my medicine.

Annie looked up and saw me. She gave me a pleading look. I heard the front door shut. Some uncle or cousin late to the big party. I was about to step in and help her out when I heard a familiar voice.

"Happy Birthday, Grandma!"

Oh shit! Oh shit! Oh shit! It was the Eater. The Eater was an hour early. Who the fuck was I kidding? Get me the fuck out of here! This was a crisis situation!

Annie realized who it was a second after I did and sprang into action.

"Come on, this way!"

She threw an apron over me and hustled me out the other door into the dining room.

"Shit! The front door can be seen from the living room, so it's a definite danger zone. We're trapped. We're going to have to take to the stairs!"

I heard a voice in the kitchen.

"Where is he?"

I was an apron blur. We flew up the stairs. There were four doors to choose from.

"He went upstairs?"

Footsteps on the staircase. I needed a place to hide. Annie opened a door.

"In here. I'll stall her and meet you out front."

She pushed me into the dark and closed the door. My heart thudded like the beat at a rave, fueled by fear and anticipation and thrill. I heard that familiar voice.

"Where is he, Annie?"

"He left."

"I know he's still here. Why did he come if he didn't want to see me? He misses me, doesn't he? Where is he?"

I felt bad putting Annie in this position. I felt worse about my own position. My eyes adjusted to the dark. Fantastic. I was crammed in the linen closet, with nowhere to go. I wondered what she was wearing.

"He's in one of these rooms, isn't he? David? David, I know you want to talk to me!"

I didn't, I really didn't. I heard her open a door.

"Are you in here?"

I was screwed. I tried fitting into the hamper. My legs stuck out. Maybe she'd think I was a novelty hamper. I was fucked. I heard another door open.

"Hello? David?"

"He's gone. Just let him go."

"I know he wants to see me. Where is he?"

There was no hope. I was going to have a mature discussion about the nature of our relationship and there was no way I could escape it. I eyed a bedsheet. Nah. Hanging myself was tempting, but it would only put off the inevitable. I'm not sure what hell is, but I'm sure it will involve the Eater in some way. I was screwed.

Another door opened. Only one more. It was over.

"Psst. Up here."

I looked up. Cousin Eddie looked down at me with an arm outstretched.

"What the hell are you doing up there?"

"Grab on."

I was desperate. I clung to his arm and he lifted me up through the hole in the ceiling. He had just replaced the ceiling tile when we heard the closet door open.

"Hello? Annie, where is he?"

"He's gone. I'm sorry, but he's gone."

The door closed again. I looked around. I was in a tiny crawl space, with electrical wires and insulation everywhere. In the center of the space sat a lawn chair. Eddie sat in the chair.

"Thanks, buddy."

Eddie looked at me. I noticed a window in the corner. I peered out onto the roof.

"Can I get down from here, do you think?"

Eddie said nothing. He must have gotten all the Aunt Clara genes. At least he wasn't checking out my ass.

"Why'd you help me out? She's your cousin."

This prompted a response.

"I don't like her. She gets on my nerves. It's about time she didn't get something she wanted."

Eddie said this without changing expression. It was very creepy. I appreciated Annie's pain more and more.

"Okay. I guess that's fair. Well, thanks."

Silence. He just kept staring at me. I started to fidget.

"Does this window open?"

Nothing. I turned and pushed. After a few tries, I forced it three-quarters open. Just wide enough to squeeze out.

"Well, I'm going to sneak out this way. Thanks again. I think the hidey-hole is a stellar idea. I'd stay here as long as I could if I were you. Until they tore the place down around you."

Eddie didn't crack a smile. He just stared. I didn't like the idea of turning my back to him, but I did, slipping my body through the window. It was touch and go there for a second and I tore up my elbow real nice, but I finally made it. One last look saw Eddie still sitting there like a statue. Poor kid. He freaked me out.

I scrambled down one side of the roof and hopped over onto the garage. After I landed, I waited for a moment, sure my loud thud would draw out the Eater like a bloodhound. When no one came, I lowered myself down the side of the garage onto some garbage cans. At the last minute I slipped and fell with a huge metallic clatter. I got to my feet in record time.

"Fuck this."

I ran.

Eventually Annie appeared at the front door and came out to the car. I could see her looking around. I whistled. She glanced in my direction, quickly looked away and got in her car. She backed out of the driveway and down the street, where I bolted out of my hiding place and leapt into the front seat, keeping my head low until we were out of Dodge.

We didn't talk for about twenty minutes. Finally, Annie spoke up.

"Are you okay?"

"Sure, why not. How about you?"

"I feel like I've been given a colonic with a vacuum cleaner, but I guess I'm okay."

"Why do you put up with them? I just don't understand. I'd be ripping them new assholes."

"They're my family. My dad's gone and so are his people. My mom's never here. They're all I have. What am I supposed to do?"

I had never thought of it like that. It made dysfunctional sense.

"I'm sorry I snuck out like that. I wasn't much of a dam."

"It's okay. I shouldn't have brought you."

"I knew what I was doing."

"Somebody called her and told her that you were here so she left work early. Hence, the surprise."

"Thanks for looking out for me."

"No problem."

"Did anyone say anything to you?"

"They all said stuff to me, but they always do. I'm used to it."

"Okay."

"She really made a thorough search. I'm impressed you escaped. How'd you do it?"

"A magician never reveals his tricks."

"I guess you weren't ready to see her."

"I guess not."

We drove on.

"Your cousin Eddie freaks me out."

"He's pod people all the way."

By the time we hit the city, I felt halfway myself again. I left the Eater behind like a scary dream. Aunt Clara, on the other hand, was a nightmare that would linger.

CHAPTER NINE

The Homeopathic Benefits of Strippers

The next morning I stood staring into my closet. My buddies Dustin and Cameron were taking me out on the town that evening. Knowing their great sense of adventure, that probably meant the Indian restaurant and a flick. I took out a disappointingly-low-key-night-out-with-friends shirt and then put it back. My nightlife attire revolved around my shirts. I only had one pair of cool pants, and who really cares about pants anyway. I may be a nonpracticing homosexual, but that didn't mean I had to start caring about pants. My party pants were black, of course, since I am a New Yorker, and I had a cool black belt that I kept on the pants at all times. I dry-cleaned the pants with the belt attached. So my pants were a given. The shirt was the adventure. I owned different shirts that said different things. One dark red shirt screamed, "I'm a freaky vampire sex fiend!" One of my favorites. My dark green shirt subtly whispered, "I have nice eyes. You are falling into a deep sleep…" My pink shirt nudged, "Hey, look at the nonpracticing homosexual.

Dance with him all night and then go home with his friend." None of these seemed appropriate for a night out with the guys. But there, behind the shirt with fringe that invited "Beat me up!" hung the perfect choice. Dark blue, businesslike but casual, it seemed to calmly say, "I am hot, and you'll never have me. Oh, and I'm rich too. And I get lots of women whenever I want. And I'm much taller than I actually am. And I can read minds! Maybe not the last one. But are you willing to take that chance?" A little ambitious for the evening I would probably end up having, but a guy can dream.

I tucked in my shirt and threw on my leather jacket. I did a quick spot check. Cell phone—check. Keys—check. Cab fare—check. Business card—check. Credit card—check. Mints—check. Origami swan—apparently check. I was ready to go.

When I got to work, I wasn't surprised to see Maureen looking good. If her shirt had been cut any lower her breasts could have waved. Harold hadn't paid her this much attention since she accidentally wore those pants with the hole in the ass. As the day progressed, the game heated up. She borrowed my stapler and bent over so low she almost left her boobs on my desk. I "accidentally" dropped a pen in front of her office and bent over seductively to pick it up. Okay, that actually set me back a little. As we neared the end of the day, I was exhausted from all the flirting. And we weren't being as subtle as we thought we were. Harold kept smirking at me. Don shook his head and muttered about how I thought he was bad. Tyrone did his happy white boy dance every time he saw me. But I didn't care. I was a guy. This would only help my reputation.

With quitting time approaching, I called Dustin to see where we were meeting up.

"Hey, dude, glad you called. I heard about this great bar over on Eighth Avenue. It's called Naughty But Nice."

"Sounds like a strip club."

"Hey, I didn't name it. It's supposed to be fun. Here's the address. Meet us out front around eight, okay?"

"Okay."

He hung up. Maureen walked in wearing her coat.

"I'm heading out."

I stared at her standing there, looking good.

"What are you doing tonight?"

"Dinner with some friends, why?"

"I'm going to this bar, Naughty But Nice. You ever heard of it?"

"No. Sounds a little shady."

"Anyway, I'm meeting some friends there. You want to come?"

She seemed tempted. But she didn't break.

"I'm sorry, I can't. You know it's not a good idea. We both know it."

I'm sure that shirt wasn't a good idea either, but you wore it anyway.

"I understand. Look, here's the address. If you want to catch up with us, stop on by."

I wrote down the address and handed it to her. She smiled.

"I'll see you on Monday, David."

She walked out, crumpling up the piece of paper absently. Oh well, I guess I'd have to wait till next week to continue Operation Shit Where I Eat. I concentrated on surfing the internet for porn until it was time to go.

⬦

I walked down Eighth Avenue, looking for the bar. I stopped in front of a doorway with a red rope in front. I looked up. The sign said NAUGHTY BUT NICE. Wait a minute.

"This *is* a strip club."

"You bet your ass it is. You need titties."

Dustin walked up, Cameron in tow. If Dustin had any more testosterone, he'd be humping legs. These manly outbursts were in direct conflict with his extremely laid-back delivery. He's the friend everyone thinks is normal until he nonchalantly mentions pussy farts. Dustin thinks titties solve everything. You should have seen the looks he got in math class.

"Dustin, I don't need titties."

"You have been moping around like a little school girl and it has to stop. Trust me, big titty women an inch from your face are just what you need to put the pep back in your step. If you don't see strippers within a few months of breaking up, you never find love again. It's a medical fact. That's why I think you should see them as much as possible, just in case. Strippers are like vitamins: if taken daily, you get big and strong. If taken sporadically or not at all, you get weak and listless."

"I didn't realize that a lap dance cured iron deficiency."

"They're using them to treat sickle cell anemia."

"Of course, an overdose could lead to a pumping of the stomach or worse."

"Look, are we going to talk like this all day or can we go get fucked up and see some nice titties already?"

What the hell. I'm only human.

"Okay, fine."

Dustin put one hand on my shoulder and the other on Cameron's.

"I don't know who needs it more, you or the twinkie over here."

Dustin may be unusual, but Cameron is the only one of his kind. I mean this literally. I don't think there's anyone else with his specific mix of genetic and cultural background anywhere in the known world. Cameron was born in Korea, where he was left at an orphanage. He was subsequently adopted by Michael McKinley and his wife, Barbara, of the Scarsdale Goldsteins. That's right, Cameron is a Korean Scottish Jew. He speaks a smattering of all his native tongues, including Korean, Hebrew and unintelligible. He knows all the good Asian restaurants in Little Korea, he can lead a Seder, and he plays the bagpipes. He's the cultural equivalent of a Swiss army knife. He goes to synagogue. He wears the kilt and marches in the St. Paddy's Day Parade. You haven't lived till you've see a Korean Jew in full skirt-and-hat regalia playing old Celtic tunes down Fifth Avenue while a thousand drunken Irishmen convince themselves that they didn't just see what they thought they saw. When they're talking about the melting pot, they're talking about Cameron McKinley. God love him.

"Hey! I am not a twinkie. A twinkie is yellow on the outside and white on the inside. I'm a lemon. Yellow on the outside and bitter on the inside."

Dustin pulled out his ID.

"Shut up and get ready to see some sweet ass, you sad little man."

As we waited inside for a table, Cameron expressed some of his bitterness.

"So she's back with her ex-girlfriend. It's all pretty much over."

We expressed our sympathy. Cameron has very peculiar taste in women. He always seems to end up dating ex-lesbians. He never knows that in advance, but he's come to expect the "talk" a few weeks into the relationship. The only explanation I can think of for this phenomenon is his predilection for women who can kick the crap out him. All of his girlfriends played some kind of sport, usually field hockey or rugby or, in one memorable instance, professional wrestling. Yet still he wonders at his lesbian track record. He's been rendered fatalistic. If you kept dating women who used to get it on all the time with other women but now say they've had enough, you'd be fatalistic, too. There goes the one perk of dating an ex-lesbian. Poor Cameron, always hearing about all these fantastic multi-female sexual experiences but never able to participate. Always a bridesmaid, never a bride...

Let me give you a quick mental picture. I was looking fine in my blue shirt and black pants. Dustin had on the Wall Street special, down to the tie clip and the shiny black shoes. Cameron had on his prep boy best, Dockers and all. We looked like the representatives of three completely separate nations brought together to negotiate a peace treaty. Over strippers, of course.

We were led to our table by a gentleman in a tuxedo. Evidently this was a classy joint. I'm sure the Rockefellers were regulars. Looking around, I was less than impressed. Even though it was a Friday, most of the girls were second-tier. This didn't stop Dustin from going immediately to work. I always needed time to acclimate before leaping into a lap dance, but Dustin equated time with money. He hated wasting either. He sure was a cheap bastard. Except when it came to strippers. He refused to spend money on groceries, but he always had a twenty for a lap dance. Five minutes after we sat down, he had his back to the wall and a bizarre-looking pink-haired girl rubbing her ass in his face. Good times.

Cameron and I were slower to partake. He ordered a shot of some kind and I offered my condolences.

"I'm sorry about the lady."

"I wasn't surprised. I knew something like that would happen. She was too cute for me. I knew it wasn't going to last."

If asked whether the glass was half-full or half-empty, Cameron would say he wasn't thirsty anyway. Dustin would demand to know who the hell had been drinking his water.

"At least you know she was a lesbian before. It would be worse if she was hetero before you and homo afterwards. That would be like her saying that your dick was so awful she never wanted to see another dick again."

"I was the first guy she had slept with. And the last."

Whoops.

"Oh. Sorry man. If it makes you feel any better, I met the woman of my dreams and not only did I sound like an idiot when I talked to her, I never caught her name. I ended up giving her my number and that's the last time we spoke."

"It's fine. If I got offended every time you inadvertently insulted me, I'd be in a constant state of pissiness. Though your troubles do make me smile."

"She still may call me."

"Women don't call men."

"The Eater won't stop calling me."

"She's not a woman. She's pure evil."

My friends didn't really like the Eater. The day I broke up with her, they couldn't wait to burn her in effigy. They came up with that effigy suspiciously quick, come to think of it. They'd obviously been embroidering for months in hopeful anticipation.

Dustin was on to his third girl. At this rate, he'd have rubbed laps with every woman in the place by eleven-thirty. Cameron and I were such slackers. The girl on stage finished her dance and the DJ got on the mic.

"Give it up for Diamond! And now it's time for our featured dancer. Put your hands together for...Dominique!"

The girl walking onto the stage had the biggest pair of fake hooters I had ever seen. These babies were like two corn silos sticking straight out into the air. They were perfectly round and they didn't so much jiggle as bounce like a basketball in a sock. I wanted to crack one open to see what kind of prize was inside. I turned to make a comment to Cameron but was stopped by the look on his face. Cameron was in love.

Dominique was a pro. She rode the pole. She did her splits. She smiled seductively at the crowd. Cameron threw a week's pay at her feet. She took notice, spending more and more time in our corner. Cameron looked like he wanted to hang a hammock between her massive mammaries and sleep there for eternity. I wondered how many women she had slept with and whether she played field hockey or soccer. The sight of those twin cannonballs barreling down the field would strike fear into the heartiest goalie. The DJ's voice broke through.

"Dominique needs a volunteer for the next part of her act. Which lucky guy will she choose?"

Another two weeks' salary hit the floor and Cameron was on stage. His face glowed, though his eyes didn't know what they could safely stare at. They tried to remain fixed on her face, but they kept giving in to those huge orbs' gravitational pull. Dominique laid out a towel on the stage and pushed Cameron gently down onto it. I looked around to make sure that Dustin was catching this. He had positioned his stripper so that he could watch both her and the floorshow at once. This was why he made the big bucks. Multitasking. He gave me a thumbs-up.

Dominique started to dance above Cameron. He looked bewildered.

"Do you mind if I join you?"

She came. Maureen came. Holy shit. I must look like the biggest pervert on earth.

"Hey. I had no idea this was a strip club. Honest. I am not a sexual deviant, I swear. I only came in for the buffet. The wings are the best in the city, really."

She sat down.

"It's okay. What the hell, right? Just don't buy me a lap dance."

"How about a vodka tonic?"

"That I can do."

I waved the waitress over and ordered. Maureen looked around.

"There are some sad-looking women in here."

"I know. How was your dinner?"

"Fine. They left for Brooklyn and I decided I wanted to stay in Manhattan a little longer. Where are your friends?"

"One is back there getting rubbed and the other one is up on stage."

"That poor guy's your friend?"

Dominique was now writhing on Cameron's lap. His arms flailed around uselessly, like a monkey doing the wave.

"Yeah, he is. And it's the proudest day of my life."

"I bet you're wishing you were up there, right?"

Dominique pulled out what looked like a shampoo bottle and began to rub it all over her body. Cameron put his legs down and closed his mouth, protecting all entrances to the fort.

"Not even a little."

The drinks arrived. I tipped well. I lifted my glass.

"To aptly named strip clubs and the people who accidentally wander into them."

"Sure, why not."

We clinked and drank.

"Poor Cameron. He doesn't always make the best decisions."

Dominique stroked the bottle at crotch level, faster and faster in a very male fashion. Cameron began to look worried.

Maureen smiled.

"Unlike you. You always make the best decisions."

"I don't know yet. We'll have to revisit that."

We watched Cameron get more and more frightened.

"So what made you stop by?"

"I don't know, really. It goes against everything I know to be smart. My mom always told me that you keep it separate."

"Probably good advice."

"Probably."

Dominique masturbated the bottle like a fourteen-year-old in the bathroom. Cameron looked openly afraid now. He tried to scurry away, but her thighs were a vise. He was trapped. She moaned louder and louder. The audience began to clap rhythmically. This would end badly, I could tell.

"What advice would your mom give him?"

"My mom would never say anything to him. She's intimidated by Asians."

Dominique was at a fever pitch. She started to scream. Cameron got caught up in the moment and he joined her. They both wailed like horror movie victims as Dominique threw her head back in one final gush of ecstasy and gave the bottle a big squeeze. Milky liquid shot out of the bottle in a beautiful arc of white like a gooey rainbow. It hung gracefully in the air and then landed all over poor Cameron. She squeezed and dribbled the entire bottle all over Cameron's shirt and face and pants, covering him in the stuff. It looked like...well, if I have to tell you what it looked like by now, you wouldn't understand anyway.

Cameron stood up slowly, dripping goo. Dominique took a bow and gestured for Cameron to do the same. I could tell that he really wanted to clock her. But instead, he bowed sheepishly and slinked off stage like a kicked puppy. He headed towards our table. I tried to make him feel better as he approached.

"So are you a spitter or a swallower?"

He walked right past me without a word and on towards the bathroom. Maureen took a sip.

"How much did that cost him?"

"Between his money and his pride, I think he's cleaned out."

"Too bad. I've got some hand cream in my bag I'd cover him with for twenty bucks."

Cameron came back. He was a mess of stains.

"I am not happy."

"That's what you get for falling in love, my friend."

"My shirt is ruined."

"It isn't ruined. What is that, shampoo? It'll wash right out."

"Okay, my fragile mind is ruined."

"Here's my brave boy!"

It was Dominique. She was all smiles.

"Look at you! You know what you need? My special T-shirt! Just for my little helpers. Let me grab you one!"

I half expected her to twist open a boob and pull out a shirt. Instead, she reached behind her and snatched up the prize. Cameron took off his damp button-down and pulled on the tee. The front was a color photo of a naked Dominique lying on an American flag, spreading her legs for God and Country. Definitely a classic. Dominique kissed Cameron on both cheeks.

"Would you like a private dance now?"

Cameron kept looking down.

"That's okay. I'm a little too soggy."

"Okay, suit yourself. By the way, the shirt is fifteen dollars."

Shaking his head in disbelief, Cameron paid. Dominique smiled and walked away.

"I'm going home."

"No way, mister! You need a dance!"

Dustin was back. He had two girls in tow. In real life, he may be a mild-mannered businessman, but here he was Tommy Lee.

"I think I'd rather go home."

"Not till you've proved to me that you're a man. The first dance is on me. Come on, little trooper!"

His self-pitying tendencies overcome by good ol' fiscal sense,

Cameron walked off to enjoy his freebie. Maureen watched them go.

"They didn't even notice me. I hope they didn't think I was a stripper."

"You're a cut or two above the Naughty But Nice employee."

"You are such a smoothie. My panties just flew away like a bird in winter."

I was liking this sexy, dirty Maureen. She ordered another drink and a round of shots.

"I never knew you were such a lush, Maureen."

"Of course you did."

"Yeah, I did. I was making conversation. I like your shirt."

"I know. It was almost worth the boss fly I attracted by wearing it."

"I hope he doesn't show up now."

"He's probably over in the corner behind the bar, waiting to pop up and toot his didgeridoo."

"That's the dirtiest thing I have ever heard."

We downed the shots. And another round after that. Cameron and Dustin staggered back. I tried to introduce them, but before I could open my mouth, they were off again, chasing an especially unattractive stripper and giggling. We threw back another round of shots.

"Maureen. Maureen. What do people call you for short? Maury? Reenie? Uree?"

"I don't have a nickname. I'm always Maureen."

"Well I'm the king of nicknames. I will give you one. I anoint you . . . Wiggy!"

I touched her forehead with my gin and tonic.

"Wiggy? What does that mean?"

"That you wig out all the time. Wait a minute. Did I say that out loud? Fuck. That was supposed to be without quotation marks."

"You little shit. I do not wig out all the time."

I gave her a knowing look. I wedged my arm between the table and my chin to make sure the look stayed on her.

"You freak out all the time. There's nothing wrong with it. It's just who you are."

"I do not freak out! Does everyone think that? Jesus, what are you guys saying behind my back?"

I started to laugh.

"Wiggy! Wiggy wiggy! You're wigging, Wiggy!"

"I can't believe you're making fun of me! Look at my shirt! My boobs are hanging out for you."

"Are you trying to distract me from my mockery? Your diversion is a failure!"

"Then why are you still staring at my chest?"

"There are so many bare ones around, I'm fascinated by what I can't see."

"Do I really wig out?"

I patted her hand.

"Yes. But we love you anyway."

Her hand curled around mine.

"Good."

"You know, I've been here for hours and I haven't gotten a single lap dance."

"That's not cool. Do you have a twenty?"

I pulled out the bill.

"Right here."

She took it.

"That'll do."

She started to dance for me. Maureen, my obsessive, oversensitive coworker who I'd worked with for years without ever a romantic thought, was dancing for me. She was awful at it. She had no rhythm and her hips kept banging into my knee. She tried to make sexy faces but instead looked like she'd eaten something strange. I loved it.

She rubbed up against me. I love alcohol! Her hand trailed down my chest. She reached for her shirt and started to lift it up towards the ceiling.

"Hey. Come on, miss, that's not allowed."

The bouncer had snuck up on us unawares. Maureen kept dancing, undeterred.

"If you don't stop that, you'll be asked to leave."

"It's a free country!"

In one fluid motion, she pulled off her shirt. Her bra, black and full of promise, sprang free. The men around us started clapping and cheering. She bowed.

"I will not be kept down! I am woman! See me strip!"

"They'll have to watch it outside, lady."

The bouncer grabbed Maureen and dragged her towards the door. I quickly gathered our stuff, shrugged in Dustin and Cameron's direction, and followed. Outside, Maureen was pulling her shirt back on and glaring at the bouncer. I hailed a cab and grabbed her arm.

"Get in before he tears off an arm and starts gnawing."

She let herself be stuffed in the cab and we rolled away. Maureen's hands ran up and down my leg.

"You're pretty frisky there. Where do you want to go?"

"Your place."

"What about shitting where you eat?"

"Fuck that."

She grabbed my head and sucked the lips right off my face.

The cab pulled up to my apartment building. We staggered out and gradually made our way up the stairwell, pausing every few inches to paw at each other. It took me five minutes to figure out how to use my keys. With a flourish, I unlocked the door and we fell into my apartment.

She skipped over to my bed, which only took a single skip. She sat down.

It's always strange when people visit your apartment. They fill up the place like this intrusive piece of furniture you never ordered. You feel out of place in your own home, because they're out of place.

I leaned against the door.

"I'm gonna hit the bathroom. I'll be right back."

With that sexy toss off, I slipped into the bathroom and closed the door behind me.

I washed my hands and stared at my reflection. I looked as drunk as I felt. I wiped my hands and stepped back out into the main room.

Maureen was already under the covers. She laughed to herself, like I was the funniest joke in the world. She pulled a little of the covers back. I could tell that she was naked underneath.

Flash.

It's a year ago. I get a call at work.

"Come home."

It was the Eater, back before she was the Eater. Back when the Eater was the One.

I hurry back to my apartment. I have my cell to my ear, listening to her tiny voice telling me all the bad things she'll be doing to me when I get home. I run up my stairs reaching for my keys. They aren't there. I yell through the door.

"I forgot my keys."

"Okay."

"Open the door."

"Fuck. Close your eyes."

I close my eyes. The door opens.

"Keep them closed."

I walk through and the door closes behind me. I hear a scurrying of feet across my rug.

"Open."

I open my eyes. She's in my bed, under my covers.

"Don't move. Watch."

Slowly, agonizingly slowly, she pulls the covers down her body. Inch by inch she reveals herself to me. I have never wanted anyone so bad. I want to dive into her and pull her over my head where I'll be warm and safe. This is all I ever wanted. And she's mine.

"David! Are you gonna stand there all night?"

Flash.

I blinked. I was back. Back with Maureen and the ever-present knot in my stomach that I had conveniently ignored.

"Come to bed."

Maureen's voice and the Eater's rang in my head as one. Fuck her! Fuck the Eater! She wanted to take this away from me. I wasn't going to let her. If I could go through with this, I would be free. I forced myself to walk over to the bed and sit down. Maureen sat up, clutching the covers to her. She gave me a warm kiss. I kissed her back.

"I can't believe I could be this lucky."

I'd said it back then. Maureen said it now. It hit me like a sucker punch to the gut. A few small tears slipped out. They seemed to wash my vision clean. The illusion I had created fell away and I could see Maureen in front of me. Maureen, who went insane over the smallest problem. Maureen, who had to be reassured every five minutes. Maureen, who smoked two packs a day. Maureen, who was just not my type. The picture I had painted in my head of the friend I could look at in a new way melted and the real Maureen sat there holding the covers to her chest. She was pretty and nice and comfortable and all of that. But she wasn't the answer. I didn't want to be with her. I had never wanted to be with her. I'd made her into someone I could be with. But the charcoal on that sketch had smudged. She didn't belong here.

"What's wrong? Are you okay? Oh, shit, what's wrong?"

Something broke inside of me. I crumbled. I didn't cry. I just collapsed.

Maureen clung to the covers. Her fantasy dissolved with mine. The reality of just how much I had used her crush on me washed over me. It was horrible what I was doing to her. I forced out some words.

"I'm sorry."

"I didn't mean to move so fast. I had a few drinks and we were, you know, in the cab..."

"It's not your fault."

"Is it your ex?"

I could only nod.

"I didn't mean to move so fast."

"It's okay. I thought I was ready. You know?"

This is where it would happen. I could tell she was cracking. Soon she'd be replaced by Wiggy and bad would become worse. I braced myself for the fallout like a guilty child. She put her hand on my hand.

"When I got dumped by the Asshole, it took over a year before I could even go out. Hey, I know all about the rebound. It's a shitty job, but somebody's got to do it."

"You're not a rebound."

"I know how it works."

The mix of compassion and pain in her eyes made me feel tiny. But I was grateful. No Wiggy. This was amazing. Maureen was amazing. I clutched her hand for dear life.

"I can picture her. I can see her and remember feeling perfect. I miss that so much."

"I know. It gets better."

"When?"

"When the Asshole gets together with your best friend and you cover his precious jeep in turpentine."

I laughed.

"I look forward to that day."

"Good."

"I'm sorry I dragged you into this."

"It's fine. I should have known better."

"I'm sorry anyway."

"Thanks."

She kept holding my hand as the pain slowly recessed back to the familiar ache I knew like my own heartbeat. I could tell by her breathing that she was crying. But she didn't wig out once.

CHAPTER TEN

My Aura

I woke up around twelve the next day. Maureen had left before morning. My head felt like it was giving birth to a Samoan. I knocked back two Tylenol and an Advil. I believe in firepower. The night before was still horrifically etched on my brain. I was pathetic. I needed a cookie.

An hour and a half later I was sitting in Annie's kitchen in Queens. Annie was mixing some emergency dough she kept on standby, for just this type of situation. Jacob leaned up against the wall with a beer in his hand. His T-shirt said, "Kill Whitey." You could see his tattoo of David Mamet poking out from his short sleeve. Jacob loved David Mamet. If you got him drunk enough, he'd recite the entire first half-hour of *Glengarry Glen Ross*. I like him, but Jacob does bug me on one front: He can do what I can't seem to. He writes tons and tons of screenplays. He keeps offering to look mine over when I'm finished. Or even as I go along, if I need the help. I'm not sure that he's needed quite yet. I don't know what he'd have to say about a character's name followed by a colon. I think you need actual dialog before you can be critiqued. His stuff is pretty good. Very personal and heartfelt. He's a little sentimental for a guy who has a cross on his chest formed out of self-inflicted cigarette burns. Reading his screenplays was like finding out that *Howard's End* was written by Ozzy Osbourne. He had a lot to say on the topic of drunken failure.

"It happens, man. I can't even count the times I've gotten so wasted I pissed on some girl's skirt. You just move on."

Annie smirked.

"Well, I can only vouch for once on the shoe, so don't look at me."

It had nothing to do with alcohol, but I couldn't let him know that. I had a little pride.

"I'm fucked at work. We're supposed to work together."

Jacob waxed philosophical.

"Hey, man, being fucked up is being fucked up. She'll understand."

He moved to stand behind Annie, watching her mix. She took a spoon, scooped out a dollop of dough, and held it up for him. He leaned forward and brought his mouth around the head of the spoon, which slid back out smooth and clean-looking. She smiled and turned to me, eyebrow raised in question.

"No thanks."

She shrugged and went back to mixing.

"She's the one I feel bad for. Who are you calling?"

I had my cell up to my ear.

"Just checking my messages. I enjoy hearing that I have no

messages. It's like probing a loose tooth. The pain reminds me I'm alive."

"You are a dipshit."

"Shit. Apparently I have a message. Love that false hope. Probably Maureen or something…"

I froze.

"Hey, this is Julie, you remember, from Maggie's party? Sorry it took me so long to call, but I've been out of town. Anyway, I had a good time talking to you. Sorry about the whole tax law thing. It was too good to pass up. I hope you can forgive me. It was kind of funny watching you come up with any phrase that could keep you from actually having to use my name, which you obviously didn't catch. Hey, don't feel bad, I couldn't remember yours the next morning either. Of course, I had a phone number and a name to remind me. But I gave you a nickname anyway. Maybe I'll tell you what it is sometime. Anyway, I'm rambling. I'm back in town and I thought you might like to grab a drink, so give me a call back. That's Julie, J-U-L-I-E in case of static, 212-555-6781. I look forward to hearing from you. Bye."

How could I not believe in God? I was an alcoholic whose sponsor called right when he was at rock bottom, about to take a swig.

Annie was staring at me.

"You look like you've been propositioned by a nun."

"That was the Goddess."

Jacob raised his glass again.

"Nice work, dude."

"Did she leave a name this time?"

I was in a daze.

"Yeah. I can't remember it right now, though."

"Good for you, man."

"I had completely forgotten about her. And then she calls. I obsessed for a week and nothing. Now she calls. Do women put chips in our brains to keep track of when we need prodding?"

"No, we just play the averages. But that long message is a good sign. Did she ramble?"

"She even mentioned that she was rambling."

"Even better. I guess you made an impression."

"I don't know if I can be Zen about this."

"Calm down. You can't call her in this state."

"What state? What's wrong with my state? Am I losing it? I'm losing it, aren't I? Jesus."

"Look, you need to think this through carefully."

"That's true. Cause I'm in a state."

"Do I need to slap you? Calm down."

Jacob patted my back.

"You need a drink."

We took a walk down to Jacob's favorite bar, Paddy's. I didn't want to drink. I couldn't see how sinking into a stupor would help me to make calm, well-thought-out decisions. I envisioned myself fucked up proper, phoning the Goddess and asking her if she would sit on my face. I couldn't see the logic. Jacob, however, could be very persuasive.

"First round's on me."

I don't drink beer. I'm more of a girly drink kind of fellow. If it sports an umbrella, then I'll down it. An orange slice on a little plastic sword floating within? All the better. Being beer swillers, Jacob and Annie both approached their beverages with an oat bran cereal mentality. I went for the fruit loops. I like the pretty colors.

The flip side of this preference is that I tend to get drunker much quicker than my plain, ordinary beer-drinking comrades. One foo foo drink and I was gone.

"I don't know what to do! What if I make the beach vagina mistake all over again? Every time I open my mouth I fuck myself over. You know I'm afflicted with verbal hemophilia. Most people are born able to stop themselves from talking like an idiot, but I am unable to clot."

"Poor baby."

Dustin walked in, followed by Cameron. Annie had called in the heavy artillery.

"Wow. You're all the way out here. I'm honored."

Dustin lives in an apartment in Riverdale because it's cheap. Dustin likes cheap. He buys everything in bulk from the huge warehouse store off of 87. He only gets the cheapest brands there. His toilet paper and his jeans are made by the same people. He keeps protesting that the pants are comfortable, and so is the toilet paper, so who cares if they're manufactured by the same company. I think it would be cool if they found a way to combine the two. Self-wiping jeans. That would be pretty sweet. Dustin is not cheap with his friends, however. He works at a hedge fund and makes a huge amount of money. His birthday and Christmas presents reflect that, God bless him. We usually get him name brand jeans and toilet paper.

Cameron came up from the East Village. The fact he actually left his apartment to see me more than once that week blew me away.

Dustin proved unsympathetic to my situation.

"You've got women calling you up asking you out. I want problems."

I defended myself.

"You know me. You know what I'm capable of."

Wry affirmatives surround me.

Jacob tried to be helpful.

"Just relax, man. You get too uptight."

"You're right. It's nothing. Of course, if I screw this one up that means I'll never be with a woman again due to my own self-destructive tendencies. I'll spend the rest of my life in a studio apartment surrounded by cats. But I'll relax. I'll be coolio, foolio."

Annie shook her head.

"Don't be so melodramatic. It's just a date. Right, guys? Dustin?"

Dustin took a healthy swig of his Corona Extra Light. I don't know why he bothers.

"She's right. So stop crying about it and call the damn girl. You're like a very special *Dawson's Creek* over here. It's just a woman. So take off your momma's panties and drop those testicles already."

Cameron elaborated, stirring his gin and tonic sadly.

"I can't get past the two-month mark with my women. It sucks. You end up looking down this dark tunnel of loneliness and there's no light at either end. After a while you just accept that life is being alone."

"What do you mean? Is that advice? I need help on how not to screw up, not on how to be depressed. Anyway, you've been having sex with Lizzie for years."

Lizzie was an ex-lesbian who Cameron liked to drown his sorrows in.

"That doesn't count. Those are just booty calls. That's not dating."

"Even you're doing better than me."

"Depressing, isn't it? I've given up on real love. Just make enough money to buy someone blond. That's my goal now."

Dustin knocked back his drink.

"I'm surrounded by pussies."

Annie interjected.

"Boys, boys! Be nice."

She looked thoughtful.

"Maybe what you need to do is not date this girl."

Cameron agreed.

"That is the smart route. You cut off the infected parts to keep the rest of the body safe."

Annie shook her head.

"No, I mean maybe you should just go out as friends."

"So when do I sleep with her?"

"You don't."

"Let me get this straight. I'm not just treating her like a friend to fool her, I'm deciding in advance that we're only going to be friends. Even if she wants to sleep with me."

"Especially if she wants to sleep with you. Look at your past. Look at Maureen. Even someone like Bendy Girl."

Dustin shook his head sadly.

"The world was a brighter place when you had a shot at her."

Cameron nodded.

"There was hope in the air, and now there's nothing."

Annie protected me.

"Will you shut your pie-holes? She wasn't right for him."

Dustin raised an eyebrow.

"She could bend over backwards and touch her chin to the back of her ankle. That kind of girl is right for anybody."

"You wouldn't know what to do with that kind of flexibility if you came across it."

Dustin laid it out for me.

"You have a great evening. You guys connect. She's laughing at all your jokes. She's tickling your hand. She's batting her eyes at you. She gets drunker and drunker. You go back to her place. She lights candles and incense. She sits right next to you on the couch and you can see right down her shirt. But you can't touchy touchy. Because you're just friends. Do you know what being friends with a hottie means? Masturbation and sadness, my friend, masturbation and sadness."

I pondered.

"I appreciate the thought, Annie, but Dustin's right. Sex is too important to be thrown aside for friendship."

"That's not what I mean. I mean, maybe, and I'm just throwing it out there, maybe you shouldn't be dating."

I shook my head.

"Nope. Not acceptable."

"Just keep it in mind."

Cameron raised a hand.

"Tell her you cut your tongue out to protest cruelty."

"Just general cruelty?"

"It's twofold. You aren't able to talk and thereby fuck it all up. And you won't have to go down on her and then talk and fuck it all up."

"So no one has any real advice for me? You are all useless."

Annie gave me a cookie, seemingly from nowhere.

"Sorry, honey, you'll just have to fuck up on your own."

An hour and a half later we stumbled out of the bar. Annie and Jacob kept playing with each other's hair. Cameron sang an old Korean poem set to a Scottish lullaby. Dustin propped himself up against our minstrel, loudly announcing his candidacy for governor. I ran ahead, laughing wildly, drunk on two Long Island Iced Teas and a Buttery Nipple. I pulled out my phone. I needed to call someone.

"No!"

The next thing I knew, my face met the pavement. Annie had tackled me.

"Give me that phone!"

I complied, pouting.

"I wasn't gonna, I swear."

"No talky talky while drunky drunky! If you think you talk stupid sober..."

"Fine. Fine, I don't care. Take it. I don't care. Hey, look!"

I picked myself up and skipped over to a nearby storefront. The blue neon sign in the window read PSYCHIC—PALMS READ AND FORTUNES TOLD. I wanted to play.

"Is it open?"

Dustin caught up.

"Dude, don't be stupid. These are all fakes. Don't throw your money away."

I tried the door. It was open.

"I want my palm read. Anybody else interested?"

Jacob looked in the window.

"I think I'd get a kick out of it. Sure, why not."

Annie laughed.

"I never thought you were the gullible type, Jacob."

"Never hurts to get a second opinion."

"Well, have fun. I'm waiting out here."

In the end, only Jacob and I went in, while the other three made fun of us and yelled out questions for the beyond.

"Ask my grandma if she remembers where she put the ratchet set. We haven't seen it since she died."

"See if Jesus wants me to grab him a parking space for the second coming. Or will it be a pedestrian thing?"

"I don't need anyone to tell me there's a toilet in my future."

The door closed behind us. I called out.

"Hello? You guys open?"

We stepped into a small waiting room. A door to our right stood slightly ajar.

"Hello?"

A voice drifted in.

"Take a seat for a moment, fellas, would you? I'm stuck on the crapper!"

We sat down. I looked at Jacob. He shrugged.

"A psychic's gotta shit, I guess."

We sat in silence for a few minutes. Jacob leaned back in his chair.

"Do you know what you want to ask?"

"No. I'll play it by ear. You?"

Jacob smiled ruefully.

"I think I'm at a crossroads. I want to see which path I should take."

"Did you do that romantic thingy yet?"

"Not yet. I'm working up the courage."

"Is that what your question is?"

"We'll see."

We sat silent for a moment. Jacob turned to me.

"Did you know Annie's dad?"

"Not really. Seemed like a nice guy, though."

"I wonder if he was still around... if things would be different."

"Maybe, maybe not. Does it matter? Maybe her dog ran away when she was five. Maybe she was dumped once by some guy who just happened to be male, just like you. What can you do about it? Nothing. She is the way she is. If you care about her, that's what you have to work with. Is it enough? You have to give it a try or you'll never know."

I meant that. I was feeling optimistic.

The voice floated in again.

"Thanks for waiting. I can feel two of you. One of you may enter."

Jacob and I looked at each other. He stood up.

"I'll go first."

He disappeared through the door, closing it behind him. I glanced around the room. I wanted reading material, but all I could find was a sad, ten-year-old *Highlights* with all the games filled out in pen. So I stewed in my own drunkenness until Jacob came back out. He looked sad.

"How'd it go?"

"Weird. She tried to sell me these clear stones for forty bucks, but I passed. Watch out for that."

"Was she on the money?"

"You'll have to see."

He brushed past me and out the front. The voice slipped in.

"Are you coming in or ain't you? I'm not the sphinx. I got other shit to do."

I took a breath and walked through the door.

I entered a deep purple room. Glass shards hung from the ceiling, casting patterns onto the wall. A wooden table dominated. On the table rested a pile of cards and a pair of hands. The hands were attached to the psychic. She was shuffling the cards without looking up.

"I am Madame Bubola. Take a seat."

Madame Bubola looked around forty. She wore all the requisite jewelry and headgear. A pair of Pumas poked out from under her robe. I could see another open door behind her. A TV flickered in the back of that next room. From the faint sound of it, it was tuned to the Yankees-Rangers game. This was spirituality I could get behind. I sat down.

"Hi, I'm David. Nice to meet you. What's the score?"

"Down by one in the ninth."

She looked up. She started.

"What?"

"Nothing."

She was looking at me strangely. Then she shrugged.

"Do you have a question?"

"What kind of question?"

"Ask me one specific question and I'll find the answer in the cards."

I thought. It didn't take long.

"Will the Goddess work out for me?"

She nodded and went to work. She shuffled the cards and laid them out one by one in front of her. In the background, it sounded like someone got a hit. I wondered if she could predict that. That would have been a silly waste of a question. Tempting from a gambling standpoint, however. She studied the cards, passing her hand over each one. Presently, she looked up.

"Okay. Your job isn't going well. You work in...it's something to do with camels. Watch out for the camels. Trust me. Okay, your parents...you haven't spoken with them in a while. You should patch things up with them. It will help you monetarily. You should try a new haircut. Don't be afraid of bigger hair. You have a girl-friend who is very beautiful. You worship her. She can do no wrong. You shower her with love and affection. But she gives none in return. You don't know what to do. Unfortunately, you don't have enough money for her. She will dump you."

Amazing. It takes real skill to be so unilaterally incorrect. Usually anybody can hit one by accident, but to get every single thing about my life wrong...that took real talent.

"Well. Thanks. Do you mind my asking, which card is the big hair card?"

"I hope I have been helpful. Good night."

She seemed distracted. I got up to leave.

"Wait. I'm sorry. Sit down one moment."

"Okay."

"I shouldn't be saying anything. It's not really what I do. But your aura is growing black."

"Black? What do you mean, black?"

"Your aura is black on the edges and it's growing blacker."

"So what?"

It's not like she's been throwing a perfect game so far.

"I have these stones."

Ah, the forty-dollar stones. It all becomes clear.

"I don't have too much money on me."

"They're free. Take them. Place them under your pillow for two weeks and then throw them in running water. That should help."

"Free? No charge? What's the catch?"

"There's no catch. I can't let you walk out of here with that dying aura without trying to do something. The bad karma would kick my ass, you know?"

Nice to know I'm that bad off.

"Well, thanks"

I walked to the door.

"They win."

I stopped at the door.

"Who does?"

"The Yankees, three to two."

In the next room, I heard a loud cheer and Michael Kay screaming.

"It's in the air. It's on the warning track...!"

The cheers turned to groans.

"And it's caught by Gonzalez. The Yankees lose two to one. So close..."

She didn't even look embarrassed. I shook my head and walked out.

The others were waiting for me on the sidewalk. Jacob smirked.

"So? Enlightening?"

"You first."

"Not bad. The thing with these psychics is that they tell you stuff you already know. Even if it is real, it doesn't really help. Her future readings were obscure at best. You?"

They all looked at me.

"That woman was full of shit."

I absently fingered the stones in my pocket.

When I finally got home, I could barely see straight. I wanted to sleep forever and ever. I thought about throwing out the stones. But something stopped me. What did I have to lose? That woman was off her rocker, true, but...it would be nice if it were true. That all I had to do was throw some stones into the river and I'd be all better. It would be so easy. I slipped the stones under my pillow. It would be nice...

CHAPTER ELEVEN

Dinner with the Goddess

I woke up on Monday morning ten minutes before my alarm went off. I didn't feel like going back to sleep. I was keyed up. Overexcited. If I called the Goddess in this state I'd probably speak in Swahili. I needed to calm down. I took a long shower and actually shaved for once. I brushed my teeth and tried not to notice my stomach hurting. An expectant, worried hurt. When I got out of the bathroom, I was shocked to see it was only 8:45. I went over and turned off the alarm that had been ringing for the last fifteen minutes. The banging on the wall stopped accordingly. I opened up my tiny closet to pick out a shirt. Normally I dress in the dim light, but today I turned on the lamp. For some reason it was important that I look nice when I call the Goddess. I picked my light blue, "He's more built than he really is" shirt. It didn't even occur to me to leave early so I could get to the office on time. I just watched the Weather Channel and played with the clear stones under my pillow until I was running late, and then left.

As I passed Victoria's Secret, I gave in and stared at the mannequins the whole time I was walking by. They were wearing some kind of hot pink lacy bra and panty combo. Some kind of Easter thing, maybe. Because there's no better way to celebrate the resurrection of Christ than playing a little hide the salami. I had a raging stomachache by the time I hit the subway.

I got to work my customary ten minutes late. I shut the office door to keep out Maureen. The last thing I wanted to do was face her after my breakdown. I took out the Goddess' number and put it on the desk in front of me. It mocked me with its promise of eventual humiliation. I pushed it aside.

Baseball! That'll take my mind off! I accessed my league on the web and checked my standings. Shit. I was in last place again. Orlando Cabrera was out with a bulging disc. What kind of injury is that? His back hurts? If he's going to sit out a game, he's supposed to have a broken leg or a ripped hamstring or a slashed aorta. I was very disappointed in the wussiness of ballplayers today. I dropped Orlando and picked up Lyle Overbay. Time to take a chance on the rookie! I called up Jim to tell him all about it.

"Hey, monkey!"

"Hey, Gonzo."

"I picked up Lyle Overbay. He's going to kick ass for me!"

"Good for you."

"His home runs are going to be staggering, since the pitchers aren't used to him."

"I hope he hits eighty for you."

"What's up with you? You sound distracted."

"There are more important things on heaven and earth than are dreamt of in your fantasy league, Horatio."

"Have you been licking stamps again?"

Something tickled at my memory. That's right! In my woman-fearing self-involvement, I had completely forgotten about my Jim kidnapping scenarios. I guess being worried about a friend's death by unspeakable cruelty comes a distant second to phone calls with girls.

"Hey, what happened to you last week? Was it white slavers?"

"No, it was something far worse."

"Color-blind slavers?"

"No my friend, it's that crazy little thing called love."

"Jesus, don't tell me that! Not you, too! Tell me you didn't have sex! I'll have to kill myself."

"The thought of me getting some makes you suicidal?"

"No, of course not. I'm just not getting any at all, and anybody who does get some is another dagger in my booty-less heart."

"I understand."

"So what happened?"

"Have you ever been baked into a cake to be served to a room full of vampire pseudo-lesbians?"

"It depends on what you mean by baked."

"So then, no. Well, I had a crazy week."

My phone beeped.

"Dude, hold on one sec."

I hit the other line.

"Hello?"

"David?"

It was the Eater. She was crying, I could tell. Her voice quivered. I was caught.

"Hey."

"What's up?"

"Nothing."

"How's work? Any new puppets?"

"No, it's the same cast. We're just doing the same thing. Same old, same old."

"Why haven't you called me?"

"I left you a message. Didn't you get it?"

"Yeah, I got it. I know you were at my grandma's party. Why did you run away from me? Do you think I'm crazy?"

"What? No, of course not."

"Then why are you treating me like I'm crazy? I can hear it in your voice."

The last word came out more as a sob than as English. I hated this.

"Look, I'm sorry I'm not sounding lovey-dovey, but I'm trying to move on."

"Why? Why are you treating me like this? I didn't do anything wrong!"

"It just didn't work."

"What does that mean? Didn't you love me? Or was that a lie?"

"Of course I loved you."

"I thought we were going to spend the rest of our lives together, and now it's just over? I don't understand. I didn't change. Did you change?"

"It's hard to explain."

"Try."

"You know how you just accept things when you're dating someone? Maybe you even tell yourself you think it's cute, in the beginning. But after a while, you have to make a decision. Can I live with these character traits or not?"

"So you think something is wrong with me. Well, you're not that easy to be with yourself!"

"I know. That's why it didn't work. We both had things that we couldn't look past."

"You were selfish and you made me feel bad. Did you want me to do it even when I didn't feel comfortable with it? Do you know what that's called?"

"Look, we just didn't match up. There are things I want that you don't want."

"Then why do I miss having sex with you?"

"Stop it!"

"How can you say we aren't right for each other? We were so happy."

"I have to go. I'll call you later this week."

"Don't do this to me. Don't hang up."

"I have to go to a meeting."

"Please..."

"Bye."

I hung up.

The phone rang again. I saw her number on the caller ID. I didn't pick up. I heard my cell phone ring. I didn't pick up. My office phone rang again. I let it ring. Eventually, the ringing stopped and it was quiet.

I grabbed the piece of paper with the Goddess' phone number on it and dialed.

"Hello, *Now* Magazine."

"Hi, can I speak with Julie?"

"This is Julie."

"Hi, it's David. The guy with the bad memory for names."

"Hey, how are you?"

"I'm good. I'm good. Look, I'd love to go out with you some-time. Maybe we can grab dinner."

"That sounds great, but the only night I'm available until next Tuesday is tonight. I'm working all weekend to finish this project."

"Let's do tonight then."

"Okay. Why not? What time? Where?"

"Let's say eight at Nissho's, the Japanese place on Ninth?"

"I love Japanese, that sounds great. So I guess I'll see you tonight."

"Sounds great. I'll see you tonight."

"Great."

"I'll see you then. Bye."

"Bye."

Completely calm and assured. Whatever happened tonight, happened. If I fucked it up, I fucked it up. Right then, I couldn't care less.

Walking to the bathroom after lunch, I noticed that Maureen's door was three quarters closed. I could hear her inside on the phone. It sounded like she was crying. I didn't want to peek. I just walked by.

Thanks to my nice shirt, I didn't have to go home to change, so I stayed late at work playing computer games. The Eater tried to call me three more times, but I wasn't answering my phone for anybody. My door opened. I couldn't avoid it all day, I guess. Maureen stepped in and closed the door after her.

"Hey."

"Hi."

She sat down.

"How you feeling? You scared me a little."

"I'm okay."

"Me too, if you were wondering."

"I'm sorry. I guess I'm a little embarrassed."

"Me too."

We both stared at our hands. She picked at her fingernail.

"So what now?"

She sounded small and hesitant.

"I guess we know it won't work out."

"I guess so."

I looked up. Her whole body was shaking as she fought to stay calm.

"Maureen, I'm sorry."

"It's fine. It's okay."

"I'm veering out of control. I didn't mean to take you down with me."

"I'll be fine."

"You're such a great friend."

"I'm sure I am."

"You are."

"Look, I'm not mad at you. I understand. I was there. It's not like I don't believe how hurt you've been. I'll be fine. It was stupid of me to get caught up in it. I broke the main rule."

"So what do we do? Are we going to be awkward around each other from now on?"

"I don't know. I guess we'll find out."

She left, closing the door behind her. I felt horrible. I hadn't even stopped to think about the civilian casualties in my war with romance. Maureen was unfortunate enough to be taken down by friendly fire. I had to learn to be less...messy. I looked at my watch. One more hour. I turned on my TV. The Yankees were playing the Royals. They're almost bad as the Devil Rays. This was "Beat Up the Children" week in Yankee baseball, apparently. I forced myself to watch the carnage. My mind wandered to the bodies littered around my road to happiness. How many more had to die? Should I even go through with this date? I knew the answer to that one. You don't stand up a goddess. But if this didn't work out, I'd have to reconsider my whole strategy. Please God, don't let it come to that. I glanced at the clock, which let me know it was already seven thirty. I thought about waiting a little bit so I could be late, but why bother? Between the Eater and Maureen, I didn't have any energy left to play games.

I headed out to the restaurant and got there before she did. I grabbed a table and stared at the lobsters floating in a tank right by my head. Their claws had rubber bands on them to keep them from fighting back. A friend of mine from college used to rant about that. She thought it was cruel. I thought the whole keeping them alive just to eat them was the real issue, but I kept my mouth shut. One of my stronger moments.

I was so wrapped up in the plight of the lobsters, I didn't notice the Goddess until she was standing right over me.

"Hey, David. Do you recognize anyone in there?"

"I think that one's my grandma reincarnated. You can tell because it keeps trying to give the other lobsters ginger snaps. How are you? Have a seat."

The Goddess sat down. She looked good, but not overwhelmingly, unreliably good. That may sound like a shitty thing to say, but it's actually a compliment. I'm not that attracted to women who look too created. It makes me fear the next morning, when her face has magically made its way onto my pillow like some mass makeup exodus. The Goddess, on the other hand, was only lightly made up. Nothing hid that darker, Mediterranean skin tone. I could see a few light lines and her lips were the slightest bit chapped. I found that very sexy. She wore a medium cut top, formfitting but not too revealing, and very trendy hip-hugging black pants. I didn't notice her shoes, since I'm not a *practicing* homosexual. I did notice her breasts though. I'll leave you to imagine them.

Maybe I can go a whole half an hour without fucking this one up.

"Have you ever been here before?"

"No, actually. It seems nice."

"Yeah, I like it."

"So you come here for the sushi?"

"No, I don't eat sushi. I like the steak teriyaki. Very tasty."

"I guess I'm on my own."

"How's the law school hunt going? If there is one, that is."

She seemed a little embarrassed, but didn't apologize.

"It's going well. I'm writing up my applications right now."

"Looking at the east coast?"

"Looking at New York, actually. Columbia or NYU."

"Cool."

"Yeah, I hope so."

Silence as she studies the menu. I feel compelled.

"So how's Opera Girl?"

"Who's Opera Girl? You mean Maggie?"

Shit. Me and my hemophilia.

"Yeah, that's just a nickname I have for her."

"Nickname, huh? Maggie's singing voice sounds like the death cry of a tortured seal. Why that particular nickname?"

"It's a little rude, actually. I shouldn't say."

"Just tell me. I'm no snitch. I won't tattle."

"Opera singers are known for singing scales. You know... 'Me-Me-Me-Me-Me-Me-Me.' And that's who Maggie talks about."

"I see. You're right. That is rude."

This talk about nicknames set off an itch in my brain. Oh yeah...

"You said you had a nickname for me."

"Yes, I do. Maggie told me of your penchant for nicknames, so I thought I'd play."

And I thought Maggie never listened. I'm never as clever as I think I am.

"What is it?"

"I don't know if we've come far enough for you to hear it. It's at least a post-tempura type of revelation."

"If you don't tell me, I'll cry."

"Chokey McCoughCough."

"That's...catchy."

"Your little 'I forgot your name so I'll pretend to cough so you'll introduce yourself' move impressed me so much I had to incorporate it into your name. Though you should have seen your face when we just stood there. Priceless."

My patented move was as transparent as my motives.

"Look, I'm sorry. I didn't mean..."

"Don't worry about it. I think it's funny."

"Why did you call me? Since I made such a fantastic first impression."

"Puppeteers are supposed to be good with their hands."

Hello.

"I wish I was one, then. I'm the producer of the show. I don't actually work the puppets."

"So what do you do, then? In actuality?"

"I sit in my office, ignore my phone and look busy. You?"

"The same. Except I do it in a cubicle. And since I'm a receptionist, I probably get into more trouble with the phone thing than you do."

"Yeah, they do get steamed about stuff like that."

"They have no understanding in their souls."

She was pretty cool. She smiled at my jokes. And made jokes of her own! None of the girls I went out with made jokes. Except for the Eater, of course. She could be pretty funny. She'd once made me laugh so hard a piece of Belgian waffle went up the back of my throat into my nose. It didn't fall back down for three hours.

"What's wrong? You look a little sad."

"Nothing. Sorry. Just thinking about a work thing."

"I'm glad I could send you off so easily."

"No, you reminded me I had to approve a script I forgot to read, that's all. It's about understanding."

"That's pretty deep."

"All of our shows are like that. One episode is about smiles. Another is about clouds. Another is about trees. Another is about the one boy with two mommies. We deal with some deep shit."

"It's better than what tiny purse that only holds lip liner goes with which pumps that you can only wear if you're a twenty-foot-tall Amazon who weighs three pounds."

"I don't mean to be forward, but you look like you can hold your own with any Amazonian featherweight."

"They wouldn't hire me otherwise. But I have to tell you, working with all women and gay men has some distinct disadvantages."

I tried to get all nonpracticing offended, but I admired her disgruntlement.

"Sometimes I feel like I'm back in junior high trying to hang with the in crowd. People go through best friends like they're Pez. And you have to look fantastic all the time. I guess I should have expected it, but I'd like to have at least one day where I can wear jeans and a ponytail. I like my hair in a ponytail. But no, it's Gucci this and Prada that. Not that I have anything against Prada. I don't want to misrepresent myself. I've spent enough money on Prada to feed Indonesia. I admit I believe in the importance of boot cut when wearing certain shoes. 'Cute' does pop up a lot in my everyday conversation. But there's something to be said for comfy flannel."

"I agree. As if I had some kind of personal style to back up my understanding."

"You look nice."

"Not as nice as you."

"Thanks."

I really liked her. Not in a "She's attractive, everybody says so" way. In a talky talky, then bouncy bouncy, and then more talky talky sort of way. Do not screw this up, David!

"If you want to get away from the soulless, why are you headed towards law?"

What the hell is wrong with me? Keep your goddamned mouth shut!

"I thought we already went through this."

"I'm sorry. I just say things sometimes. I get caught up in this 'trying to be funny' thing that isn't funny at all."

"I just want to do something important, like all of your sad friends."

"So you are a do-gooder."

"Whatever you want to call it. The money doesn't hurt, though."

"I'm not being a smartass when I say this. Please, stay away from tax law. Whenever you're doing something for a reason, remember that reason. Or you'll end up doing something that's just different enough to beat you down while fooling yourself into thinking you're on the same path you started on. Trust me."

"You sound pretty emphatic."

"I've seen it happen a lot. You start out working on a specific short-term goal that will help you get to where you want to be eventually, and then that goal takes over. You forget that it's just a stepping-stone and you end up, I don't know..."

"Producing a puppet show for TV."

"Could be."

"I'll try to keep that in mind."

"Good."

"How old are you?"

"I'm twenty-seven."

"That's pretty young."

"Disappointed?"

"No, but it's still pretty young."

"What about you, if you don't mind."

"Twenty-four."

I glanced at her hands. No liver spots. Just checking. Women have been known to lie.

"What are you looking at? Are you checking my hands?"

"I like your nails."

"Oh. Thanks. Are you gay?"

"Why would you ask me that? Do I seem gay to you? Is it my hand gestures? They're fey, aren't they?"

"I'm kidding. It was the nail thing. So you have a gay complex, huh?"

"It's just this hand thing I do. I don't mean to. When I gesture to myself, I do this."

I put my hand on my chest like a shocked housewife.

"I see what you mean."

"It's unconscious. But it raises questions."

"So are you or aren't you? It's good to know."

Who am I kidding? A nonpracticing homosexual who's been sneaking peeks down the Goddess' blouse all evening? I don't need to practice to see I have no aptitude for it.

"No. I'm straight. It'd be easier, I think, if I was gay."

"Why is that? Because life is so simple for the marginalized?"

"Gay guys are always hitting on me."

"That's because they know you're straight. If you were gay, you'd be no challenge. And once the challenge is gone, they're left with . . . you."

"That's a low one."

"Ah, well."

"Are you gay?"

"I went down on a girl in college. It wasn't my thing."

The sexy thought of her with another woman warred with the disappointment that it would never happen again.

"Maybe you could answer a question for me. You can see it from both sides. If someone went down on you on the beach and then said that they had a taste in their mouth that was half sand and half you, how would you react?"

"That was a pretty stupid thing to say, David."

"I know, I know. But would it bother you?"

"Was it a good taste?"

"Yes, it was."

"Then it would bug me that I must have sand in me and I'd probably get an infection."

"That's what you'd think about?"

"I wouldn't be thrilled, but it wouldn't bother me. I have it on good authority that I taste wonderful."

Good to know.

"Super."

"You're a weird guy."

"Thanks. I'm amazed you called me."

"You did say some stupid stuff, you know."

"I did. It's my trademark."

The waiter showed up. The Goddess ordered a bunch of different sushi rolls like a pro. I ordered steak teriyaki like a sad, staid little man. She gave me a thoughtful glance.

"There was something about you that seemed...off balance. Like you weren't really there. I thought about it, and I remembered that Maggie, sorry, Opera Girl, had said you'd just broken up with some girl. So maybe you weren't used to being in that situation. Where you have to talk to a girl like a normal person while trying to be perfect. I'm not too good at it either, actually. I broke up with my boyfriend of three years last fall. I don't know how to talk sometimes. So I kind of understand. And that choking thing was pretty funny. So I thought I'd give you a try. For shits and giggles. There it is again. That sad look."

"I'm sorry about your breakup. Any shits and/or giggles so far?"

"A few. Though I won't tell you which."

"Do you still talk to him?"

"He sends me e-mails trying to get back together. He keeps asking me to feed his fish while he's away. I only fell for that one once. It's hard, but I'm a lot better."

"What went wrong?"

"Sex, I guess, was a big issue. He's older, and he doesn't want it so much."

"Meaning only three times a week?"

"Meaning once every three weeks or so."

"Is he eighty? Is he dead?"

"He's forty."

"Forty? Is he all flabby and droopy? That's nasty."
She laughed.

"Stop mocking my ex, he has a beautiful soul."

"Good for him. He and my grandma have a lot in common. He likes bingo, doesn't he?"

"I like sex. I'm not a weirdo about it, but I like it. I want to have sex at least twice a week."

"That's your right as an American."

"Sometimes I would start to, you know, go down on him, and he wouldn't even stop typing."

"Was it prosthetic? Maybe it got shot off in the Civil War."

"And he wouldn't go down on me."

"That is just a crime! Every woman should get flowers once a month and oral sex once a night. Oral sex brings us closer together as people. And you can do it in the car."

"I love giving blowjobs. They say that only thirty percent of women like doing it, you know."

"I don't like those odds. What is the issue? I may be a picky eater. I may not like to try new foods all the time, and I may make some women feel bad by eating less than they do, but when it comes to the important culinary duties, I am a gourmand. Women taste wonderful. And how can you not love the way a woman moves? The way you sometimes have to chase her around the bed because it's just too much. The uncontrolled sounds she makes. You know what I'm saying from both ends of it."

"I know what you're saying. I just like things in my mouth. Lollipops, straws, pens, cock, it's all good."

"You are the greatest woman I have ever met."

"You're just saying that because I'm in that coveted thirty percent."

"I like meeting someone who understands what I'm saying. People get so hung up on sex. My ex thought that her dog was watching us and it freaked her out."

"Really. What kind of dog?"

"A shitzu. Cute little dog. He never barked. And I never saw that dog less interested in us than when we were making love."

"It sounds like she was a little ashamed of sex. How old is she?"

"Twenty-one."

"There you have it. Still a little immature. She'll grow up."

"I hope so. There are so many better things to be weird about than sex. I was in love with her. Sex had never been better than with her because of that. Even though she would only go down on me if I promised to tell her a good five minutes before I came so she could run in the other room. But sex was beautiful. The way it's supposed to be. So why was she so screwed up about it? I don't understand that. It doesn't hurt anyone, unless you get confused about what goes where. I wanted to play, you know? I didn't want a one-night stand. I didn't want to finish up quick and go to sleep. I wanted to try everything. I wanted to spend two hours being sexy together. I wanted excitement and passion and her. I didn't feel dirty about that. I don't feel dirty about any of it. Why does she?"

"There are so many reasons."

"I know. Objectively, I know them all. I just want to be with someone who likes to feel sensual, who wants to help me feel sensual. And I don't want to feel like I'm a pervert because that's important to me."

"She really made you feel bad, didn't she?"

"I mean, it's not like she's in the wrong. If she doesn't feel comfortable, she doesn't feel comfortable. But she'd stop right in the middle, say she felt weird, and that would be it. She didn't feel like she owed me anything. She told me that if I was so hot and bothered than I could masturbate and she'd be okay with it. Like that's not humiliating, you know? Why am I talking about this? I'm sorry, this isn't proper dinner conversation. I don't usually go on and on about my sex life with my last girlfriend at my first meal with someone I barely know. I usually wait until we're in bed, you know, to maximize the embarrassment potential."

"Don't feel bad. I understand."

"I'm still figuring a few things out, I guess. I don't think she could see things from my side. When her eyes flinched after I said something stupid, my gut would clench up like she'd punched me. But she could tell me that I could masturbate and it wouldn't bother her. She's a beautiful girl, but not as beautiful as she thinks she is."

"Ouch."

"I know that's a shitty thing to say, but that really bothered me. I like girls who are a little more beautiful than they think they are. Otherwise, none of my compliments will mean anything. I think it's that unselfconsciousness that elevates those girls. She was attractive, but every time she told me that, she made it less true. Every time she told me that someone was jealous that she was so pretty, I noticed a pinched nose or a weak chin or blotchy skin. Every time she told me how everyone liked her in high school I heard a whine in her voice or saw this arrogance in her face. She was her own worst PR."

"Who broke up with who?"

"Can't you tell?"

"No, I can't."

"I broke up with her."

"Then why do you still care?"

"I don't know. I thought I had made it. I thought I had finally found it. So it really pissed me off when I finally took a hard look at what my subconscious had been screaming about. What about you? Do you still care?"

"Of course. But I'm not bitter anymore. It's just life. I'll find someone else, someday. But I'm not going to waste my time worrying about it."

The waiter arrived with our food. My steak teriyaki looked

great. Nissho's shines at presentation. The steak comes arranged on a plate made to look like a cow. You lift slabs of pink meat right out of its stomach. This might bother some, but I am a dedicated carnivore. I only wish we had sound effects.

The Goddess' sushi came in a boat, which was a little less visceral. Ah well, I think she liked it anyway. A big trout plate that flopped around would have been cooler, but you can't have everything. She could still enjoy watching me eat out of my cow.

We veered away from the sad ex stories and talked about work and family and stuff like that. Her parents were still together. They were into board games, just like my family. My dad lived for our after-dinner games of Outburst and Balderdash. He's sick when it comes to vast amounts of useless knowledge. He can name the only pitcher to throw back-to-back no hitters. I don't know why we reward this kind of sad, obsessive behavior, but if it's something we'll never have any use for, we'll remember. Calculus goes through us like Metamucil, but the winner of the 1962 Best Actor Oscar stays with us always.

We understood each other's family lives. We both had siblings, though she was a middle child and I was the elder. We both lost our virginity at seventeen, though hers drifted away on a bed covered in flowers and mine was cast aside on the ninth hole of the Scarsdale Country Club golf course. She liked to dance, I liked to dance. She liked to ski, I liked to watch girls ski. The only thing that seemed slightly worrisome was that she had slept with over twenty guys, while I had only slept with seven women. You factor in her last three-year relationship and that was some serious booty time she was making. Twenty guys in four years. Of course, she went to a very liberal college, which can inflate your numbers, much like the Colorado Rockies' hitting stats at home. The ball really carries there.

So I was digging the hell out of this girl, to say the least. I hadn't met anyone who I felt I could actually spend some time with like this since the Eater. We finished up our meal and headed outside. I didn't want the date to be over. I wanted a kiss. So much it hurt. There was no way I was going to sleep with her. Not for a few dates. But I needed that kiss. Otherwise this was just good conversation. The kiss was the line that needed to be crossed.

"So, do you want to hit a bar or something?"

"Actually, I should probably head home. It's almost midnight."

So it was. Damn. She noticed my disappointment.

"But I had a great time."

"Me too. I'm glad you didn't just stick my card in your bicycle spokes like so many women before you. We should do this again sometime."

"Sure."

There was no ambiguity here. We had been talking like old friends all night. She looked beautiful under the neon light from the restaurant sign, which is not easy to do. I needed that kiss, and there were nothing but positive signals shooting my way. I called her a cab while I steeled up my nerve. Then, as I opened the door, I leaned in...

"David."

At this point, is it really a surprise?

"David, you're not ready for this."

"What? Of course I'm ready for this, whatever this is. Unless you mean you're recruiting for some kind of Mars probe mission or you turn into the Hulk when kissed."

204 | SCOTT MEBUS

"No, I mean it. I really like you. A lot. But I can tell from the way you were talking about your ex, you're not ready. And I don't want to be the one who proves that to you. Because that would ruin everything. Let's be friends for now. And we'll take it from there."

"How can you tell me whether I am or am not ready to move on?"

"I don't mean to hurt your feelings. I really like you. But now is not the right time. But let's grab a movie or something. Maybe this weekend."

"I thought you were busy."

She smiled.

"That was before our nice dinner. Weekends are precious, you know."

"Oh."

"Give me a call. Bye."

She gave me a hug, got in the cab and was gone.

What the fuck just happened here?

How the hell does some girl who barely knows me reject me by telling me I'm not ready? What is she, the ultimate relationship champion? Do you need years of training to be prepared to date her? Well, fuck that. I don't need that. I couldn't believe my bad karma. I meet the perfect girl (they always become the perfect girl when it doesn't work out) and she tells me that I'm not ready. I feel lower than I ever have. I thought I was at the end of the tunnel, and it turns out there might not be an end after all. Goddamnit!

What if she's right?

⟡

I couldn't get to sleep that night. I tried watching Cinemax After Hours, but it just depressed me. All the pseudo-porn actors were so in love, it was obvious from the way they simulated the sex, and I was alone. I played a mournful version of "Twinkle, Twinkle, Little Star" on my guitar. I tried to read the Bible, thinking it would put me to sleep. Instead I got wrapped up in the Letter to the Corinthians until three in the morning. I took a shower. I rearranged my CDs. I even took out those clear stones from under my pillow and tried to juggle them. I hoped whatever spirit they were hooked up to wasn't a big stickler for his rules. I stuck them back, anyway. By now it was four-thirty. Finally I turned on my computer. The only way to deal with the pain was to pour it out onto the page. I would transfer my sorrow onto the unfortunate souls who would one day read my screenplay. I brought up the file and began to type.

After an hour, I had written ten whole pages, which was a shitload for me (my previous high at one sitting had been a meaty three quarters of a page). I felt good about the plot so far. The two characters had a nice flow to their conversation. All in all, something good was coming out of my night of a thousand kicks to the crotch. I read it over one last time. It's amazing how much better I felt. I had sucked out a little of the poison and turned my pain into the art I knew I could make. It was all for a reason. If it hadn't have been for the Goddess, I would never have been able to start writing. I pressed quit.

Shit, oh man. I had forgotten to save, but, thank God, it asks you automatically when you close out. I pressed okay.

I pressed okay again.

I pressed it a third time.

I could move the little arrow around all I wanted, but nothing happened when I pressed okay. I frantically stabbed the enter key over and over again.

Nothing.

It was frozen. My catharsis was frozen. I couldn't save it. I couldn't trap it and keep it safely locked away. I had to hit force quit. Maybe it saved automatically? Except that it didn't. I had finally started writing and it was all gone. I felt the poison seep back into me. I couldn't bear to try writing it all again. The inspiration was gone. Now I just wanted a cookie. I climbed into bed thinking that I had finally one-upped myself. This was officially a night of a thousand and *one* kicks to the crotch. And it's the last one that's the doozy.

CHAPTER TWELVE

Jim Gets Some

My mom called me at work the next day.

"So, how did the date go?"

"All right, I guess."

"That doesn't sound too enthusiastic."

"Leave the poor boy alone."

"Ed, I'm just asking about his date. I'm not grilling him."

"I know how you can get."

"I'll never be as bad as you, Ed."

When I was eleven, my dad decided it was time for me to learn about sex. I had stupidly mentioned that I kinda liked this girl, Tiffany, from school. So he arranged a special "talk" in order to inform me what all the equipment was for so I would be prepared for any eventuality. He treated it very seriously. He booked an hour with me one Tuesday night. I sat waiting in my desk chair, not quite sure what was going to happen. I heard him upstairs getting revved up like a motivational speaker. My mom encouraged him while he walked around, boxing the air. Finally he deemed himself physically fit enough to talk to his son about sex and came downstairs. He was wearing sunglasses to help preserve his game face. I had been doing homework, so only my desk lamp was on and it shined into my face. He came in and started pacing. I couldn't see him very well. I could only make out the glint of the light off his sunglasses.

"Son, do you ever have...thoughts?"

"All the time, Dad. I'm having some confused ones right now."

My smart-aleck comment seemed to derail my dad a little bit. At least the sparkle on his glasses stopped moving for a second. Then he started up again.

"Do you ever think about girls?"

"In what way?"

I was screwing with him on purpose, just to see what he'd say. He got a little more flustered, and when my dad gets flustered, he visibly calms down and talks real intently. He has an automatic switch inside that turns on the cool when he starts losing control of a situation. This was not passed on to me. As he feels himself losing it, he uses larger and larger words and gets more and more logical. When he starts to sound like a clinical psychologist, you know he's about to punch you.

"I'm trying to ascertain where your thoughts about women lie."

"You lost me there, Dad."

"Do you ever feel the need to...explore?"

"I like climbing things."

"When you reach a certain age, young males such as yourself begin to exhibit certain reactions to the opposite sex."

"Like what?"

"One begins to see their feminine playmates as possible objects of mental imagery which can make one exhibit certain physical responses that may dismay you. These responses are not to be feared. It is a normal reaction."

"You lost me at 'objects.' "

We slipped into a rhythm. The harsh glare of the desk lamp coupled with my dad's dark glasses made me feel like I was in some war movie being interrogated by the SS. I could almost hear my dad's voice shouting out short, staccato, German-accented demands.

"Haf you had impure thoughts?!"

"I will never betray my country!"

"Ven did you begin to notice de female breast area, you swine?!"

"I'll never tell, Nazi bastard!"

I'd be damned if I'd tell the head of Hitler's secret service that I had a *Playboy* hidden under my bed.

"Son, it's nothing to be ashamed of. It's a biological necessity of nature."

He was close to cracking. If I could just hold on a little longer...

"I don't really know what you mean, Dad."

"Have you or have you not had 'special dreams'?"

"I don't really remember. I'm sorry, Dad. I wish I could help."

His shoulders slumped. He took off his glasses and I got a good look at his tired eyes. I felt a little bad, and a little exhilarated. I had beaten my old man.

"If you want to talk about it, you come talk about it. Good night, David."

"Good night, Dad."

As the vanquished Nazi interrogator left the room, I had to smile. It was my first real victory. It got even better the next weekend when my dad left a book on my bed, titled *Boys and Sex*, which explained in detail everything my Dad couldn't get out. I studied it for a week, and then I rented it out to my friends for five bucks a night. I made a good fifty bucks off that book.

My parents were still arguing. They'd moved on to the internet.

"Ed, every time I open up the mailbox, there are hundreds of messages."

"Well, I don't know what I can do about that."

"I know I don't go to porn sites. So where are these messages coming from?"

"Hey, the porn sites are all you."

"Stop it, Ed, you know that's not true. You even made David show you how to download."

"David, did you tell her that? Well, it's not all mine. You're the one with the lesbian thing."

Not this again. Dad loves to bring up Mom's alleged "lesbian thing." Like the song says, he's the king of wishful thinking.

"I can't keep up with this today. I'll talk to you later, David."

Mom hung up.

"So how did the date go, really?"

"Fine, Dad. Just fine. She was really nice."

"So, grandkids, right? Your mom wants grandkids. She's started buying huge stuffed animals for strange toddlers at the mall. People are talking."

"Patience, Dad. I'm young."

"You're not that young."

"None of my friends have kids."

"What about Paula Jenkins?"

"She was my English teacher. She's at least forty."

"But you guys were friendly. You said she was your favorite teacher. And she has three kids. And she's been married twice already. Only forty and already divorced twice. Why can't you be more like her?"

"I gotta get back to work, Dad. I'll talk to you later. Bye."

I couldn't get any peace. I checked my scores to try to lift my spirits. No change. Monday was apparently a big off day throughout the sporting world. I called Jim to complain.

"Hey, monkey."

"Why did you hang up on me yesterday?"

"Oh, shit, I'm sorry. I totally forgot."

"It's nice to be a priority."

"I'm sorry. Listen, I have to tell you about my date last night."

"Why should I listen to you when you didn't even care enough about my week to call me back? I was a human cake! Doesn't that pull you in?! Isn't that noteworthy? Doesn't that beg the story? I mean, Jesus! What do you have to do to be interesting around here? Dump you, apparently."

"That was a low blow."

"So was hanging up on me."

"Look, I'm sorry. Really. Let's grab dinner tonight and you can tell me all your baking stories and I'll lay out my last disaster. Cool?"

"Fine. Nissho's?"

"Hell, no. I'm in pain."

"Diner it is. See you tonight."

I spent the rest of the day pretending to work. I couldn't focus. I felt like Charlie Brown about to get his football snatched away at the last minute—pensive, yet fatalistic. My phone rang.

"Yes?"

"Hey, David."

It was the Goddess. Great. She's a dirty fighter, hitting me when I'm down.

"Hey."

"I am so sorry for last night. I had a great time. I really did. And the look on your face when I got in the cab made me feel awful."

So I was pathetic, too. Kicks to the crotch, they don't stop.

"I understand. It's fine."

Now is when she says, "No, it isn't! We are soul mates! I was afraid! I feared love! But I'm not afraid anymore! I won't fear love! Your love is better than chocolate. It's better than anything else that I've had!" Basically a lot of exclamation points and Sarah McLachlan lyrics. Of course, what I got was:

"That makes me feel better. Whew. We should grab a flick this Friday. You up for it?"

I managed a curt reply.

"Sure."

"Okay. Call me Friday then. I'm sorry again. But I think we'll be great friends. Bye."

Great friends? Are we British? Something was going on here. Usually when women just want to be friends, that means they don't want to ever see you again. Ever. But the Goddess not only wants to see me again, she's setting it up. She's actively trying to spend time with me. But, why? Could she really just want to be friends? Isn't that just a little farfetched? I'd rather assume it was some kind of spy thing. She's a spy and she's afraid I'll get caught in the crossfire. Well, whatever it was, I wasn't going to let it go. I don't come across connections like that often. There was something there. I just needed to find out what.

I met Jim at the Westwood Diner after work. He was sitting in the back by the bathrooms. He was sipping away on his soda. Seeing him there without his long black coat it struck me how ordinary Jim looked. Throw the black coat on him and it eats him up. Either way, he's the loner in the corner. I've only seen him really let loose when he doesn't think he'll see anyone around him ever again. When we spent a week down at Mardi Gras, for example, he went crazy with the beads. I couldn't believe the stuff he got girls to do for plastic on string. I gave most of mine away. Jim, on the other hand, came home with pictures of him doing all sorts of stuff with bead-hungry women. Really cool, kinky stuff involving whipped cream and tongue rings. He's the toughest negotiator around and he really got the most for his beads. I don't understand what the bead attraction is for these women. It's not as if they can trade them in for prizes like at the arcade. That would make all the flashing worthwhile—if at the end of the trip you turned your beads in for a giant Pooh bear. I wonder how many of them wake up the day after Mardi Gras, look down at their piles of useless plastic, and vow to never drink anything named after a natural disaster again. I'm sure those beads are a nice consolation when they show up on *Girls Gone Wild*. That's an argument that'll hold up with Dad.

But most of the time, Jim fades back. Jim is made for the internet. And this Goth thing he's gotten into is perfect for him. These girls *like* a guy in a black coat standing in the corner watching. That's their fantasy. He's smart, a little arrogant, and he went to Catholic school. He's their sex god.

I sat down, signaled the waiter, and ordered a Coke.

"Hey, man."

"Hey. I'm ready to order, so pick something out."

"I am sorry about yesterday. Really. I'm dying to know what happened."

"Tell me about your date first. I know you won't be able to concentrate until you do."

I laid out the previous evening in full. I tried to describe the goodbye rejection thoroughly in order to best represent my conundrum. I finished up with today's phone call.

"Pretty strange, huh?"

"Maybe she's still with the other guy. She doesn't want to scare you away, but she doesn't want to cheat on him."

"Maybe she's with a girl! But I'm making her doubt her lesbianism."

"No more *Chasing Amy* for you. I don't think trying to manipulate your situation into a threesome is going to help you. It doesn't sound like she's gay. It sounds like she's conflicted."

"But she's saying I'm conflicted."

"Maybe that's what she's conflicted about."

"I actually have a headache now. How do you do that?"

"It's your brain trying to keep up with me. Like Scotty says, you just don't have the power!"

"*Star Trek* references only make you look sad."

"So you're going to go out on Friday?"

"I'm not sure."

"Don't kid yourself. You have the willpower of a puppy."

"Yeah, I'm probably going. I want to know what's going on."

Our food arrived. Jim chose that moment to unbutton his shirt.

"Look at this."

"I don't want to see your nipples again. I told you last time, they don't look like volcanoes."

"Just look."

He pulled down his collar to reveal two strange tattoos, one on each shoulder. One was a funny little caricature of him dressed as a devil, pitchfork and all, giving a big thumbs-up. I looked at the other shoulder. The same devil sat there, also giving the thumbs-up.

"What the hell were you thinking?"

"These are my guardians. When I have a decision, I look at each shoulder and ask them their opinion. I think two devils is more appropriate for the kind of choices I've been making the past week, so I left out the angel."

"I can't believe it."

"Watch how it works. 'Should I make fun of David's female problems?' That's a yes from the devil and, let me check, yes, it's a go for it from the other devil. All votes are unanimous."

"Did you get those in Providence?"

"Yep."

"How did you get talked into it?"

"There was this girl."

"Oh, my God. Did she make my little boy a man?"

"She made me a man all right, and I almost missed my bus because she was busy making me a man in the bus station bathroom."

"Way to go. I'd be jealous if I hadn't seen the inside of a bus station bathroom before. I don't wish that on anyone, even if sex is involved."

"I have to tell you, I am good."

Jim's Unbelievable Story

Jim headed up to Providence for one reason only. He wanted to have sex with Janine. It didn't matter that she didn't want to be seen in the same room with him. It didn't matter that he couldn't even tell anyone they were getting it on, which is half the point of getting it on. He was willing to play by her rules. He didn't care as long as he got to fool around. A lot had changed since the last time he had gotten some. Presidents for example. Hairstyles. Bare midriffs went out and came right on back in. He kept his dignity the first year he went without sex. By the second, he became overly interested in his friends' sexual exploits, asking probing questions while leaning. By the third year, all pretense of playing it cool was gone. Jim regressed into a *Porky's*-like state. He visited tons of chat rooms. He didn't care what the heading read; he did not discriminate. On any given night, he was a foot fetishist, an eighteen-year-old lesbian and a nun. He went along with the perversion of the day. He didn't mind. He finally hit pay dirt with the Goth group. They were mostly lonely girls in need of sun and a solid meal who tried to be more sexually adventurous than they were actually capable of. They wanted to strip, but couldn't even watch themselves in the mirror. They bit their lovers with passion, but then immediately ran out to buy hydrogen peroxide. They had whips that they carried around with defiant authority, but didn't really know what to do with. They were fascinated by lesbianism, but only kissed other girls when everyone was watching. In truth, they were one painful candle wax burn away from suburbia and minivans. Jim was like a fox in a henhouse with these girls.

His first night in Providence, they threw a dildo party. He had suggested it the week before and they all thought it was a good idea. So they went out and bought dildos of all shapes and sizes. Big bulbous ones. Long bumpy ones. The kind that filled both needs. Double-sided. Pink, white, green and fluorescent blue. They even found one that glowed in the dark. I'm sure that one contributed to some psychological complexes over the years. When Jim got there, he was pleased to see the party was in full swing. And by full swing, he meant there were four girls in latex costumes sitting on the couch holding wine coolers, two guys in white face makeup over by the snack table eating chips, a bunch of girls wearing corsets holding plastic cups in the kitchen and a small group of gimps straight out of *Pulp Fiction* playing Jenga on the dining room table. It was junior high with nipple rings. Oh, and there were dildos everywhere, just lying around looking sad.

Jim smiled to himself. This was a party he could own. Everyone looked up when he entered and they oozed desperation. Katalina, one of his on-line friends, came over wearing a worried expression.

"Jim, it's not working. Everyone's bored. And no one's even touched the dildos!"

"Don't worry. It's early. Besides, the dildos are for later. Right now, we need to get these stiffs loosened up."

"What do we do?"

Time for Jim to take control.

"First, turn down the lights. Those guys by the chips look like they just came from Barnum and Bailey's under your fluorescents. Good. Now, turn off the Depeche Mode. Depeche Mode hasn't been sexy since they came out. Throw on some trip hop."

These demands were met, and the white-faced vampire guys looked up gratefully from their Doritos.

"So now what?"

"I think some ecstasy is in order."

Ecstasy is a tricky drug. Jim and I both agree that some drugs are worse than others. Pot is the perfect example of this. If alcohol and cigarettes are fine, then pot should be too. It's no worse than either of these. In fact, the government should be encouraging us to smoke pot. High people are easy to control. They don't get violent like drunks and they eat more food, which helps the economy. Most potheads don't even consider smoking up to be a drug-related activity. They get just as offended as anyone else by drug addicts shooting up or snorting at their parties. They'd sit there taking long hits off the pipe while pointing out the cocaine user to the cops who raided the place.

"That's him, man. That's the dude. You should put those drug addicts away, man. You gotta protect our streets!"

Now ecstasy is an interesting drug. It's supposed to be herbal in nature, but due to the type of people who tend to sell it, it usually isn't. Many times ecstasy has been cut with plenty of strange substances. Everything from cocaine to Drano has been found in

E. But if you're lucky enough to get the herbal kind, it's an interesting evening for you. Maybe you'll get horny as hell. Or maybe you'll just be extremely happy. But as long as you keep drinking your water, you will have a night to remember. (By the way, make sure you don't have some terrible secret, because it's tough to keep your mouth shut on E. It's the kind of drug that would have Norman Bates telling Janet Leigh "Guess what? It's not my mama! It's me in a freakin' dress! Isn't that crazy! Doesn't this knife look cool under the lamp? So how many nights are you staying? Hey, where are you going?")

Katalina had begged Jim to come up with some way to spice up her party, and Jim had complied. The relief on their faces when he pulled out the E was almost pathetic. They'd have fun tonight the only way they knew how, artificially induced.

An hour and a half later, the party was in full swing, for real this time. The two white-faced dudes were being whipped by some of the corset girls. A latex girl outlined her breasts in frosting. The gimps were sword-fighting with the double-headed dildos (you can't help everyone). And Jim was making out with both Katalina and Janine, though it was in the dark part of the room where no one could see. Everything flowed perfectly to plan when suddenly, time stopped. There, on the other side of the room, dressed in red leather, stood the most beautiful woman Jim had ever seen. She had dirty-blond hair and almond-shaped eyes. She smiled as she surveyed the room. Jim forgot the two girls beside him; the world around him came to a standstill in deference to this magnificent woman. If this was a normal party, Jim would have probably stepped back into the corner and watched her without daring to approach. But this was Jim's crowd. Jim's party. These were Jim's people! He was a god here! Anyway, he was fucked up and he had more E. So he left Katalina making out with Janine and walked right up to the hottest girl in the universe.

"Hey. Welcome. I'm Jim."

"Hi, Jim. I'm Asia."

"That's huge. I have E. Interested?"

"I think I am."

It was that easy. By the end of the night Jim was sticking it to the hottest girl in the world. It was the greatest sex he had ever had. And then, when he woke up, she was gone.

Jim was frantic. He asked the girls about her. Janine had no idea.

"I don't know anyone named Asia. Katalina?"

"I seem to remember one of the gimps telling me he had invited his friend. I think the name was Asia. It was probably her."

"Do you remember which gimp?"

"They're gimps. They're all the same."

"So I'm never going to see her again? I need to find her."

Janine was a little peeved.

"Why do you care? She was just some weirdo, anyway."

"It's none of your business. You didn't even want me to let anyone know you invited me, and I made the party."

"I don't care what you do with this girl. But it's pretty telling that she left before you woke up. It sounds like she doesn't want to be found."

"Janine, be nice. Look, Jimmy, why don't you come to my party on Monday? Maybe she'll be there."

So he did. He went to the dominatrix party on Monday. She didn't show. He went to the amateur stripper party on Tuesday, but no dice. He did have to do a quick dance with a feather boa before they let him leave. There is no dignity for a man in love. He attended the vampire lesbos extravaganza on Wednesday, and though he got nibbled on by someone he hoped was a girl, there was no Asia. He even went to the drag queen soiree on Thursday, just in case, but no Asia. He did find out that he looked good in a beehive wig and that walking in heels was suicide. But his search for his love was in vain.

Throughout the week, Janine began to pay more attention to Jim. She started by caressing his arm and whispering in his ear, and by Thursday, she was dancing topless on his lap. But he only had eyes for the empty spaces where he wished Asia would be. Janine got pissed off. Jim didn't realize how pissed off until Saturday rolled around.

The theme for that evening's party was sexy food. Katalina had gathered together all manner of eclairs, oysters, bananas and whipped cream. She asked Jim for help with the centerpiece.

"It needs to be something outrageous. Something everyone will be talking about."

"Okay let me think. What's the sexiest thing you can do with food? Eat it off of someone's body! So how about this? We make a cake out of someone. We bake the cake and put a naked person inside it. As we serve pieces of the cake, more and more of the person inside will be revealed until he or she, hopefully she, is completely naked!"

"That's perfect! But who should we put in the cake? How about Alexis?"

"She's too fidgety. Nobody likes fidgety cake."

"What about Raymond?"

"He's too hairy. Not very appetizing."

"How about you?"

This came from Janine, who was standing in the doorway. Jim laughed.

"I don't think so. I don't have a cake type of body."

"Well, I came in here to tell you I found which gimp knows your mystery lady, but I guess you don't want to know."

"You found him? Send him in here!"

"I don't think so. I think I'd rather send him over to that guy inside the cake. I think that would be cooler."

"You are a bitch, Janine."

"Do you want to find her or not? Then put your icing where your mouth is."

Katalina laughed.

"I think she's got you, Jim. So will you be our cake boy?"

Jim nodded, glowering at both of them.

"I won't forget this. Fine. Bake me up."

They spent the next four hours baking dozens of flat sheet cakes. Then they deftly arranged them around and over Jim's naked body. Halfway through, Janine paused to look down at Jim, surrounded by the moist cake.

"This is the greatest moment of my life."

"Just ice me up and get it over with, Satan."

They took two hours covering him in icing. By the time they finished, only half an hour remained before the guests were scheduled to arrive. Katalina and Janine stood back and took a good look at their handiwork.

"I think we created art, Katalina."

"I think you're right."

Jim was a mermaid. His entire body was covered in icing fins, icing breasts, icing seaweed. Only his head stuck out, upon which they had placed a small tiara. Janine took a picture.

"I think I have a Christmas card."

"So where's this gimp?"

"He'll be here. I'll send him over."

Jim knew she'd probably wait until the end of the night. There was no way she'd give him a chance to get up before the cake cutting.

The guests started to arrive, and they were universally impressed with the Jim cake. Various ladies came over to stick a finger in and pronounce him "tasty!" Two hours passed and no gimp came by. Jim started to get pissed. His neck hurt, his arm was asleep and he had icing up his crack. He called Katalina over.

"She's not fucking with me, right? There is a gimp who knows Asia, right?"

"Don't worry. She pointed him out to me. You're fine."

"If you know, send him over!"

"In due time. I don't want to ruin the party."

Another hour passed, and it was finally time to cut the cake. They made a huge ceremony out of it. Katalina added a nice little touch by cutting the first piece right by his crotch. Of course, no one wanted to eat that one. Piece by piece, cake was cut away and handed out, until Jim lost his breasts and his tail. Finally, his middle was exposed for all to see, and he received a nice round of applause. He sat up, all covered in cake crumbs and icing, and had a taste. It wasn't half bad. He looked up. A gimp was there.

"Hey, that was pretty cool, man. I know I couldn't do it. You made the party, man."

"Are you the gimp who knows Asia?"

"That's me."

"Is she coming tonight?"

"Nah. She doesn't usually come to these things."

"Can I have her number?"

"Nah, she asked me to never give it out. But she will be at the Blue Ghetto tomorrow night around seven. You can check her out there."

"Did she mention me at all?"

"Nah, but she doesn't really talk to me that much. I'm just a gimp. Good luck, cake boy!"

The gimp scampered off. The Blue Ghetto, huh? Jim wondered what kind of club that was. He asked Katalina.

"The Blue Ghetto? I have no idea. You'll have to go there and see. Thanks for being such a good sport. You made the party."

"I always make the party. That's my job."

"And you are good at your job, my little Betty Crocker. You are good at your job."

The next night, Jim hopped in a cab and headed out to find the Blue Ghetto. His heart beat double time. Was this love, he wondered? Or just lust? Did he really care? She was hot, for Christ's sake. The Blue Ghetto ended up being this dinky little bar, a true dive. One patron played a lonely round of strip poker on the machine in the back. The bartender was an older guy with three missing teeth. What was going on here?

"Hi."

"What'll you have?"

"Could I get a Guinness?"

"Sure thing."

He filled the mug halfway, let the foam settle, and then topped it off. Jim took a swig.

"Thanks."

"Sure thing."

"Do you know if a girl named Asia is here?"

"She should be here any minute. You know her?"

"Yeah. I was told she'd be here."

"Well, she will."

"Do you know her well?"

"Not really. She just comes in, does her thing, and then leaves."

"Oh."

Jim was just about to ask what Asia's thing was, when the door opened and in she walked. She didn't look quite as magnificent as she had under the dim lights and E, but she still rocked his world. She didn't seem to recognize Jim.

"Hey, Ted."

"Hey, Asia."

"Pour it."

Ted drew another Guinness.

"This guy is here to see you."

"Just a sec."

Ted handed the mug over. Asia took a long, hard swallow.

"Now let me look at the spigot. Everything seems to be in order. Sign here. All right."

She was a beer tester! For the greatest beer of all time! Jim's angel had just become a seraphim.

"So, who are you? What do you want?"

"I'm Jim. Hi. We met last weekend at that dildo party. I gave you E and you had sex with me. I don't know if you remember."

"Oh yeah. Sure. Hey, good to see you. How are things?"

"Good. Good. Anyway, I'm sorry to surprise you at work, but I wanted to see you again."

"That's sweet. You doing anything now?"

"No, not really."

"Well, I'm going to the tattoo parlor. You can come if you want."

"Sure. Okay."

Jim got in Asia's van and they drove to a very seedy part of Providence. She pulled up to a little storefront next to an abandoned Domino's Pizza. A blinking red sign flashed TATTOOS. He followed her inside.

The largest man he had ever seen sat at the counter.

"Hey, beautiful."

"Hey, Fatso. This is Jim."

"Hi, Jim."

"Hi, Fatso."

"The name's Milton."

Jim had obviously angered it.

"I'm sorry, I just thought..."

Asia stepped in.

"Fatso, I need a tattoo."

"What this time? A naked Powerpuff girl?"

"It's not for me. It's for my friend Jim, here."

Jim took a step back.

"Hold on. I'm not getting a tattoo. I thought you were getting a tattoo."

"I've got enough tattoos for right now. Whenever I met someone I think is kinda cute, I check out their tattoos to see what kind of person they are. You can tell a lot about a guy from what kind of tattoos he has. So you need to get one so I can check it out. Otherwise, how will I know anything about you?"

"You can ask."

"Men lie. But tattoos are forever. You can't lie about them. So, which tattoo do you want?"

"How about I tell you which tattoo I would get, and then not get the tattoo."

"It needs to be permanent. Otherwise, you'll lie. Go ahead, choose away."

Jim was frozen. Sure, this girl was cute and all, but a tattoo? That was going too far. He would just turn around and walk away. But he had stayed here all week for her. She was different from any other girl he had ever met. She fascinated him. And maybe he needed a tattoo. He always planned out these crazy schemes, but he never went through with them. He never had the guts to actually do anything unless he could control what would happen. He'd known he'd own that dildo party because he had the drugs. Would he have been so cocky if he had been empty-handed? Of course not. He wouldn't have gone near a girl like Asia. This whole week had been about doing things differently. He was a different Jim in Providence. Maybe a tattoo could help him bring that Jim back to New York. And then he saw it.

"That one. Right there. That's the one I want."

"I like it, Jimmy. I like that one a lot."

Jim was finished with his sandwich. I had barely touched mine. I couldn't believe what I was hearing.

"I got the one devil on this shoulder, so when I was afraid to do something I could ask him and I'd know what he'd say. Then Fatso mentioned that I could chicken out by asking the other shoulder where the angel's supposed to go, so I got a devil on the other shoulder just to make sure I went through with whatever I was questioning myself about. Asia loved the tattoos, went with me to the bus station, and screwed my brains out in the bathroom. Then I kissed her goodbye and left. It was fantastic."

"That's amazing. I can't believe you let yourself be a cake."

"Life as a cake is not very complicated. I enjoyed it for an evening."

"So are you going to see her again?"

"I hope so. She wouldn't give me her number, but I know she'll be checking Flannigan's Pub next weekend, so I think I'll meet her there."

"So you're going back to Providence."

"Yes I am. This is the greatest thing that has ever happened to me."

"I hope it works out."

"Me, too."

"Did you see her tattoos?"

"Yep. She had a tiger on her back and a bleeding rose on her inner thigh."

"What do those mean?"

"Who cares? I'm in love! I'm not going to jinx it by overthinking things."

"She sounds a little smarter than you on this subject, Jim."

"Maybe. I'm happy. That's all that matters."

✧

I was walking past Victoria's Secret on my way home when I stopped up short and blinked. The clothing had changed again, with very sexy garter belts on display, which made me feel especially bad. But that wasn't what stopped me short. What I saw threw me off balance a little. I didn't know what to make of it. I didn't know how I should feel about it. One of the mannequins wasn't wearing any panties.

I know I shouldn't have cared one way or the other. I understand she's not real. She's just a mannequin. But the sight of that smooth, plastic space between those legs shook me. It was too real. It was a scratch in the gold bar revealing the dull iron beneath. A well-concealed hole in the wall of the fantasy. It stood up in front of the promise of sexual delight and whispered that this was all a farce. A lie. A cover-up. This isn't romance, it's plastic. For some reason I thought of the Eater.

I forced myself to start walking again, and I left the shop window behind. But the image of the panty-less mannequin stayed with me long after I had made my way home and crawled into bed.

CHAPTER THIRTEEN

Wussy French Films

The next morning at work, I tried to call Jim, but he wasn't in yet. Looking over my scores, I found that I had risen a little in the baseball standings. I was now in fifth. Not bad. If I could only grab that one player who would carry me to the title. If I could get him now, with over a hundred and forty games remaining, I could dominate. I needed to think about who I wanted.

Maureen strode in, closing the door behind her. I sat frozen, waiting for the heavy talk to begin.

"Relax. It's about work."

My stomach unwound.

"What's up?"

"There's a problem with the puppets. The designer working on the special yoga versions called me to say he's behind."

Our puppets didn't have legs, so we needed to design and make new ones that did. See, we think of everything.

"Okay. So what does that mean?"

"It means we won't be seeing them until the day of the shoot."

"So you can't rehearse with them?"

"No."

"But we'll have them by the shoot."

"Yeah, that should be no problem. I hope."

"So is that it?"

For a second I thought she was going to hit me.

"Yeah."

She turned to leave.

"Wait. Hold on. Do you know what I think? Don't tell Harold. Just keep rehearsing. I'll deal with the camera angles on the day. We've done it a thousand times before. We'll be fine."

"Thanks, David."

"No problem."

She stood there for a second. I shifted uncomfortably. She turned and left, slamming the door behind her. I will never know how to deal with women, no matter how many Lifetime movies I fall asleep watching.

As the week passed by, I found myself waking up with my hand under my pillow, fingering those clear stones. I counted the days down in my head. Eleven days, ten days, nine days until I could toss them and be free. I laughed at myself, at how I grasped at the flimsiest of straws. But I still did it.

Friday came and I called the Goddess.

"Hey, Julie."

"Hey, David. How's the yoga?"

"It's going. Do you do yoga?"

"Nah, I'm more of a kickboxer. It's more useful. If a mugger came at me at two in the morning I don't think I could fend him off with my extreme flexibility. Thugs aren't as scared of the leg-behind-the-head trick as they used to be."

"Yoga relaxes you. That can be handy."

"Knowing I can break a man's neck with my palm is pretty relaxing, too. I sleep like a baby."

"Remind me not to mug you without at least three of my swarthy underworld companions in tow."

"What about you? Do you do yoga?"

"I'm a board. I can't even touch my knees, let alone my toes. I don't bend, I break. I work out though. At least twice a week every other month or so."

"Stop it, the mental picture is too exciting for me."

"You still up for tonight? You mentioned something about a movie."

"You know, I've been thinking. It probably isn't a good idea for us to just go out together. A little too tempting. Would your friends be coming?"

So I was too tempting. It's a start.

"Of course. Is there anything you'd like to see?"

"How about that French film playing at the Angelika?"

"Is that the one about the charming young woman? And the men who love her?"

"Are you making fun of foreign films?"

"I love French films. I'm a big reader. What time is it playing?"

"Let me check on-line. There's a seven-thirty."

"You wanna meet at the theater?"

"Sure."

"How about seven? The Angelika gets pretty crowded."

"Good idea. I'll see you then."

"See you then, Julie."

She hung up. French film, eh? Who could I get to go to this one? First, I needed info. I called the expert on everything.

"Hey, monkey."

"Hey, Gonzo."

"What do you know about the new French film, *Angeline*?"

"Critics love it. Only playing in two theaters in New York. Stars a hot French chick with big eyes. People have used terms like 'lyrical' to describe it. Avoid like the clap."

"Well, I'm going tonight with the Goddess. You want to join us?"

"Hell, no."

"Come on. Be supportive."

"But it's foreign."

"Be open-minded. I know the only good foreign films are the kung fu flicks…"

"Hey. Those aren't foreign. They're American movies that happen to be made in Hong Kong in Mandarin Chinese. They still count as domestic."

"If you say so."

"Don't even try to lump *Iron Monkey* in with those European disasters."

"They are badly dubbed."

"It adds an immediacy to the action. They wanted to keep the combat pure by keeping away good acting. It's all about purity."

"*Rumble in the Bronx* was supposed to be set in New York. There were mountains in the background."

"So you wouldn't be distracted from the ass-whuppings. It was all a delicate dance."

"Help me out. Hey, there may be nudity."

"That is what the French do best. They've mastered the art of justifying gratuitous nudity. You've got to respect that."

"So back me up."

"Fine, what time?"

"Seven at the Angelika."

"See you there. You owe me big. Bye."

"Bye."

Next on my list was Dustin. I told him about the foray into culture I wanted him to join. He wasn't as enthusiastic as I would have liked.

"Jesus, if I had known I was talking to a woman I would have called you ma'am. Will this girl not leave you any balls to speak of?"

"It's supposed to be very lyrical."

"That's film critic speak for 'ass-suck.' Dude, is she really worth subtitles? You know the rules. If it's in another language, it has to have kicking in it."

"I'm trying to get some lovin'."

"Is it worth my respect?"

"Of course. I'd trade your respect for a pat on the ass and a quarter."

"There are so many other films to see. There's an old silent film from the twenties overdubbed by the Wu-Tang Clan playing in the village. You haven't lived till you've seen Douglas Fairbanks as voiced by Old Dirty Bastard."

"This is the one she wants to see. Anyway, there's supposed to be tons of nudity in it."

"Really?"

"It's French. From what I heard, it's boobies from start to end. All three Bs."

"All three? Honest?"

"Yep. So are you going to help me out or not?"

"Fine. But you'd better get some."

"I'm going to do my best."

"Just remember, your friends' vicarious thrills rest solely on your shoulders. Don't let us down."

"It's a heavy burden."

"If she drops you after, we can go catch strippers."

"Be at the Angelika at seven."

"All right. This better be good. All Bs, you promised"

"Bye, Dustin."

"Bye."

Unfortunately, both Cameron and Annie proved unavailable. So the motley crew of Jim and Dustin were to be my backup. This had disaster written all over it.

Wussy foreign films notwithstanding, the Angelika is my favorite movie theater in the city. It's not the size of the screens, that's for sure. My dad's big-screen TV is wider. It's not the sound system. I guess since they show so many films with subtitles, they don't think they need good surround. The main allure of the Angelika is the feeling you get standing in line overhearing the conversations around you. The patrons of the Angelika love movies. They know a lot about them. They know how to talk about them. And when you see a movie at the Angelika, you're one of them. You're one of the cultural elite. That almost makes up for all the reading.

I was a little early, so I grabbed a hot chocolate and a scone from the café inside. The theater has a coffeehouse feel that adds to its cultural elite aura. I pulled out a book to make like I belonged.

"Is that a *Dragonlance* novel?"

She had snuck up on me again.

"It's well written."

"It has a man in a loincloth on the cover."

"He's a warrior. That's what they wear."

"Put the book away before you embarrass me."

The Goddess looked good. Her hair was back in a ponytail. I don't know why I found this attractive, but I did. Focus. Concentrate on intelligent conversation.

"So this movie's supposed to be good, huh?"

"The *New York Times* described it as 'beautifully lyrical' if that means anything to you."

"I love the lyrical stuff."

"I come here a lot. I love foreign films. They're so much better made than American ones."

"I like them, too. Makes you think."

I swear I could almost feel Dustin's foot kick my ass.

"Where are your friends? You didn't make them up, did you?"

"No. Actually, here they are now."

Dustin and Jim came towards us from different locations. Dustin gave me an approving nod.

"These are my friends, Dustin and Jim. Guys, this is Julie."

Jim shook the Goddess' hand.

"We met at that party, remember?

"Of course."

"I've heard a lot about you since."

I flicked him where the Goddess couldn't see.

"I mean, he's barely mentioned you. He's way too busy and important."

The Goddess laughed again. It calmed me.

"Yeah, I can tell."

Dustin looked skeptical.

"The movie poster doesn't look very sexy. Are you sure about this?"

"You're gonna love it. Trust me."

The Goddess nodded towards the theater.

"You guys ready?"

"Bring it on."

We grabbed our seats, sat back and watched a beautiful film. It sucked me in from the first shot. The young girl was struggling with her identity, and the young man she was obsessed with didn't even know what she looked like. I was laughing and crying. And the language! Truly...lyrical. Even though I had read it off of the screen, the translation soared with such vivid imagery I could only guess at how beautiful the original French was. As the credits rolled I looked to my right to see the Goddess crying. Jim wiped his eyes secretly, then made like he'd seen better. I looked over at Dustin. He waited a second, stood up and pointed at us one at a time.

"You're gay and you're gay and you're gay."

I was indignant.

"It was a good movie."

"It was a gyp. There wasn't a single areola to be seen. Not one! Not a single B!"

"It didn't put a lump in your throat?"

"No one even kicked anyone! What kind of foreign film is that?"

"A good one."

"I couldn't even pay attention, it was so dull."

The Goddess stood up,

"That's too bad. While you're guarding your testicles from outside influences, you're missing some great movies."

We headed out of the theater. The Goddess was talking to Jim.

"I saw you tearing up. What got to you?"

Jim was quiet for a second.

"The most powerful moments in cinema are so often the simplest. It's such a simple thing. The girl breaks out of her shell and is able to seek out and hold the love of the boy. She brings herself to go out and get what she wants. It doesn't seem like anything new. It seems pretty obvious, actually. But it's so simple that it's everything. So it gets you."

"I know. The scene at the end where they're dancing got me. I've always equated dancing with love, so it worked perfectly for me. I was crying like a drunken Irishman, which I can say because I'm part Irish. It's a small part, but valid."

"As an almost full-blooded drunken Irishman, I absolve you."

We stopped outside the theater. We stood for a second and I tried to think of something cool to do next.

"So, anybody want to grab some coffee or something?"

Dustin shuffled his feet.

"I should get going."

Jim took the hint.

"Yeah, I'm pretty tired."

To my surprise the Goddess looked uncertain.

"You're right. I should probably be heading home."

No! Too early! Must stop! Needed some form of physical affection!

"It's so early. We can grab some coffee, we don't need these jokers."

"No, I should get some sleep. I'm not much of a coffee drinker."

I couldn't believe this. This wasn't the plan. I had no idea what to do. Jim gave me a look.

"You know what would be fun, now that I think of it? There's salsa dancing at Tortilla Flats on Friday. Have you been?"

What the hell was Jim talking about? The only time I'd ever seen him dance was when I accidentally lit his coat on fire. The Goddess, however, looked interested.

"No, I haven't. But I love to salsa."

"You'd love it. Dustin and I have been a few times."

If Dustin danced it was alone in his room. Men don't dance. There's no kicking in it. Unless you're Michael Jackson, and he isn't really the manly gold standard. I appreciated what Jim was doing but it was going to derail here. Masculinity was at stake.

"Um, yeah. Jim talked me into going and I had a good time. Dancing with the girls, that is. Not Jim."

I owed Dustin a mental apology. Which I gave him. The Goddess looked interested.

"David, do you salsa?"

As a matter of fact, I did. I had learned it at a wedding a few years back. Talk about fortuitous.

"Yes. I love it. Let's check it out."

"Well, if you're all going."

Jim put his arm around Dustin.

"Of course we are."

Dustin looked a little more uncomfortable now.

"Sounds peachy."

I sealed the deal.

"Let's go."

We hopped a cab over to Tortilla Flats. A kind of "blink and you miss it" type restaurant, Tortilla Flats proved to be packed. We only got in because the Goddess used her magazine ID to pretend she was doing a piece on the place. She was quite useful. We got a table near the floor, where the movement was in full swing. We're talking sweaty bodies, saucy hips, teasing heel flips: pure sex. I leaned over to Jim under cover of the live salsa band.

"I owe you again. You saved my ass. How did you know about this?"

"There was a flier on the lamppost right behind you. This is as far as it goes, however. I am not dancing. Too many people could get hurt."

"Fair enough."

Dustin checked out the crowd. He approved of the bared midriffs. He shouted in my ear.

"Not bad. Do you think any of these ladies give lap dances?"

"I don't know. Why don't you ask? I'd love to see what they'd say."

"I think I'll get some margaritas instead. Jim, why don't you help me?"

"Sure."

They disappeared into the crowd. The Goddess danced in her seat. I brought my mouth up to her ear.

"You want to hit the floor?"

"Give me a second. I need to assimilate."

We waited for the drinks to come. After a few minutes, we starting talking a little bit about nothing. I asked her about her brothers.

"They're both bigger than me. By a lot."

"Why are women's brothers always over seven feet tall?"

"They're great. They're both married. Hayden has two kids and my little bro Peter is expecting one in a few months."

"Man. Do you feel left out?"

"I don't need kids yet. I've got a few more years of hormonal balance to enjoy before I tackle that mountain."

"Does that have anything to do with the ex?"

"Maybe, I don't know."

"You don't have to talk about it. I just understand about that kind of thing."

"Maybe you do and maybe you don't. It was weird."

"What's his name?"

"Carl."

"Not Carl the bastard, or Carl the ball-less wonder?"

"No, just Carl."

"How are you dealing with things?"

"All right, I guess. I'm just sad. We were supposed to get married, you know."

"No, I didn't. You didn't mention that."

"That's what ended up breaking us apart. He wanted a prenup."

"Ouch."

"He makes a lot of money, so I guess I can understand. But he didn't make me feel like he trusted me, you know? If you want me to sign a paper that admits the possibility of failure, you have to do it with a lot of love. He never reassured me, or downplayed its importance, or even tried to make it seem like the prenup was supposed to protect both of us, you know? I could make a lot of money as a lawyer and he could have phrased it like that. But he just wanted to protect his money. How can you love someone who acts like that?"

She seemed to be genuinely asking me.

"I don't know if you can, I guess."

"So I broke it off. And now he wants me back and he's so, so sorry. But I can't trust it. He had his chance and he blew it."

"So you're over him."

"I'm getting there. I know it's for the best."

We watched the floor. I stood up and grabbed her hand.

"I think we need to dance."

Dancing with someone for the first time is often awkward. You don't trust each other. You don't know the other person's preferences or quirks. You spend the first few dances just trying to figure each other out. Sometimes you never get in sync. Toes are stepped on and timing is forever off. Salsa is especially difficult because of the hips. Both your hips had to move together. I've been told that if you want to know if someone would be able to move with you in bed, then dancing the salsa is a good way to find out. You can tell if you follow the same choreography. If that's true, then sex with the Goddess would be a Fred Astaire and Ginger Rogers movie. It was that perfect.

She moved when I moved. Her hips and my hips swayed to the same metronome. Effortless. It felt effortless. We wrapped the music around us and disappeared. I didn't have to look down. We locked eyes and just let go. Our movements were crisp and arrogant. I felt sexy. It was so easy.

We tore through at least five songs in a row. When we finally made our way back to the table, Dustin and Jim had downed both their drinks and ours. They pretended like they had already danced and now they were resting. I wouldn't have noticed either way and I had a feeling she felt the same. Her face remained flushed throughout the rest of the evening. She tapped Jim on the shoulder.

"May I have this dance?"

This was going to be good. Jim froze.

"I'm kinda tired. Maybe some other time."

I had mercy.

"I think Jim's a little tired out."

Dustin, however, had none.

"Dude, it's just one dance. Show her how it's really done!"

Jim shrank back.

"Maybe next time..."

Dustin unveiled an evil grin.

"You keep telling us what a dancing machine you are. Now's the time to prove it."

The Goddess pouted.

"Come on. I'll let you grab my ass."

A war raged in Jim's eyes. The Goddess fired the last shot by pulling him onto the floor before he could dig his feet in. They began to sway. I tried to keep a straight face. I owed Jim for this evening. The least I could do was keep my lips pressed together. But Dustin started to giggle. And once he started to giggle, I was lost. It wasn't pretty. By the time the song ended we couldn't breathe. We tried to compose ourselves. As they walked back towards us, Jim looked a dagger into me. A stray chuckle escaped me as he sat down.

"Hey, I'm not embarrassed. Did you get to touch her ass? Hmm? No you didn't. So shut it, you sound like you're high."

The Goddess patted Jim's hand.

"That was fun. I can tell you enjoy it. And that's what's important."

I risked an aneurysm trying to hold back the snort. Dustin had to turn away. What a great evening.

A few drinks later, Dustin and Jim both announced they were leaving. I was certain the Goddess would stay. After all, we had practically made love. And we were good at it. She sighed.

"I should head home, too."

To her credit, she looked reluctant. But I didn't push it. Something else lurked beneath the surface and I wasn't going to screw with it. We pushed our way to the door.

Jim and Dustin said goodnight and leapt into a cab, leaving the Goddess and me to say our goodbyes alone. They were good friends. Everyone should be so lucky. She looked at me.

"So when does the yoga thing happen?"

"Next week. You know what? You should stop by."

"I don't know."

"You can check it out during your lunch hour. It'll be fun."

"Maybe. We'll see."

I didn't kiss her. It didn't seem like the right moment. After our dance, a kiss was too small. It was all or nothing, and since I wasn't getting it all, nothing it would have to be. For now. So I hailed her a cab and said goodnight. She gave me a wave and was gone.

On the ride uptown, I couldn't nail down how I felt. I decided to concentrate on the hopeful signs. The positives. She was in the same place I was. She wanted to move on as much as I did. She just needed to feel comfortable with me. She needed to see me as a better man than her bastard ex-boyfriend. That shouldn't be too hard. I'm successful with a cool job. I'm good with kids. I'm fun at parties. I'm not old enough to be her father. And we have obvious chemistry. She just needed to see me the right way. This was some kind of divine sign. I was being told that this was my game to win or lose. And I was good enough to win. The Eater hadn't torn that part of me down. I just had to play it cool and I was going to win over the Goddess. I needed to believe that.

CHAPTER FOURTEEN

The Bubble-Ass Hummel Boy

"This doesn't sound too promising, David."

That was Annie. We were grabbing dinner at an Italian restaurant she likes in Little Italy. This place was built for fun. Hundreds of photos lined the walls like wanted posters, showing a guy who had to be the owner with every celebrity who existed, ever. There he was with James Caan, with Al Pacino, with Ed Koch, with Bjork. Bjork? I guess even Icelandic oddballs gotta eat. I had never been there before and I eyed the strange object hanging from the ceiling with some trepidation. I had been warned.

Dustin shoveled pasta into his mouth while Cameron ogled a busty woman two tables over. He was being very obvious. Dustin had been twenty minutes late because he couldn't find a parking spot on the street. He refused to park in a garage and drove around until he found a spot a mile and a half away, and then took the subway over. He was very proud of the spot and kept commenting on it throughout the evening. Cameron was only ten minutes late, though he had almost bailed because he had to be up by nine o'clock the next morning for his bagpipe band practice. It wasn't even seven in the evening yet. He's the copout king. Once, before he moved into the city, he had driven in from Westchester to attend one of Annie's parties in Queens, circled the block once, couldn't find a parking space, so he went home. We called to see where he was and he had already changed into his pajamas. My friends really know how to party. I was amazed they both had made it out for dinner. They must need to borrow money or something. I had just told everyone about my conversation with the Goddess.

"Why? She's just like me."

"Women will never be just like you. We don't have penises. We can only imagine the depths of stupidity those tyrants drag you down into. Our breasts just aren't as demanding."

We had caught Cameron's attention.

"Look at that girl's rack."

We all looked. Annie nodded.

"That is a nice rack. I don't even think it's fake."

"Of course it isn't fake. Those are proof that God exists. And he is a great and glorious God."

Dustin looked back down at his plate.

"I'm in the mood for ice cream. We should grab some later."

I waxed nostalgic.

"You know who had great breasts? Stephanie Mangini. She was a grade below us, you remember?"

Cameron got a faraway look in his eyes.

"Of course I remember. She was in my French class. I had to wait for five minutes after class let out before I could even stand up."

Dustin sighed.

"She was on the swim team with me. She was naturally buoyant. It was unfair to the other teams, actually."

"Well I got to second base with her back in junior year."

Annie snorted.

"Second, David? Do you still use baseball terminology? If second is boobage, than which base is oral sex? Or anal sex?"

"Well, anal sex is a perfect game. Everybody knows that."

"I always thought basketball was better for sex. Slam dunks, three pointers, high free-throw percentage—those are metaphors that work."

Dustin was impressed.

"Damn, Annie, I didn't know you had such a sports streak in you."

"A gal needs to know if her guy can score in the paint."

"Anyway, I was just saying that I got to touch Stephanie's boobies. And it was cool."

"So what? We give tits away."

Cameron looked at Annie sharply.

"What do you mean?"

"A girl doesn't really think of her breasts as some kind of temple. I've let guys I barely like feel my breasts just to shut them up. And they get all happy like little monkeys."

"So why haven't I felt up more breasts? Plenty of girls barely like me. Why don't they try to shut me up with their rack?"

"I don't know what to tell you."

"Dammit, if girls don't care, I want to be feeling more boobies."

"Maybe you need to work on getting a girl to sit next to you, then you can move in on the boobies."

"Women suck."

I steered the conversation back to what was important—me.

"So how is the Goddess not like me? We danced perfectly."

"And that's a big plus. But I bet you she's still hung up on her old boyfriend. That's probably why she's holding you at arm's length."

"She barely even mentioned him. I had to bring him up."

"I don't want to bring you down, David, I'm just trying to give you a different perspective. She could very well be hung up on her old man."

"She just needs to forget him."

"I don't want you to get hurt because she's an emotional mess."

"We're all emotional messes. If I let that get in the way, I'd be cutting off everyone I've ever met."

Dustin stabbed another stuffed mushroom with his fork.

"So what's the plan? Roofies?"

"I invited her to my taping on Wednesday. That'll be perfect. She'll see me in control. She'll be awed by the exciting world of television. A woman can't resist a powerful man."

Cameron tore his eyes away from the cleavage.

"Is this the yoga puppet thing?"

"Yeah."

"You're going to be directing puppets doing yoga and you're inviting a girl you like to watch? Sometimes I think you want to fail!"

"It's a kids' show. She knows that. The important thing is that she sees me calm and in control of an entire television show."

"If you say so."

Annie smiled.

"If you want to impress her, you should bring her by the play-group on Friday. She'd see how good you are with kids."

"You know, that's a good idea! When she sees me standing there with three kids dangling from my forearms by their teeth and me not doing a thing about it, she'll see what a kind nurturer I am."

Cameron agreed.

"Maybe you can tell her that autism is catching and play with her breasts. She won't be allowed to react. It'll be perfect."

Annie speared a piece of mozzarella with her knife.

"Cameron, you need to get laid. The longer you go without it, the more fixated you become on it. Soon you'll be like Rain Man. 'I definitely need some titties. Definitely want to suck on some titties. I need to watch Judge Julie on Playboy at eleven-thirty. Definitely titties at eleven-thirty.'"

Dustin interjected.

"What's that old guy doing with the butt doll?"

Three ancient Italian men had appeared at the back of the restaurant. One played an accordion. Another banged on people's plates with what looked like a small white dildo. The third, who was the one Dustin pointed out, had some kind of mooning Hummel figure in his hand. He danced to the front of the restaurant, aimed the figurine's anus at one of the tables, and pushed on its head. Bubbles flew out of its butt. The old guys let out a cry of joy.

"Ayyy!"

I turned to Annie.

"What the hell is going on?"

"They own this place."

The butt guy danced over to our table and we got a closer look at the figurine. It was a little boy wearing a Robin Hood hat, bent over with his pants around his ankles. The old guy smacked the boy's head and bubbles shot out into Cameron's face. Dustin was laughing so hard he couldn't talk. All the while, the plate guy clanged away while the accordion guy played a rustic Italian tune. I turned to Annie.

"Is this a tradition? Because I would hate to think of how it got started."

It got better. The plate guy must have gotten bored with plates, because he ran to the center of the restaurant and pulled on a string. A huge papier mâché penis lit up and shot out confetti. The Italians are a festive people.

Cameron shrugged.

"I guess this is the extended version of the penis ritual."

"Annie, your people have issues."

Dustin had tears running down his face.

"I want one for my apartment. And the bubble-ass Hummel boy. This is the greatest restaurant ever!"

It took five or ten minutes, and another round of food, before we could get Dustin settled. Finally, I turned to Annie.

"So we can help out at the playgroup?"

"Sure. Just tell her the rules. I need all the help I can get."

"You know what? I'll bring my guitar! I can play children's songs for the kids!"

"They have autism, they're not catatonic."

"They'll love it."

"If they start to cry, I'll make you stop. I spend a lot of time trying to pull them out of themselves. I don't want you sending them screaming back in."

"Have faith. I'll have them all singing along."

"Sure. Why not?"

"Cool. I'll ask the Goddess on Monday."

"Don't overwhelm her, though. Since you're just starting out with her you have to tread lightly with plans. Jacob tried to book me up solid and it drove me crazy."

Dustin cocked his head.

"Where is the shy boy, anyway?"

"He had something he had to go to."

"Is he still coming with you to your family's Easter extravaganza?"

"He knows better than to skip out on that. I need the moral support."

Cameron sighed.

"I really want to suck on a nipple right about now."

Annie shrugged.

"I'd give you mine, but I don't know. I just don't wanna. I don't know what to tell you."

"You women just want to see me cry."

"It's a tragedy. You repulse that which you love most. Forever denied that which you crave. You're like the Trix bunny. 'Silly Cameron, tits are for kids.' It's a sad, sad thing."

Annie had a book on autism she wanted me to read if I was going to show up at her playgroup, so I accompanied her back to Queens to pick it up. I reminded her that I had helped out before. She said she remembered. That's why I needed to read it. As we rode in the cab, I asked the question that had been preying on my mind.

"Is she still calling you?"

"Yeah."

"I'm sorry I've stuck you with her."

"It's fine. She'll be fine. I just wish she'd make these conversations quick. Do you know how long the last call was? Four hours! Her calls last longer than your whole relationship did."

"What does she say?"

"She's confused. She contradicts herself."

"Does she hate me?"

"A little bit. That's the good part. I think she could even hate you more."

"I don't like the idea of her hating me. I don't hate her."

"She needs to hate you. That's why you need to talk to her. She needs to know that she can hate you. She still talks about getting back together, you know."

"Shit."

"Sometimes you need to be the bad guy, even though I know you don't want to be. You need to make her cry and have her burn all your photos and stick pins into a doll."

"But then why did we date at all? If it's just going to end up with all this anger."

"We're bulls in the china shop. That's the way we're all built. The only people who can break up painlessly never really cared. When you fall in love you sink a little of yourself into someone. When you break up, you yank it out. Or it gets yanked out for you. There's no pretty way to do it."

"That's kind of harsh."

"But sometimes you leave a little bit of yourself behind, and she leaves a little bit of herself, and maybe you're better for it. Eventually, anyway."

"I haven't called her. I told her it's over. What else does she want?"

"I don't know. Maybe she'll be okay on her own."

"She's going to have to be. I don't think I could take talking to her again. It's too hard."

"It's up to you. She's young. She'll move on eventually. I'll just have to find something to do during her marathon David laments. Knitting or reading or something. I always wanted a nice quilt."

"You are such a guilt machine."

"A huge quilt. Depicting the entire Spanish-American War."

"What do you know about the Spanish-American War?"

"I have plenty of time to read up on it, now don't I?"

We pulled up to her apartment building and got out. She looked up at her dark window.

"That's strange. I thought Jacob would be home. Is that a reading lamp? What's flickering?"

Oh, shit. Why tonight? Why'd he have to pick tonight?

"Look, maybe I should grab that book another time..."

"What the hell are you talking about? We're already here. Come on."

She opened the front door and headed up the stairs. I slinked in after her. I didn't want to see what Jacob considered a romantic gesture. My imagination couldn't even attempt a mental picture. Annie reached her apartment door, unlocked it and swung it open. She stopped dead in her tracks. Curiosity got the better of me and I snuck up beside her. She had a look of abject terror on her face. I gazed past her.

Candles filled her living room from wall to wall. They flickered everywhere. But not in the colors you'd expect. Black, silver, blood red: all the colors of the troubled-youth rainbow cast an ominous glow on the walls. In the corner huddled a punk band, looking awkward in ripped-up tuxedos and torn bowties. But the real spectacle stood in the center of the room, where Jacob had decided to make his grand romantic statement.

It wasn't really a tuxedo. It wasn't really typical punk wear either. What Jacob chose to wear that evening looked like the bastard love child of a seventies prom tux raped by Johnny Rotten. I even saw some torn Prince-esque ruffles on the cuffs. This kind of clothing monstrosity could only be conjured up by someone caught in the throes of love, or a severe addiction to painkillers. Annie couldn't move. Jacob bowed to her formally.

"This is for you, my love."

He nodded to the band. The guitarist flicked on his amp and spent five minutes trying to get his guitar to feed back. Eventually, he coaxed a sad little whine out of the box and the drummer took that as a cue. Like the Sex Pistols being pushed down a flight of stairs, they began to play. The music hit me, kicking me in the balls. The sound beat me up like it wanted my lunch money. Hurricane Upchuck swirled around in my stomach. While fighting to keep my family-style Italian dinner down where I had paid to put it, I noticed something. Though muffled by the blood trickling out of my ears, their music seemed somewhat familiar to me. Annie spoke out of the corner of her mouth.

"Please tell me this isn't what I think it is."

"I wish I could."

Jacob grabbed a mike, got down on one knee, and began to sing with the voice of an angel being slowly pushed into a food processor.

"*Love. I get so lost sometimes.*"

Annie still hadn't moved her head, but her voice drifted my way.

"Please make him stop."

"But he's doing it for you."

"It's horrifying."

"So? At least it's sincere."

"*All my instincts, they return.*"

"What's wrong with a card?"

I didn't want to answer that one.

"In my wildest dreams, I never thought he'd do something like this."

I didn't know if that was a good thing or a bad thing. I was too busy trying not to pass out under the audio assault.

"*In your eyes, the light, the heat.*"

It wasn't that their rendition of Peter Gabriel was bad, per se. They played competently enough, as punk goes. It was just that the whole package was so *wrong*. A love song was never meant to be beaten into submission that way. When the bass guitarist sang backup, he sounded like a cat being strangled. The rhythm guitarist kept kicking the sofa like he hated its guts. The lead guitarist kept screaming "Fuck the Police!" at the top of his voice. And through it all, Jacob sang, in his strangely hypnotic way, sounding for all the world like he was starting a riot and not telling the woman he loves that he loves her. Apparently even badass punks can get the Say Anything Syndrome. I only hoped Annie didn't chuck the VCR at his head.

My nose was starting to bleed. It had to end soon, right? The two guitarists had stopped playing and were now beating each other over the head with their instruments while screaming "In your fucking eyes!" The bass player passed out. The drummer gamely pounded on, until Jacob gave him a signal, upon which he launched into a huge solo, while Jacob ran around screaming into the mike. Eventually, the drummer's arms must have locked up, because he just stopped abruptly and slumped forward, spent. The two guitarists had long since been rendered unconscious. Noticing that the music had stopped, Jacob threw himself at Annie's feet.

"In your eyes, Annie! I love you!"

With that he ripped open his shirt. Annie drew back in shock. I gasped. A beautiful rendering of Annie was tattooed across his chest. Above the picture was the legend "I Love Annie." Underneath, because he couldn't resist, read "Down With Government." All in all, I had to admit that this was true love.

"What the hell did you do to yourself!"

Annie, I fear, was less forgiving.

"I love you, Annie. I've been afraid to say it for a while now, but..."

Don't mention me. Don't mention me.

"...recently I've decided I had to go for it."

Thank God. Annie stood there speechless. Jacob stood up.

"Are you going to come in?"

Annie walked in like a zombie. I followed, closing the door behind me.

"Hey, Jacob. Cool song."

"Thanks. Annie? What do you think?"

Annie looked at the most permanent example of commitment

she had ever seen and did the only thing she could bring herself to do. She walked right past Jacob, into the kitchen, where she turned on the oven and grabbed the cookie sheet. Jacob followed her.

"Annie? Are you okay?"

She didn't answer. She pulled down a bowl and opened the flour. The band members had come to and were silently packing up their stuff. I gave them a thumbs-up. In unison, they shot me the finger and went back to their instruments. I walked over to the kitchen, where Jacob was trying unsuccessfully to get Annie to talk.

"Don't you have anything to say? I needed to let you know how I felt. I can't keep going on like this. Pretending to be all nonchalant and friendly about it. I want to be with you. I want to wake up next to you every morning. I love you."

This got a response.

"Why? How can you love me like this? We're not even going out! This is crazy. Crazy people do stuff like this. Look at your chest! How could you do that?"

"I had to risk it."

"But you don't even know how I feel!"

"Well, this is how I feel. I needed to tell you. And I wouldn't give you the chance to doubt it. There's no doubt here. It's written on me, for Christ's sake."

True. Jim's friend Asia would be all for this. Annie was obviously in shock. She had no idea how to handle this. Either way, her life had been changed for her.

"What am I supposed to do with this? Am I supposed to say it, too, or you leave? Do I get a gargantuan tattoo? I'm painted in the corner!"

Jacob closed his shirt. His shoulders slumped a little.

"You've always been painted in the corner. We both have. This was my way of breaking out of it. It's up to you what you want to do with this. I'm not asking for you to say anything you don't want to say. I just wanted you to know. And now you know."

He kissed her on the cheek and walked into his bedroom, closing the door behind him. Annie collapsed in the kitchen chair, clutching the cookie bowl in her arms. I sat down next to her.

"What are you going to do?"

She brought her tearing eyes up to meet mine.

"I don't know. I don't want to do anything. I don't want to leave this kitchen."

"Do you love him?"

"I don't know."

I gave her a hug.

"I guess now you're going to have to find out."

"What if I don't?"

"Then you don't."

"But then I lose him."

"That's true."

"He does make me feel comfortable. I like being with him. What if this is the best I can ever get? What if I break up and move on and never find anyone to love me ever again? Or I never even feel comfortable with someone like this again? What if I'm alone forever because I make the wrong decision?"

"You'll never be alone. Don't worry."

She started to cry. As I held her, my mind flashed to the Eater of Souls. I knew exactly how Annie felt. I wished I knew the right answer, for both of us.

CHAPTER FIFTEEN

Dancing in the Mind

Walking to the subway on Monday, I found myself staring at the couples heading off to work together. I blinked and could almost see the tendrils reaching out and connecting them, body to body. I imagined myself surrounded by connected people, striding along in concert, linked together. They were all around me, fleshy ties floating between them. And I was alone, with a small piece of what was once a tendril flapping helplessly on the side of my chest. Everyone was connected except me and the mannequins in the Victoria's Secret.

Annie had eventually gone in to talk to Jacob. I don't know what she said, but it seemed to work, because they both came back out to the kitchen and started baking. I caught a ride with the band back into Manhattan. They were good guys. Just really mad. When I talked to Annie later, she seemed better. She told me she was trying to figure things out and she'd fill me in when she came to some kind of epiphany. She also reminded me to read that book on autism. I told her I'd try. I couldn't even remember where I'd put it.

When I got to work I felt a restless energy. Thankfully Maureen was at the rehearsal space working with Bendy Girl, so I didn't have to go out of my way to avoid her. I made a few calls to make sure everything was set up for Wednesday's shoot. I still felt jumpy, so I pulled up my fantasy baseball board. I was in last again. I had fallen over the weekend. All my players were under-performing, so I decided to take some drastic action. I would engineer a blockbuster trade, fleecing some poor owner of his best players for my slumping ex-superstars. But who? There he is. The Riverdale Raiders. He has the players I want: Delgado and Piazza. But who should I give him? Who is playing for shit? Hudson isn't pitching well. Neither is Roger Clemens. Billy Wagner only has one save. But he'll probably want a little more. Delgado is hitting .400 and Piazza is the best catcher out there. Well, Mark McLemore is hitting well, but he's old. He's bound to slump. So I'd throw him in. This looks good. The trade of the year! I'll be in first place by next week!

I got so wrapped up in my eventual dominance of the baseball league that it was mid-afternoon before I remembered that I needed to make sure the Goddess was coming. That would be nice. I called and got the voicemail. I left her the info and directions and told her to let me know. She never called me back.

The end of the day loomed and she still hadn't called back. I shouldered my bag and was about to close my office door when the phone rang. I raced over and picked up.

"Hello."

"Hey, David."

"Hey, son."

Somewhere up above, God laughed into his hand.

"Hey, Mom, Dad."

"David, sweetie, are you coming home for Easter?"

"Yes."

"Of course he is, Elaine."

"I'm just making sure. Your brother's coming home, so that should be nice."

"We're doing an egg hunt."

"But no Easter baskets this year. Your father isn't allowed to have candy."

"I can have some candy, if I want. It's a holiday."

My dad has diabetes. Not the kind that you take shots for, but it's still diabetes. My father refuses to follow the rules of diabetes. He has the willpower of Pavarotti in a pastry shop, and he loves candy. Trying to keep him away from it is right up there with alligator wrestling for highest chance of losing a limb. My brother got in the way last Easter and he still twitches when faced with Mallomars.

"Ed, you can have the sugar-free kind."

"Do you want to kill me? That stuff is worse than Montezuma's Revenge. I'll be shitting till Tuesday."

"Watch the language."

"I think he's old enough to hear it."

I felt kind of cool about that. Whenever my dad curses around me I feel like he's saying, "Now you're a man!" It's the next best thing to him buying me a whore.

"You're not having candy. You want me to be a widow by the time I'm fifty-five?"

"You're overreacting."

"No, I'm not. You wonder where my stress comes from."

"You are such a hypochondriac."

"You are not having any candy if I have to tie you up with duct tape and lock you in the cellar. And then you'll miss the egg hunt, and you'd hate to miss that. Hello? Ed? He hung up. So what time are you going to stop by?"

"I'll be there around eleven on Sunday."

"It'll be nice to have you and your brother home again. I miss my boys."

"It'll be a great Easter."

"How are you doing? Have you heard from that girl?"

The Eater will always be "that girl" to my mom.

"She's still leaving messages."

"If you need to take some time, you can always stay with us for a while."

"I'm fine. Really."

"Okay. If you say so."

"I'll see you Sunday."

"I can't wait. Bye, honey."

"Bye."

So the Goddess hasn't called me. My life is dictated by the damn phone! I'm tired of calls. I wish we could go back to the old days when we'd send manservants back and forth bearing messages. Though my apartment is so small, my manservant would have to sleep in the oven. Life is always rough for the help.

The next day passed slowly. I felt strapped onto a torture machine, a medieval rack that slowly pulled my limbs apart. I tried to be

negative to protect myself. Of course she wouldn't call. I'd be surprised if she did. My stomach told the truth. Night faded in. I
headed home on legs that weighed tons. Midnight slipped by. I lay
in my bed, giving up, ready to sleep off my disappointment. The
phone rang.

"Hi, Davey."

Does the Goddess have me followed? Did she plant a heart
monitor on me to determine just the right time to contact me? It
was uncanny. I affected nonchalance.

"Hey, Julie. What's up?"

"I'm sorry I didn't call back right away."

"That's fine."

"It's just that I wasn't sure what I wanted to do."

"Do you know now?"

"I'm still thinking."

"This isn't a huge thing. You get to watch television being
made. It's the stuff of dreams."

"I don't ever want to be the girl who dreams about puppets. Or
television being made."

"So what do you like to dream about?"

"I don't know. I know what I like to daydream about."

"What?"

"Sometimes at work I close my eyes and imagine I'm dancing
on the sidewalk."

"I like to imagine you dancing, too."

"When it's sunny out, I daydream I'm swing dancing. When
it's raining, I two-step. When it's snowing, I waltz. You always
move slower in the snow. When I work really late, I tango under-

neath the streetlights. The dances change, so does the man's hair color, but it's always dancing."

"That sounds tiring."

"It's not that I'm a dancing addict or something. I just find that thinking about dancing calms me down. I think if I was ever really scared, I'd grab the nearest partner and salsa until it passed."

"I can just see you, war all around, bombs dropping everywhere, and you're swaying back and forth with some surprised revolutionary to 'The Way You Look Tonight.'"

"I love that song."

"It's a great tune to dance to. I enjoyed dancing with you."

"Me, too. You don't think my daydreams are strange, do you?"

"When I get nervous I tell jokes to myself. Sometimes I even laugh. And people look at me strange. So I get more nervous. I need a new system."

"What do you dream about?"

"I have vivid dreams. I'm always being chased by something. I must come from a long line of frightened townspeople. I've even died in my dreams."

"That's not good. You're not supposed to be able to die. They say that if you die in your dreams, you die in real life."

"Total horseshit. I got chased by this huge head once and it bit off my face and I died. Then, nothing. A huge blank nothing. I was bored out of my skull. I was just surrounded by blackness with nothing to do. Apparently death is just chillin'. I kept waiting to see if I'd be reincarnated as yet another terrified villager, but nothing happened. And then I woke up."

"That's really weird. Were there any long-term effects on your dreams after that?"

"I was afraid of that so I fell asleep the next night clutching a Gameboy. Just in case I had killed off my dream self and needed something to do. But I ended up having a dream about hijacking a nuke and forcing the world to make a definitive decision between cake and pie. I think they were leaning towards pie when I woke up."

"Strange. Which are you for?"

"Oh, pie. I'm a huge pie man. It's that creamy filling. And I love whipped cream. Whipped cream never seems to work with cake. Plus I heard somewhere that Hitler liked cake."

"Is that true?"

"No, but I'm spreading the rumor to sway world opinion towards pie. It's what I did in my dream. I'm pretty sneaky when I want to be."

"I had a dream once where I was running from French noun to French noun, pulling down their pants to see what gender they were."

"Kinky in a grammatical sort of way."

"I woke up when I displayed to everyone that the French word for house was neuter and it got embarrassed and clocked me."

"You should have danced with it."

"That only calms me down. It can piss other people off."

We talked for a while about other stupid things. I really liked talking to her, though my stomach still flopped around like a fish on the floor of a boat. I didn't want to say anything stupid. So I did.

"Have you been hearing from your ex? What was his name again?"

She got real quiet. How could I be so dumb? One of my brain cells must have learned it was going to die and was trying to take me with it.

"Carl."

"Is he still e-mailing you?"

Stop it! I don't want to talk about this. Why am I talking about this?

"Yeah. He's kind of messed up by the breakup."

"Are you doing any better?"

"I'm depressed a lot. You know."

I did know.

"I'm sorry I brought it up."

"It's not like it isn't in the back of my mind all the time anyway."

"Are you ever going back to him, do you think?"

"No. It would never work. I know that intellectually. If I start believing what he's telling me then I'm just making up a Carl in my head that I want to be with. Because the Carl I almost married wasn't someone I could be with."

"I've been told you should try to hate him. Apparently when you hate them, you heal faster or something."

"How can I hate him? Sometimes I hate him for not being who I wanted him to be. But that's not really his fault. Do you hate your ex-girlfriend?"

"I don't know. I don't think so. I'm mad at her for putting me through this. I'm mad at her for being just close enough to what I want to tease me."

"I know what you mean."

Neither of us spoke for a minute. I wished she was there in the room with me so I could see if she had a broken tendril floating off her chest, or if it was still whole and shooting off into the distance towards this Carl person.

"Well, whatever happens, at least you're moving on."

"Yes, I am. I'm not going back to that. I'm moving on."

"So have you decided if you're stopping by tomorrow?"

"You know what, I think I will. I'd like to see the world of children's television. Does everyone talk all polite and correct?"

"Not exactly."

Hopefully the crew would behave tomorrow. There weren't any kids on set, though, so it could get ugly. Puppeteers get creative when kids aren't around, and it ain't always pretty.

"Well, I'll stop by anyway."

"Thank you. I'm excited. This should be fun."

"It sounds fun."

"All right."

"All right."

And that was it. She was coming. She was going to see me in my element and in control. This Carl guy she was carrying around in her head didn't stand a chance. Not against the grandmaster of Public Television. That's me, by the way, not Barney the Purple Dinosaur. I hate it when people get that mixed up.

CHAPTER SIXTEEN

Puppets Can't Do Yoga

The next morning was a whirlwind. I oversaw setting up the soundstage, making sure the crew did a little work in between coffee breaks. If you've ever worked with a union, you know that getting them motivated is like getting your ex-girlfriend to make out with your present girlfriend while you watch—it ain't gonna happen without a lot of effort and bald-faced lying. I always make sure that we have plenty of coffee and food around. If you let a union guy step out to grab coffee, you will never see him again. The next time you hear anything, it'll be when he's invoicing you for the day and asking for overtime because he got lost. I always make sure that there are more than just donuts and candy bars to eat. I've made that mistake before. I shot a side project once about swimsuits. The craft services table was filled with cinnamon buns and Rice Krispie treats. When the rail-thin swimsuit models showed up, they went insane. They ate everything, including the napkins. The modeling shoots they normally do serve shit like melon slices and tiny bagels the size of my thumbnail. They didn't know how to handle the Sara Lee Factory that was our catering table. By the time we were ready to shoot, half of them were on the floor twitching, overdosing on Bavarian creme. Thankfully I always keep plenty of adrenaline shots handy, so I was able to revive them, but it was touch and go there for a half hour. More importantly, only three of the models could stand up, so we had to prop the others up against each other. No one noticed. But ever since, I make sure I have plenty of fruit on the catering table.

It took most of the morning to set up. We didn't have too much time, so we decided to shoot the rehearsal. Then we'd just have enough time to do a few fixes in case something falls off while the puppets were bending. The set itself was pretty cool. In order to mix puppets with live actors, we built a platform for the actors and the set to stand on. The puppeteers stand underneath these platforms and manipulate the puppets while speaking the lines. We do everything in one take, though we can overdub the voices later if we have to. But that would cost money, which we always avoid, so I try to do it all on the day. That's right, I'm one of those slave drivers who sacrifice artistic integrity to bring the project in under budget. Whenever the artist inside me starts to make a fuss about all the corners I'm cutting and the children's lessons I'm botching, I just pop in a tape of one of my episodes and say to myself, "It's about pirate puppets who teach children how to tie their shoelaces. You couldn't have artistic integrity on this show if you wanted to. So close the door of the office that you have all to yourself and take an artistic nap!" It is funny to see how hoity-toity some people get about this stuff. When we won an Emmy last year (We win every year, as I mentioned. It's either us or LeVar Burton, and he's the Susan Lucci of children's television.

The academy would rather give an Emmy to Larry Flynt than LeVar Burton. Of course, Susan finally won one, so here's hoping, LeVar!) one of our writers, Alex Feldman, actually cried as he accepted the award. The episode was entitled "Too Close to the Faucet" and it was about peeing yourself. Captain Blueboots advocated telling the other kids that you stood too close to the faucet and got splashed. I shuddered uncontrollably the entire time we shot it. I think Harold sent it in as a test just to see what would happen. He went around calling the academy his "little Emmy bitches" for a month after the ceremony. If I were Alex Feldman, I would have had someone accept it in my honor just so no one knew what I looked like. Hell, I'd have had LeVar pick it up for me, just to give the old boy a thrill. The point being, we have fun jobs filming silly things. We should be happy to be allowed to do that. There's no reason to get all serious about it.

Our set looks like a huge pirate ship viewed from the side. There's a flag hanging from the mast, though on our flag instead of a skull and crossbones we have the word "smile" written in big pink letters. There's a crow's nest where, get this, a *crow* named Johnny Crowsfeet pops up and tells the captain stuff like "Ahoy there! I spot me a boy! I do believe it's Jimmy, Captain!" And Captain Blueboots pops up and says "Ahoy there, Jimmy! Come aboard!" And the guest star walks on visible from the waist up and is quickly surrounded by the crew. First Mate Jigglebelly is very orange. Cook looks like a mop that's seen too many clogged toilets. Aargh is a hamster who only says "Aargh!" And then there's Mr. Beard. I'm not sure what he's supposed to be. Maybe he's Blueboots' accountant. He looks like a huge hairball coughed up by a giant mutant kitty. If Paul Bunyan had a cat, this would be its hairball. With googly eyes. Did I mention the googly eyes? They all have googly eyes. I won't tell you the dreams I've had concerning these puppets, but let's just say that googly eyes played a significant and psychologically damaging role.

We had to reconfigure things for today's episode since we needed to see Bendy Girl's entire body. We built a little poop deck with boxes on it that the pirates could stand on. This way Bendy Girl could stand among them, and you could still see her feet. The puppet designers had to be very creative to figure out how to do the pirates' legs and feet. Our puppeteers had never had legs and feet before. What they came up with looked very Kermit-ish from what I had been shown, but I had yet to see them in action, so I reserved judgement.

We use the same crew as much as possible, so I was used to working with everyone there. Tyrone the sound guy was there, as was Big L the cameraman. I hate Big L. He's the worst cameraman I've ever worked with. He shoots like he's going into an epileptic fit. The camera shakes so much I feel like I should pour a shot down his throat to take the edge off. I've ended up restricting him to a camera on a tripod, or sticks as we call it, just so he can't ruin the shot. He still manages to make you feel like you've got an inner ear infection. So why do we use him? Somehow, and I don't know how, he manages, on the establishing shots, to make the boat look like it's really floating. It's only for a few wide shots a day, and that may seem like a lot to put up with for a few shots, but we can't find anyone else who can do that shot. That shot's become our signature. Industry insiders speculate amongst themselves about how we manage it. No one tells them that it is the product of a truly awful cameraman who's so bad he comes out the other side. Big L has convinced me that everyone truly has their place in this world. If he can be a cameraman, than maybe one day I'll finally get to pitch for the Yankees. Big L also has a mouth on him. So does Lizzie, our production coordinator. Her favorite word is "Cockgobbler." Hearing that word shoot out of the mouth of a five-foot-one, eighty-pound Asian girl is either very disturbing or very hot. Hell, who says it can't be both?

Harold wasn't on the set. Which meant he was probably in the dressing room with Bendy Girl making innocent comments about her unitard. Whenever we had pretty guest stars, Harold would suddenly show up to "answer any questions they might have." This is a blessing for me, since it meant I didn't have him in my ear making inane suggestions like "Wouldn't this flow better if he was eating mashed potatoes instead of French fries?" or "He should wear a cape, like in Batman" or "The cook should have a Spanish accent. Wouldn't that be funny? He could say *si* all the time. And call everyone *señor*. Throw tamales at the First Mate. Foreigners crack me up. We should do that. Do it. Right now." It's like leaving a dingo alone in a room with a baby. You've told it not to eat the baby. It knows it's bad to eat the baby. So you come back and guess what? It ate the baby. And that shouldn't surprise you. So I love days like today, when a hot girl keeps him busy. I just hoped he didn't get it into his head to boss me around in order to impress her. We had a very well-known actress on once and he made me get him coffee all day long. I got him back, though. He only likes natural sugar and I used Sweet 'N Low. I was laughing behind my hand the whole time. Try to order me around...

I was a little worried because I still hadn't seen the routine. I knew what was supposed to happen and where, but I had no idea what it would look like. I tracked down Maureen prepping the puppeteers. Say that ten times fast.

"I know the legs are a little clumsy. How are you guys feeling about that?"

There were mumbles of "Okay, I guess." And "It'll be fine!"

"Okay. Just try to make it look natural. If it looks awkward to you, just try throwing in a line about it being a little tricky to figure out, but it feels great. Or something like that. Oh, hey, David."

"You just about ready to go?"

"Yep. I think we're done here. Have a great show, everybody."

The puppeteers filed out, leaving me with Maureen.

"So how's it looking?"

"Fine. It's looking fine."

"Does Kelly look comfortable around the puppets? Does it look unnatural?"

"It'll be great. It's the first time we've seen the puppets, Kelly isn't sure what she's doing, everything's going fucking fantastic!"

"Calm down. It'll be fine."

She shot me a look.

"I need to check on some things. Call if you need something."

She hurried off. It didn't seem to get any better with her. I stopped in the dressing room to say a few encouraging words to Bendy Girl. Just as I got there, I heard Harold's voice.

"So how do you take that thing off? Do you pull on this part here?"

I quickly butted in.

"Hey, Harold. Hey, Kelly, you ready?"

Bendy Girl looked happier than I had ever seen her. She also looked hotter than I'd ever seen her. She was all done up and wearing a black unitard that clung a little too sexy for our show, but who's complaining? She smiled wide when she saw me.

"I am ready! I am so excited, David. Thank you so much. This is going to be great."

"You had a good time working with the puppeteers this week?"

"They are so nice. It was great. I think you'll love it."

"I'm sure I will. Are you going to keep her company, Harold?"

I swear I saw a brief pleading look cross Bendy Girl's face but then I blinked and it was all smiles. Harold patted her back.

"I need to make sure she gets everything she needs. We're here to make you comfortable, Kelly."

He patted her again. Kelly smiled gamely.

"Thank you, Harold. Do you need me yet, David?"

"I'll send someone over when I do. It won't be long. Have a good show!"

I walked out shaking my head. Thank God that man wasn't a priest.

I walked into the control room. We shoot four cameras at once, and I checked all four monitors. The puppeteers set up their puppets and we did a quick test run to check out the legs. They did look a little funny, but better than I had expected. Maybe this wouldn't be so bad.

In the back of my head this whole time floated the Goddess. God, I hoped nothing got fucked up. And I hoped she came. She wasn't here yet, but it was still early. She'd better come, or I'd... well I would have to... give her another chance. Hot women always get the benefit of the doubt.

I watched the director go over some things with the camera

crew. The director of a television show isn't like the director of a movie. On a television show, the director tells the cameramen what to do and sets up the shots, but on all things creative and financial he answers to the producer, which in this case is me. Our director is at least fifty. He has a daughter who's only a few years younger than me. I feel bad sometimes that he has to take orders from a little snot like myself. But then I give the orders and I don't feel so bad anymore.

Bendy Girl walked on set so we could get a look at her through the camera. Everything looked great. I was getting excited. The puppets looked pretty good, actually. This was going to work. Harold walked into the control room and sat next to me.

"How's it looking?"

"Good. Everything's looking good."

"I told you this would work. And you scoffed at me. There's a reason I win all those Emmys, you know."

"I know. We're almost ready to go."

"Okay."

"Go sit in your chair."

"Okay, Daddy. You need to be a little less sensitive, Davey."

After one shoot with Harold, I made a deal with him. He doesn't sit next to me, I don't gut him like a trout. I still hear his whispered comments in my ear, but at least I don't have to look at him.

There she is! I spied her in camera 4, over by the door. I walkeed a PA and told him to escort her into the control room. A few minutes later, the Goddess stepped cautiously into the room where I'm standing foolishly like an eighth grader at the dance.

"You made it! Great. Come on in."

"Thanks. I can only stay an hour or so."

"That's cool. You have perfect timing. You should be able to catch the whole first take."

"I'm excited. So this is where you work?"

"Ahem."

Harold actually said "Ahem." If human beings were given one chance to mentally burst someone into flames, I'd have used mine up right then.

"I'm sorry. Julie, this is my boss, Harold. Harold, this is my friend, Julie."

"Nice to meet you, Harold."

"Likewise. Believe me."

Just what I needed. I forgot my boss would be there to creep my would-be girlfriend out. I just thanked God she wasn't wearing a leotard. My walkee beeped.

"David. We're ready to go out here."

"Okay. Get everyone in position."

Harold took the Goddess' arm.

"You should sit back here by me. David doesn't like anyone sitting next to him while he's working."

"Okay."

Great. I just hoped she wasn't wearing anything with a zipper on it. Accidents do happen.

"You can watch the monitors, Julie. I'm sure Harold will answer any questions you may have."

"I'm sure he will. I am sure he will."

I felt one brief flash of guilt at trapping her with him, but then my walkee beeped again.

"We're set to go. Everyone is at places."

I put on my headset so I could listen to the camera crew.

"We're ready to go."

The director nodded.

"Cue jib. Pull in. Nice. Go to 2.

I heard Harold behind me.

"I like your top. Is that a zipper?"

I winced.

"Cue Blueboots."

And we were off.

The Puppeteers Episode 89 Scene 1

Captain Blueboots walked onto the ship. He bent over to tie his big pirate boots and then stopped halfway.

"Ouch."

Johnny Crowsfeet popped his head out of the crows' nest.

"What's wrong, Captain Blueboots?"

"I am stiff, Johnny! I can't even bend over to tie my big black boots. And do you know what happens when you don't tie your boots?"

"You fall down!"

"That's right. You fall down. So always tie your boots. I wish I could tie mine."

First Mate Jigglebelly ambled onto the deck followed by Aargh.

"You don't know how to tie your boots? I can show you how!"

"Aargh!"

"That's right, Aargh can help me!"

Aargh bent over and fumbled with Jigglebelly's feet.

"Thank you, Aargh! See, that wasn't so hard!"

Jigglebelly takes a step forward and falls flat on his face.

"Aargh! You tied my shoelaces together! That's not nice."

"Aargh!"

They all laughed.

Blueboots lifted a hand.

"I know how to tie my own shoelaces. I'm just too stiff."

The Cook burst onto the deck.

"Hola! Perhaps the Señor would like some of my tortilla soup!"

"There are some things even your tortilla soup can't fix, Cook."

"Que? That is loco!"

"I just need to be more flexible."

"Si?"

Mr. Beard strode on.

"Did I hear someone say flexible?"

"Yes, Mr. Beard. I need to become more flexible."

"Then we need to visit New York City. My friend Kelly can help you. She is a master of something called yoga! I think you'll find that it will help your back."

"That sounds great! Hard to port, laddies! We're off in search of a treasure called yoga!"

Dissolve to shot of open sea. Johnny Crowsfeet is up in his nest. He begins to caw.

"Land ho! I spy your friend, Kelly!"

Offscreen, Bendy Girl's voice drifts in.

"Permission to come aboard, Captain!"

"Permission granted."

Bendy Girl walks on in her black unitard.

"Hi, Mr. Beard!"

"Hi, Kelly! Kelly, this is Captain Blueboots and First Mate

Jigglebelly and the Cook and Aargh and that rascal up there is Johnny Crowsfeet."

"Hello, guys!"

They all answered at once.

"Hello, Kelly!"

"I hear someone's feeling a little stiff."

"Aye, I sure am, lassie. And I hear you know a magical thing called yoga!"

"Aargh!"

"Yes, I do. Yoga helps you get in touch with your body and your mind. Would you all like to get in touch with your body?"

"We sure would. I'm tired of being so stiff all the time."

"Well, you guys follow me, and I'll help you feel really good! You with me?"

"I'm with you."

"Yes, young lady."

"Sure."

"You bet."

"Si."

"Aargh!"

"Then let's begin."

"And cut!'"

The director spoke over the intercom.

"Move to the yoga set."

On set the stage manager herded the cast over to the new poop deck. I heard Harold behind me talking up my girl.

"So what do you think so far? Pretty cool, huh?"

"Yeah, it looks fun. I'm sure the kids love it."

"Do you do yoga? I only ask because you look so fit."

I stepped in.

"Everything okay so far?"

Harold nodded.

"Yeah, it looks good."

"I'm impressed, David. This is a real job. You get a headset and everything."

"They just give me that to keep me from crying. It's an electronic pacifier, really."

My walkee beeped.

"All set on set two."

I beeped back.

"Places. Whenever you're ready. Time for the yoga fun to begin."

The director counted it off.

"Camera 2. Pull in. Cue Kelly."

It started out innocuously enough. Bendy Girl ran through some of the basic yoga poses while the puppets stood on their boxes and watched. She was very good. It was actually interesting to hear her explain what the poses did in simple terms. She turned to Blue-boots and told him to try the Downward Facing Dog. He did.

"Sweet Jesus."

My headset came alive with the entire crew's voices.

"Do you see what I'm seeing?"

"I think I am. That is not natural."

"Is it supposed to look like that?"

"I don't think so. Unless there's something about yoga

nobody's been telling me. If I knew it was this fun, I'd have started years ago."

Blueboots is a puppet. And there are some things a puppet was not meant to do. One of those things was Downward Facing Dog.

"I think he's getting a mouthful."

For those who don't know, Downward Facing Dog looks like someone making a bridge with their body, their stomach facing the floor. Kind of like someone doing a pushup with their ass way up in the air. The puppeteer was having trouble keeping Blueboots from sliding out of that position, so he kept moving him back into it. The end result of which was that from the outside it looked like Blueboots had not only conquered his flexibility issues, but was in fact giving himself quite the energetic blowjob.

"Now that's a cockgobbler."

The worst part about it was his fixed smile and googly eyes. He looked ecstatic about this BJ he administered himself. I would too, I guess, if I could do what he was doing. I looked around the control room. Jaws were dropped everywhere. I didn't dare look behind me. I wanted to tell the director to cut, but the car wreck mesmerized me. Then it got worse.

"Now everyone try it!"

Have you ever wondered what a puppet orgy would look like? Picture the googly eyes.

"How does that feel?"

"Wonderful!"

"Aargh!"

Don't the puppeteers realize what they're doing? I needed to stop this! But I couldn't. I had to see just how bad it could get.

"Blueboots, you're not quite getting it. Let me adjust you."

Yoga instructors often adjust their students to ease them into the correct position. With Downward Facing Dog, this meant getting behind the student and pulling their pelvis up and in. This looks okay with humans...

The headset went crazy.

"Holy shit."

"Is it me, or is she humping Captain Blueboots?"

"Doggystyle!"

"This girl is fucking him from behind!"

...but with puppets, not so much. And all the while Captain Blueboots kept smiling with his googly eyes.

This was enough. It couldn't get any worse than this. I had to stop it. Just one more minute...

"Okay, now we move into Upward Facing Dog. Bring your hips down to the floor and thrust upwards."

And five puppets began humping the floor.

"Señorita, this feels muy bueno!"

"Aargh!"

"Really feel it. How's the stiffness now, Captain?"

"I'm working it out. This is great!"

Even more huge smiles and googly eyes.

My headset no longer contained English, just insane giggling and religious testimonials. I had to stop this.

"Mr. Beard, you need to stretch more. Let me help you."

It seemed like slow motion as she walked over to the huge hairball and straddled him...

"Cut! Cut! Stop the tape!"

Everyone in the control room just sat there, shocked. They

turned to look at me. I realized that it was my own voice that had shouted.

My headset squawked.

"Should we come in close for the money shot or what?"

"What does puppet sperm look like, anyway?"

"I hear it looks like soup."

"I feel the urge to watch a Jenna Jameson movie."

And that's what it was. It was puppet porn. I was a purveyor of puppet porn. And the Goddess had seen it all. The director broke the silence.

"What do you want to do?"

"Give me a minute."

I felt Harold's hand on my shoulder. Stay calm! He's going to fire me! Stay calm! Don't pee yourself, there are no faucets nearby.

"Why'd we stop?"

What?

"What?"

"Well, since we are stopped, you should tell them to try to be a little smoother. They looked a little jerky."

A muffled snort erupted from the other side of the room.

"What? Yeah. Yeah, you're right."

"But she's good, right?"

"She's great."

"It's looking good."

The Goddess' cheeks were so red I expected blood to just shoot out of her face. I swear I saw tears building up in her eyes. I was so screwed.

"So are we starting up again?"

"Give me one minute."

I raced out of the control room and bumped right into Maureen. She was practically crying. Looking in her eyes, I could see that there was no more Maureen. There was only Wiggy.

"Am I fired? He fired me, didn't he? I told you it would be a problem. I told you it would be a fucking problem. But no! You said it would be fine! Why did I listen to you! I have rent due next week, I can't be fired. I don't want to move in with my mother! She keeps trying to feed me pasta at all hours of the day. I'll weigh three hundred pounds. Jesus Christ, we're so fucked."

"You're not fired."

"Oh, my God, did he fire you?"

"Nobody's fired. Harold has just proved himself completely insane. He thinks it's going great."

"What? Is he blind? It's Muppets Does Dallas out there!"

"I know. Let me talk to them. Give me a sec."

I left Wiggy to pull out her hair and ran into the dressing room. Bendy Girl was crying her eyes out in the makeup chair. The puppeteers stood around looking uncomfortable. When I entered, they all began to talk at once.

"Quiet. Keep it down, it's not as bad as you think."

Bendy Girl looked up.

"I look like the Robin Byrd of children's television. I can't believe it came out like that. I am so sorry! I didn't even know until I got back here and everyone told me what it looked like. I didn't mean for it to be like this. I am so sorry."

I thought fast.

"Don't worry. We obviously can't do that version. Not unless we get Kelly a huge pimp hat."

They all laughed nervously. They were calming down.

"Here's what we're going to do. Kelly, do the routine yourself. The rest of you, just watch."

The man behind Mr. Beard looked skeptical.

"Won't that look like we're some kind of perverted freaks?"

"Don't worry. We'll barely show you guys. This is about Kelly showing you yoga. As long as you take it seriously, it'll all be fine. At the end, Kelly, tell them to try it a few times a week and they'll be more flexible blah blah blah. It'll be fine, trust me. You look great. We're going to try this again. You ready, Kelly?"

"I guess so."

"Why don't you touch up your makeup. You look great out there. You are good at yoga. Extremely good. And you look good doing it. As long as we concentrate on you, the show will work perfectly. Just do it like you always do it, like all those classes you've taught. They all trust you and we trust you. So trust me."

"Okay. Let's try it."

"Okay. See you in five."

I ran back to the control room. Maureen had stepped in. I addressed the director.

"We're going to focus on Kelly. The puppets won't be doing the exercises."

"Thank God."

"Just make sure you keep any cutaways of the puppets watching as short as possible. We don't want it to look like we're in some pirate strip club."

"No prob."

Harold walked up to me.

"What do you mean, no puppets doing the exercises? That's the whole point. The puppets are doing the exercises."

"Harold, it won't work. You said it yourself, they look unnatural."

"Not that unnatural. You could tell what they were trying to do."

"I know. That's very true. But the point of yoga is its grace. Its fluid motions and elegant postures. We don't want to destroy that image. Don't you want yoga to look as good as possible?"

"Yes."

"Then let's focus on the one who accomplishes that. Kelly looks great doing yoga. We spotlight her and turn the pirates into we, the viewers. We're learning as they're learning. Trust me, if you want to make yoga look good, this is the only way to do it."

Harold was caving.

"It just doesn't seem right..."

"It doesn't seem right to try to show the world the inherent beauty of Downward Facing Dog with the rough imitations of a puppet. They're doing a good enough job, but I don't want to be just good enough. I want it to look the best it can, don't you?"

He was defeated.

"Yes. Do it your way."

"Thank you."

I sat down. Thinking fast always tires me out. Maybe it dehydrates me. I needed a Gatorade. Too late. Time to try it all again.

The second time through it went much better. It didn't look that creepy to cut away quickly to the pirates watching. Except Mr. Beard, but he always creeps me out. It's as if what clogged up your sink could talk. We did some pickups and wrapped the entire show in an hour and a half. All in all, it didn't go that badly. It wasn't even that bad a show. Harold clapped me on the back.

"Good job. You and Maureen did a real good job."

"Thanks."

The seat next to Harold was empty.

"Where's Julie?"

"She slipped out about five minutes ago. She didn't want to get in the way. She said she'd call you. She's a cutie. You are a horny bastard."

I walked out of the control room and was assaulted by a wildly hugging Maureen.

"You saved my life. You rock forever!"

"My pleasure. What did you think?"

"Much better. Still not the best show in the world, but not the worst. From now on, I do at least one rehearsal with the puppets. That much I've learned. Those right-wingers are right. Porn is everywhere!"

She stopped jumping and gave me a serious look.

"Thank you. Really. You are a good friend."

She kissed me on the cheek.

"You too."

"Then we're friends."

"I'm glad."

"Good."

She walked away whistling "I Will Survive."

I walked to the front entrance and stepped outside. The sun shone down approvingly. The building we were shooting in was nondescript. Could have been anything going on in there. I sat down on the sidewalk. Now that the high of shooting the episode was fading, I realized that I had probably blown it completely with the Goddess. I thought I was going to show her what a bigshot television producer I was, and instead I bring on the porn. And trap her with Zipperboy to boot. She left without even tapping my shoulder. It was over. My streak was unbroken. I had found a completely new way to fuck it up. You gotta tip your cap.

"Not bad. I didn't realize puppets could be so...instructive."

She had snuck up behind me.

"I thought you'd left."

"I had to pee."

"Good. I mean, I'm glad you stuck around."

"I liked it."

"So you had a good time?"

"Yeah, I did. I actually stayed half an hour late I was having so much fun.'

"I'm sorry. I hope you don't get in trouble."

"I'll be fine. Your boss cracks me up."

"I am so sorry about that. I know he's a pig..."

She stopped me.

"Don't worry. I had my taser ready to go, so if he had really tried anything, I would have shot it right into his nipple. He actually played with my zipper! How pathetic is that!"

"Pretty pathetic, it's true. Though he does play a mean naked didgeridoo."

We stood there for a moment, uncertain.

"I've got to head back to work."

"Cool. Thanks for coming. Really."

"Thanks for inviting me. You impressed me by the way."

"Completely by accident. How did that happen?"

"It just did. Anyway, about Friday's outing, I think I'd like to come. I'd like to see what this playgroup is like."

"Okay. Cool. I'll call you tomorrow with the details."

"Sounds good. Well, I need to get back to work."

"Yeah, of course."

"Bye, David."

She kissed me on the cheek, extremely close to my mouth, and walked off.

"Bye."

Women are like pitchers. The successful ones know that the key isn't overpowering the hitter. It's changing speeds. She had a great time. She wanted to go with me on Friday. I just saw Captain Blueboots hump the poop deck.

I leaned my head back and laughed till my eyes swam.

CHAPTER SEVENTEEN

The Teepee

The entire next day found me lying on the floor. Was this falling in love? It didn't feel the same, but I've always been told that it's different every time. So maybe this is a different form of falling in love. It felt like a way out.

I resisted the urge to call the Goddess. Instead, I pulled up my baseball league to check on my trade. The guy I had offered it to had come back to me with a slightly different offer. Instead of Mark McLemore he wanted Edgardo Alfonzo. That seemed like an awful lot to give up. But I felt reckless. I knew it was too much, but I wanted to just press the button and see what happened. So I clicked "accept." I immediately felt a wave of regret, but you had to be willing to risk in order to win. Or maybe the saying should be, never make a baseball trade while confused about women. Only time would tell. I called Jim again.

"Hey, Monkey."

"Hey, Gonzo."

"I made a big trade."

"I can see that."

"Dude, this trade is going to put me on top."

"David, let me explain something to you. There are one hundred and sixty-two games in a year. We've played twenty of them. This is a game of patience."

"I'm in last place. I need to do something drastic."

"You have no patience! Sometimes you need to wait and see what happens. You can't just keep changing things around. You need to just let things happen. Make small changes. But most of all, you need to trust your players."

"I'm making the trade. I need to make something happen."

"Okay. But you'll never win like that."

"I'll play the game the way I want."

"I don't know what you're thinking, but I'm not going to interfere. Maybe you know something I don't. All I can say is you'd better hope Piazza hits sixty home runs this season."

"I felt like taking a risk."

"I don't know if jumping out a window is technically a risk. It's more of a certainty. But it's your team."

"Yes, it is. How was Tiger Lady, by the way?"

"It was great. We did it everywhere. She is an animal."

"You didn't get another tattoo, did you?"

Everyone's getting tattoos. Maybe I should get one. I could cover myself in question marks.

"I didn't have time. I was too busy worshiping Dionysus."

"You're too geeky to be allowed to score."

"She tied me up."

"You're kidding me."

"Oh, yeah."

"How does one go about doing the whole bondage thing, anyway?"

"Well, first you decide on a safe word that you can yell out in order to stop the action."

"Why not yell 'Stop!' "

"Apparently acting all pissed off is part of the fun. So the safe word is supposed to be something you wouldn't normally yell out in the throes of passion."

"So what was it? 'It broke?' "

"Sadly, that is something that has been yelled out during sex."

"It would make you stop."

"No, the word was 'watermelon.' "

"Really? That's odd. I use that word all the time when doing the nasty. It just pops out."

"Funny."

"So did you use the word?"

"Nah. It didn't get that crazy. Actually, to be honest, and I'd never tell her this, but bondage just isn't my thing. We didn't have handcuffs or anything, so we used some neckties her ex-boyfriend used to wear. I could have slipped out of those without squirming. And she didn't tease me enough. You know? I always thought bondage was about driving the other person crazy. But I think she just wanted to get my hands out of the way."

"I thought she was a crazy sex lady."

"She is. She's just bondage impaired, I guess. Hey, don't get me wrong, any sex that ends in me popping a cap in her ass is a good time. I just didn't like feeling like a piece of meat."

"That's all you are to the ladies, man. A piece of meat. When will they love you for your mind, Goddamn it!"

"I'm heading up there Friday afternoon. I figure I'll sneak out early and be up there by seven, ready to party. She's gonna be at this Irish pub."

"You didn't get her number."

"It's more exciting this way."

"Meaning she won't give it to you."

"She's waiting till she knows me better."

"So until then you just follow her scent."

"I'm a booty nomad, aren't I?"

"Uprooting yourself to follow the poontang across the plains."

"She's worth it."

"Well I hope you get her number someday. Just don't let her borrow your lawnmower, cause you'll never see her again."

"If she wanted my lawnmower she could have it."

"Where's your pride? That's right, it's nestled in her pocket-book, resting comfortably against your balls."

"I don't see anyone handling your balls."

"Fair enough. Well, good luck. Just remember to listen to your tattoos and you should be golden."

"I am a wild man."

"The next time you do the bondage thing, make sure you tie her up. You know what she can use as a safe word? 'I'm coming!' "

"I'd be tying and untying her all night. Please. Give me some credit. I'm a bad boy. I get the job done."

Not much I could say to that. Without being mean.

⟡

That night I sat looking at my guitar. I needed to practice if I was going to rock the playgroup's world. I banged on the wall. I waited till I heard the hum of an amplifier click on. Then I picked up my guitar and sat down. Time to get funky.

I'm going to be honest with myself here. Make a note, because later bravado will set in and I'll deny I ever thought this.

What we did to "London Bridge is Falling Down" was not mere butchery. That would be far too kind a label for such an atrocity. It wasn't even just cruel to both the song and the memory of the songwriter, unknown though he may be. I think the word that best describes the damage we did to the musical world that night is unholy. Our rockin' version of "London Bridge is Falling Down" waged a jihad on God and all he holds dear. No one in our building complained because they were too busy hiding under their beds waiting for the screaming demons to get bored with feeding and fly away. All the car alarms on our block began to shriek right after we started, and then shut off in shocked silence as we hit the second verse. There was a feeling in the pit of the stomach like you'd just been punched in the balls by The Rock, hard. I couldn't get the corners of my rug to curl back down again for weeks afterwards. When we finally finished, the whole world held its breath in silence, praying that the assault was over. After about five minutes, all the sounds of the city switched back on and the world was normal again. But somewhere in their subconscious, buried for the sake of their own sanity, lay the memory of our version of "London Bridge is Falling Down" which, in later years, would cause them to scream at the sight of a Raffi record and hide in the closet.

I knocked on the wall to say good jam and lay on my bed. I

wanted to call the Goddess. I don't know why. Of course I know why. She was going to see me Friday. Where she would be subjected to the kind-hearted side of David. The autistic-children-loving side of David. The nonthreatening, "such a sweetie must be dynamite at the boingy boingy!" side of David. To call her now, however, would be to weaken my position. Because whatever commanding image she has of me now would quickly dissipate under the stupidity I was capable of unleashing, especially at that moment. I'm always at risk to dress up as Hitler for the Hanukah party, but over the years I've learned to sense when I am most likely to make a dead-guy joke to the girl whose dad had been hit by a bus that very morning. Right now was one of those times. So I needed to play it cool and not give in to this need to call her for another hit of approval like some sad junkie. As long as I waited till this window of stupidity passed, I'd be all right. She answered on the third ring.

"Hello?"

"Hey, it's David."

"Hey. I thought you were calling tomorrow."

"Yeah, well, I ended up calling tonight."

"Okay."

A moment of silence. She broke it.

"I have to admit I'm a little nervous. Are the kids hard to handle?"

I pictured the bite mark on Annie's wrist.

"Not really. What can kids do? You just have to be sure not to react to them when they act out and you'll be fine."

"Don't react, huh? I guess I can do that."

"You'll do fine. I'm bringing my guitar to play for the kids. I was just practicing, actually."

"I love the guitar. How are you sounding? Good?"

"Yeah, it went well. I'm doing some kid songs, you know. I'm not a master guitarist or anything. I just noodle. But I think I can play well enough for the kids to like it."

"I can't wait to hear it. You'll have to play for me sometime. Something besides 'Twinkle, Twinkle, Little Star.'"

There goes my best tune. I know, I know. This will end badly. But she likes the guitar. I should sound okay for Friday. I may not sound the best right now, but I've got another night to practice. It'll be fine.

"I'd love to. So, are you thinking about dancing?"

"Nah. My feet hurt. I'm looking at brochures for teepees, actually."

What the hell?

"Teepees? Like the Indian houses?"

"Native American."

"The tents?"

"Yeah. I'm leaving the magazine by June. I just can't take it. So I lined up a job in Westchester for the summer and I'm going to live up there for a few months. I can't really afford an apartment on my own since I'll be paying tuition for the next three years, but I refuse to live with my parents. I've moved out and I am not moving back in. So I figure I'll set up a teepee on their property and live there. I'll be living rent free, but I'll have my own place."

"You're going to live in a tent all summer? When I was a kid, I'd pitch my tent on the front lawn fully intending to sleep outside, but then, well, it would get dark, and I'd be in my own bed by nine. I'd still build a fire, though. My room got cold at night."

"This isn't some tiny tent. It's huge. It's the size of a studio apartment."

I looked around my apartment. I think even my old Boy Scout tent had it beat by twenty square feet.

"Okay..."

"I can fit my dresser and my four-poster bed in it. And I'll have a plush chair and a reading lamp. I'll run an electric cord out to it for power and I'll work the fire pit to keep warm. I'm going to have a ball."

"So outside it's a teepee, but inside it's your bedroom with sloping walls."

"And a fire pit."

"Of course. Well, I think that's great. It sounds like a party."

"You're making fun of me."

Think fast if Chief TalkDumb wants wampum with Little Tent.

"No, I love it. You're the only person I know who'd even think to do it. I think it sounds like good times. Really. I'd love to see it."

"You'll have to stop by sometime."

"I will."

"Well, I've gotta go. See you Friday."

"See you then."

"Bye."

"Bye."

She hung up. A teepee. Who the hell thinks to live in a teepee with a four-poster bed? You had to admire the thought process. My first impulse was to put a crazy check next to her name. But the more I thought about it, the more I liked the fact that she wanted to do it. It was definitely creative. Maybe she'd dress up in a cute Indian princess outfit. That would be hot. What can I say, I'm attracted to eccentricity. That won't stop me from bringing my kung fu just in case, since, after all, an eccentric is just one badly folded towel away from a psychotic. But I won't mock the teepee. Not when I'm paying a grand to live in a crawl space on Third Ave. She's smarter than I am.

I woke up in the middle of the night. My face was wet. I don't know what I was dreaming about. I looked around my apartment. Everything looked familiar. I was okay. But I felt so empty. Something was missing. My stomach hurt. My arms curled around me, trying to substitute for what I had given up. I hated the feeling. I felt like I was in a room without doors. Every way I turned was the same featureless wall. I had nowhere left to go. I was overly conscious of my shallow breathing. Was this a panic attack? I remembered holding vigil while the Eater suffered such an attack. Her mom had said something awful to her and she had come by my apartment to escape from it all. She sat on my bed, so fragile, and I could only look at her. I couldn't do anything, so I said something stupid. Something about looking at both sides. You don't say something like that to a crying woman, to a crying anyone. Logic is not wanted. Love is wanted. Unconditional love always tells you that you are right. That's what you need when your guardian angel slaps you in the face. I was never any good at unconditional love. I think too much. I can't keep my damn mouth shut. So I was a safety net that tore. And she looked at me with these shocked eyes and began to wheeze. She couldn't breathe. I didn't know what to do. I went to touch her but she jerked away. I snatched my hand back like she was a hot stove. I was useless. I was part of her problem. Just like everyone else in her life, no better than her mother. I tore. So I started to cry. I repeated "I'm sorry! I'm so sorry!" over and over again. And gradually she began to breathe normally. She stopped shuddering. I poured her a glass of water and sat on the far end of the bed watching her. She finished the glass and looked up at me. I felt like a frightened rabbit. She told me she was okay. It was a panic attack. But it had passed. And there I sat with tear-streaked cheeks feeling like the weakest coward in the world.

I wonder if she had felt like this. Surrounded by walls. How did she get out? How do I get out of here? I needed something worth hoping for. I needed a line of floor lights to lead me to the exit. I needed something to make me feel like me again. Like someone who could love.

I was sweating. Why was it so hot in here? I looked to the center of my apartment, and there in the center of the rug burned a fire. The smoke rose upwards towards the ceiling. I followed it with my eyes until it disappeared out the hole in my roof. When I looked back down, I noticed that the walls had gotten round. I was in a teepee. And there in front of me was a flap leading to the outside. I stepped through it.

I was in the hallway of my building. I could breathe again. I looked back into my room. It was just my room. I was no longer shaking. I stepped back inside, closing the door behind me, and got into bed. I was okay. Two hours later, I fell asleep.

CHAPTER EIGHTEEN

The Amazing Carlos

I met Annie at the elementary school in Queens where she held her workshop every week. The Goddess hadn't shown up yet. Annie looked tired.

"How you holding up?"

"Fine. What about you?"

"I'm still trying to figure things out. I don't feel good talking about it right now. Did you read that book?"

What book? Oh yeah. The one I never read.

"Sure. Very interesting stuff."

Her eyes let me know she knew I was full of shit, but she didn't say a word about it.

"Cool. The kids will be here soon. So that's your guitar, huh?"

I patted the case.

"Yep. It's ever so pretty. I have a list of songs. Here, take a look. What do you think?"

I handed my handwritten list over. She glanced down at it.

" 'London Bridge.' Good choice. The kids like to sing that one. 'Twinkle Twinkle, Little Star.' Okay. I'm sure they all know that one."

"Everyone knows that one."

"That's it?"

"That's it."

"You don't have to play, you know. It's enough that you're showing up to help. That means a lot."

"They'll love the singing."

"It's not the kids I'm worried about. It's hard enough to get qualified people to come and help me out. If you drive some of them insane, it'll be a bitch to replace them."

"It's going to be fine. God, will you relax?"

"Is the Goddess coming?"

"Yes, she is. So be nice to her. Try to keep her away from the biters and the wrestling superstars. I'm not a caveman who needs to have his woman knocked out in order to get her home."

"You know you're weak when you have to let a small child with autism knock your women unconscious for you."

"I'm small-boned."

"You're all bone."

"Maybe I'll hit you with a chair."

"You'll fall over backwards the minute you lift it over your head."

"When you get your boobies grabbed, I'm not going to help you."

"Were you planning on helping me before this spat?"

"No, but now I'm definitely not going to. So when do I play?"

"Right after snack. They'll be less likely to ignore you if they're full."

"Do I get snack?"

"Yes, you get snack."

"Sweet."

"Is that your girl?"

The Goddess was half a block away, walking towards us. She'd done up her hair in a ponytail. I repeated my mantra under my breath.

"Don't fuck up."

She reached us. She smiled. I crossed myself inside.

"Hey, Julie. This is my friend, Annie."

"Hi, Annie. Nice to meet you."

"You too, Julie. Thanks for offering to help out."

"I'm looking forward to it. Is it just us?"

She looked a little worried.

"Oh no. My assistants are inside setting up. Don't worry. They're just kids. Let me handle any problems and you'll be great."

"Are there some rules I should follow?"

"Actually, there are. Come on in and I'll explain them. They're very simple."

We walked through the doors and into the classroom. It was a typical elementary school classroom. The walls were covered in children's drawings and unhealthily happy alphabet letters. Everything smiled. The dinosaurs in the toy chest, the fruit on the health chart, even the word "House" on the flashcard grinned like a crazy person. Everyone was happy. You'd think that would be welcoming, but strangely enough the fiercely smiling faces made me uncomfortable. I felt like the fruit knew something I didn't. And it made them laugh. Annie was going over the rules.

"First off, most of the kids can't really talk very well. The point of this playgroup is to get them accustomed to playing with other children. Children with autism pull into themselves and live in their own little worlds. They can't connect with the people around them. They want to, but they don't know how. We're trying to teach them. So what we'd like you to do is play with the children and get them to play with each other. None of these kids are problem children, so you don't have to worry about them getting violent or anything. They may scream or throw a tantrum if they get worked up, but if that happens just send for me and I'll deal with it."

"That sounds easy. This will be great. Thanks for trusting me."

"David gave a glowing recommendation. Oh, and one other thing. Sometimes the kids do act out a little. When they do, it's important not to react in a negative way. Say one child comes over and smears a cupcake on your arm. Don't pull your arm away and yell at him. That will only reinforce the behavior. He'll keep doing it since it got a reaction. If something like that happens, just walk away to get me. Cool?"

"Cool."

"How about you, David? Cool?"

"Of course. I've helped out before. I know the drill."

This wasn't technically a lie. I had helped out on the first day of the playgroup. Of course, this was when only two children were enrolled and Annie had hired ten counselors. My job consisted of hitting on a cute assistant. She treated me like a child with autism—she didn't react.

"Good. Well. I've got to finish getting ready. The kids will be here in a few minutes. It would be great if you could help set up the chairs. Thanks!"

Annie walked away. The Goddess and I started unstacking the chairs. I tried sitting in one.

"These are tiny."

"They're for children. If you need to sit down, you can always use one for each butt cheek."

"Are you saying I have a fat ass?"

"I'm not going to say anything about your ass."

I let that one go.

"Are you nervous?"

"You ask me on the weirdest dates."

"I thought we weren't dating."

"We're not. And I'm happy to be doing this. It's just an odd suggestion from a guy."

"I'm not your typical guy."

"Is that so? I'll let you know when you do or say something original."

Annie asked everyone to gather around.

"The kids are here. They've still got their nametags since we have some new counselors today. Katie, could you look after Sam? Jenna, you've got Carlos. Carla, grab Stan. Yolanda, I'm giving you Megan. You all know David. David, you've got Matthew. And this is Julie. Julie, you've got Christian. He's a sweetheart, you'll love him. Have a great playgroup, people."

With that, she opened the door and a kid ran in. His worried mother followed right behind him. She spoke quietly with Annie while her son raced straight to the blackboard and picked up a piece of chalk. Jenna poked me.

"David, that's Matthew. Go over and say hi."

I didn't want to leave the Goddess, and I definitely didn't want to be the first one to approach a kid. I thought I'd hang out and watch everyone else do their thing while I got a sense of how things were done. Maybe the Goddess and I would get a kid together or something. But instead, I was the guinea pig. The Goddess looked at me.

"He's so cute. Go over and say hi."

"I'm going. I'm just thinking of my opening line. You need a good opening line with these kids, or they eat you alive. Okay, now I've got one. So here I go."

As I walked over, I could see little Matthew's mom watching me. Great. Knowing my luck the kid would turn around and bite off my nose. I wondered how many noses were lost per week. I should have asked Annie that before I set this up. Matthew was writing something on the blackboard with his chalk. He was obviously very intent on what he was doing. This wasn't fair. I should have gotten some kind of dossier on Matthew before I got here. I needed to know his statistics. Could I touch his chalk? Did he like to draw? How often did he kick, and was the crotch his area of preference? These were things I needed to know. I stood right behind him. He ignored me. Everyone was watching. I squatted down next to him and looked at what he was writing.

"Hey, Matthew, what are you working on over here?"

Nothing. He just kept on writing.

"Do you like that color chalk?"

Still nothing.

"My name's David."

Finally he reacted. He reached for a piece of chalk and quickly wrote out something on the blackboard.

"D-I-V-A-D. Hey, that's my name spelled backwards! That's pretty cool. Can you spell your name backwards?"

He quickly jotted out W-E-H-T-T-A-M. I was impressed.

"What about your mom's name?"

M-O-M. Bad example.

"Okay. What about Annie?"

E-I-N-N-A. Annie. Wow. This kid was a genius. I felt a tap on my shoulder. I looked up at Annie.

"Hey, Annie. Look, it's your name backwards. This kid is cool!"

"I'm glad you like him, David, but we're trying to get him to stop doing that. We want him to interact with kids and having essentially his own language doesn't really help with that."

"Man, I'm sorry. It's just really cool."

"If you want cool, you should talk to Carlos. If you give him your name, he'll spell it in numbers."

"Like A is one and B is two?"

"Yep."

"Won't that be encouraging him?"

"It gets him talking. Hey, Matthew! Do you want to play some basketball with the other kids? Come on!"

She took the chalk out of his hand and led him over to the mini-net in the corner. I followed. I looked around for the Goddess. I spotted her sitting at a table with a small round boy. That must be Christian. He had his arm around her. He was engaged in a smiling competition with the fruit and the dinosaurs. He reached out and touched the Goddess' nose. She laughed and gave him a hug. He was muscling in on my girl! I'd have to deal with that later, after I played mini-basketball.

Matthew loved playing basketball, though he sucked at it. I

lifted him up so he could dunk it. He still managed to miss and knock me in the head. We all laughed, though I made sure Annie helped him dunk the next time. He was a cute kid. He smiled absently, like he was laughing at a joke we couldn't hear. He didn't talk much. He made a lot of sounds, though. Mostly squeals when despite his best efforts the ball went through the hoop. The other kids lined up to play. I ended up helping all of them. Annie walked up leading a small boy with dark, wavy hair and eyes that always looked away.

"Carlos, this is David. David, say hi to Carlos."

"Hey, Carlos."

Carlos didn't say anything. He stared at something a few inches to the right of me. I almost turned to look, but caught myself in time.

"Hey, Carlos, do you want to play a game with David? David, why don't you play the name game with Carlos? He loves the name game."

This got a reaction.

"Gimme!"

I squatted down.

"What? What do you want?"

"Gimme gimme!"

Annie patted his head.

"He wants a name."

"Okay. David."

"David. 4. 1. 20. 13. 4. David."

"Wow! That's amazing."

"Yes, it is. It's amazing, Carlos."

And it was. But something about it rang strange to me. Julie walked over with Christian. Christian had his arm around her waist. He was a pimp daddy.

"Who's this little man?"

"Julie, this is Carlos."

"Hello, Carlos. I'm Julie."

"Julie! 13. 21. 16. 10. 6. Julie."

Wait a minute here.

"Gimme!"

"Matthew."

"Matthew. 16. 1. 20. 22. 11. 7. 25. Matthew."

Something was fishy here. I stood up.

"Annie, doesn't that seem a little off to you?"

"What do you mean?"

Julie looked over.

"I think it's amazing."

"I don't think it's right."

"Of course it's right."

"But Matthew has two 'T's in it, and he didn't repeat any numbers. Let me see something. Carlos?"

"Gimme!"

"Annie."

"Annie. 1. 17. 16. 7. 5. Annie."

I stood up again.

"The letter N can't be two different numbers. Did anyone even check to see if he's right?"

"Kids with disabilities often develop other skills like math and drawing to make up for their deficiencies."

"He's just making up numbers. He's a con artist! Watch. Carlos."

"Gimme."

"Tim."

"Tim. 21. 10. 19. Tim."

"That wasn't even close!"

The Goddess shook her head.

"Well, I am very impressed, Carlos. David, it doesn't matter if it's true or not. As long as it gets him talking."

She walked away. I swore Christian turned to smirk at me as he held her hand. Annie laughed.

"He fooled me. The wrong numbers. Who would have thought? Well, David, maybe you should get back to Matthew. Though I don't know how impressed Julie is so far. She seems a little more into my little buddy, Christian."

"He's smooth, I'll give him that. But it's early."

I spent the next hour playing with Matthew. He grabbed a truck and started tossing it back and forth with me. It wasn't a baseball, but he caught it, so I guess it was all right. I got him and Carlos to toss to each other a little, though I think Carlos was still mad at me for blowing his cover, because he got me on the foot with an errant throw. I didn't react, though inside in my head, Carlos felt the fury. It only felt like five minutes before Annie called everyone together to hand out snacks.

Ah, snacks! Why did we ever get away from it? Like naptime, snacks should be a valuable part of every workday. Annie asked me to hand her the Doritos. I opened a bag and grabbed a handful. Without thinking I tossed them in my mouth. The Goddess smirked.

"I think we're supposed to give them out."

Annie looked back.

"He can have some if he wants. He'll make a fuss if he doesn't. Hand me the bag, Julie, before he eats the rest."

This wasn't making me look particularly good. First I call a kid a liar and then I eat their snacks. I took a sip from my juicebox to console myself. It just wasn't fair.

These kids loved their snacks. They fought like hyenas over a carcass. This must be where most of the biting happened. We made it through unscathed, though the Goddess almost got her pinky mistaken for a cheese puff. Or at least, that's what Christian made it look like...

Snack was winding down when Annie got everyone's attention.

"Hey, guys, you want to sing some songs? Well, David here has brought his guitar and he's going to lead us all in a sing-along. You ready?"

I grabbed my guitar from its case and pulled my list out of my pocket. Time to rock.

"All right, you ready to sing?"

What did I expect? A rousing "Hell, Yeah?" A few of the counselors managed a weak "Yes." You should never say "Yes" in a group-yelling situation. The "s" robs the word of all its power.

"The first song is 'London Bridge.' Here we go!"

And I began to play.

The kids didn't sing along. The counselors didn't sing along. They didn't stop me either. I don't think they could have if they'd wanted to. Annie had a tear running down her cheek. I wished someone would sing along. Wasn't there a little dance with the bridge? But no one got up. The kids just stared at me, immobilized by this strange new noise. Some of the counselors clung to each other unthinkingly. When I finished, no one spoke. I broke the silence to say I was going to do "Twinkle, Twinkle." My audience flinched. That's when the Goddess grabbed my guitar.

"That was great, David. Do you mind if I play one?"

She caught me flatfooted. I nodded weakly and she sat down to play. Who was I kidding? Every note I played probably set Annie back a year with these kids. The only way this could have gone worse was for me to have gotten up and beaten the children with my guitar while screaming "The London Bridge is coming down, motherfuckers!" I was so bad the Goddess thought she could play. I prepared myself to be supportive. Then she began to strum.

Holy shit. The Goddess played guitar like an Indigo Girl. And I thought I was going to impress her? She began to sing "Old McDonald" in a sweet alto. The kids that could joined in. She played "Bingo Was His Name-o" and "Here We Go 'Round the Mulberry Bush." The kids loved it. The counselors loved it. She led everyone through "Row, Row, Row Your Boat." I felt a hand on my leg. Matthew was trying to climb up into my lap. I lifted him up and we all sang. She was great.

When she finished, the kids dispersed to play some more mini-basketball. I walked up to her.

"You play fantastic. Why didn't you say you were so good?"

"It's just a hobby."

"Thanks for saving my ass."

"It wasn't that bad."

"I made Annie cry."

"You just need to practice. For a few more years. Ten or twelve, to be safe."

I had to laugh. Right then, Matthew ran up and threw a truck at me. I caught it just in time.

"I think somebody wants to play some basketball."

"Christian, do you want to play some one on one?"

I don't think Christian was much of a sports guy. He was more of a lover than a fighter. He played a little, though, before he got pouty. We ended up sitting at a table, coloring. For both Christian and Matthew, lines were something that happened to other people. While they massacred the World of Disney, the Goddess and I engaged in a little coloring war of our own. We started out drawing a little scene of two cows eating what looked like Ellen Degeneres, but ended up scribbling at each other till the paper was pitch black. She kept borrowing my crayons. That's a good sign, isn't it? I'd have to ask Christian. He knows about these things.

Finally time was up and we said goodbye to the kids. Matthew actually hugged me goodbye. He was a good kid. I'm sure once he starts writing forward he'll be all right. The room was almost empty when I heard the Goddess' voice from the corner.

"David. What do I do?"

"Why? What's wrong?"

"Just come here."

I walked over to her and had to sit down to keep from falling over laughing. Christian had decided to make his move and stood there holding one of the Goddess' breasts in each hand.

"I don't want to reinforce this, but the only way I know how to react to this in a positive manner is just not going to happen. What do I do?"

"I knew that boy was trouble. I think you led him on."

"Could you get Annie?"

"She's talking to some of the parents. I don't want to butt in."

"Just get her!"

"Okay! Hold on a second. Both of you."

I grabbed Annie and brought her over.

"I think Julie needs some help."

"Christian! Your mommy's here. Come on!"

Once Christian saw his mom, he let go and ran over to give her a big hug. I couldn't stop laughing.

"I'm sorry. It's just so funny."

Annie apologized.

"I should have warned you about that."

"So Christian's one of those booby grabbers you've been talking about."

"Yep."

"I didn't do anything wrong, did I, Annie?"

"No, Julie, you did everything right. You were great. You play a mean guitar on top of everything else. I have to get these snacks back home, so I have to run. It was great to meet you, Julie. See you, David. Thanks for your help."

Annie left. We followed and strolled towards the subway.

"Matthew cracks me up. I think he was starting to like me."

"You two looked like you were having a good time."

"He's a cool kid. So you had fun?"

"It was fun. Really. I want to do it again."

"Annie would be happy for the help."

"Thanks for inviting me along. This was a great not-date."

Amazing. I had made a complete fool of myself, played guitar so badly that even kids with autism begged me to stop, and called a six-year-old a fraud, and she was still digging me. Her eyes shined and her hand kept brushing up against mine as we walked. It could have been an accident, but I didn't think so.

"Do you want to grab some dinner?"

She stopped and looked at me.

"You know what, I'd better not. Let's just call it a day, okay?"

What the hell was going on?

"Okay, if you want to. Maybe we can get together next week?"

"I'd love that. Anyway..."

She was slipping away. What did I have to do? I was going to explode!

"I had a good time. Thanks for coming."

"Thanks for inviting me."

There was an awkward pause.

"So I guess I'll be seeing you."

Just then, my cell phone rang. I picked it up while the Goddess stood around waiting to finish up the goodbye ritual.

"Hello?"

"David, can you get a car?"

It was Jim. He sounded stressed.

"What's wrong?"

"I came up to surprise Asia and she didn't like the surprise. And now I'm stuck in a biker bar in the bad part of Providence and I can't feel my face. I need a ride."

"How did you know where to find Tiger Lady? I thought she was a mystery."

"Well, I found out why. Anyway, I just called a bunch of bars until I hit the one she was working at."

"How long did that take you?"

"It doesn't matter. Look, can you help me?"

"Man, I don't have a car."

"Shit, what am I going to do? These biker guys have tattoos that could kick the shit out of me."

"Jesus, I'm trying to think if I know anyone with a car who's around this weekend."

The Goddess interjected.

"Is your friend in trouble?"

"He's stuck in a Providence biker bar and he fears for his life."

"I have a car. I'll drive you up."

"You sure? It's a long drive."

"It's no trouble. I can hear him from here. He sounds desperate."

I was nonplussed.

"Thanks. This is really nice of you."

"No problem."

"Hello? David? Help?"

"I've found a car. I'm coming up."

"Thank you! You're saving what's left of my ass."

"Good to know. I need directions."

"I think they're tattooed on the bartender's arm. Let me see. Yep. Here's what you do . . ."

Jim gave me the directions. He hung up after telling me to hurry. I wondered what had happened. And how he had gotten the bartender to show him his tattoo.

"He sounded really scared."

"So let's get my car."

"What kind of car do you drive?"

"You are such a guy. Your friend is in trouble and that's what is on your mind?"

"Just asking. Jeez."

And we were off to save a life.

CHAPTER NINETEEN

Dancing at the Red Dog

The Goddess drove a Jetta. As we cruised up I-95, I filled her in on Jim's tumultuous relationship.

"Wow. That's a kinky friend you have there."

"He's not really like that. It's just since he started heading up to Providence that he went a little wild. He's always been the quiet guy in the corner."

"Those are the ones to look out for. It's a cliché, but it's true. So now he's a sex fiend."

"He's not a sex fiend. He just wants a little adventure. We all want a little adventure. Some of us have less experience dealing with it than others, that's all."

"Would you have been baked into a cake and gotten a tattoo?"

"Under the right circumstances and under certain narcotics I guess I would. I hope I wouldn't get a devil giving me the thumbs-up, but who knows what my subconscious wants. Maybe I'd get something worse. A naked Charlie Brown with a huge package on my inner thigh, just to punish myself with the comparison."

"That is pretty messed up."

"My subconscious and I haven't gotten along in years. We only talk when the nice lady with the clipboard makes us. I think it's jealous. That would explain all the sabotage going on in my life."

"We've all sabotaged ourselves at one time or another."

"You've done yourself in with a boy?"

"Hell, yeah. Many times."

"What's the worst screwup?"

"I once was talking to a guy while I was on the toilet and I made the horrible mistake of telling him where I was."

"Oh man! Okay, that's pretty bad."

"I didn't think it would be a big deal. I felt really comfortable with him and I thought he'd be flattered."

"I think you might be falling short of that doctorate of the male gender you've been studying for."

"I didn't know you men were so delicate."

"We prefer to think of our women as disposing of waste magically, without ever having their pristine bottoms touching the harsh, cold porcelain."

"Well, he woke up in a hurry from that particular pipe dream. He broke up with me the next time he saw me."

"That's pretty harsh."

"I didn't think it was that big a deal."

"Do you mind my asking?"

"It was number one. Don't worry."

"Number one is okay. If you ever, completely by accident,

become comfortable around me, you can call me while doing number one."

"I'm honored."

"One request, though."

"Yes?"

"If you have to do number two, just tell me you're lifting something heavy."

"You suck. I'll give you a blow by blow, just for that."

She laughed and lowered the window. The breeze felt nice on the abnormally warm April evening.

"What's the worst breakup you've ever instigated?"

She shuddered theatrically.

"I don't think I should say."

I nudged her.

"Come on. I won't think any less of you. It can't be any worse than mine."

"What's yours?"

"You first."

"I'm driving. I could leave you by the side of the road to hitch-hike up to Providence. You'll probably be murdered and eaten."

"I'll tell after you do. I promise. Come on. It can't be that bad."

She tapped the steering wheel with her fingertips and gave in.

"I was a freshmen in college and I had been dating this boy, Kevin, since the end of high school. He was a nice enough guy. He really liked me. When we were about to head off to our separate colleges, he told me he thought we should break up. Because we should start fresh, he said. But he really liked me, you see. He was trying to save himself from being hurt. I thought he was nice, but I wasn't in love with him or anything. So I should have said yes. But

I wasn't finished yet. I know that sounds horrible, but I wasn't ready for my fling to be over, so I convinced him to stay together.

"We kept dating. He'd call every other day and he'd always be careful to not pressure me or anything like that. He was great. He even felt compelled to call me before he came up for a "surprise" visit, just so I wouldn't be caught off guard. It was nice. But I finally realized that I wasn't excited by the relationship anymore, and I knew I had to end it when I got home for Christmas.

"So I get home and he calls three times and leaves messages. But I never call him back. I can't bring myself to just call and end it. I hadn't broken up with anyone before and I didn't know how to do it. So I avoided it, and him, for a week. He came by the house and I told my parents to tell him I wasn't home. On Christmas Eve he stopped by one more time and dropped off a present for me. Then he left. I opened it. I love the Beatles. I have all their stuff. I listen to them continuously. Kevin knew that, of course. So he had bought me a limited-edition live concert album that was only available in England. He had sent away for it. It was a great present. Which made the whole thing suck even more. There wasn't any way you could look at the situation without pegging me as the bad guy. I knew I had to end it. Yet a week later, when he called to invite me out for New Years, I answered the phone and told him my parents were insisting I spend it with them. I jilted him on New Years. The worst was when he called some of my friends to see if he could come to their party, and they had to tell him no with some lame excuse because, of course, I was there hanging out with them.

"The next morning I finally worked up the courage to do it. So I drove over to his house and rang the bell. He came out onto his porch and I could tell by his eyes that he knew what was coming. Hell, my dentist knew by this point. But he had given me a gift, so I felt like I was in his debt. Even though I was breaking up with him in horrifying fashion, I couldn't let him have me in his debt. So I gave him a Christmas present, a double album by his favorite band, The Who, and I dumped him. And that's why I am a horrible person."

I couldn't lie.

"That's pretty horrible, I'll agree."

"Thanks."

"Kids can be cruel. What can you do? I still have you beat, but that was a brave fight."

"How can you possibly beat that?"

"O, ye of little faith. About five years ago I met this girl at a party. She was a friend of my buddy, Cameron. Very pretty Chinese girl with the voice of a newscaster. A younger Connie Chung if you will. I was intrigued at the prospect of that voice talking dirty to me. Very exciting. The party was at Cameron's parents' house. They were away doing something or other. So this girl and I really hit it off. We eventually find our way upstairs. Cameron graciously allows us to stay in his brother's room. So she tells me that Cameron had warned her that I was a player. I have never thought of myself as a player, so I tell her I'm not. I mean, I have the game of Jerry Lewis. But this seemed to reassure her and we start to make out. I like sex. Sex is fantastic. And I really believe that it's important to know if you have sexual chemistry before you jump into a big relationship."

"So you slept with her on the first date."

"No, I didn't. She had this rule that nobody was allowed to

orgasm on the first date. So we messed around and not only did she deny me orgasm, she denied herself orgasm. It went against everything I believed in. And what was worse, she went so slow that I would get bored. She was going down on me and I let my mind wander. I started to think about Monty Python sketches and I found myself trying to remember which member was in which skit. At one point I did the entire Parrot sketch word by word in my head. Needless to say, this didn't make her feel particularly good about herself. By the end of the evening, we were both pretty frustrated. But she still seemed to like me. A lot. And I attributed the whole slow thing to her not wanting anyone involved to be blowing their tops.

"So for the next two weeks I talk to her every night on the phone. We're getting along great. I get to hear her CNN version of the Penthouse Forum. Then we get together again. We end up fooling around, and I bring out a condom. She's taken aback and says she's not really ready for sex. I tell her that it's just in case. I'm not pressuring her, I'm just letting her know that that option is available. Pretty slick, huh?

"So we're getting to it, and once again she's going excruciatingly slow. We are talking glacier slow. The Atlantic Ocean expands quicker than this girl goes at it. I start to get bored again. I ask her if the orgasm ban has been lifted. She grudgingly agrees to come. I go down on her and she's doing great. Then she goes down on me and once again, surprise surprise, it's ridiculously slow. I just can't keep my concentration. I start thinking about how much I like Eggo Waffles, especially the Cinnamon Toast ones. So now I'm hungry, and not at all excited. This is obvious to her. And then I get worried. What if this isn't her fault at all?

What if I'm losing it? This thought scares me, so I redouble my efforts on her. I'm kissing her, I'm touching her, I'm closing my eyes and trying to think sexy thoughts. All I can see are sandwiches. With all this increased frenzy, she must have thought I was mad with passion, because she grabs a condom and puts it on me. There was no turning back. Somehow I manage to picture a fairly sexy roast beef sub, so I'm able to perform. We finish. Very unsatisfying. An obvious mistake. I should never have let it happen. I blame that whole orgasm ban coupled with fears about my virility. Excuses aside, I needed to get out of there.

"I fled home and didn't call her. She called me that night and asked me what was going on. I invited her over, saying we needed to talk. She arrived pissed off at me, and I made it worse by breaking up with her. I told her I just wasn't ready for a relationship. She, of course, throws up her hands and declares that she knew it! I was a player! I was just doing whatever I could to get into her pants. I'm not a player, I tell her. It just happened. She points out the condom. I have no excuse for that. Eventually she storms out, convinced that she had been the victim of a womanizer. When I had never meant any of that to happen that way. I just couldn't stay excited around her. So I had to have sex with her. It made perfect sense at the time. So I think I'm a much worse person than you are."

"That's pretty bad, but I don't think it even approaches my breakup."

"Oh, did I forget to mention that when she got home she found out that her mother had died?"

"Ouch."

"I've always had impeccable timing."

"I think we have to call a draw. We're both assholes."

"I guess we are."

"Well, I'm being paid back now."

"Me, too. In spades. Karma's a bitch."

We passed through New Haven. The water lay on our right, twinkling under the harbor lights. A closed-up van with the words "Roses - $10" painted on the side sat parked on the grass. I felt the urge to jump out and knock on the door for a dozen reds after hours. I enjoyed the silence, and then broke it to tell her so.

"I love driving with the radio off."

"I'm sorry, I was thinking."

She reached over to turn the knob.

"No. I wasn't being sarcastic. My first car didn't have a radio so I got used to it. I find the sounds of the wind blowing by as we drive in silence comforting. Helps me think."

"Have you heard from your ex?"

"She's left a few messages. I'd hoped it would drop off by now, but I think she's having a hard time. I feel bad, but I think the worst thing I could do is call her back."

"How are you doing? Okay?"

"Yeah. I guess. I'm over her, if that's what you're getting at."

"I don't buy that."

"I'm just telling you. I may be a little sad sometimes, and I do think about her, I won't lie, but I'm not in love with her anymore. I'm fine and ready to move on."

"I'm sure it feels that way. Wait until the relapse."

"Has that happened to you? The relapse?"

"I was like a werewolf who needed to be strapped down for the full moon. Thank God I called a friend instead of him."

"You sound like a junkie."

"He was a hard habit to kick."

"So you're over him now."

"I think so. He still e-mails me. And I get sad for no reason and think about things we used to do together. I miss his backrubs and the way he'd laugh at my jokes so hard that he'd run out of breath. And I miss reading in bed while he was working at his computer. I liked looking up and seeing him there."

"But you're over him."

"Mostly. I know it wasn't right. It still hurts."

"The best thing you can do is move on. You'll miss the future if you keep walking backwards watching the past. I've stubbed my heel a few times these past few months, so I should know."

She laughed a little.

"Yeah, I guess you should."

"I guess you'd say we're in the unique position of understanding each other's trauma. If anyone can commiserate, it's us. We've made mistakes, we've been bastards, we've been hurt, and now we should be all paid up. Maybe it's finally time to be happy. Our karma is all settled and our past transgressions have been wiped away. We can start fresh, wiser but unbowed, ready to love again."

"You sound like you're on Oprah."

"She knows her shit."

"Maybe you're right. Maybe I'm just scared."

"Of course, I'm right."

"You don't need to be cocky."

"Just think it over. I'm not going to let a little ache in my chest keep me from being happy. I'm not going to let her do that to me."

She didn't say anything. We rode along in silence. Somewhere in Rhode Island, around exit eight, she slid her hand into mine and we continued that way on into Providence.

The directions led us down into a seedy part of town. The type of neighborhood where if your car broke down, you just gave it up for dead and ran your little white ass off. If someone starts messing with you, that's when you follow my grandpappy's advice. You yell, "Herpes" while pointing to yourself and then pass out. Hopefully they'll just take your money and leave you alone. I passed this advice over to the Goddess.

"Something tells me you'd be more likely to find that herpes is something you two have in common."

"I thought you were a lady."

"You didn't check the package. I'm kidding. Don't worry, if someone attacks us, I'll save you."

"You have a real rapport with the swarthy underworld thugs, do you?"

"No, but I can shoot mace like Spider Man."

"Good to know. I guess I'll have to go the watermelon route with you."

"What?"

"Nothing."

"I think that's it up ahead."

I pointed to a shacklike building across the street. You couldn't even see the front for all the bikes surrounding it. This was the kind of place where guys like me walk up, lean on a bike starting a domino effect that knocks down everyone's ride, and then get the living shit kicked out of them after a hilarious chase through the surrounding streets. A blinking red neon sign in the corner of the window flickered RED DOG. This was probably it.

The Goddess looked at me.

"Your friend is a fucking idiot."

"Love will do that to you. Or maybe it was the tattoos. It's tough to tell which is which sometimes. Do you have a club or something for the car?"

"No, I have an old trick that I use to keep my car from getting jacked."

"What?"

"Positive thinking."

"And how's that working out for you?"

"I'll let you know when we walk back out."

We got out of the car and crossed the street. I half expected a guy to be chucked through the window at our feet. I was tense and ready for action. My right hand made the shape of a karate chop, just in case. I avoided the parked bikes by over a mile. The Goddess walked behind me. She held my other hand. Or at least I assumed she did, since her kung fu grip had long since squeezed out any feeling I had there. I opened the front door tentatively and we walked inside.

The Red Dog wasn't much. It had a bar, a little backroom, and around eighty drunk Hells Angels with ZZ Top beards and ugly girlfriends. The bartender was a hugely fat black dude with the biggest Afro I had ever seen. That was probably where he parked his bike. He had on a wifebeater that barely covered the myriad of tattoos that completely blocked out the skin. I wonder how many different sets of directions he kept on his body. He must never get lost. Three girls danced on the bar. The one nearest us was pretty cute, so I avoided looking. No need to start trouble with the only person in the joint on my side.

"Do you see him?"

"No. You?"

I did a sweep.

"No. Unless someone is sitting on him or molesting him in the bathroom I don't see him. Shit. I hope he's okay."

"Let's ask the bartender."

"I don't wanna. What if he grabs me and sticks me in his hair? That could be the portal to Narnia!"

"Just ask him."

I walked boldly up to the bar. If anyone asked for my woman, he would get her without a fight. I leaned over the bar. I suppressed the urge to call out "Barkeep!"

"Excuse me?"

I got his attention right away. As if everyone in there hadn't been staring at us since we walked in.

"Yeah. You're not looking for Asia too, are you? That wouldn't be such a good idea."

"No. No, I'm not. But my friend was in here before looking for her, and I'm picking him up. Do you know what happened to him?"

The bartender laughed. I flinched back in case stuff started flying out of his Afro.

"You want to take away one of my bitches. That's not cool."

Oh, no. Jim was somebody's bitch. This was not good.

"He needs to go home. His father, the President of the United States, is worried about him."

The Goddess kicked me. It was worth a shot. The bartender

laughed again. I flinched again. I was going to get whiplash from this guy.

"I don't think he wants to go home. He looks so happy."

The bartender pointed. There in the corner, trying desperately to get down from the bar before we saw him, stood a figure in a pink dress. I had assumed it was one of the dancing ladies. The figure turned around. There, in full hoochie mama makeup, was Jim.

"Hey, guys. Thanks for picking me up."

Holy shit.

"Jim? Tell me they did this to you. Tell me this isn't a new job gone horribly, horribly wrong."

"I don't want to talk about it."

The bartender patted Jim on the head.

"It's okay. I just thought the little homewrecker needed to see how the other half lived. So he's been doing a little dancing for us. But I think that he's learned his lesson. Bye, Darla! We'll miss you!"

"My name is Jim! I'm a man, damn you!"

As we led Jim out of the bar, the patrons turned to say good-bye.

"Good luck, Darla!"

"We'll miss you, girl."

"No one has legs like you, Darla!"

"My name is Jim!"

The bartender waved in a friendly manner as the door shut behind us. The Jetta was still there. The Goddess looked relieved.

"The power of positive thought wins again."

We helped Jim to the car. His makeup job was truly hideous. He looked like Tammy Faye Baker crossed with Tim Curry.

"You look hot."

"Fuck you, David."

The Goddess took pity.

"Here's a tissue. You should wipe your face."

"Thanks.

"I never met a guy who loved to dance so much."

We got in the car and started her up. Jim's forlorn voice drifted up to the front seat.

"Please get me the hell out of here."

"Not to worry, young damsel in distress. Your shining knight is here."

"I'm going to have to kill you once we hit Manhattan, you know that."

"It's so worth it."

We made our way back to 95 without incident. I was bursting with curiosity. Finally Jim cracked.

"I came up to surprise Asia. She had told me the names of a few of the bars she hit every month and the Red Dog was one of them. When I called, they told me she'd be there around eight. So I headed on up."

"How'd you get to that part of town?"

"Taxi. I thought I'd be leaving with her. And I didn't realize what kind of bar it was until I got there, and by then it was too late. The minute I saw that dude's hair I knew I was fucked. He was going to pull some A-1 sauce out of that topiary, pour it over my head and take a bite, I could tell. I snuck into the corner of the bar where I could see the door. I almost got raped by the barmaid when I asked for a Corona. Apparently, I wanted a Bud. Lucky for me, I guess, it was only about fifteen minutes before Asia showed up. She looked fucking hot, too. So I walked up to her and grabbed her shoulder. That's when I felt the hand on my neck. It turned me around and I was face-to-face with, I kid you not, a fucking professional wrestler."

"Really?"

"Okay, not really. But he was that fucking huge. And I hear Asia behind me call out my name and then Andre the Giant says 'You know this guy?' And she says 'Yeah, I've been fooling around with him. Try not to break him.' And he lifts me up by my neck until we're face-to-face and says the worst sentence I have ever heard in my life. 'You fucking my wife?' I almost peed all over myself and him. I think the only reason I didn't was because the rest of my body was numb from the neck down."

The Goddess turned around to stare incredulously at Jim. I had to kick her to get her to watch the road.

"How did you not get killed?"

"That was the freaky part. Because then Macho Randy Savage starts to laugh. 'This was the best you could do?' he asks Asia. Asia tells him 'Yeah, he was persistent. And he's cute. Don't you think so?' I wanted to scream 'No! I am not cute! I am hideous! Hideous! Please don't kill me!' But The Rock just laughs and says 'You have some weird taste, honeybuns.' And he puts me down. Asia looks at me and she's half-smiling and she says, 'That was so cute of you to try to surprise me. Thanks. But I never date guys who have met my husband. That's just not right. So it's over. But thanks for the fun times!' And she kisses me, leans over to check the Guinness, finds everything satisfactory, and leaves. And I'll never see her again."

"But why are you in a dress?"

"While she was checking the beer, I called you guys. I thought I was okay. But Rowdy Roddy Piper didn't leave when Asia left. Turns out he loves hanging at the Red Dog. And he may not say anything to her about their little arrangement, but I don't think that he's completely cool with it. 'Cause he forces me to put on this dress, he and the bartender make me up like a Vietnamese hooker and they tell me to dance on the bar. It was horrible. Every time I tried to get down, they'd pour a beer on my head and threaten to swallow it. And if I hear 'The Devil Came Down to Georgia' one more time, I'm going postal."

"How long were you up there for, buddy?"

"Time has no meaning up there on the bar. It's just one long hellish dance. You guys were lucky. Super Fly Snooka had just left before you got there. Otherwise you'd probably be decked out in your summer finest boogying to 'Honky Tonk Women' right along with me."

He looked so forlorn.

"I'm sorry, man. I know you liked her."

"This was the worst night of my life. I knew it wasn't going to last, but married? That's not fair. I thought she liked me."

"She did like you. A woman like that doesn't get it on with a guy like you unless she likes you."

"Is that a compliment?"

The Goddess put in her two cents.

"At least he didn't kill you. Or harm you in any ungodly ways. You're basically okay, right?"

"I guess so. I just really liked her, you know."

I passed him another tissue.

"I know."

"Thanks."

"Jim?"

"Yeah?"

"You're still wearing the dress."

"I know."

Jim clutched his shirt and pants to his chest as we drove on in silence.

We dropped Jim off at his apartment building. He disappeared into his front doorway without turning around. The Goddess turned to me.

"I'll drop you off."

"Thanks."

"Do you think he'll be okay?"

"I have no idea. This is kind of uncharted territory. I've dealt with heartache and betrayal, but never crossdressing bar dancing. I hope so. He's a strong boy."

"I feel bad for him."

"I still can't believe he ever even got close to being this crazy. Part of me feels awful for what happened and another part is saying 'You go, crazy boy! Break down the walls!' I'm glad he wasn't sitting in the corner for once."

"I guess that could be a good thing."

"We'll see how he reacts to this. He still has those tattoos. They may not let him sit in the corner again. Devils can be quite tricky."

"Too true."

We crossed through Central Park.

"Thanks for doing this. It turned out to be scarier than I thought it would be, and I'm sorry I dragged you into it."

"Don't worry. I'm glad I could help. I wasn't scared, really. I had you to protect me."

"That should have been scarier than the bikers. Anyway, it was really nice of you. I appreciate it, a lot."

"No problem."

We turned up Third Ave.

"This is me up here on the left. Right here is cool."

"Okay. So, give me a call next week."

"I will. Definitely. We can grab food or something."

"That would be great."

"I'm glad I got to spend some real time with you, even though it was under weird circumstances."

"Me too. It felt good to get to know you a little better. And it was nice to see how much you care about your friends. Between helping out Annie and going to Jim's rescue, you're a good friend."

"Wow. I keep impressing you by accident."

"That's the only way."

Her eyes shone green under the faint streetlights. My hand was shaking.

"You're impressing me right now."

"Am I?"

She smiled softly. I touched her hand. I couldn't tell if I was making it shake or if it was shaking all on its own. She turned her head away, but her fingers curled into mine. I leaned forward and kissed her lightly, and then stronger as she pressed her face towards me. I reached up to cup her cheek and she moved her lips under mine in perfect rhythm. It was a fucking good kiss. She pulled away and kissed my hand. She smiled.

"Still impressed?"

"Very. You have impeccable taste in lip gloss."

"Max Factor. Write it down."

"Duly noted."

"I have to head home."

"Okay. I'll call you tomorrow?"

"Call me next week. After Easter and all that."

"That sounds good to me."

I opened the car door and turned back. She was already there, giving me a last deep kiss. I touched her forehead with my lips and got out of the car. I waved once as she drove off. Her hand popped through her open window to match me. And then she turned right and disappeared.

I guess I should have walked into my apartment, smiled softly to myself and laid in bed with my hands behind my head replaying the kiss over and over in my mind. That would be the romantic path. As I think I have demonstrated over and over, however, I have very little class. So I, of course, called every single person I had ever met to brag.

Annie:

"Good for you. Now let me sleep."

Dustin:

"Dude, you let the ball drop. You could have hit that!"

Cameron:

"Cool. You sure she doesn't have a boyfriend or girlfriend or something? There's gotta be something."

Jim:

"Yeah, I'm in the mood to gossip. I'll talk to you later when I've bought some self-respect."

Mom and Dad:

"Hello? You know what, I don't care who this is. It's too late to listen to you bastards. Leave us the hell alone." Click.

Hunan Four:

"That's nice. Your order?"

Hey, I was hungry.

CHAPTER TWENTY

Easter

My father is insane when it comes to holidays. I don't mean a little kooky, I mean clinically insane. Easter is my Dad's second favorite holiday after Christmas, so he goes all out. At the center of the maelstrom lives the Egg Hunt.

My father's Easter Egg Hunt is massive. It's bigger than the one they do for the town. Hell, it's more involved than the one they do in Central Park. He has more eggs and better prizes than the City of New York. Plus there're only two kids involved: me and my brother. And before my brother exploded into the linebacker he has since become, I was bigger than he was, so I kicked his ass and won every year. And when you won, you really won. Some of the prizes I've collected over the years: a CD player, tickets to a Broadway show, a free massage from a spa, a dirt bike, a year's supply of jelly beans and a spelunking helmet with a light on the brim. My dad can't help himself. If there aren't any cool prizes, he's not interested. But don't think that my abuse of my brother has left him empty-handed. Hell, no. The eggs are plastic like the ones at Central Park, and like the Central Park variety, some of them are filled with candy. The others, however, contain money. Good money. Take-the-family-out-to-brunch-at-the-Hilton-type money. On a good year, a kid can make a cool seventy to eighty bucks doing one of my dad's hunts. That's good cash for a Sunday.

Don't get the wrong impression of my dad. He's not some spendthrift who just throws away his money. Okay, so maybe he is. But he never simply handed us cash. We always had to find it under a bush or hidden in the fireplace or floating in the back part of the toilet. I think he'd forget how much he put in the eggs since he always seemed as surprised as we were when we counted it all up. Dad was a genius at draining any spiritual qualities left in our major religious holidays. The one time he took us to church for Easter, we spent the first half of the sermon searching the pews for eggs. We had to leave after my brother was dragged from the confessional clutching what looked like a pantyhose container. Priests. They live in a place called a rectory, so what do you expect?

So I was home again for Easter and I was excited. I may be in my late twenties, but I still get all revved up about the Easter Egg Hunt. I could really use the cash. And maybe the prize this year will be a new car or something. The funny thing about all this money my dad spends on presents is that you'd assume from his purchases that he was filthy rich. But he isn't at all. He just buys a lot of shit. He doesn't have a huge wad of cash locked away somewhere. He's too busy making sure we're all having a good time right now. Some people may bemoan the lack of inheritance that this will obviously leave me and my brother. I look at it like he's been giving me little bits of my inheritance all along. I like it better his way.

My dad must have been awake for hours before us, hiding the eggs throughout the house and the front yard. Of course that wasn't such an amazing feat of discipline, since by the time my brother and I finally dragged our sorry asses out of bed, it was one o'clock in the afternoon. That's right, in the *afternoon*. The great thing about moving out of the house was that every time I came back home, I was given a twenty-four-hour grace period before I had to act like a member of the family. Just because they missed me. This meant no cleaning, no mowing, no painting the house, and most importantly, sleeping late. My brother had been away at college, so he received the golden day as well. Taking advantage of this on Easter may seem a little ungrateful of us, especially seeing as this entire egg hunt was for our benefit, but hey, that's life. We were tired.

Dad was excited, as always, while Mom just kept repeating, "My boys!" and smiling. It was a little cloying, actually, like a *Little House on the Prairie* episode, but that's my family. Of course, during our opening credit sequence, I trip halfway down the hill and take out my brother while shouting out obscenities in slow motion. And my dad laughs his ass off the whole time. More of a cable program, really. Anyway, we sat down at the kitchen table to go over the details that we already knew by heart. My brother downed a Red Bull for extra egg-hunt energy while I tried to check out the living room in the reflection in my Mom's glasses. I could pick out four eggs just sitting there. Alex didn't have a chance.

Alex is my little brother. And little is only a word I use out of habit, since the boy is huge. Not fat, just big. He couldn't have looked any less like me if he were black. As has been established earlier, I am a slight individual. I'm not short, but I am very thin.

The muscles I've developed through my haphazard gym appearances don't fill out my frame at all. They're more like individually wrapped snack cakes in a box. You can make out every one if you try. Alex, on the other hand, is a behemoth. He's a little shorter than I am, but his shoulders could form the beam of a barn. Occasionally I'll get the suicidal urge to wrestle with him, which always ends with me dangling upside down from one of his gigantic hands. He played some football in high school and he did well because of his sheer size. He had no instinct for it, however. He was always the last guy on the pileup, jumping on sheepishly. So he turned to his real love: computers. It's kind of funny to seem him stabbing at the little keyboard with his gargantuan fingertips, but he's actually pretty good at it. He's a junior at RPI upstate, and if he remembers to register for all the classes he needs, he'll graduate next year with a pretty impressive grade point average. Much higher than mine. He got the brains and the brawn in the family. I got the neuroses.

Alex and I get along really well. Part of that is my instinctive desire not to anger the beast coupled with his innate submission to the elder sibling. But we also share a similar sense of humor. You may not know we're brothers when you look at us, but hear us laugh and you'll be hard pressed to tell us apart. It's amazing how close people can be based solely on what they find funny. Of course, we have the same parents. And only we know how unique that situation really is.

The doorbell rang. I got up to answer it but Dad pinned me with a glance.

"Don't think you can sneak a peek. Sit your ass down. Your mom will get it."

Mom shot him a look and trudged over to answer the door. She came back looking surprised, with Annie in tow. Annie's face was pale and drawn like she hadn't slept in days. She was wearing a nice summer dress that hung awkwardly. She opened with an apology.

"I'm sorry to barge in like this."

"What's wrong? Aren't you supposed to be at that huge Easter brunch with the peeps?"

"I was. I had to leave. I couldn't take it any more."

My mom touched her shoulder.

"Did something happen? Are you okay? Here, sit down."

Annie took a seat.

"I'm fine. It's mostly family stuff. And Jacob stuff."

"Who's Jacob?"

I answered for her.

"Her not-boyfriend."

"Oh. Where is he? Is he okay?"

"I can't believe what he did to me!"

My dad nodded sagely.

"Say no more. This is a romantic-bullshit-free zone."

My mom snorted.

"Speak for yourself."

Annie smiled.

"Thanks. I just needed a place to not have to hear it any more, you know?"

I wanted to know.

"So what happened?"

Dad held up a hand.

"Not now. We have more important things on our plate."

Dad handed her an Easter basket.

"Here there are no problems. There are no blow-offs or blow-hards or endless questions. Here there is only the hunt. Let me explain the rules."

"I don't want to impose. I just wanted to get away from my aunts..."

"Shh! Rule number one: no bitching. No one wants to hear it when they're preparing for the hunt."

My brother and I nodded agreement and grabbed our baskets. Or at least, Alex grabbed his basket. Annie had mine so I had to settle for a plastic bag.

"Rule number two: there are eggs in the living room, the dining room, the porch, the hallway, the bathroom, the guest room, the front lawn and the driveway. There are no, I repeat, no eggs in the chimney, due to last year's humorous mishap. So confine yourself to those areas. Rule number three: no planting eggs to boost your score. This means you, David. I know how many eggs there are. Rule number four: no buying eggs off of the younger, stupider participants for shiny bottle caps."

I protested.

"Dad, I haven't done that for ten years."

"Or for promises of stock options."

Alex shook his head.

"As if I'd trust someone who can't work his calculator to sell me stock."

"Rule number five: no luring anyone into the closet with trails of jelly beans and then locking them inside. And rule number six: no biting or sticking each other with dirty needles."

Annie moved her basket away from me.

"David, you're a bastard."

"I play to win, Annie. I suggest you do the same. Have I mentioned a new company called Fortech? They're primed to explode, you know."

"David. You know the rules. Annie, do you understand the rules?"

"I do, sir."

"Good. Then get ready...set..."

Dad always waited a good two minutes before saying...

"Go!"

And we were off. I tripped Alex at the door to the living room and the game had begun.

And an hour and a half later, it was over. My shirt was ripped and Alex's ear was bleeding, since Dad couldn't watch us the whole time. Annie had proven to be irritatingly good at grabbing eggs. I had to accidentally bump into her and "help" her pick up her eggs and put them in her basket. My egg total went up by four. The front yard looked like an insane badger had torn through looking for her baby. The dining room and living room both had overturned furniture, though this year only one vase got cracked. Dad had actually gotten the potter to bake the clay around the egg. Props to Alex for finding that one. My face was all sooty as, in the heat of battle, I had forgotten the fireplace prohibition and repeated last year's humorous mishap. I did get the egg tucked in my Dad's front pants pocket, though I don't think I'll ever sleep the night through again.

We all sat down at the kitchen table to count up the spoils. Once again, I was robbed monetarily. Alex always sniffed out the biggest wads of cash. This year was no different, with the little bastard taking home a cool seventy-three bucks. Annie picked up thirty, while I amassed a less than impressive five dollars and three cents. But there still remained the main prize that went to the most eggs collected. We waited breathlessly as they were counted up. Mom did the honors, since she was supposedly impartial. I leaned back quite confidently, as I'd slipped her a handwritten early Mother's Day card with a crisp single inside the night before. Can't buy me love, my ass.

Mom and Dad walked into the kitchen with solemn faces. Mom put the two baskets and the bag on the table.

"I recounted three times just to be sure. Most years are close, but this one was a photo finish. The champion of this year's Easter Egg hunt, and winner of an amazing prize is... Annie!"

"This is bullshit!"

It came out of me before I could stop it. They all stared at me.

"Sorry, gut reaction. Congrats, Annie. Couldn't have happened to a better blah blah blah. So what didn't I win?"

"Annie, you are now the proud owner of a new DVD player!"

Annie was dumbstruck.

"I can't possibly... that's too much."

Alex patted her hand.

"This is nothing. Why do you think there's a no biting rule? Do you think we risk infection for nothing?"

Dad handed the package to Annie.

"This is our tradition. This year you won it fair and square, so enjoy it."

"It's too much. I feel awful."

"Don't. This is how we do Easter here."

"It's not that. It's just... after what happened this morning..."

Mom sat down next to her. My phone beeped, so I picked it up. I read the display.

"Jesus, I have twelve missed calls!"

Annie looked down.

"That would be my cousin. I should explain."

"Don't tell me. Okay, I guess you'd better."

Annie began nervously sticking various jellybeans and marshmallow peeps in her mouth while she talked.

Annie's All Too Believable Story

Annie never liked to admit that she needed Jacob at all, but there was one thing he did for her that she counted on. She needed him to protect her from her family. She'd never been with a guy who was willing to brave the jackals for her before, and at first she didn't trust it. She pictured him setting up a tab of good deeds that she would one day be asked to repay. After a while, however, she grew used to it. Even depended on it. Definitely depended on it. And he never let her down.

Then came the day before Easter.

Jacob always stayed out late and he often came home drunk, but when the clock hit three, Annie began to worry. She couldn't fall asleep, which bothered her. She spent hours wondering what that meant, but came up with no answers. Eventually, at five in the morning, Jacob rolled in.

He was hammered. More than hammered. He'd come out the other side of drunk into the realm of sick honesty. You don't ever want to have a serious conversation with someone who's reached that state. There's no telling what things they'll blurt out that you just don't say. Jacob flopped down on the bed.

"You don't love me."

Annie couldn't move. He repeated.

"You know it. You don't love me."

"I don't know."

"Of course you know it. I'm so fucking stupid. You haven't said a goddamn thing to me about it all week long. We're right back to where we started. You know what? I'm gonna give you one last chance. This is your final window of opportunity. I'm sorry for all the pressure and everything, but I can't live with the pain in my gut anymore. It's not worth it. I can move on if I have to."

"But the tattoo..."

"You let me worry about that. I need to know right now."

"Are you quoting 'Paradise by the Dashboard Light?' "

"This isn't a fucking joke. Jesus! Why can't you answer the fucking question?"

Annie pulled herself up into the corner of the bed, trying to escape.

"You're drunk. I don't want to do this when you're drunk."

"Copout! Fucking copout! Do you want me to run outside and walk the fucking line? I'll fucking run down the center of the street straight as a fucking arrow! I may be drunk, but I'm here. Really here. Are you here?"

Annie didn't move.

"Of course I'm here..."

"Enough of this shit."

Jacob worked his way upright and planted himself in front of Annie, forcing her to look at him by his sheer presence.

"Just do it like they did it in Roman times, when the gladiators fought. Thumbs up or down. Make it easy."

A thousand thoughts flew threw Annie's head. This couldn't be it. Oh shit, this is it. She wasn't prepared. She didn't know. How could she hedge her bets? She needed more time. She needed a few years to figure this out. Of course she knew the answer, but what if it's wrong? Jacob's eyes tore into her, demanding. It had to end now. Annie had to toss the dice. She had no choice. But she couldn't let go.

"I'm sorry, Jacob. I'm not like you. I'm not so sure all the time. It's not a black-and-white world for me. There's no right way or wrong way. There're no good guys and bad guys. There are just shades. And I need more time to figure out…"

"Bullshit!"

It ripped out of his throat, hard and angry. Jacob leapt off of the bed.

"Jacob?"

"This is black and white. It's not even about how you feel. Maybe you need to work that out. But I'm talking about making a choice. Do we try or not. Am I worth that to you, or not. Do you think you might ever love me, or not. And I can tell. I hate it, but I can see it. It's not. And I wish you had the fucking balls to just tell me that."

He stormed through the door and slammed it. Annie heard him in the next room, stomping around. She wanted to get up and go to him. She was wrong! She could try! She could learn! Don't leave! But she didn't.

As dawn broke, she lay awake, staring up at the ceiling while her body wracked violently with sobbing that could have been a reaction to her cramping stomach or her cramping life. And the whole time her mouth stayed closed, a thin line padlocked against the flow.

When she woke up a few hours later, Jacob was gone. Annie had never felt so tired. She poured herself into her car and drove up to her Aunt Antonia's house in Nyack. Mom was in California. She was all alone. By the time she drove up to the house, she had dipped into a kind of suicidal funk. She didn't know it, but she just needed a match. One match. And her family was like a group of businessmen at a bar surrounding a beautiful woman with an unlit cigarette.

She steeled herself and rang the doorbell. The Eater answered it. Annie was surprised.

"Hi. I didn't know you were coming to this thing."

"Mom's making me. Where's Jacob?"

"Not coming. Had to do his own family thing."

The Eater looked somewhat satisfied that she wasn't the only one alone. The Eater was the favorite. The pretty one. The cheerleader. And once I was out of the picture, Annie could admit that she didn't like her very much. She definitely didn't want to commiserate over ex-boyfriends.

"So...how's David?"

Amazing. Annie wasn't even in the front door yet.

"Okay. You know."

"Has he mentioned me?"

"I should probably go in and say hi to everyone."

"Cool. But I want to talk later."

Fantastic. Annie would rather be shaved by an epileptic at a rave.

This was probably the only time in her life she actively sought out her aunts. They were all in the kitchen arguing, as usual. The talking stopped when she entered. They looked around for Jacob and saw that he was not present. Their faces lit up. They were the Stepford wives and Annie had forgotten her cross. It would not be pretty.

"Annie!"

"So lovely to see you, honey."

"Where's your man? With his family! And where did you say they lived, Harlem, was it?"

"Poor boy. It's probably better that he's not around to see you eat the cake. I swear, you would make any man run in fear for his life the way you put away your cake. He'd be afraid he's next!"

"You can tell me, Annie. Did he run away with another girl? You shouldn't be too surprised. He was very handsome."

"That's true. We were all surprised at how handsome he was. You're better off without him. You two didn't look right together anyway."

Annie replied to all the arrows with a firm "We're still together" and "He just needed to spend this one with his family." But they weren't buying it. They could smell despair on her breath. It was their meat and they were ravenous.

The morning passed in a blur of thinly veiled insults and false sympathy. With each barb, Annie's heart beat faster. By brunch, she felt like her head was going to explode.

"It almost doesn't feel like Easter without that lovely Jacob. He was such a smart boy."

"And funny! I almost split my side right in half. It's better that he isn't here, because I wouldn't be able to keep the milk from squirting out my nose! I knew this would be a dull Easter when I saw you standing there alone, Annie."

"Don't worry, Annie. You'll find another boy. Someone a little more suited to your type. You should always try to stay within your means. You reach too high and you'll never be able to hold on."

"Too true."

Annie tried to concentrate on her plate. Just eat and leave. That's all she had to do. Her stomach was killing her. She couldn't swallow.

"What's wrong with my waffles, Annie! You are so particular. I guess my handmade waffles aren't good enough for you. I swear, I hope you put your sweat and tears into something some day so I can turn around and turn up my nose to it."

Annie's blood roared louder and louder in her ears. Everything else faded into the background. Nothing seemed real. It was like she wasn't there. She was dreaming. That must be it! She was dreaming.

"It's not like you're your cousin. Now she has something to cry about. That ungrateful boy just dumping her like that without any warning. Now that is unfair."

The Eater had something to say about that.

"It's not so bad. I can tell he's just taking some time. I can tell he's regretting breaking up with me. Of course, I don't know if I'll take him back. He was an asshole. Annie agrees with me. But he's just moping around his apartment thinking about me, so it won't be too long before he's crawling back."

"I know you're right, dear. You're so beautiful, how could he stay away?"

"That's true, honey. No boy could keep away from your pretty face. No boy worth having."

That was the last thing Annie heard. The unfairness of it all overwhelmed her. The sensation that this was some sick nightmare pervaded her. Her head felt like it was overfilled. And just like that, it exploded.

"This is bullshit!"

All conversation stopped. They stared at her like she had mutated into a donkey right before their eyes.

"You go on and on about how beautiful she is! How special she is! How every boy would be crazy to stay away. And what about me? What am I? I'm not the one who was dumped by my boyfriend months ago and still holds on like some pathetic schoolgirl. I'm not the one whose husband would rather change religions than stay married to me. I'm not the one who's browbeaten my spouse and child into a coma. I'm happy! I'm good at what I do. I'm smart. I have a good life! And I don't need to hear about every little fucking thing that's wrong with me every fucking time I show up at one of your demonic houses. It's like I was born into a family of harpies! Pecking away at me! It's horrible. You dried-up, bitter women are driving me insane. I'm sick because of you. Physically ill. And I know you don't care. You probably look at it as some kind of sick trophy. But I'm tired of just shutting up and letting you do this to me! I'm tired of it. I'm not going to let you ruin me. I've been a good little girl for the sake of the family. Well, you know what? Fuck the family! A family is something you feel safe inside. It's not supposed to tear your colon apart. I'm on lithium because of you witches. The only reason I don't go to therapy is because I don't want to let you depress any more people than you already have. Well, I'm finished! I am done! I am walking out that fucking door and if you have anything to say about that, you can tell it to my fucking ass, because that's the last you'll be seeing of me for a long time. And by the way, little miss perfect. David hasn't been moping in his room crying over you. He never talks about you. I met his new girlfriend the other day, and she's great. He's completely over you. And he's happy. So stop calling me! Happy Easter!"

And with that, Annie walked out.

Nobody knew quite what to say. Me included.

"I'm so sorry about Jacob."

"It's my own fault."

"Don't say that."

"Of course it is. But at least I stood up to my family. I did something good today. And you guys made me feel better. Thanks."

My mom handed her a tissue and smiled.

"Are you okay?"

"I don't know yet. I'll tell you tonight after my mom calls."

"I mean about Jacob?"

"Same applies."

Silence for a moment.

I looked back down at my phone.

"So that's why she's calling? It's about the Goddess?"

"I am so sorry, David. I was just so mad it kind of flew out of me."

"It's not your fault. It's not your job to keep secrets for me. What does she want, do you think?"

" I don't know. You'll have to check the messages."

"I don't know if I have that kind of time."

My mom patted my shoulder.

"She always was a determined girl."

Dad laughed.

"I think bitch is the word your mother's leaving out."

"I would never say that, Ed. She and I didn't always get along but that doesn't mean I wish her pain."

"She sure was a pain. If you ever go back to her, David, I am going to have to neuter you."

"You will not. Your dad is full of it, David. He would never neuter you over something so silly. We want you to make your own choices."

I looked at my phone. I picked it up and pressed the voicemail button, brought the phone up to my ear, and braced myself for the worse.

"Hi, David. How are you? I haven't talked to you in a while. Hope you're doing okay. I've heard through the grapevine you're dating again. That's cool. I hope you're happy. Anyway, I really need to talk to you. I've been having trouble moving on. I'm dating and stuff, of course. I've seen a bunch of cool guys. I've had no trouble with that. I just really think I haven't had a chance to say everything I need to say. So I want to ask you, as a friend, would you get together with me this week? To talk. Please, I really need this. Just so I can have some closure. Please let me know you'll do it. Thanks. Glad to hear you're doing well. Bye."

Next Message.

"Hey, David. Look, I want to talk. Please give me a call. I'm here all day. Bye."

Next message. Her chipper tone was gone, replaced by a subdued quiet.

"I'm sorry I keep leaving you messages like this. I'm just having a really hard time. I heard you were seeing somebody, and that's cool and all, but it's . . . hard. I'd really appreciate it if you'd call me back. Bye."

Next message. Her voice trembled out of control.

"I'm not crazy or anything, I just need you to talk to me. Please. If you ever cared about me at all, you'd call me back. I need to talk to you one more time. I need this. I can't handle it. Please don't just ignore me. I know you probably hate me now or wish you'd never met me, but can't you just remember how we used to be for one second and see it from my side? Please. Call me back."

I looked at the phone helplessly. This had to end.

Annie had fallen asleep in the guest bedroom. She didn't want to head home and I didn't blame her. My phone kept ringing, all day long. Thankfully my mailbox filled up so the messages stopped. Even though I'd moved on, it hurt me to hear her in so much pain. I sat around the kitchen table with my parents and Alex. My mom put a bag of original Goldfish in front of me.

"What are you going to do?"

"I don't know. I don't want to do anything."

Mom opened up a bag of potato chips and grabbed a few.

"I don't know if that's possible, any more."

Dad popped a Mallomar in his mouth. Mom shot him a look.

Dad chewed defiantly as Mom pulled the package away from him. Dad swallowed with a grin.

"Don't you have that other girl? The one you were telling us about?"

"That's true."

Alex swallowed a mouthful of Cracker Jacks. If you couldn't tell already, we're a snacking family.

"She always seemed a little high-strung, but I never knew she was this wack."

I absently rolled a single Goldfish between my fingers, toying with it.

"Was I crazy to date her?"

Dad smiled while snagging another chocolate marshmallow delight.

"She was cute. Young. I don't think I can fault you that one, David."

Mom shot him an annoyed look.

"We would never say anything, David. It's your life."

"But you didn't like her."

"No. But that doesn't mean anything. You did."

"Did I really? It gets confused."

Mom leaned in over the smattering of as-yet-untouched Doritos in the center of the table.

"You were in love, David. I could see it. If you weren't I would have spoken my mind about her. But it was never our place once we could see how you felt. You can doubt everything else, but don't doubt that you were in love. That's something to be proud of. You gave everything to that girl. You should never be ashamed of that. It doesn't matter who she ended up being, or whether she was worthy of it, or any of that. What matters is that you loved someone. That's a great thing."

"Look what it got me."

She returned to her chair, snagging a Dorito on the way. Dad went over to pour himself some Diet Coke, musing as he walked.

"David, what do you want? Do you think talking to her will get her out of her life? Or will it fan the flames? Do you want her out of your life?"

"Of course I do."

"Then it seems pretty simple to me. Talk to her and let her go. Elaine, where's the lemon?"

"In the fridge."

This wasn't what I wanted to hear.

"But it's not fair. Why does she keep pulling me back in? I'm over her. It's not my problem anymore. I don't see how meeting with her and letting her crap all over me will help things out."

Alex got fed up with my lack of Goldfish consumption and pulled the bag over towards him.

"Are you afraid you'll still like her?"

"No. Of course not."

"Then what's the worst that can happen?"

Dad laughed.

"She can handcuff herself to his ankle."

"No, really. What's the worst that can happen? Didn't you just say that you were over her? You've moved on. I know it may be hard to face her, but come on, what do you care?"

What did I care? I didn't care. Then why was my stomach twisting up like a wet towel being wrung dry? Alex continued relentlessly.

"And maybe you do owe her something. Two years together buys her something, I think. What does this do to you, really? Makes you a little uncomfortable for an hour or two? Makes you go over a few painful memories you've pushed down? So what? At least once you're through, it'll be over."

He made sense, but everything inside me rebelled. What would this do to me? It wouldn't be as simple as he made it out to be. If I looked deep enough, I could see the source of my little internal storm. Fear. I was afraid of the Eater. I didn't want to see her ever again.

"I'm not sure I believe this will really help her, you know? I don't know what else I can tell her that I haven't already. If she isn't better by now, why would she suddenly drop this obsession after talking with me? I would think the best closure is never seeing me again. Forgetting me."

Mom took up Alex's flag.

"That's not closure, David. That's closing your eyes and hoping it all gets better by itself."

It will. Of course it will.

"This isn't my problem any more."

Mom looked at me sadly.

"Do what you feel you need to do."

My family lapsed into silence, absently munching. I sighed.

"It'll be my last trial before my wonderful new life."

Mom patted my hand. Dad walked over behind her and massaged her shoulders. As my brother and I watched my dad give my mom a backrub, I found myself wishing for a world where sons don't grow up and their mothers always wipe their streaked faces dry without fail.

I sent the Eater an e-mail that night when I got home letting her know I would be willing to speak with her, and suggested a restaurant. She e-mailed me back five minutes later. She wanted to see me tomorrow at her apartment. I e-mailed again, suggesting a neutral place like a park or something. She came back with my apartment. We finally agreed to meet at Annie's apartment the following evening at eight. I would treat it like a Band-Aid: the quicker the pull the less the pain. I almost went to sleep before I remembered to ask Annie if it was okay.

CHAPTER TWENTY-ONE

Thank God for the Goddess

When I woke up the next morning, my forehead hurt. Rubbing my brow I noticed that I had tossed aside my pillow during the night. The clear stones lay there. Their irregular shapes matched the imprints in my forehead. I picked them up. How fitting was this? Today was the day. I was supposed to throw them in the river and I'd be free. I sat there unmoving for a moment, staring at the translucent rocks and thinking about my black aura. What did it look like now? I wondered. I'd toss them in the East River on my way to Annie's. I could confront the Eater with a clean aura, whatever that means. I slipped them into my pocket and got ready for the day.

Thank God for the Goddess. That thought reverberated through my head all morning long. I wanted to call her, just to give me a confidence boost before the evening's entertainment, but I held off. Maybe during the afternoon. It was only ten in the morning, anyway. If she was anything like me, she wouldn't be able to form complete sentences for another two hours. I hoped I could catch her before I left for Annie's. Just to remind me of what my future really looked like. I needed all my thoughts racing along the same lines. I would call her after lunch. During lunch. Easy, tiger...

I couldn't concentrate on work, so I perused my baseball league. I was in dead last. I didn't want to jinx myself, so I quickly signed off. My stomach still hurt a little.

The phone rang. The voice of the Goddess greeted me.

"Hey, David."

She called me! Looking good, David, my boy.

"Hey, girlie. How was the big Easter blowout? Find any eggs?"

"I'm actually really busy today, so I can't talk too much right now, sorry."

"That's cool. I'm just glad you called."

"Are you free for lunch?"

How about that. She can't go any longer without a David fix. Well, this pusher likes to keep his customers coming back for more.

"Sure. What about the Bull Moose? Do you know it?"

"Yeah, I do. Twelve-thirty?"

"See you at then. Looking forward to it."

"Bye, David."

"Bye."

She sounded pretty off-kilter. I felt bad for her. She must be crazy busy. I figured we could have some food and talk for an hour or so and I'd forget all about what's coming up. It actually worked out for the best, as now I would have the taste of the Goddess fresh in my mouth when I arrived for my Eater meeting.

The Bull Moose was fairly empty when I arrived. It was more of a bar than a restaurant. I just really like their chicken fingers. I walked around the pool table looking for the Goddess. There she was, sitting in the corner by the jukebox. She had a half-drunk martini in her hand. An empty martini glass sat on the tray of the waitress walking away from her. I sat down with a smile.

"Fancy meeting you here, pretty lady."

"Hey, David. Thanks for coming."

"Thanks for coming? What are you, CIA? Do you have a mission for me?"

"No. I just know you're busy."

"Never too busy to encourage you to get drunk. Do you want another?"

"No, I think this will be enough."

She really was beautiful. I took a mental picture to bring out later on.

"So what's up? How was your Easter?"

"Actually it was very...confusing."

"It's that whole egg-and-bunny thing, isn't it? I never understood it myself. Unless rabbits have changed since the time of Christ when they could and did lay plenty of eggs. Maybe they laid plastic eggs filled with candy! Now that's a religion I can get behind."

The Goddess didn't laugh.

"No, it was other stuff."

"I'm not liking the vibe I'm getting from you. Did I do something wrong?"

"No. You didn't do anything. You've been great."

My heart sank.

"Shit, this isn't one of those 'It's me' speeches, is it? Fuck."

"Well. Not exactly. I...Carl came over to my apartment Saturday night and we started talking and somehow, I don't really know how, we ended up sleeping together. I'm really sorry."

I sat frozen. Just when you thought it was safe to take off the cup, WHAM! Another huge kick to the crotch.

"Jesus. How did...how?"

"I don't know. It just kind of happened."

"So you're back together?"

"I don't know. I don't think so. I'm all fucked up right now."

"Your timing is fantastic."

"This was what I was trying to avoid. I wasn't being completely honest when I said you weren't ready. I mean, you weren't, but I wasn't either. I'm still not. I'm all messed up. I like you, David. A lot. But I don't know what I'm doing right now. I'm just trying to get through the day."

"But I know all about that. I've felt like that, too..."

"I've been thinking and...I can't be with you the way we would both want it. There's too much shit in the way."

"I can help you. We can get past all of that. We're the same, you know..."

"I can't do it. I don't think you can either, though you sure won't admit it."

"I wouldn't sleep with my ex."

Silence. I regretted.

"I had another relapse. I told you they were tough. I'm sorry if I hurt you; I never meant to. I'm a train wreck right now and it'll take me a while to sort out the wreckage."

"So what do we do now? Should I call you in a few weeks?"

"I'll call you, David. Please, let me call you."

"Okay."

Silence.

"I should go. Take care, David."

"Okay."

"Bye."

And she got up and walked out.

It was all falling down. And it wasn't even my fault. At least when I was fucking up, I had the hope of someday learning to do things right. So that when I met the right girl, I would have gotten all of my fuck ups out of the way and everything would go perfectly. But this had nothing to do with me. I didn't fuck anything up. It just wasn't allowed to happen. Forces completely out of my control decided to keep me alone. There was nothing I could do. She was gone. And it wasn't even my fault.

I snorted. Listen to me, all high and mighty, thinking how nice it was of me to meet with the poor Eater of Souls. I would sit on the couch, protected by the knowledge that I had officially moved on. I could condescend at will from such a thick-walled fortress. Of course, I had nothing now. No protection at all. I would never have agreed to meet with the Eater under these circumstances. I was all soft underbelly. She was going to rip me apart.

I trudged back to my office and closed the door. I couldn't go through with this. I'd call the Eater and cancel. I'm sorry, but something came up. Something left, actually. Something I needed. So you and your closure are just shit out of luck. I picked up my phone. And put it back down again. I couldn't call now. She'd answer the phone. I'd have to talk to her. I'd wait until later, when she'd more likely be in the car or something. I didn't know. But I had to cancel. Unable to focus, I brought up my baseball league again.

Unsurprisingly, I remained in last place. Why did I have such shitty players? Why did my team suck so hard? It seemed apparent. I made bad choices. I thought I saw potential where there was just shit. Everything I planned went wrong. Letting the season play out would only make me feel worse. It would be better just to give up now. Admit defeat before I embarrassed myself. One by one, I dropped my players until my team was empty. I imagined the surprise of my fellow fantasy baseballers when they checked the boards to see Piazza and Delgado available to be picked up, just like that. I had no use for them. Playing only brought out my inner loser for all to see. If I didn't play, only I'd know.

I was still staring at my empty team roster a few hours later. My phone remained untouched. There was a knock at my door. I looked up. It was Jim.

"Hey, man, what's going on?"

I didn't want to say anything about what had happened to my life that day. I needed to pull inside like a turtle.

"Nothing. What's up with you?"

"I was in the neighborhood, so I thought I'd stop by."

"Don't you work during the day?"

"I used to, yeah."

Shit.

"Oh, man. What happened?"

Jim grabbed a seat in front of my desk and smiled.

"Today at ten-fifteen my boss made it known that my services were no longer required. When I asked him as to the reasoning, he proceeded to inform me that I have been less than reliable the past few weeks, especially considering the precedent I had set with my long hours the months before."

"I told you all you needed was to do a bad job."

"So I've finally done it. Of course, I've been working half the hours I used to recently, so my unemployment is minuscule. But hey, you can't have everything, right?"

"Shit, man, that sucks. So what are you going to do?"

"Daddy isn't sure. I can't afford to live here anymore."

"You can get another job."

"I think I'd rather live off of unemployment for a while and see what happens."

"Dude, that's only for six months."

"Then check up on me in six months if you're so concerned."

"So you're just going to run off without any idea of what you're going to do? That's how people end up selling their bodies. And the buck fifty you'd get for that won't last too long, even in Providence."

Jim gave me a hard look.

"You can be an elitist bastard sometimes."

I was taken aback. Jim had obviously cracked. It creeped me out a little bit. He radiated calm, sitting in the ugly orange chair in front of my desk.

"Why are you so relaxed? You got laid off, man. Your whole future is up in the air."

Jim cocked his head to the side.

"You know, the whole time I've known you, you've lorded this whole 'goals' thing over me. You think I'm some poor sap caught in a dead-end entry-level job with no prospects. And now that I'm finally free of that job, you continue to give me shit. Now I'm the poor unemployed sap."

I didn't need this right now.

"Dude, that is not fair. The only thing I've ever done is encourage you to find a direction."

"Fuck direction. Maybe I don't want a direction. Maybe I'm fine just taking life as it comes. Who are you to tell me about direction? You aren't even doing what you really want to do. So what if you're successful? You're not happy. I don't even think you really know how you got here. You'll probably be here as long as they'll let you stay because you could care less about going any-where else. You say you want to write, but do you? What are goals worth if you never try to reach them? Hell, I may have no goals to speak of, but I'm having a fucking good time."

"Yeah, I saw what a good time you were having doing the ass shake in full Ru Paul regalia."

"I don't regret it. So I had a scare. What's life without a scare or two? In the end, you know what I did? I slept with a married woman! That is pretty fucking cool!"

"You still don't have a job."

"You know what I think it is? It's all about instincts. Everyone says 'Trust your instincts.' That's the mantra we're fed from day one. Trust your instincts. So I did. I'd see a hot girl, but my instinct was to do nothing, so I stayed in the corner. I'd be bored in my job, but my instinct was to stay comfortable, so I kept work-ing. Instincts are false messengers. They lead you astray. They're knee-jerk reactions like pulling your hand away from a hot stove.

They keep you safe. What has safe gotten me? Maybe the pain is a good thing. Maybe it clears the head. Maybe the pain is a needle in your arm drawing a tattoo that can save you from your little life. These two devils here are my watchdogs against instinct. I can give you the address of the parlor if you want."

Jim was raving. He had fallen over the edge.

"What are you talking about?"

"Seems to me like your instincts have ruined many a promising relationship, but I could be full of shit. Wouldn't be the first time. Hell, if I really knew what I was talking about, I'd have a job and goals and I'd be ridiculously unhappy like you."

"Fuck you. I've been nothing but supportive of you. I know you're probably all pissed off because of the unemployment check thing, but that's no reason to take it out on me. I'm your friend."

"And I'm your friend. So here's some friendly advice. Instinct is not your friend. You know what my instinct is now? To go home to my parents and save up some money and then try to get another assistant editing job. But then I check my little buddies here, and they say something different. They say that I'm heading up to Providence to hang out with some kinky ladies and have a fucking good time. I'm gonna die someday, I know, but I don't have to spend the rest of my life practicing. I'm sure I'll do fine without rehearsal."

"Well, good luck, Hugh Hefner. But a month from now, when you go to pee and it feels like your dick is a blowtorch, think of me sitting in my office laughing my ass off, safe and secure."

Jim stood up. He looked unfazed.

"Give me a call in a week or so when you've excavated that

stick from your ass. I know your instinct will be to avoid the confrontation, but try to ignore it."

"Sure. Whatever."

"Yeah, whatever. I'll see ya."

He walked to the door. He stopped.

"Why did you drop all of your players?"

"You saw that, huh. Why do you care?"

He turned around.

"I want to know."

"I was tired of playing. I was only going to lose anyway."

"So what?"

"So I didn't want to play anymore. I made some stupid trades
and I was tired of playing."

"It's still fun to play."

"No, it isn't."

He stood there watching me.

"You had a whole season ahead of you."

"She broke up with me."

He didn't seem surprised.

"When?"

"This morning. And now I can't do it. I can't face her like this,
you know?"

"Face who?"

"I'm supposed to see the Eater tonight."

"Okay. Why can't you face her?"

"I'm not in a position of strength anymore."

"You're over her. That's your position of strength. Right?"

I said nothing. He nodded.

"Of course. So now you're going to avoid another confrontation?"

"I can't do it. I have to cancel. This isn't the way I wanted it to be. I just know it will go badly. I can feel it."

"Why don't you ask me what you should do?"

"I know what you're going to say."

"I won't say anything. Just ask me."

"Fine. Should I meet with the Eater tonight? I don't want to, remember that."

Jim reached up and pulled down his shirt over his shoulder. A grinning devil defiantly gave me a thumbs-up.

"But wait, you should get a second opinion."

He switched sides, pulling down the other arm and exposing another thumbs-up from a second, identical demon.

"I think the shoulders have spoken."

I couldn't help it. I laughed.

"They sure have, haven't they."

Something about those devils centered me. I could almost see what Jim was talking about.

Jim turned to open the door.

"Good luck tonight, man. I hope everything goes okay."

I jumped in before he could leave.

"Listen, Jim. I am sorry you got laid off. I hope you have a good time up in Providence, I really do. I just don't want you to end up broke and feeling like a fool."

Jim smiled.

"But fools have all the fun. It's a proven fact."

He walked through the door, closing it softly behind him.

I didn't reach for the phone again. The devils had spoken.

On my way out, I walked by Maureen's office. I slowed. The door was open just a crack. I could see her inside on the phone. She laughed at some unknown joke with her entire body. I considered knocking on the door. Instead, I brushed my fingers along the door, trailing onto the wall as I walked away.

I took my time heading out to Queens. I rode the local train. I tried to read but I couldn't concentrate. Would I end up just like the Goddess? Would I succumb to the Eater's comfortable charms? Was I due for a relapse just like the Goddess said? Of course, she wasn't the Goddess anymore. Now she was simply Relapse Girl. She had lost all Goddess privileges. Just like Sandy and Bendy Girl and Opera Girl and all the rest. Just another girl with a funny nickname. I had been so wrapped up in whether I should do this or not that I hadn't spent any real time preparing for it and now I felt the sting. What would I say? What if she looked good? What if it still hurt to see her cry? I had no idea. I was a twig in the river now. Carried along.

I got to Annie's a good twenty minutes late. I knew that the Eater waited inside. She was a punctual girl. I took a deep breath, said a prayer to every god I thought might take an interest, and rang the bell. Annie buzzed me in and met me at the door.

"She's in there."

"Thanks for letting me use your place."

"No problem."

"Is Jacob here?"

"I haven't seen him."

I was stalling.

"I'm sorry. But maybe it's all for the best."

"I don't know. Now that I know he's gone, I really miss him. I

was just so used to it. To what we had. And now...maybe that
was my shot. I guess I'll never know. Anyway, you'd better go in.
I'll be back in a few hours."

"Thanks."

She left. I walked into the apartment, through the living room
to the kitchen and there she was.

CHAPTER TWENTY-TWO

The Eater of Souls

She looked a little paler than I remembered. She was dressed in a
low-cut sweater and tight jeans. She wore a little too much makeup.
I had forgotten what a nice body she had. My chest stung me as I
took her in. I wasn't ready to handle wanting her. She looked
apprehensive and excited. She stood up when I entered and made
as if to hug me. I let her.

"Hey."

"Hey."

"Thanks for seeing me."

"No problem."

"How have you been?"

"Okay, I guess. Just working and getting by. You?"

"Pretty good. I've been dating a little."

"Good for you."

"Yeah."

Silence. She sat back down again.

"I wanted to talk to you again. To let you know exactly how you made me feel. I don't think I've gotten to say everything I wanted to."

"Okay."

"You should grab a seat. We're going to be here a while."

Fantastic. Just fantastic. I sat down on the other side of the kitchen table. I was walking on broken glass, waiting for the sting of the first cut.

"Okay. What do you want to say?"

She gathered her thoughts, looking for all the world like she was reviewing some internal script she had drawn up.

"I don't think you've been very fair to me. I did my best to be a good girlfriend, and I think I was. I did everything I could. When you broke up with me, I thought for a while that I might have screwed up somewhere. That was definitely the way you made me feel. But the more I think about it, the more certain I am that there was nothing I could have done better. I gave you everything I could, and it really hurts me that you blame me."

Did I blame her? Of course. As she spoke, I found myself tracing her neck with my eyes. Such a beautiful neck. Graceful and long, like a swan. This wasn't fair. I wasn't prepared for this.

"Don't you remember all the good times we had together? Don't you remember how happy we were?"

I felt like I was in front of the Victoria's Secret again, held fast by the dreams of perfect happiness posing for me in the window. And every mannequin bore the Eater's face. *She* was what they promised me, what they had always promised me. I could hear the mannequins speaking to me. Their beautiful promise whispered in my ear.

"Isn't she more beautiful than you remember?"

"You remember kissing her? Watch her lips as she speaks. Remember how they moved under yours in perfect unison. Remember running your tongue across first the top lip and then the bottom. Don't you want to taste them again?"

"Look at her body. Watch how it moves under her clothes like a belly dancer behind a screen. It's promising you something. Everything. Look at her face. You could kiss away those tears and it would all be all right. If she stood up, shed her jeans and sweater and beckoned, wouldn't you trip over yourself in your rush to reach her? To touch her? To fit inside her perfectly?"

I tried to push those voices out of my head. I had to focus on the pain, the anger, the downward spiral. The Eater kept talking.

"You used to swear to me all the time how much you loved me. You'd call me ten times a day just to say it. Where did that love go? How can something like that just go away?"

I had missed her voice. I was so afraid. But of what? Love? Was I just like Annie, ready to throw it all away rather than face whether I was even capable of love? The mannequins' voices slipped seductively into my ear.

"Are you going to keep staggering around blindly hoping you happen to come across the perfect woman? Or are you going to open your eyes and see you've got someone good enough right here? Open your eyes and look at her."

I stared at the Eater. She seemed to glow, making it hard for me to make out her features. Looking into her light, I could see shadows, flickering like memories.

Flash

We stand on the boardwalk by the ferry in Battery Park, looking out at where the Hudson and the East River intermingle. I've just met her, so I don't want to presume. I surround her with my body as she leans over the rail, but I don't touch her. It's too soon. I stare out at the Statue of Liberty, which will forever smell like freesia to me. Her hair blows in my mouth and I don't pull it out.

Flash

We sit across from one another at La Mela. The waiter tries to show her how to break open the lobster, but fails spectacularly. She puts her entire body into one huge crack and a claw shoots across the table into my lap. I look down at it nestled in my crotch. She makes a joke about sinking her claws into me. I hand her the lobster shard, telling her she had to do better than that. But she didn't.

Flash

I visit her home in southern New Jersey. Her mother and brother are out, so we make out like teenagers on her mother's bed. She whispers into my ear that she likes my arms. I whisper that I like her ass. We go through dozens of body parts, trying to find one to agree upon. We have to settle for eyelashes.

Flash

She goes out with another boy. I try to take my mind off it by watching the last game of the World Series. I can't focus. Not even the Yankees can overpower her. I'm lost. I call her and tell her I love her. She tells me that the actor in the movie they saw reminded her of me. My heart leaps.

Flash

We make love for the first time. She made me wait forever. I waited. I couldn't have turned away. She whispers in my ear that she loves me. She loves me. Someone loves me. We move together smooth and perfect.

Flash

We lie underneath my parents' Christmas tree. Everyone else sleeps. The world is still. The blinking lights illuminate her face sporadically. I look up at the angel atop the tree. My father had bought such a huge fir that the tip pushed up against the ceiling, forcing the angel into a suicidal lean. It seems like she blesses us from above.

Flash

We go romping in the snow down Fifth Avenue. The largest snowfall in years blankets the city, trapping the cars in white cocoons and leaving the city empty for us to play in. We plow our way to Washington Square Park, where we try to build a snowman. We get bored and have our picture taken next to someone else's snowman. We tell everyone we show the picture to that it had taken us hours.

Flash

She dances for me. I can't tear my gaze away from her eyes, teasing me. She owns me. I sit helpless under her movements. I can't speak but to thank God for her. She twirls, wrapping me in her promise. I never want to be untied.

Flash

We lie on the beach in Montauk at midnight. We decide to make love, but every time we get going, someone walks by on the beach. We picked the most popular stretch on the peninsula. After a group of fishermen passes by yelling out helpful advice, we give up, contenting ourselves with the stars.

Flash

We kiss for the first time. We had left Battery Park hours before. I drove her all the way home. We stand in her front yard for hours. We talk forever. She sits on my lap. I look up. Her face is in shadow with the moon directly behind her. She wears a halo. I can just make out her smile. I put my hand on her cheek and guide her to me. She resists, leaping off me and running. I follow. I catch up at the side of her house. She leads me on. She doesn't want to be easy. She never is. I trap her in the corner. She places my hand on her breast as a peace offering. We kiss.

Flash

She sits in front of me in Annie's kitchen, crying as she speaks. I can barely see her for the blaze of memories surrounding her. These promises get in the way. I want them to come true.

I felt such a wave of loss and sadness. My throat closed up. I had forgotten. The scar tissue proved new and easily shed. The wound still bled. I pushed down an overwhelming need to kiss her.

That was the moment. The moment I could have cracked. It would be so easy to slip right back in. My fingers curled around the clear stones in my pocket as I tried to keep my footing.

"Can I ask you something?"

I had caught her mid-sentence. Her train of thought derailed, she nodded.

"Why do you love me?"

She seemed taken aback by that simple question.

"Right now? After everything you've put me through? Why do you think I still love you?"

"Well, you're angry at me. You think I was unfair. You didn't want it to end. So you must love me. Otherwise we wouldn't be here, right? Otherwise there'd be no point. So why? Why do you love me? Why did you ever love me? What made me special?"

She recovered well, thinking hard as she gathered herself for her final pitch.

"I guess I loved the way you listened to me. The way you were always there when I needed you. I loved the way you'd drop everything to give me a backrub. I loved the way you were nice to my dog. I loved the way you treated me, like I was special. I loved the way you would take me shopping, even though I know you hate shopping. I loved the way you would try anything for me, even oysters. I loved the way you always talked about going on trips with me. You wanted me to see the world. I loved how important it was to you that I laugh at your jokes. I was important to you. I loved . . . you."

She paused to wipe her eyes.

"But then you changed. Love is work and you just stopped trying. I stayed the same. But you changed somehow. You started treating me differently. Badly. Like you didn't care. It made no sense. I didn't do anything differently. I know I didn't. You're the one who changed."

Something seemed off about her description of her love. I didn't seem to be involved. She loved the way I treated her and the way my loving her made her feel. But did she love me? Not the me who listened or shopped or was nice to her dog, but the me who watched baseball games and loved to read and knew obscure Monty Python quotes by heart. The me who wished he could play guitar and wanted to write and cried at wussy French films. The me who existed whether she was there to see it or not.

"What is your favorite memory of me? Not of us, but of me?"

She thought for a moment. Then she smiled.

"Do you remember back before we were even going out, we

had kissed but nothing official or anything, do you remember I got sick? They didn't know it was food poisoning yet. You called in sick to work and looked after me all day long. And then, right before you went back into the city, you gave me this big bouquet of flowers. It was beautiful. That's when I fell in love with you. When you put those flowers on my table and told me you hoped I felt better. That's my favorite memory."

She sat back, eyes shining at the memory.

But that could have been anyone. There was nothing of me in that moment. That was a nice guy who wanted to get laid. But it made her feel special. She fell in love with someone because he loved her. So who was I to her? Why did she care if I moved on? I was easily replaced. My job requirements were not hard to fill. But maybe she and I had the same fears. Holding out for more took a lot of courage. Settling was so much easier on the stomach. So why wasn't I settling?

Flash

She's sleeping after we both stayed up watching TV. We haven't said or done anything different this night than on any other evening. It could have been just like the others. Only this night I can't sleep. I prop myself up on one elbow and look at her sleeping face. I know what I'm supposed to feel. She looks like an angel, peaceful and still. I should be awash in a wave of love and contentment. That's how love works. But that's not what I feel. Watching her sleep, I feel empty. Restless. Like I'm staying in a friend's spare bedroom a few days longer than I should. I feel out of place. I try to imagine myself in thirty years, gazing down at this same face. How would I feel then? With a start I realize how angry I would be. Not sad, not lost, but angry. Because the thought first and foremost in my mind is that I don't want her to wake up. I want her to stay perfect. And once she wakes up, she becomes real.

Flash

It wasn't that she was a bad person. She just didn't make me happy the way I needed to be happy. It's hard trying to be happy. Much harder than just getting by. But at least the doubt was gone. The glow I had imagined around her subsided. The desire faded. The Victoria's Secret mannequins' voices faded...

"Look at her."

"She's so beautiful."

"She's what made you happy."

...until it was just the two if us sitting in Annie's little kitchen. I understood why she spun this tale of our breakup that sounded nothing like the one I remembered. Because we didn't experience the same breakup. Just like our relationship, the reasons for our breakup were dressed to our specifications. But whereas I could see that, she never would. To admit that would mean she was as responsible as I was.

"Lots of other guys asked me out. Sometimes I wanted to go out with them, have fun, you know. But I didn't. Because I loved you. And what did I get for it? I loved you the best I could, but it was never enough for you. You always wanted more. I gave you everything. But you always made me feel like it was never enough. Nothing was ever enough for you."

I wanted to argue with her. Not because I wanted her back, but because I wanted what she wanted. I wanted her to acknowledge my truth. I was dying to speak up. I could feel it building up inside of me. I couldn't keep quiet; it wasn't in my nature. I always said what I thought. That was my instinct. Speak up and tell her my truth. Ram it down her throat. She'd never accept it, but that's not really the point, is it? At least I'll know I defended myself. And then, a week later, she'll call, still stung, needing another closure session, another shot to get me to agree that she hadn't changed. That she'd done nothing wrong. Because she needed to be reassured, like the child of divorcing parents, that it had nothing to do with her, since deep down she fears it did. One dissenting word and we would be off again, dancing the blame tango until the end of time.

I said nothing.

Part of me, the pride in me, was livid. Why was I keeping my mouth shut? Protect yourself! But eventually even the pride quieted down. Eventually even the pride noticed the circles under her eyes. The chewed fingernails. The nice clothes that seemed out of place on her, like she was playing dress up. Watching her work herself in and out of hysterics, I recognized who she really was. She wasn't some sick, evil Eater of Souls put on this earth to torture me. She never had that kind of power. Whatever power she had over me I gave to her. She wasn't the evil creature I'd imagined, nor was she the perfect match I feared she might be. She wasn't an extreme at all. She was a twenty-one-year-old girl who couldn't get over the fact that the guy she thought was gaga over her had left her. She was young and fairly immature and not worth any of the pain I'd put myself through over her. Like the song says, she was just a girl. She wasn't the Eater of Souls. She was Elizabeth, Beth for short. I had enjoyed my time with her, but it was over. It hadn't worked and now it was through. And no amount of truth and argument would change that. So I ignored my instinct and said nothing.

Eventually she finished. She looked wary, waiting for the explosion. The subway train rattled by as we sat in silence. She jumped a little as the room shook at its passing. I chose my words carefully.

"I'm sorry about the way I treated you. I'm sorry I hurt you. I'm sorry it has to be over. I'm sorry about all of it."

She looked at a loss. She had trained hard for a fight and never had to dodge a punch. She managed a wary reply.

"Thank you. That's what I wanted you to say."

I stood up. She got to her feet as well, suddenly awkward. Before she could say anything else, I gave her one last hug, turned and walked out without looking back, leaving her and her mannequins in that cramped kitchen in Queens.

I haven't seen her since.

I don't know if she ended up happy or not. You can argue that I made it worse for her by allowing her to keep her misconceptions. I argue that it is no longer my affair. I did what I could and I can't do any more. Some things can't be fixed, especially by the ones who helped break them.

CHAPTER TWENTY-THREE

After the Storm

It's amazing what you can make yourself believe. I spent months certain I was leaving Beth behind. I comforted myself in the thought that every woman I broke bread with carried me further and further away from her. But I was the boy lost in the woods. I travelled through the wilderness certain I'd walked halfway to Boston, but all the while, just through the trees, my house waited a stone's throw away. The end of the trail deposited me right back at my front door. All my twists and turns served only to keep me close. She was always in my head, leading me in circles. But now I had an aerial view. I could see the tiny path that wended through the small patch of forest. It was all so small from up here. I could also make out the path that led away. I took it. And morning would find me miles away.

I sat on the front stoop of Annie's apartment building. Annie joined me with a sigh.

"She's going to sleep over."

"Okay."

"This was a good thing you did."

I didn't answer for a moment. I looked out at the subway trestle lifted up above the street. The N train rumbled by, obliterating all sound in its wake. Eventually, like frightened animals returning to the forest, the noises of the city returned. I looked down at my hands.

"It worked out for me too. I needed it more that I thought I did. I always thought closure was overrated, but..."

I trailed off. Annie nodded.

"It's probably a feng shui thing. Something about leaving open doors behind you. Lets all the good spiritual energy out. Closure is the emotional equivalent of your mom yelling, 'What were you, born in a barn?' and making you shut the door behind you."

"I guess that's it. Otherwise, your mind goes crazy and you make up a whole bunch of crazy shit. You can blow people all out of proportion that way."

"Yep."

A gypsy cab pulled over to the side of the road trying to pick up a fare. I could hear them haggling. The worth of a ride to midtown is always negotiable. The guy decided against the gypsy. From what I could hear, he would have been ripped off anyway.

"Is Jacob coming back to get his stuff?"

"I'm moving out, actually. My friend from college is getting a new place so I might move in with her."

"I'm sorry. Maybe you can still work things out. Now that you know you want him..."

Annie shook her head.

"I still don't know anything. And it's too late, anyway. He won't trust my intentions. And he's right not to."

"I think it's better that you're leaving. Comfort can turn into contempt pretty easily without something stronger to fall back on."

"I guess I'll never know. That's what I regret. That answer. Next time, I guess. I won't be able to mistake it next time. The sheer force of the passion will knock me on my ass."

"Hey, I may never reach perfection, but I can get closer than this. So I'll go on being a booty nomad."

"We're booty nomads all."

Some kids yelling at each other in lightning Spanish ran by. Four boys with a young girl running after. A tennis ball bounced around them without ever seeming to touch anything. They turned a corner and only their voices, like echoes, remained, until they, too, faded. I lay back on the step.

"I'm tired."

"You should get some sleep."

"Give me a second. I find your block soothing."

"I'll be sad to leave."

"Maybe you could move into Manhattan."

"That would be nice."

"Yeah."

We sat on the stoop, watching the world slide by.

On my way home from the subway, I stopped in front of the Victoria's Secret and took a long hard look at the mannequins. Despite everything that had happened, despite all my newfound resolutions and knowledge, I still felt a twinge when I took in all that promise. I don't think I'll ever grow immune to that. I know it's a lie, but it's such a sexy lie. I can't help but dream of the day I strip the lingerie off and dive into the warm fulfillment of my wandering. No more bitterness. No more lost meanderings. Instead, I'll be one of those smug bastards with tendrils floating off into the distance, safely tethered. Who needs lingerie then?

I took the stones out of my pocket. I walked east. It was late, but I didn't care. When I reached the East River, I leaned out over the railing. The Triboro Bridge sparkled in the distance. I drew my arm back and shot those stones in a glittering arc out over the water. I heard a soft splash and they were gone.

The next week I gave my notice. No more puppets, no more Harold, no more strange drug forays in wilderness. I knew I'd find something, somewhere, if I looked. I'd adjust to the water well enough. Harold said he was sorry to see me go. He asked me whatever happened to my friend, Julie. I told him she was living with another woman. I considered it my severance thrill. Maureen gave me a bigger hug than I thought I'd get. She'd be the only one I'd miss. I told the editor to send me some of his soup. He told me to kiss his ass. Tearful goodbyes....

I had enough money to last me a few months, so I didn't look for a new job right away. I didn't really know what I wanted. I spent a lot of time sitting in my apartment and jamming with Rory. Neither of us got any better, though we did meet some policemen a few times. Any contact is a good contact in the music industry. I didn't even try to date. I wasn't inspired. Every once in a while, I'd be in the mood to salsa, but I did nothing about it.

Jim moved up to Providence. Even with his unemployment checks being half of what he had planned for, he could afford a gigantic one-bedroom apartment. He lorded it over me mercilessly. I visited him once. That one girl, Katalina, was cute, but that whole Goth thing scared me off. I'm nobody's bitch, thank you. Jim seemed happier. He didn't look for a job either. He just lived it up. He'll probably die from some latex-induced asphyxiation accident, but I know that's what he would want. An embarrassing sex death would cap his life nicely.

Annie moved in with her friend, though she didn't quite make it to Manhattan. Actually, she moved into an apartment four streets over from her old place. She ended up having an affair with the father of one of her kids. She had a crazy two months of excitement before she dumped him. It was too much for her. So now she's in Arizona. It's only for a few months or so, supposedly, but who knows? She went home for a quick visit with her family where she told them exactly what she thought of them. They didn't take it very well. Apparently she's been banished or something. I thought this would make her stomach feel better, but she told me that some days it's just as bad. But some days it's not. At least she's trying. No matter what, she's got us.

One day, I woke up antsy. I felt like vomiting, or giving birth, or jumping up and down until I passed out. Instead, I fired up the old computer. I started writing. I needed to put all my thoughts into order. I needed to connect the dots. Before I knew it, Memorial Day passed, as did the Fourth of July. Eventually, I finished. I didn't know if it was any good. It didn't really matter if it sucked. I had finished it. I could take that to my grave. I wanted to tell someone. I picked up the phone and dialed. Relapse Girl answered on the third ring.

"Hello?"

"Hey, it's David."

A pause.

"Hi."

"I know you told me to wait until you called me, but I have no patience at all."

"That's okay. I'm glad to hear from you."

"I just wrote a story."

"Good for you."

"I wanted to tell someone."

"I was your first choice?"

"I thought you'd appreciate it."

"Well, I am impressed."

"That's the general idea. It doesn't matter if it's good or not, so long as it impresses you."

"What's it about?"

"Stuff."

"Am I in it?"

"You'll have to read it. Are you still with the senior citizen?"

"No. I haven't seen him in a while."

"Are you over him yet?"

"I'm getting there."

"Fair enough."

"Are you over your crazy woman?"

"Well on my way, I think."

"So."

"So."

"Do you feel like dancing?"

◈

I'm going on a not-date with Julie. I need to pick my shirt. I think I have a special not-dating button-down in the back. I haven't shaved for two days, so my stubble is in good shape. I'm leaving all of my expectations in my apartment, though the place is so small I'm sure I can grab them at a moment's notice should we find our way back here later tonight. I check myself in the mirror. Looking...half-decent. Good, but not too good. The picture of non-pressure. So off I go. As I step out my door and lock it behind me, I start humming. I'm feeling pretty good. Now, if I can just keep myself from fucking this up...

Acknowledgments

This book never would have happened without the support of the people around me. At least, that's what I'm telling those people. My super-agent, David Dunton, who somehow managed to remain a real person amongst the wolves, did a great job of getting the book out there (once he got around to reading it). He and the rest of the crew at Harvey Klinger made me feel all warm and protected, especially Harvey, who's like a big fuzzy bear. Special thanks to Susan Hobson, and Mary Anne Thompson, of Mary Anne Thompson Associates, for spreading the word so quickly and enthusiastically. Extra special thanks to Jacob Hoye for getting me in touch with Dave and for having such an expressive soulpatch. And now we come to Miramax, as does everyone ere the end. A reverent bow to the best book division in the known corporate universe: Jonathan Burnham, Kristin Powers, Hilary Bass, Kathy Schneider, Bruce Mason, Jaime Horn and the rest of the crew. Thanks to Peter Borland for giving the book an editorial polish. I also bow to the lovely Miramax film folk who gave me a chance to try my hand at the screenplay: Jennifer Wachtell and Steve Hutensky. I also want to thank Harvey Weinstein because something tells me it's a smart thing to do. Thanks also to Sheri Smiley, a super-agent and real person in her own right, and the lovely folks at CAA for introducing me to a whole slew of people who bought me lunch.

Thanks to my co-workers at MTV for not telling anyone what I was really doing in my office, especially Kim Noone (who taught me all about the power of soap operas, footwear and being fabulous), Maggie Nemser (for critiquing an early draft) and Hillary Cohen (because I said I would). A huge messy gush of thanks to my great circle of friends, many of whose character traits and jokes I outright stole. I won't tell you who's based on who, because even my closest friends would have no qualms about suing the hell out of me, but suffice it to say that they are all much funnier than I am. So thanks to my funny, understanding friends, especially Peter Vaughan, Ed Finegold, Allison Werner-Lin, Ezekiel Arlin, John Magovern, Josh Marks, Melanie Penn, Brian Hennessy (thanks for helping me navigate the tricky waters of Hollywood while crashing on your couch), and Justin Burk (who'd always wanted to be thinly veiled and once stood up in a movie theater after a particularly wussy film to declare for all to hear what he saw as our obvious sexual preferences). Special thanks to Karyn Silverman for listening to me read the first page over the phone and telling me that it actually wasn't all that crappy. Thanks to Nik Anderson for reading an early draft and for always being there to help me bring some crazy new project to life. And super secret extra special thanks with lemon to the incomparable Christina Burk, who read and critiqued all eight drafts and without whose editorial genius I would have had no plot at all. Thanks to my extended family for always supporting me even when my language got a little risque: Uncle Stan, Aunt Sonya, Susan, Kathy, Colleen, Jeanne and their respective families, and Jeanie and her family. Thanks to my sister Alison for her unconditional love. Thanks to my brother Derek for looking so opposite from me on the outside and being so similar to me on the inside. And thanks most of all to the two people who always knew I'd make it, even though they ended up completely wrong on what I'd make it doing: Mom and Dad. With love and support like yours, it's impossible to fail.

Damn, could I have made this any longer? I think I forgot to thank Al Sharpton and the guy at my deli.